BEWARE THE LAUGHING BLACKBIRDS

SENJA SUUTARI

Boilerplate Books, llc | Maine

For my partner, Jouko Vainio

CONTENTS

Chapter 1 1
Chapter 2 7
Chapter 3 13
Chapter 4 19
Chapter 5 23
Chapter 6 37
Chapter 7 49
Chapter 8 59
Chapter 9 69
Chapter 10 81
Chapter 11 93
Chapter 12 105
Chapter 13 119
Chapter 14 127
Chapter 15 135
Chapter 16 143
Chapter 17 151
Chapter 18 155
Chapter 19 165
Chapter 20 179
Chapter 21 187
Chapter 22 191
Chapter 23 193
Chapter 24 201
Chapter 25 209
Chapter 26 221
Chapter 27 229
Chapter 28 247
Chapter 29 257
Chapter 30 271

Chapter 31 287
Chapter 32 293
Chapter 33 303
Chapter 34 315
Chapter 35 319
Chapter 36 329
Chapter 37 333
Chapter 38 337
Chapter 39 351
Chapter 40 361
Chapter 41 367
Chapter 42 373
Chapter 43 377
Chapter 44 385
Chapter 45 391
Chapter 46 399
Chapter 47 405
Chapter 48 411
Chapter 49 419
Chapter 50 423
Chapter 51 431
Chapter 52 437
Chapter 53 441
Chapter 54 445
Chapter 55 455
Chapter 56 467
Chapter 57 483
Chapter 58 491
Chapter 59 499
Chapter 60 509
Chapter 61 525
Epilogue 535

CHAPTER 1

Fidelia Lemerriant opened her eyes in the darkness. She lay still, barely breathing, straining to hear, her pulses pounding. What was that? Was someone coming? She whimpered, burrowed down under her handmade quilt; then, when nothing happened and no one came, she pulled the edge of the covers down so she could breathe more easily.

Wide awake now, she became conscious of pressure in her bladder, tried to ignore it, but couldn't. She threw the quilt aside and sat up on the thin cotton pad that served as a mattress, slipped out of bed and felt around for the small enameled chamber pot underneath it. Her hand encountered nothing. She, herself, had emptied the pot that morning, carried it to the outhouse to dump out the contents — but then had forgotten to bring it back. Where had she left it? Oh yes, now she remembered that she'd set it on a stump while she'd wandered off to look for wild berries.

Fidelia had walked along a path through a hayfield, on through to where grasses, salal, and Labrador tea grew sparsely. There had been no rain and the ground was dry, the vegetation crispy under her feet.

Blackberry brambles grew along the edge of the forest, their thick thorny canes forming an impenetrable tangle, but the berries weren't ripe yet. She'd walked on past a small thicket of hemlock to where there was a narrow opening into the deep woods.

There, under the canopy of huge cedars and firs, where the light dimmed to a green glow, the air was always cool and still. Fidelia's attention had been caught by the sight of a large black slug lying as if asleep on a rock. She'd been prodding it gently, watching it extend its antennae and begin a slow oozing movement along the stony surface, when her mother's voice had called her to come help with the wash. Now Fidelia could picture the chamber pot — rounded, white, with a blue lip and a handle to carry it by — still sitting on a stump in the moonlight.

Barefoot and shivering, the little girl picked her way across the plank floor to the rough-hewn wooden doorway. She moved quietly so as not to awaken her brother, then remembered that Elphique no longer shared a room with her. Eight-year-old Fidelia now had the tiny room off the kitchen to herself. "It is not fitting for brother and sister to sleep in the same room," her father had said, probing her with eyes that were sharp with anger, and with something else that seemed even more threatening.

Fidelia's mother had protested weakly. "Brazeau, s'il te plaît! They are just children, and Fidelia becomes so frightened at night if she's alone."

"It's time she outgrew that," Brazeau Lemerriant had said. "From now on her brother sleeps in the barn."

There was no point in arguing. There was never any point in arguing with Brazeau Lemerriant who ruled his family with his roar and his fists — except, of course, for Elphique, who was becoming so elusive that nobody could quite rule him — not anymore.

Her room had no door, just a curtain — a piece of cotton cloth threaded through a rod and tacked over the doorway. A floorboard creaked as Fidelia made her way across the deserted kitchen, through a square of moonlight that spilled through the window onto the gray planks and briefly framed her tiny shadow. The moon was bright and full as she moved toward the window and climbed up to stand on the wide sill in order to look out.

There, illuminated, lay the hay field — ripe heads of timothy ready for harvest, palely ablaze in a wash of luminescence. The hay had been planted all the way up to the window, in the style of the times, when every available scrap of cleared land was expected to be productive. There were no beds of flowers or ornamental plantings on the Lemerriant farm. Narrow pathways led where needed, and the only area not given to hay was the vegetable garden planted mostly in potatoes and other root crops — their greens a target for the island deer.

Fidelia stood on tiptoe and leaned forward as her eye caught a flicker of movement. Something was in the hay field! At first it looked a little like the scarecrow her mother had made of old clothing stuffed with straw. She had set it in the garden, mounted it on an old broomstick, and when the wind blew it flopped from side to side. It had never scared away crows or deer but it did frighten the dog, Lacrosse, a bony, cringing mutt that ran whimpering when the scarecrow moved, and then turned to bark loudly at it from a safe distance.

But what Fidelia saw was no scarecrow. Its movements were rhythmic and it was coming toward her. It was swinging from side to side almost like a dancer. As the figure approached, Fidelia could see that it was a man cutting hay, swinging the scythe expertly, with the skill and grace of one who had done it all his life.

It was her father, Brazeau Lemerriant. His figure in the moonlight was ghostly, a little nightmarish. Fidelia rubbed her eyes, half believing she was dreaming. Fidelia sometimes didn't know whether she was asleep or awake, and her dreams were populated with such horrors that she often cried out. If she were to say, the next day, "I saw Papa cutting hay at night," would Brazeau pin her with his hot eyes and say, "The young girl, she is crazy, *n'est-ce pas?*"

But wasn't it crazy to be out cutting hay by the light of the moon? Fidelia made no such judgments. She was too young to know that the entire village considered all the Lemerriants to be mad — especially her brother, Elphique.

The figure was cutting a swath, advancing toward her. *Swing, swish, swing, swish.* Was that the sound that had awakened her? Fidelia shrank back. She didn't ponder why the sight of her father out there should send an icy chill down her spine; she only knew she didn't want him to find her, not now, not here, not when she was alone.

Both she and her brother usually tried to hide whenever they saw their father approaching. Built like a bull, although not a tall man, Brazeau would strike a child as quickly as he'd slap a mosquito, then order them to do some unpleasant or difficult task. He established dominance with the authority, if not the compassion, of a silverback gorilla, and both Fidelia and Elphique had become adept at staying out of his way during the daytime.

It was the evenings they dreaded. Whether drunk or sober, Brazeau was an elemental force, his rages escalating like hurricane winds, abating only when he had drunk himself into unconsciousness. Sometimes he would become playful and that was, perhaps, the worst of all. While his wife, Dauphine, alternately cowered and pleaded, he would "play" with the children, scoop them up, then threaten to drop them, blow cigarette smoke in their faces, or force them to drink his illegally distilled moonshine, laughing when they choked.

Her bladder contracted again, and Fidelia desperately did not want to go outside and risk being seen. But something had caught Brazeau's eye, some movement of her white nightgown perhaps. He was coming toward the window and Fidelia stood frozen. Brazeau, with measured steps, still swinging the scythe, was cutting as he approached. Suddenly he was at the window, looking at her, his eyes glinting in the moonlight. As the blade caught and flashed a reflected beam, Fidelia saw him raise the scythe higher, as if he would strike the window and cut down the girl behind it.

Fidelia gasped and clung to the frame. She saw Brazeau make a sweep with the scythe, then, just as he might have shattered the glass, he stopped short. His thick lips twisted into a smile, and he brought the tip of the blade to the window pane, inches from the top of Fidelia's head, then began to draw it downward slowly, slowly, the sharp metal scraping across the glass while he followed it with his eyes. He then raised his head to look at her, lifted the point of the scythe, and with it gently tapped the glass. *Tap. Tap. Tap.* He threw back his head and laughed. The laughter seemed to fill the night. Once again Brazeau Lemerriant raised the scythe as if to strike, scraped it slowly, agonizingly, downward — a sound Fidelia would never be able to forget — then again, deliberately, stopped and tapped the pane. *Tap. Tap. Tap.*

Fidelia jumped off the sill and fled, leaving a trail of bodily fluid.

CHAPTER 2

WILLIE HAAPALA pulled a weed out of the purple aubrietia on her rock garden wall, musing at the ability of weeds to mimic whatever plant they were entrenched in, making it almost impossible to recognize them. Her glasses had slipped down on her nose, and Willie carefully pushed them back in place. She had only recently begun to find it necessary to wear glasses other than for reading. Gardening had been more fun when she didn't need bifocals. *So had everything else*, she thought ruefully. She was grateful that her rock wall — a ha-ha built into a hillside — allowed her to work upright instead having to assume what she called the missionary gardening position: hands in soil, head down, rump in the air.

Now in her early eighties, Willie was still spry enough to do active gardening, although since Jeremy Banks had come for a visit (and then had returned to become more or less a permanent houseguest), she had his willing help in all things. It was nice to have a man around the house, particularly when rain gutters needed cleaning, or when a tree blew down in a storm and blocked the driveway.

A couple of years ago, Willie had sold her house in the town in which she'd lived and taught school most of her life. Trusting that she would be able to maintain it despite her advancing years, she had returned to live in her childhood home on Broom Island, a small dot of land off the Canadian Pacific coast.

Jeremy Banks was a retired professor of astronomy whom Willie had met two years earlier when he'd made an offer to buy her property as a place to live out *his* retirement years. Willie had decided not to sell, but the two had become friends, and Willie had invited Jeremy to stay with her while he looked for a suitable place for himself. Now, a year later, Jeremy was still Willie's houseguest. Both acknowledged that the arrangement was temporary, but Willie was glad of Jeremy's company. Broom Island, beautiful as it was, didn't afford a great deal by way of entertainment or social life, and the house, although built to last by Willie's grandparents, needed more upkeep than Willie had realized.

Willie also took wicked pleasure in the faintly improper appearance of a man and woman, unmarried, living under the same roof, even when both were senior citizens — although, goodness knows, these days, among the young, it seemed to be the norm. The only people scandalized would be people of Willie's own generation, and there lay the fun in it. Willie never explained. She referred to Jeremy as her visiting American friend, and allowed the village gossips to think what they chose.

Until he arrived on Broom Island, Jeremy Banks had never spent much time outdoors or working with his hands. Whether it was the climate, the sheer beauty of the place, or the desire to make himself useful and to keep fit, Jeremy had discovered the joys of gardening and outdoor work.

In the past year he had repaired fences, fixed a hole in the roof, and cleared out storage sheds. He had acquired a collection of garden tools, ostensibly purchased for his own home, once he found one. He liked to see them neatly arrayed, each in its designated spot, laid out on workshop counters and hanging on walls, each tool scrupulously cleaned, sharpened and oiled. Willie knew that if she left the garden hose on the lawn, Jeremy would silently, and with maddening neatness, reel it up on the hose caddy so that it looked as though it had just come from Home Hardware. If Willie left her garden snips sitting on the corner of a compost box, Jeremy would find them on his evening patrol, take them into the workshop, then leave them, sharpened and oiled, tucked into a pouch in her canvas garden bag — the same bag Willie left hanging on a hook in the greenhouse all summer long, only to find it, in the fall, full of the clay nests of mud dauber wasps.

Jeremy's love affair with garden equipment had led him to purchase a new power mower, a garden tiller, and the tool that gave him near erotic delight — the Troy-Bilt chipper/shredder he'd had shipped from Port Casper. With it he produced dozens of bags of garden mulch, each lawn & leaf bag tied with color-coded marine tape, each tagged and labeled with the date and the type of material used. The bags were stacked in chronological order in the utility area, and were viewed by Jeremy with the pride of a squire taking pleasure in his wine cellars.

Willie, herself, preferred a spading fork, a hoe, and the rattly reel-type lawnmower that had been her father's. Her approach to gardening was more freestyle than Jeremy's, and it made Jeremy wince to see Willie buy a shrub from Bloomers nursery, then carry it around the yard, looking for a place to plant it. Jeremy felt that one should draw plans on graph paper, consider the height and breadth of the mature tree or shrub *before* making a purchase, and dig the hole well in advance of bringing the plant home.

It had taken the summer of 1996 for Willie and Jeremy to get used to each other's ways. Although their approaches were different, there was little friction between them. Now, with the 1997 season upon them, Willie would have been glad of Jeremy's help. Unfortunately she hadn't been getting as much of it lately.

Willie stopped short to stare at a patch of Corsican mint — a flat, creeping ground cover that blushes tiny pink flowers in spring. She ran her fingers over the foliage then sniffed them, surprised, as always, by its powerful fragrance. Willie had planted the mint in hope that it would form a lush green cover that would flow over and between the rocks to cascade over the edge of the wall, but the herb seemed to have a different agenda. Last spring the mints had spread to dinner-plate size patches of green, but then the summer dry spell caused them to retreat like polar ice caps. Some had died out, only to reappear as haphazard bits growing in crevices in the side of the wall. Now, nourished by spring rains, surviving plants were once again spreading out, and it was at one those that Willie now stood staring. It had happened again!

There, in the center of the emerald patch, sat a small dark object — a lump of coal — charcoal, to be exact — a briquette, the type one would use in an outdoor barbecue. It was a small lump, about an inch square, partly burned away. Willie picked it up. Underneath it, the mint was green with no yellowed spot, indicated that the coal had been put there only a short time ago. She put it back. *Okay, how exactly did that get there and where did it come from?* Willie had an outdoor grill on which she and Jeremy barbecued steaks and salmon — but it was a gas grill, fueled by propane, lined with ceramic rocks. Willie didn't even know of anyone nearby who owned a charcoal grill. Her neighbors were far enough away so that she couldn't see their houses for the greenery, so it seemed impossible that anyone could have *thrown* it into her yard.

Children? Yes, there were mischievous children on the island, and one right in her own neighborhood. Yes, it was possible that a child walking along Kaunio Road could have opened her gate, run up the hill without being seen, and deposited a single black coal on her bed of mint — but *why?* Some childhood ritual? Childhood, she recalled, was filled with ritual. "Step on a crack and break your mother's back." This was not the first time Willie had found such a lump of coal. It had happened twice before this spring. She had found one on top of a bale of peat moss next to the greenhouse, and another neatly deposited on the railing of the porch of the old log sauna. The coal had appeared, like a message, in a place where it should not have been — a place where it had to have been *put*.

At first, Willie had suspected Jeremy of playing games, but when she mentioned it to him, he just stared at her blankly; indeed, it was difficult to picture Professor Jeremy Banks playing puckish tricks. When Willie had tried to impress upon him the strangeness of lumps of coal appearing out of nowhere, Jeremy had suggested that a squirrel or a bird could have dropped them and had appeared utterly disinterested. They had agreed to blame the "house gnomes" — the ones who occasionally hid household objects or their car keys.

Willie picked up the coal again. Maybe it *had* been dropped by a bird, a raven, perhaps. Why would a raven be carrying a lump of coal? *That, on this island, would really be a switch,* Willie thought, remembering an old chant from her childhood. *If they don't stop laughing, throw a lump of coal.* The origin of that chant had been one of the saddest — and most terrifying — legends of the island. It had affected four generations of children, and Willie remembered how, when she was a child, they'd all carried lumps of coal in their pockets. *I wonder if kids still do that.* Childhood rituals get passed on long after everyone has forgotten how they got started. Willie turned the coal over in her hand, then hefted it, feeling its weight. A raven could have carried it easily. She looked up, almost expecting to see coal falling from the cloudless sky. She saw none, but there were a couple or ravens flying overhead, heading for the top of the tall, old-growth Douglas fir that flanked the driveway. *Okay, you have my attention. Are you trying to tell me something?*

Deep in thought, Willie walked toward the vegetable garden area. She started to toss the piece of coal into a compost box, then changed her mind. Instead, she carried it to the bench by the greenhouse and dropped it into an empty clay flower pot — empty, that is, except for two other lumps of charcoal. *Why am I keeping these?*

CHAPTER 3

THE VILLAGE of Satama on Broom Island had been founded by Finns escaping tsarist rule in the early 1900s. The name, Satama, means harbor or haven, and to the early settlers, Broom Island had represented the hope of a better life. Most of them were unprepared for the harsh conditions they found in this strange raw land, so thick with huge trees that it was near impossible to cut one down because there was no place for it to fall. With only their hands and primitive tools, but fueled by that Finnish quality known as *sisu*, they set about carving out lives. The cost was high. Many died of disease and lack of proper medical attention. In their efforts to establish industry that would sustain the little colony, some were victims of storms at sea, and of logging and mining accidents. Many left, disillusioned by the hard life, and also by the power struggles among, and surprising incompetence of, the colony founders, who ultimately either deserted the island or were invited to leave. A few of the settlers had stayed, and it was their descendants who established Broom Island, first as an agricultural, then forestry and fishing area, and now, increasingly, as a growing tourist attraction.

The village was no longer purely Finnish. The Old Finns were dying out, their children scattered to the mainland in search of better opportunities. Where Finnish once had been spoken on the streets, younger people now had forgotten the language that had given both the village and themselves their names, names that in the slim Satama telephone directory could be recognized by their double vowels and consonants: Pikkusaari, Riittamäki, Sillanpää.

The Finns had not been the first to settle Broom Island. An even more ill-fated religious sect from the British Isles had attempted to establish itself in the 1800s, but had also ended in failure. Its legacy was the wildfire growth of the shrub called Scotch broom, the seeds of which, it was said, had migrated to the island in cattle feed and had given the island, first its unofficial, and now official name. Hardly anyone remembered the original: Strathclyde.

During the sixties, there had been an influx of American draft avoiders and flower children. "Hippies," they were still called by the Old Guard in Satama. Indeed, any newcomer to Broom Island would be often so termed, regardless of wealth, social position, or their decade of arrival.

Only fifteen miles long and about three wide, Broom Island now housed two separate settlements: Satama village and Tranquil Bay. Tranquil Bay, at the southern end of the island, was a growing community of wealthy homes. It also provided a scattering of rental cabins to the rich and famous who flew in to enjoy the spectacular scenery, charter fishing, and whale watching at Whale Point — the southernmost tip of the island where orcas came to rub on the pebble beach.

Willie's house by the sea stood on the connecting road (Kaunio Road) about halfway between Tranquil Bay and Satama, which non-Finns incorrectly pronounced *Su-TAH-ma* instead of giving each syllable equal emphasis.

There were three places in which Satama and Tranquil Bay met and mingled: The Co-op, the only grocery and general store on the island; the post office, where everyone had to pick up his mail; and the restaurant on the main floor of the Broom Island Inn. The restaurant had been run by a number of owners under a number of names, and the quality of fare and service had varied dramatically with each. Through the years, it had been known as The Eagle's Crest, The Ocean View, The Speckled Crab, and The Blue Oyster. The current owners, Larry and June Nyquist, called it, appropriately, the New Broom.

The Inn also housed a pub that had always been called The Sea Hole. It was shunned by conservative Old Finns, particularly the women, and was frequented by tourists and loggers and those who had nothing better to do with their evenings than enjoy beer, billiards, and boozy conversation. It was hardly a "den of iniquity," except by the standards of the most conservative Satama residents, and represented nightlife on Broom Island. Willie and Jeremy, who might have enjoyed an occasional game of billiards, avoided the place because of its smoky atmosphere.

"Nothing in the mail but a couple of bills and an L.L. Bean catalog." It was Jeremy. He had hiked to the village post office and now stood before Willie with the mail tucked inside the sling that supported his right arm. He withdrew the folded catalog and envelopes. "God, I'll be glad when this cast comes off. It itches like the very devil." He pulled off the sling.

"You're not supposed to use the sling after the first week. Isn't that what Dr. Swallow told you?"

"I only put it on to hold the mail and garner sympathy."

"You're lucky it wasn't worse. You could have killed yourself."

Jeremy grimaced, nodded, and looked upward. The old house had three stories with a widow's walk along the topmost. If he hadn't landed on that walk, he could have plummeted all the way down to the flagstone path below. "I guess I'm too old to be scrambling around on rooftops."

"Especially that one."

Jeremy sighed. "With all the trees around, I thought I'd get a better view if I climbed on the roof. And I did — briefly."

"Maybe next time you should consult an astrologer before you try something like that. Anything new in the village?"

"Not much. I'm always late picking up the mail when I have to walk. I suppose I could have ridden my bike."

"*I* could have picked up the mail. Or I could have given you ride to the post office."

"I know. And I could have taken my car although I'm not supposed to drive with my arm in a cast. Insurance won't cover me if I have an accident. But it was such a nice day and I needed the exercise. Anyway, I did stop at Pearl's for a cup of coffee. The buzz in town is that some writer from the mainland is coming to Satama to do an article on Broom Island. We're all going to be famous!"

Willie groaned. "Not again!"

"It's happened before?"

"Like the grunions. Every so often somebody 'discovers' Broom Island, comes over and takes a lot of photos, interviews the residents, writes an article that gets everyone upset because of the inaccuracies, and sometimes results in a flurry of visiting gawkers."

"But doesn't Broom Island benefit from the tourist trade?"

"Not much. Those that cater to the rich don't need that type of publicity. Oh sure, I suppose the Co-op sells a few Satama T-shirts, but there's really not much here for tourists. At least not yet. Tourists are like visiting relatives. You have to put up with them but you just wish they'd lose your address."

"Well, Pearl said she'd be arriving tomorrow."

"She? It's a woman?"

"Yes. Pearl told me her name but I can't remember it now. She's booked a room for a week."

"At the Inn?" Willie gave a whooping laugh.

"What's wrong with the Inn? Isn't it the only hotel on the island?"

"The place should be condemned! Haven't you ever been in there?"

"Only in the shop, the pub and the restaurant."

"It's noisy. There's usually a bunch of loggers having a party. The roof leaks. The johns rock from side to side when you sit down. The carpets are impregnated with athlete's foot fungus. The rooms smell of stale cigarette smoke, and if you leave the balcony door open to let in fresh air you're apt to be joined in bed by the owner's cat. That animal has come close to giving several people heart attacks. She won't be staying very long!"

"Pearl said you could expect her to look you up. I mean, as the resident authority on the Pacific Northwest and as a native Broom Islander."

Willie groaned again. "Oh God! I'll probably have to give her a cup of tea while she tries to get the spellings of our names right. I don't suppose the woman speaks Finnish."

"I don't know. I wouldn't think so. She has a *very* odd name. All I can think of is opossum."

"Possum? Could that be Ooms-Possum? Celeste Ooms-Possum?"

"It could have been. Do you know her?"

"I *met* a Celeste Ooms-Possum once in Seattle, years ago. It's not a name you forget. I was there lecturing on genealogy at a private school for girls. My topic was Fitting Into Your Genes. She wasn't a student; I think she was working there. She seemed to be an intense little thing. Kept following me around. She did tell me she wanted to be a writer and asked if I thought she should change her name. I said it was up to her, but that her name would certainly be memorable on a book jacket."

"Then it might be she. How many Ooms-Possums could there be?"

"We'll see." Willie reached into the clay flower pot and pulled out the lump of coal. "Found another one of these again today."

Jeremy looked at it. "Where was it this time?"

"Right in the center of a patch of Corsican mint."

Jeremy whistled the *Twilight Zone* theme, then laughed.

CHAPTER 4

LITTLE WILHELMIINA Haapala, age eight, sat at the breakfast table. Her mother, Pirkko, put a bowl of porridge in front of her and poured a cup of coffee for her husband, Ebra. Nobody was talking. Wilhelmiina looked, big-eyed, from one to the other of her parents. Something was going on!

There had been commotion in the night. "Miina" had awakened, gotten sleepily out of her cot, and crept downstairs into the spacious main room — the *pirtti* — the center of activity in the house. Her mother had quickly led her back to bed, but not before Miina had seen the girl. Now, with a wisdom born of experience, Miina asked no questions. She'd learned that while grownups would never answer you directly, if you acted as if you were busy doing something else, they didn't seem to think that you could hear them, and would talk freely in front of you. She scraped up the last of her porridge, swallowed her milk, then left the table, and settled on a bench in the corner with a coloring book and crayons.

"That poor, poor little thing," Pirkko was saying. "Somebody should do something about that family."

"They're all crazy, the lot of them," Ebra said. "It's not the first time!"

"No, but when I think of that twelve-year-old child making her way through these woods, running away from God knows what —"

"She was drunk."

"No, she *couldn't* have been drunk! She was having convulsions, hallucinating."

"*Juoppohulluus.* She had the DTs."

"No, and it's not her fault. It's Brazeau Lemerriant's fault. The sins of the father, like the Bible says. The father is a drunk and he's passed his sins on to his innocent daughter. Now she has to bear them."

"Well, when I see a girl screaming that little devils with flashlight eyes are trying to make her eat shit, to me that's the DTs."

"Shh!" Pirkko glanced toward Miina who, by now, was humming a little tune and coloring furiously. "Nobody knows what goes on in that house."

"That's because nobody dares go near them. That old bastard, Brazeau, would shoot you as quick as look at you. That wife of his is just barely alive anymore, and his son is crazy as a loon."

"The children should be in school."

"You remember what happened when the visiting school inspector went up there? Barely escaped with his life when Brazeau pointed a shotgun and threatened to set the dog on him. Where's the girl now?"

"Fidelia?" She pronounced the name as Finns would, Fee-dee-LEE-ya. "She's still asleep."

"In the Russian church, you mean," Ebra said, the Finnish euphemism for sleeping it off. "What are you going to do with her?"

"I don't know. She can't stay here. They'll come looking for her."

Miina pricked up her ears. The Lemerriants would be coming? Here? Elphique Lemerriant would be coming? She was terrified of Elphique. All the island children were terrified of him. Elphique, at 13, had inherited his father's build, as well as a tallness gene from his mother's side of the family, and towered over other children.

"They probably will, but we can't keep her here."

"Well, it just isn't right. We should notify someone."

"Who? Who on this island wants to take on Brazeau Lemerriant? Besides, it's none of our business, Pirkko."

"Maybe so, but look at how they live! Decent people can't even imagine what kind of homelife those children must have. And the son, they say he's mentally deranged."

"Kid gets knocked around enough, he's apt to be."

"He spends his life in the woods, like an animal. They say he sleeps in caves and under trees even in winter. They say he eats raw meat. They say he catches rabbits with his bare hands and howls at the moon with the wolves. Some even say he can turn into one!"

"He's a kid. He's only thirteen."

Pirkko's voice dropped to a whisper. "A lot of people think it was Elphique who killed the little Jaakobsson boy."

"People gossip. The boy wandered into the woods. Cougar killed him."

"But the body had been torn open and the eyes pecked out."

"Cougar did that, and ravens go for the eyes. Don't you remember? They shot the cougar."

Pirkko sighed. "It's a bad, bad business, Ebra. I would help if I could. I *tried* to help. You remember. I tried talking to Dauphine Lemerriant that time when she came to town. I was trying to be friendly, but all I got was abuse for my pains. She told me she didn't want to talk to me, and then Brazeau showed up and used the most *awful* language!"

"The woman's scared of him. She knows if she talks to you, he'll only beat her up again when they go home." Ebra reached for another piece of *pulla*. "What do you want me to do? You want me to take her to town and have the doc take a look at her?"

"Oh, yes! That's a good idea. But let her sleep for now, poor child."

But Fidelia never did get to the doctor. Her family did come for her, but it wasn't Brazeau or even Elphique who came to fetch her. It was Dauphine. She came to the door, a pale, worn woman who looked much older than her 37 years. She offered no greeting to Pirkko who opened the door, and merely glanced furtively around the room until her eyes lit upon Fidelia who, by then, was sitting quietly with Wilhelmiina. Miina had given her a picture book and the girl was leafing through it, staring dully at the pages.

Pirkko Haapala showed her disapproval only by the stiffness of her back as she invited Dauphine to come in. "Mrs. Lemerriant, please stay and have a cup of coffee."

Dauphine shook her head. "*Merci, madame*, but no. We must go."

Pirkko took a deep breath. "Mrs. Lemerriant, about your daughter. She is ill. She needs to see a doctor."

Fidelia looked blankly at her mother. She was a child, but it was obvious that the entity who lived in the small thin body had long since left childhood behind.

"Fidelia, come."

"But Mrs. Lemerriant, surely you can see how desperate your daughter's condition is. She traveled here last night all alone through the woods. She had a fever. She had convulsions. This is not normal for a little girl. Won't you let my husband take her into town to see Doctor Seppänen?"

"No, *madame*. We take care of our own. Fidelia, come."

Fidelia let the book fall and slowly walked toward her mother who took her firmly by the hand, turned, and walked out the door.

"Well! That's gratitude for you. She didn't even thank us."

Ebra, who had been watching in silence, shrugged. "Did you expect her to?"

Wilhelmiina picked up the picture book. "Fidelia was supposed to take this home. Guess she forgot. Mother, what's the deetees?"

Pirkko looked sharply at her daughter. "The curse of the devil, that's what it is. And you, you have no need to know of such things."

CHAPTER 5

Celeste Ooms-Possum sat in her car, wishing desperately that she had a cigarette. It had been a week since she'd quit smoking, and she was vacillating between bitterly regretting her decision and pride at having gotten this far. Now her fingers drummed on the steering wheel as her car sat in the ferry lineup in Port Casper. She felt a rising impatience as she watched the *Island Empress* maneuver into dock and disgorge, first a huddle of foot passengers, then a succession of motor vehicles.

"Roll up your window, Gabi. The wind's too cold."

Without taking her eyes off the Game Boy in her lap, the little girl beside her reached over and closed the window just as the signal turned green. As the car moved forward, Gabrielle Choate, aged 10, looked up, her expression impassive, as if trying to decide whether there was anything interesting to see. "So where's this place we're going again?"

"Broom Island, Gabi. This is the ferry to Broom Island. We'll be able to see it from the boat. Once we park the car we can get out and take a look."

The ferry worker in his orange bib with a big white fluorescent "X" motioned them to a parking lane, and Celeste turned off the motor. "It'll probably be windy on the water, but I want to get a few shots of the shoreline." She got out of the car with her camera. "You want to come, Gabi?"

Gabi put down her game and got out as well, but not with any enthusiasm or even curiosity. "It's too cold."

"Put on your jacket and come *on*. See? It's the first time you've been on a ferry. Look, over there, that's Broom Island. That's where we're going. See all the houses along the shore? That's the village of Satama. Your great-grandmother used to live on that island."

"What are all those logs doing in the water?" Indeed, the surface of the choppy strait was bobbing with floating pieces of wood, and Celeste could hear a jarring thud whenever the boat hit one of them.

"I don't know, but logging is a big industry here. You'll see a lot of wood washed up on beaches. This is probably debris from a log boom." Celeste was focusing her 35mm Pentax at the distant shoreline.

"It's too cold out here. I'm going back in the car."

"Yes, okay. I'll be there in a minute myself. I just want to get a few more pictures." It *was* cold. The day was sunny with a few light clouds in the sky, but the wind was brisk and chilling.

The ferry ride took less than half an hour. The boat swung into place at the dock and, under the eyes of the ferry crew, jockeyed into position. A ramp was lowered and an assortment of foot passengers walked off. Celeste turned on her motor and waited to be motioned ashore. There seemed to be a number of people milling about, and a line of cars waiting to board; Celeste carefully drove off the boat, up a hill, then made a left turn into the parking area in front of the Broom Island Inn.

She was in the heart of Satama. The Broom Island Co-op was across the street from the hotel, and along the short stretch of what was obviously Main Street, Celeste noticed a few buildings that seemed to be businesses: a tiny gas station, a small café that looked to be closed, and a B&B, also closed. Would they open in summer during tourist season? Or were they businesses that had failed and been abandoned? Beyond the main drag clustered a village of small houses.

"Come on Gabi, let's go register. We can bring the bags in later."

Gabrielle followed her silently, then stopped to pat a large dog that was snoozing in front of the Inn entrance. The dog opened one eye and seemed to smile.

"Gabi, don't pat strange animals."

They entered a small room with a few chairs placed along the walls and a low table in the middle piled with old magazines. It reminded Celeste of a dentist's office. A glass door led into a small shop, and it turned out that the registry desk was the shop counter. It was a mini-general store with a cold drinks machine, shelves stocked with canned and dry goods, even a refrigerated glass case with bouquets of live carnations for sale. In one corner stood a coffee urn surrounded by styrofoam cups. A dark-haired woman behind the counter eyed Celeste with solemn curiosity.

"I'm Celeste Ooms-Possum. I believe I have a reservation."

The woman smiled, instantly transformed from wary to friendly. "Yes, we've been expecting you. And that's your little girl. She's a cutie." Celeste turned, expecting to find Gabrielle at her elbow, but saw that the girl had wandered to the back of the shop where she was investigating a small shelf of movie rentals.

"Yes, that's Gabi. She's ten. I'm afraid she's going to be at loose ends until she finds someone her own age. Are there many children on the island?"

"Oh yes, there are lots of them. They're still in school — either here or in Port Casper. If you're going to be here a while, I'm sure Gabi will get to meet some. I take it the schools in the States let out earlier for summer vacation?"

"Gabi goes to a private school, but she *is* out early. I wanted to take her with me on this assignment." Celeste spoke carefully. No need to tell everyone about Gabi's problems.

"Well, we hope you'll enjoy your stay. You're booked for a week, but if you need to extend that, it's okay. We're not busy this time of year." The woman handed Celeste two keys. "This one is to your room, upstairs, number 5, and this one is to the front door in case you're out after we lock up for the night."

"Oh! Yes, well . . . thank you. It's my first visit to Satama, and I may need help in finding my way around."

"Anything you want to know, just come ask me. I'm Helen Laine, the town gossip." She grinned, and Celeste noticed that she had kind brown eyes with little laugh lines around them. "I can tell you where everything — and everyone — is, but then, so can anyone in Satama. We all know each other's business here."

"It looks like a charming little town and the scenery is breathtaking! You probably don't have any such thing as crime, do you?"

"Oh, don't you believe it. Only yesterday someone stole the wooden eagle off Oliver Sylvester's fencepost. Big city people bring big city ways. You can't just leave your doors unlocked anymore."

"Do you have a police force?"

"We have one RCMP constable. They rotate them every two years. Our last one just left. We had a farewell party for him last week. I haven't met the new one yet, but he and his wife have just moved into that house on First Street." Helen pointed through the window. "The station's across from the post office, next to the health clinic. The constable always lives in the house beside it."

"I'll have to walk around and get to know the town." Celeste glanced down at Gabrielle who had been tugging at her mother's sleeve. "What is it, Gabi?"

"There's nothing here. You should see the movies. They're *ancient*."

Helen laughed ruefully. "I'm afraid that's true, Gabi. But the good news is there's no VCR or television in the rooms anyway." Gabrielle looked stunned. Helen said to Celeste. "No telephones either, I'm afraid, but there's one in the lobby. It's a pay phone but you don't have to put money in it. If you make any long-distance calls, get the charges and I'll add them to your bill."

"I have my cell phone, and I guess I can plug in my laptop computer, can't I?"

"Oh sure. We're still a bit basic here, but we do have power, but no Internet service yet here at the Inn. One of our guests nearly died laughing when he asked for a wake-up call and I handed him a windup alarm clock. I guess Satama takes a bit of getting used to, but you know something? Everyone who lives here loves it."

"I can see how they would. Come on, Gabi, let's get our stuff out of the car. Thanks, Helen."

"Oh, by the way, watch out for the cat. If you leave your sliding glass doors open at night, you're apt to find a big gray tabby in bed with you."

Celeste stopped and stared, half-smiling.

"Oh yes! The cat may visit and we don't want anyone going into cardiac arrest. He belongs to the hotel manager, and likes to climb on the roof, jump onto the balcony railing, stroll in the door, and leap on your bed at night. I'd keep the glass doors closed if I were you, unless you're *really* fond of animals."

"Yikes! Thanks for the warning. Oh, is there such a thing as a town archive or town hall where records are kept?"

"If you mean the old records of the early Finnish settlers, you'd have to go the Finnish museum. It's not open. It's never open. You have to call either Amanda Vuorisaari or Willie Haapala. Either of them will come and unlock it for you. There's no admission charge but there's a donation box." Helen scribbled on a scrap of paper. "Here are their phone numbers."

Celeste took the piece of paper: Willie Haapala. That name looked easier to pronounce than the other. It even looked vaguely familiar.

* * *

"I hate this place. It smells."

"Well, Gabi, it's not Club Med, but I'm afraid it's the only place in town." Celeste had unpacked their bags and situated clothing into drawers and onto bent wire hangers. She surveyed the room which, like the Inn itself, was old, run-down and weathered. While the room didn't appear to be overtly dirty, there was a dreariness and impersonality that seemed to repel even her clothing, which hung sparsely in the doorless closet as if not wishing to come in contact with walls. The smell of stale cigarette smoke pervaded everything, even the clean towels in the bathroom.

"And there's no TV!"

"That's okay, Gabi. We won't be spending time here except to sleep. Oh, Gabi, keep your shoes on. God only knows what's in this carpet."

"I have to go to the bathroom."

"You do that, and then we'll go out and explore. We'll find a place to have lunch." Celeste opened the draw drapes, revealing sliding glass doors, a small wooden balcony, and a postcard view of water and mountains. "Come and take a look at this, Gabi." She slid open the doors to let in fresh sea air.

"Mom, the toilet jiggles."

A bit hesitantly, Celeste stepped onto the balcony, wondering if it, too, would jiggle. It seemed firm underfoot and had a stout railing. The view was dominated by water which had now calmed to ripples. Across the strait she could see the town of Port Casper. "See, Gabi, that's our ferry going back." In the distance were mountains whose slopes were covered with evergreen and their peaks with snow. Below her, the beach of clay-colored sand and pebbles was patterned with the footprints of a child and a dog at the water's edge. It was deserted now except for a few gulls and a couple of ravens.

"What's that stuff in the water?" Gabi pointed to a floating mass.

"Kelp. See, there's some that's washed ashore." There was a pile of large yellow-green glistening leaves with a long coiled stalk, thick as a fire hose, lying in a heap of a size that might be crammed into a lawn

& leaf bag.

"It looks like something from outer space."

"We'll walk along the beach later so you can see it close up. Right now we'd better find food before your blood sugar drops."

Celeste learned that unless she and Gabi wanted to sip soda and nibble drying pastry in the Inn shop, the only place to eat seemed to be the restaurant. The door was open but the room was deserted. Nobody was at the till, but a young man emerged from the kitchen. "I'm sorry but we're closed till five. That's when we open for dinner."

"You don't serve lunch or breakfast?"

"We open for breakfast at seven-thirty, and stay open till one. Then we open again for dinner, but if you ask me, it's a waste of time. Hardly anybody around this time of year since the logging industry's been dying."

"Oh, dear. We just got in on the ferry and we haven't had lunch."

"Well, I was just on my way home, but I could fix you a sandwich, I guess. Or you could try Pearl's across the street."

"Is that the place with the 'Closed' sign in the window?"

"Don't pay any attention to that. She never remembers to take it down. She's in there."

"Thanks. In that case we'll check out Pearl's, and I expect we'll be back tonight for dinner."

Pearl's turned out to be a small diner with four booths and a counter with no stools. The place was surprisingly lively. Celeste and Gabi slid into an empty booth next to the door — so recently vacated that the vinyl seat was still warm. The others were occupied by men who were lingering and chatting over coffee. The conversation seemed to have to do with logging and fishing and government interference. The woman behind the counter (Pearl?) was adding her opinion of the Prime Minister and the NDP party, and looked a tad annoyed at the interruption when Celeste and Gabi came in. She addressed them with an upward tilt of her chin, "Yes?"

"We'd like to order lunch, please."

The woman pointed to a small blackboard on which was scrawled: Soup and Sandwich Special: $6.95. "Today it's corn chowder with a salmon sandwich."

"Is that our only choice?"

"That's it today, unless you want tinned meat."

"No, no, we'll each have the special. I'd also like a cup of coffee and a glass of milk for my daughter."

"*Salmon* sandwich?" Gabrielle hissed. "I *hate* fish."

"Pretend you're in the jungle and the chief of the tribe is serving grubs. If you don't eat them you die."

Pearl cleared the table of used cups and saucers, gave it a wipe with a damp dishcloth, then brought the food. The corn chowder had come from a can, but the salmon sandwich turned out to be delicious. This was salmon country, and the wild sockeye had been cooked fresh, then lovingly mixed with mayonnaise and onion and herbs to make such a tasty filling that even Gabrielle had eaten most of hers. Celeste sat sipping her coffee, inhaling second-hand smoke, and wishing she had a cigarette, while Gabi finished a small dish of ice cream.

The crowd had thinned. One by one the men had drifted out. Now the door opened and a woman entered. Celeste gave her a casual glance, then did a double take: the woman had a live crow sitting on her shoulder! What was this, some local version of a bar joke? So this guy walks into a bar and he has a crow perched on his head, and the bartender says, "Why do you have a crow on your head?" And the guy says, "Because the parrot was always correcting my grammar." Ba-ram-bam! Rim shot.

Trying to keep a straight face, Celeste watched as the woman settled in the farthest booth. She was obviously a regular, as Pearl greeted her casually, then brought her a cup of tea. The bird stood its ground, neatly keeping its balance on her shoulder whenever the woman moved.

She could be part of the Addams Family, Celeste thought. The woman or young girl — it was hard to tell — looked to be in her late teens or early twenties with hair as black as her bird's wings. She was deathly pale with dark circles around her eyes and was wearing a long black coat and a misshapen black felt fedora — the sort of thrift shop clothing affected by many young people of the day. Celeste thought of it as Boutique Macabre. The woman had been carrying a book with a black cover under her arm, a book that she now laid on the table and opened. She began running her fingers over a page, and Celeste realized the woman was blind; the book was in Braille. Gabi, who had turned to stare at the woman behind her, opened her mouth; Celeste gave her the international sign mothers give children when they sense they're about to say something unfortunate. Gabrielle lowered her voice to a stage whisper. "But Mom, that woman has a bird on her shoulder. And what's the matter with her eyes?"

"Shh! It's not polite to stare," said Celeste who, herself, couldn't help staring — and now realized to her dismay that the blind woman seemed to be staring back at *her*.

The voice was sharp and ringing — that of an evangelist commanding sinners to repent: "Come over here so I can see you better."

A little aghast at being singled out, Celeste's first impulse was to leave, but she got up, with Gabi close behind, and walked over to the woman. "Good afternoon. Please forgive us for staring, but I'm afraid we were both fascinated by your pet bird."

The woman tilted her head backwards and squinted her eyes. She apparently had some degree of vision. "This is Blackjack. He's a Northern raven. Say hello to the people, Blackjack."

To Celeste's astonishment, the bird spread its wings, made a little bow, and said "hello."

"He can talk!" Gabi exclaimed.

"He can say a lot of words. He could say more if his tongue had been split. And he has the intelligence of a child of five, don't you, Blackjack. *Don't touch him!*"

Gabrielle had extended her hand. She snatched it back. "He pecks," the woman said. She tilted her head again and tried to focus on Celeste.

"I know you, don't I?" It was almost an accusation, and Celeste was beginning to feel uncomfortable.

"I . . . I don't think so. It's my first visit to Broom Island."

"I know you."

"We couldn't have met. I think I'd remember. But people are always mistaking me for someone else. I guess I have one of those faces." Celeste realized that she was chattering nervously.

"Don't *lie* to me. I know you. I know *both* of you."

Gabrielle edged behind her mother. Celeste glanced at Pearl, who shook her head slightly and nodded toward the door as if to say, maybe you'd better go.

Celeste murmured something polite about perhaps meeting again and nearly tripped over Gabi as she stepped backward — at which point the bird flapped its wings, took flight, and to Celeste's horror, landed on Gabrielle's head. Gabrielle screamed. Celeste made a grab for the bird who with wings beating rose into the air, pulling out strands of blond hair in its claws, then landed back on the woman's shoulder.

"See?" the woman shrieked. "I *do* know you. And *he* knows you!"

Celeste scooped up her daughter who was now crying hysterically, pulled out a twenty dollar bill and tossed it on the table as she fled.

* * *

Why? Celeste asked herself back at the hotel, why am I such a magnet for *nuts?* It was true. In any public place, if there was anyone acting strangely, that person could be counted upon to approach Celeste. Whether it was a drunk, a vagrant, a street evangelist, a beggar, or someone just wandering around in a state of disorientation, that person would invariably make a beeline for Celeste. It had gotten so that she tended to keep a wary eye on crowds in shopping malls, and if she spotted a little old lady dressed in a tutu, with a bunch of keys rubber-banded to her wrist, Celeste would try to retreat before the woman noticed her.

It didn't always work. The nice-looking young man at the next table in a mall coffee shop, when Celeste returned his polite "good afternoon," had turned out to be mentally disturbed and ended up screaming obscenities, until his escort materialized to usher him away. The dignified elderly gentleman, who had stood next to her at a clothing counter, had gone on into a loud and frothing rage at the prices the store charged for such shoddy workmanship — and why were these foreigners in Taiwan making clothes for Americans, when Americans were out of work? Of course he had addressed those comments to Celeste who had edged away under cover of a T-shirt, a shirt she'd then had to buy in order to get out of the store.

Celeste, who cringed at being publicly embarrassed, always felt that, once the scene had occurred, everyone seemed to think that somehow *she'd* been the one who caused it. Pearl at the diner had looked at her exactly that way.

Now Celeste was trying to calm her own nicotine-deprived nerves by contemplating the view. Gabrielle, at least, was napping. Celeste had managed to quiet her down, and given her the medication Dr. Sitwell had prescribed — although Celeste didn't like the idea of a child having to take drugs. It seemed unnatural. She looked at her daughter, angelic in sleep. What dark things swam around in that sweet little head? What caused the horrifying dreams that had begun to plague Gabi? School, this last year, had been a nightmare for both of them. There had been any number of calls to "come pick up your daughter" because she was causing some sort of ruckus — attacking another student, throwing things in the cafeteria, having a tantrum. When Celeste had told Gabi's teacher that she wanted to take her out of school early, Mrs. Mitcher had been unable to mask her relief.

Now Celeste wanted to spend the summer with Gabi. She had to find out what was going on with her. She was not about to abandon her to any medical system, or place her at the continuing mercy of psychiatrists. She'd had enough of that. Gabi, in the past, had been a sunny little girl, sweet-tempered and outgoing. Celeste tried to remember when it had all started to go wrong. It was only in the past year that Gabi had begun having nightmares and exhibiting disruptive behavior, but maybe it had been slowly building up.

Perhaps it had started with the divorce. Gabi had been five. At the time she'd handled it surprisingly well. Perhaps that, in itself, was a sign. Gabi had become — well — quieter. Celeste, grateful that Gabi seemed so strong, had gone on to concentrate on her own career, while Gabi had, perhaps, spent too much time in daycare and with babysitters.

Her father, a high-profile attorney — Choate, Choate, Palmer & Dix — didn't seem to have time for Gabrielle, especially now that he had married the former legal secretary (with whom he had been having an affair) and had two new children. His phone calls to Gabi, assurances that "Daddy loves you very much" had begun to ring hollow, particularly since there seldom seemed to be a good time for him to come see her, or for her to visit him. ("Cynthia hasn't been feeling well.")

Cynthia, Bixby Choate's new wife, had been pregnant twice in the five years, and while Gabrielle had, of course, seen her half brothers, she had shown cold interest in them, said little, and wanted to come home.

Celeste gently pushed back a lock of Gabi's blond hair. There must have been a sense of abandonment. She'd felt it herself when she realized that divorcing Bixby meant divorcing the whole family and most of their friends. To the Choates, she suddenly didn't exist, and she'd haughtily returned the name like a library book; Ooms-Possum hadn't been an easy name to grow up with, but it was *hers*. Gabi would be a Choate, of course, not that they seemed to have any time for her. *And I never had enough time either, did I? Dear God, did I fail to notice that under that cool little-girl self-sufficiency my child was hurting? Was I so distraught and self-absorbed that I failed to see that she was coping with much too much? Well, I hope it's not too late to make up for that.*

Celeste glanced at her watch. She should call one of the women about the museum. It would probably be best to get her assignment done and go back home as soon as possible. She was to do a piece on Broom Island for a travel magazine — which would make the trip tax-deductible — but that was not her only reason for being here. Celeste wanted to try to uncover something of her own family history; maybe some of it would explain her own strange childhood, and perhaps even Gabi's.

She tried Willie Haapala's number but got no reply. There was no answer at the Vuorisaari house either, a bit to Celeste's relief that she didn't have to struggle with pronunciation of the name. It was probably too late today anyway. She stretched out on the other bed and stared at the smoke-yellowed ceiling tiles. It had been a long day, a long trip. Maybe she should nap a bit as well. Then they could both shower, change clothes, and go see what the Inn restaurant had to offer.

Outside, the sea had turned calm. A black Labrador dog loped along the water's edge, stopping to sniff seashells, and making half-hearted charges at gulls, putting them to flight. A gray tabby cat was sitting on the balcony railing, licking its paws. A ferry was coming into dock, and had Celeste stepped outside, she would have seen that there was some commotion. A group of people had gathered. There was a police car there as well. A typical late afternoon in Satama? Or was something going on?

CHAPTER 6

Showered and changed, Celeste felt better as she and Gabi made their way down the dark-carpeted stairs to the lobby, out the front door, and down the sidewalk to the entrance of the restaurant. Celeste studied the menu tacked to the heavy wooden door. "I see they have fried clams. I haven't had fried clams in years. I used to love them."

"Is everything in this place seafood?"

"No, they have meat loaf and pork chops and cabbage rolls and — "

"Can't I have burger and a coke?"

"Oh, I'll bet you can. Let's go on in."

From what the young man had said earlier, Celeste expected the dining room to be empty, but it wasn't. You couldn't call the room crowded, but several tables were occupied by both adults and children, giving the place the look of a typical family restaurant.

"See, there are lots of kids on the island," Celeste said as they chose a table by the window. There seemed to be no one in charge of seating.

Gabi looked around disdainfully. "They're just little kids."

Celeste smiled. At no time was the age difference so important as in childhood. In the pecking order of children, a year or two could form an effective barrier against comradeship. This was strictly enforced by social mores so that the only "little kids" you could play with (and only when you were forced) were your own siblings.

Gabi was, however, correct. Most of the children dining with their parents *were* little kids — and not well-behaved ones either. A small boy in a restaurant high chair was squealing and writhing to get free while his parents seemed not to notice. A couple of children who looked to be five or six were racing around the room, chasing each other. Celeste wondered to which of the unconcerned couples they belonged. *The children's hour! It wouldn't be so bad if their voices weren't so shrill.*

The young man she'd seen earlier came to their table. "Hi, ladies. What'll it be?"

Celeste greeted him with a smile. "Looks like business is brisk tonight after all. Are you here all by yourself?"

"Almost. The missus is cooking in the kitchen, but I'm going to need roller skates. I guess the excitement this afternoon brought people out."

"Excitement?"

"Yeah, uh, there's been some trouble." The man looked a little uncomfortable, as if he'd rather not stop to explain, and made a show of poising pencil over pad.

"I'll have the fried clams and can my daughter have a hamburger and a coke?"

"Sure thing." He was gone.

Celeste looked around the room. A few people at tables seemed to be looking at her with open curiosity. At least the woman with the bird was nowhere in sight! Across the room she noticed an elderly couple engaged in conversation. They looked a little out of place. The woman was wiry, white-haired, dressed in a skirt and blouse while most other women in the room were wearing jeans. The man had his arm in a cast.

As Celeste sat watching them, wondering how uncomfortable a cast must be, the white-haired woman looked back at Celeste. She said something to her companion, then got up and walked toward Celeste's table.

Oh no! Not another local nut! Celeste quickly turned away, hoping the woman would walk on by.

"Excuse me, but you must be Ms. Ooms-Possum. I think we met once, many years ago. I'm Wilhelmiina Haapala. I used to do some lecturing when I was teaching school in the States, and I think we met in Seattle."

Celeste opened her mouth in surprise. "Of course! It was at the Cumberland School for Girls. I was working there as an assistant to the librarian! Imagine you remembering me after all these years!"

"I probably wouldn't have. My memory isn't what it used to be. But the jungle telegraph has nothing on us. When I heard your name it rang a bell."

"This is wonderful. I just tried calling you this afternoon. Won't you join us? This is my daughter, Gabrielle — Gabi. Gabi, say hello to Ms. Haapala."

Gabrielle whispered a hello; Willie smiled warmly at her. "Professor Banks and I are just having dinner. Yours hasn't been served yet, so please, both of you, join us."

Celeste and Gabi moved over to Willie's table. Introductions were made, the food arrived, and Celeste was beginning to feel more relaxed in the company of this pleasant couple.

"What happened to your arm, Jeremy?" Gabi asked.

"Gabi, that's Professor Banks. Manners . . . manners . . ." Celeste murmured.

"Oh, please, everyone calls me Jeremy these days. I was Professor Banks for much too long, and he was a stuffy old coot. You call me Jeremy and I'll call you Gabi."

"Yes, and I'm Willie to this crowd. We might as well not stand on formality. Goodness knows no one else seems to." Willie almost had to shout over the shriek of child at the next table.

"But what *did* happen to your arm?" Gabi insisted.

"Well, Gabi, I fell off the roof and broke my wrist. I was looking at the stars through my telescope, then thought I'd get a better view of the Hale-Bopp comet if I climbed on the roof. I lost my footing."

"You have a telescope?"

"Yes I do. Perhaps you'd like to look through it sometime. You can see the stars as they looked a long time ago."

"Speaking of the past," Celeste said. "That was the reason I called today. Helen Laine, at the Inn, told me I should contact you if I want to see the Finnish museum. I'm doing an article on Broom Island for *Off the Beaten Path.*

"Oh, sure. We can do that in the morning. I'll meet you there at ten o'clock. Give you a chance to sleep in a bit and have a good breakfast. The sea air usually makes people sleepy and hungry. How's your hotel room?"

"Oh, I guess it's okay. It does have a nice view. Of course Gabi is devastated that it doesn't have TV."

"I can remember a time when we didn't even have power on this island. Everything ran on gas. Lamps, washing machines, even flatirons. We didn't get electricity until 1951, and there were no telephones till 1957. We all went to school in a one-room schoolhouse that only went up to the eighth grade. Just when I was ready for high school, they expanded it to a three-room building and added four more grades so I was able to finish high school here."

"Was the school conducted in Finnish? I mean you were a Finnish settlement, weren't you?" Celeste asked.

"No, that was part of government regulations. Schools had to be in English. And it's just as well. I don't care what they say about teaching children in their native tongue, if I hadn't had to learn English, I'd probably have spent my life on this island, talking to my flock of chickens in Finnish. Anyway, there were other nationalities around, even then."

"There was a French family on this island, wasn't there?"

"There were three, as I recall. There was a Leblanc family, the

Guindon family — and there were the Lemerriants. They're all gone now."

"Would there be anything in the archives about any of those families? Or has the Finnish museum only a record of Finns?"

"I'm not sure. Just about all the early records were lost in a fire in 1927, but anything after that should still be available. Let's find out when we go there tomorrow." Willie looked around. The restaurant, now, had almost emptied. "I guess we should be leaving so Larry can close up and go home."

"Yes, I promised Gabi we'd take a walk along the beach before going to bed."

Willie frowned. "Uh, I hate to say this, but that might not be such a good idea. Not tonight."

"Why on earth not? Isn't this the safest place in all the world?"

"Usually it is, but something happened today to get everyone upset, and since we don't know just what it was, perhaps we should all be careful."

"The young man here — Larry, is it? — mentioned something about some excitement. What's going on?"

"We hope it's nothing, but a little girl had a fright. She was walking along a footpath through the woods and she says something chased her."

"Did she say what it was?"

"She was incoherent, hysterical, scared to death. All she said was she'd been chased by the Loogy-Roo."

"Loogy-Roo?"

"Ah, yes, well, the Loogy-Roo is the island version of the Boogey Man. Dory Michaels is ten years old. I don't know if she actually saw what chased her, but something terrified her. She was on her way to school but whatever it was frightened her so much that she ran back home. She insists that she was followed. Her parents and their neighbors searched the area but found nothing, and the child's father came into town this afternoon to notify the constable and to alert the village."

"Could it have been another child? Children do play tricks on each other."

"Right now it could have been anything, but her father was all upset. To my mind, if another child had been trying to scare her, it would have happened on her way *home* from school." Willie laughed. "Kids usually barely make it on time as it is."

"Isn't there a school bus?" Celeste asked.

"For such a small island, we have several. The older children have to travel by bus now that the high school is in Port Casper. Another school bus brings in the kindergarteners and elementary school children from Tranquil Bay, and there's one that circles around the logging roads and picks up the half dozen children from the more remote farms. The kids in the village walk to school. Dory's parents, Chad and Weena Michaels, live some distance from town. The bus drops Dory off at a stop along the road and she usually takes a shortcut along a footpath to her house. It was there she says something chased her. A couple of weeks ago, one of their guard dogs disappeared. We all thought that was odd." Willie glanced at Gabrielle who was all eyes and ears. "Of course, we islanders do tend to overreact sometimes. You always hear such awful things on the news. We like to think of Satama as a safe place."

"It's hard to picture anything sinister here," Celeste said.

"The thing is, everyone on this island knows everyone else. Things like this shouldn't happen. When a stranger comes to the island, everybody knows it. Like you. You may not have met many people yet, but I'd bet that old Mr. Lindfors, who's lying in a coma in the geriatric ward of the retirement home, is the only one who *may* not know you're here.

"The town will be wanting to get a look at you. Why do you think so many people showed up here tonight? Jeremy and I don't usually eat out. We came because we thought you'd be here — and also because of the disturbance. Trouble brings people out into the streets."

"Couldn't it have been an animal? Someone's dog maybe? Are there wild animals on the island?"

"If there's something chasing children, we're going to have to find out what it is. Cougar attacks on children have happened on this island — though not for many years. But until it's sorted out, it's best not to be walking around at night."

"I certainly didn't expect to find anything like this. Of course I didn't expect to meet that strange woman in Pearl's café either."

"Oh yes, I heard about your adventure with our local Cassandra. I'm so sorry. I know she frightened Gabi."

"Who is she, anyway?"

"Her name is Sybil Weeks. She's the daughter of Kirsti and Rome Weeks. They live on Kaunio Road, not far from me. Sybil has always had problems. She's on heavy-duty medication, and if she forgets to take it, things can get very unpleasant. She's legally blind, you know."

"I saw her reading a book in Braille."

"That's her Bible. She takes it everywhere. Well, now that I've thoroughly spooked you, are you going to be okay for the evening?"

"I have work to do on my laptop. Gabi can make do with her Game Boy."

* * *

It was at one in the morning, after she'd finally fallen into a fitful sleep, that a shrill scream jolted Celeste awake. Gabi! The child was having another of her nightmares, thrashing about and shrieking. Celeste sprang out of bed and gathered her daughter in her arms. "Gabi, Gabi, it's all right. Try to wake up, Gabi." Celeste was holding her daughter close. "Wake up, sweetheart, you're having a nightmare."

Gabi's face was frozen in terror. Her eyes were open but glazed, staring but not seeing. She screamed again, and Celeste clasped her tightly. "It's all right, Gabi, it was just a bad dream. You're safe with me."

Gabi blinked, looked confused, then began to cry. "The birds were coming and the scary man with the big knife."

"Shh, Gabi. He's gone now. It's okay." She rocked her daughter back and forth.

There was a loud knock on the door. *Oh, dear heaven, now what?* Celeste laid Gabi down on the bed and went to door, but didn't open it. "Who is it? What do you want?"

"Everything in there okay, lady?" The voice was slurred and sounded drunken.

"Everything's fine. My little girl had a nightmare, that's all."

There was another knock — or was it the thud of a body colliding against the door? "You sure? If you need any help . . ." the voice trailed off.

"Thank you. That's very kind. I do *not* need help. Please go away."

Celeste could hear the man mumbling his way down the hall. She returned to Gabi who was now awake but still shaken. "There was this man and he was cutting hay with a big knife thing and then the birds came at me and the man was laughing and the birds —"

"Shh, Gabi. It was just a bad dream that's all. They're gone now. They're all gone." She got into bed with her daughter. "I'll stay with you and keep the bad dreams away." Celeste made her voice soft and soothing. "Tomorrow we'll do all kinds of fun things. We'll walk along the beach and look at seaweed. We'll visit the museum. Maybe we can even take a drive around the island. Won't that be fun? We can go exploring. And we can do some shopping. We'll find you a baseball cap that says Satama on it."

"Can we go see Jeremy? He said he'd show me his telescope."

"Maybe. Maybe we can even go see Jeremy." Celeste began to hum softly — a lullaby her own mother had sung to her. Celeste, as a child, had also had nightmares. Why, she wondered, do children, innocent and pure of heart, sweet and beautiful in their newness, seem to go through the tortures of souls in hell when they close their eyes?

Celeste didn't recall what type of nightmares she herself had suffered from, but she'd gone through a period of walking in her sleep. There were several instances in which she'd awakened terrified, and once found herself out of doors in the middle of the night. Her parents had installed bolts, high up, so little Celeste couldn't reach them.

But that hadn't been all. There had also been the blackouts. They were at their worst in her early grades in elementary school, and gradually diminished as she grew older. She would suddenly feel herself snapping back, as if from sleep, only to find that time had passed, recess was now over, and the rest of the children had gone back to class. Once, she found herself standing up after the morning ritual of pledging allegiance to the flag. Everyone else was sitting. Her teacher kept nodding at her, indicated for her to sit down, but Celeste, disoriented, continued to stand. Finally the teacher came over, put her hands on her shoulders and gently pushed her down into her seat. The rest of the class laughed and Celeste turned red from embarrassment.

The worst was the time she'd gone to the bathroom, and when she came out the room was dark, school had closed, and she'd missed her bus. Luckily, the janitor was still there and kindly gave her a ride home, where her parents were becoming frantic.

So, had I been abducted by aliens? Did the little gray guys come for me? Were they coming for Gabi? Not bloody likely. Celeste didn't believe in alien abductions but there *was* some wild and alien thing that seemed to run through the women of her family. Her own mother had suffered from migraine headaches. Madeleine Ooms-Possum experienced what Celeste later learned was the aura that precedes migraines. To the little girl it had been frightening to see her mother suddenly stricken with the inability to speak. Madeleine would be carrying on a normal conversation, and suddenly she would look wildly around her, as if seeing something no one else could. (She described them as jagged lights.) Then her speech would become unintelligible, and then the crushing pain would follow.

After a time, the family became accustomed to the phenomenon, to the point where a teenaged Celeste used to find humor in her mother's garbled speech. "Mom's talking Chinese again!" She and her father would lead Madeleine off to bed, where she would lie with a cold washcloth on her brow until the headache relented.

Once, and only once, had Madeleine let slip that her own mother, Fidelia, had suffered from "fits." When Celeste asked about it, Madeleine had refused to discuss it.

Celeste had never been told much about her mother's family. Her questions met with a curt, "They're all dead. There's nothing to tell." Still, Celeste had a nagging feeling that there must be a great deal to tell, and wondered why all the secrecy.

It was only recently that Celeste had discovered that her family once lived on Broom Island. It was after her mother died of a brain tumor, that her father handed over to Celeste some of Madeleine's papers. Mostly they were notebooks, diaries, haphazardly kept, but with major family events documented, as if Madeleine had intended to compile some sort of family record. There she learned, for the first time, that her Grandmother Fidelia's last name was Lemerriant, and that she'd lived on Broom Island, and had died of tuberculosis in 1938 when Madeleine was ten.

There was no mention of Fidelia's parents — father, mother, siblings — nor any of a husband or a married name. Madeleine must have been an only child; Celeste knew of no uncles or aunts on her mother's side of the family. Why had Madeleine included so little information about her own mother? Was it because she, herself, didn't know? Or was there some dark secret?

Madeleine had been secretive about her own childhood as well. Celeste didn't even know who had raised her after her mother died. Had Madeleine grown up in an institution? In foster homes? If she'd been adopted, wouldn't Celeste have had adoptive grandparents? All Celeste knew was that her mother had married Charles Ooms-Possum in 1956, and had given birth to Celeste in 1962.

Gabi had drifted off to sleep but Celeste was now wide awake. Her mind was racing like a greyhound; she wished she could turn on the light and read, but was afraid of awakening her daughter. She wished she could open the doors and listen to the lapping of waves. The ferries stopped running at ten. She and Gabi had watched the last one from the balcony, as it sailed in through the darkness like a huge candlelit birthday cake — lovely to see — to dock and let off a few stragglers on foot, and a couple of cars. It had then sailed back to Port Casper.

The room felt a bit too warm and rather close, haunted by the smell of stale cigarette smoke. Somewhere a card game must have been in progress. She could hear the buzz of men's voices — loggers? — punctuated by whoops of triumph, groans of despair, and belts of raucous laughter. *Well, cat or no cat, I'm opening the doors, at least for a while.*

Celeste quietly slid open the glass door and stepped out onto the balcony. The night was still, with stars overhead, but a fog now obscured the lights of Port Casper across the way. She listened to the rhythmic splash of waves until she started to feel chilly, then came back inside and closed the door — almost. She'd leave it ajar hoping the sound of waves would mask the sound of the card game.

Gabrielle was breathing quietly. Celeste crawled into her own bed, but sleep would not come, and the room was now beginning to feel too cool. She got up and closed the door again. The card game was still going on, and she turned over on her side and put a pillow over her ear.

She must have dozed a bit, but then a persistent noise burrowed into her consciousness and brought her awake. What *was* that? It sounded a little like a telephone ringing somewhere — or maybe a fire call summoning volunteer firemen. It went on for a while, then stopped. *Thank god.* Celeste tried to get back to sleep but then suddenly the noise was back. It was a high pitched, maddeningly persistent *beep, beep, beep.* It went on interminably, it seemed, as Celeste lay in the darkness, wondering who would keep a phone ringing in the middle of the night. Once again it stopped, only to resume a few moments later.

God damn that thing! Celeste got out of bed, opened the glass door and stepped onto the balcony. The noise out there was much louder — so loud that it made her recoil. It seemed to be coming from everywhere at once, but Celeste could see absolutely nothing: no lights across the way.

Fog! It was now so thick that, to Celeste, it was like being in goosedown. Above her there were stars in the sky, but in front of her the dense fog made it impossible to get any sense of distance. Celeste tried to gauge where the noise was coming from, and concluded it was somewhere off shore. Dimly she could just barely make out a very faint pulsating beacon of red light. *Foghorn. Has to be! It must be activated by the density of the fog and that's why it keeps going on and off.* Celeste closed the door, drew the drapes for added insulation against the noise, got back in bed — she was really chilly now — and pulled the heavy motel bedcovers over herself. She finally managed to doze off into a sleep fraught with chaotic images.

CHAPTER 7

Celeste opened her eyes. It was morning. The curtains had been drawn back, the glass door was open, and the sun was shining. *What time is it?* She glanced at her watch. Eight-thirty! She could see Gabrielle in her pajamas, curled over the balcony rail, balancing on her stomach while she looked down.

"Gabi, be careful!"

"Look, Mom, there's a bunch of fish out there."

Celeste could, indeed, see something in the distance. A school of — but no, they weren't fish! "Those are porpoises, Gabi. See, they're leaping out of the water." There must have been a dozen of them, boiling up out of the sea, their wet backs glistening in the sun. Celeste and Gabi watched, charmed, until the activity subsided as the school moved on. "If we're lucky, we might even see whales while we're here. Right now we'd better get dressed and find breakfast. We have to be at the museum at ten."

Celeste, after a night of little sleep, was feeling headachy. No, she told herself, I do *not* crave a cigarette. What I need is Ibuprofen, and of course I don't have any with me. Maybe I can pick some up in the Inn shop.

Helen Laine was not on duty. There was an older woman at the desk, and Celeste learned that several women in town took turns working at the Inn. "I'm afraid we don't have any Ibuprofen here."

"That's okay. I'll pick some up at the Co-op."

"They won't have any either. There's a law that says you can't stock it unless there's a licensed pharmacist on duty. You'd have to go to a drug store in Port Casper."

Celeste helplessly shook her head; she didn't even feel up to commenting that you could buy Ibuprofen in any drug store without ever laying eyes on the pharmacist. "I'll try coffee. If it doesn't work, I'll take an aspirin. Where can I find the Finnish museum?"

The woman pointed through the window. "You can't see it from here, but if you go left, up the street, you'll see a big white building next to the water. Go around the back. You can't miss it. There's a Finnish flag and a big iron anchor next to the entrance."

After juice, toast, and coffee at the New Broom, Celeste felt a bit better as she and Gabi hiked to the museum. It wasn't a long walk, and the exercise felt good. Last night's fog had cleared and there was, once more, the magnificent view of mountains and water. Celeste stopped to take photos of the scenery and of the ferry dock. In the light of day, she could see, some distance offshore — farther away than she'd guessed — a buoy with a light. *I'll bet that's what was keeping me awake last night.*

The village was bustling with morning activity. A truck that had come in on the early ferry was delivering produce to the Co-op. People were going to work. Nothing, it seemed, opened before nine-thirty except the restaurant — and maybe Pearl's café, which Celeste planned to avoid. A number of people, mostly women, were going into the Co-op to do their shopping. The scene was peaceful enough. Had yesterday's excitement died down?

Celeste mused that people in small communities, like this one, must be much more sensitive to any disturbance than those living in a city on the mainland, where crime is commonplace. Wouldn't living in a place like this make you timid? Soon you'd be afraid to go anywhere. Just driving your car in city traffic would be scary. A kid gets a bit of a fright and the whole community overreacts. Living here would be charming and safe and beautiful, but wouldn't it be a little like Shangri-La? You'd turn to dust if you tried to leave it.

Ah! She and Gabi were approaching a white building that had to be the museum. A Jeep Cherokee was parked in the lot and Willie Haapala was just getting out of it. "Good morning. Did you get a decent night's sleep? I'm sorry about the foghorn. I was hoping it wouldn't go off while you were here."

"I finally figured it out, but at first I didn't know what it was. It sounded like a phone ringing."

"One visitor heard it, and the next day she said she'd been listening to some little animal crying for its mother all night."

"I guess that thing is all things to all people," Celeste said, casting a baleful glance in the direction of the buoy.

They climbed a flight of steps to the front door where the anchor marked the entrance. Willie fitted key in lock. "When I was a child this place was never locked."

They went inside. It smelled musty, like a used-books or antique shop. A small foyer led to a hallway with doors leading from it. Willie opened one and Celeste looked in, then sneezed. There was the smell of old books and dust. "This used to be a schoolroom." The walls were lined with shelves of books, although they didn't look like school books. Celeste stepped inside and looked at the titles. Most of them seemed to be in Finnish, with crumbling covers and yellowing pages: ethnic reading material. They looked like romance and adventure novels, some with English titles of the lurid kind: *The Dance of Death and Other Tales, Wolf Blood*, and *Curse of the Werewolf.*

"I don't think there's anything in here but old novels circa the '30s and '40s. I don't know why we even keep them, but this room wasn't being used for anything else. If it were up to me, I'd toss out the lot." Willie closed the door and opened another. "These rooms are used for different things. Meetings. Girl Guides had their cookie drive stuff in here. Band practice. We used to have dances, but when we built the town hall across the street this building became the museum." Willie opened another door, and Celeste entered a room the size of a ballroom. It, too, smelled faintly musty. Inside lay a jumble of the artifacts of a culture, and Celeste was a bit taken aback by the impact it made on her: an ancient printing press set with the Finnish alphabet, a spinning wheel, a wooden butter churn with a dasher, and carved wooden dishes — bowls, spoons. An old galvanized washtub stood on the floor, in it a wooden washboard with a corrugated glass face. There were tools used by loggers, fishnets and floats, hand-hooked rugs, an ancient accordion, an upright piano with chipped keys of yellowed ivory, coal-oil and gas lamps, paintings of grim-faced old men (the founding fathers?) and landscapes that must have been of Finland, rampant with birch trees. There were sheep shears, carding combs and balls of homespun yarn; an old camera on its tripod, its leather bellows dried and cracked. There were boxes of old photographs. Some had been mounted on a bulletin board on the wall — old black-and-white snapshots of early settlers. Some were marked: Mimmi and Jukka Väisänen on their wedding day, June 1, 1928. Others weren't identified at all, and others only in a general way: "Aho family reunion, April 3, 1933." and "Raising the barn, May 6, 1939." Nameless faces caught in a moment of long ago.

There were handmade wooden buckets for just about any purpose — some to hold water, used in kitchens and saunas. Some were so small that they could only have been used at table. They had a longer stave sticking up on each side to act as a handle, so one could pick up the vessel by the staves, raise it to mouth and drink out of it. Celeste picked one up and found the handles cleared her head easily. There was also one very large tub in the same style, and Celeste wondered if it had been used for bathing. Then she saw a photo of two women, wearing white kerchiefs on their heads (the *huivi* that married women wore) bent over the task of mixing bread dough in a similar tub. There were tapestries from Finland — dark thick rug-like wall hangings — the *ryijy* — as well as cloth made from flax (*pellava*) that had been used to make tablecloths, bed sheets, towels, clothing. There was even a wooden rod near the ceiling, and on it, loaves of bread: Finnish rye bread — a round loaf with a hole in the middle so it could be threaded onto a rod to dry. Celeste took a photo and wondered if the bread was real or a plaster copy. It looked authentic enough. Dried, it would probably outlast plaster anyway!

Celeste found her senses assaulted by the personal possessions of people long dead — implements of daily living that had been left behind. Celeste had often been in museums, but this one affected her differently because of its intimacy. The artifacts weren't in sterile glass cases, they were strewn about as they might be in a grandmother's attic. And there, indeed, was grandmother's steamer trunk (the one she brought from Finland?) and grandmother's clothing — dark dresses with long skirts. And what was this, a widow's weeds? The skirt and jacket were black and there was a black hat and a black veil worn by a mannequin.

There were so many items that Celeste couldn't take them all in, but she was taking photos as she walked around the room, knowing that a camera records more than the eye can take in. Willie stood to one side, silently watching. She had brought people to this museum before, and found that they reacted in one of two ways. Some showed little interest, dismissed it all as a pile of old junk, and couldn't wait to leave. Others, like Celeste, seemed to lose all sense of time as they walked about, pausing, touching, gazing. Some visitors were full of questions. Celeste seemed not to be asking any, at least not yet. Gabrielle, also, seemed hushed by her surroundings. She was, Willie saw, engrossed in looking at some old dolls in Finnish national costumes — beribboned, aproned, with skirts of multicolored vertical stripes.

Celeste now trained her camera on the most dominant feature in the room. Without it, the museum might have seemed somber and a bit funereal, but on the back wall was a theater stage! Scenery — large painted backdrops — hung there. The painting had been nicely done, probably by talented amateurs. The topmost was a scene of the inside of a log cabin. Celeste climbed the short flight of steps onto the stage, lifted the edge to see another hanging behind it, depicting woods, and beneath that hung yet another of a grassy area with a small cabin in the background.

"These are charming," Celeste called to Willie. "I didn't realize you had theater on the island."

"Oh yes. We had quite a lively amateur theater group, and we had some talented people. I remember this scenery. It was for a play that was written by my own Aunt Hanna. It was called *Suotorpan Annikki. Annikki of the Cabin in the Bog* would be the translation. Our plays were either broad comedy or Finnish tragedy, which is always heavily laced with morality. I was just thinking we should do a revival of this one for our midsummer festival — *Juhannus.* We'd have to translate it into English now, I'm afraid. I don't think we'd be able to find a cast that speaks Finnish anymore, and even if we did, most of the audience wouldn't be able to understand it. My aunt used to write plays so she could appear in the starring role. This one is about an innocent young maiden who spurns the lecherous advances of a libertine."

"Really? I've read that Satama was founded by proponents of free love."

"Oh god! Yes, *everyone* has heard that. First of all, as I always tell people, love is *never* free. Secondly, it's true that the founding fathers were communistic rather than churchgoing, and they held views that were shocking to the people of the times — like a woman had the right to have sex and bear children without being owned by a husband, and that a child born out of wedlock shouldn't be labeled a bastard and shunned.

"However, the people who settled here, came from God-fearing

Lutheran stock for the most part and brought their values with them. We didn't have an established church, and no one seemed to feel the need of one. Visiting pastors held services in this building. It was also the town hall, the dance hall, the theater, the center of all community life. This isn't the original building, of course. That burned down in 1927 and several people died in the fire. This was built in 1928."

"What of the records of the early settlers? Where would I find them?"

"As I said, much was lost in the fire, but we do have some old family records — Bibles in which people used to record genealogy, family histories that have been compiled by the Historical Society, old photographs donated by the children when their parents died. They'd all be in the library here, but I'm afraid it would take some time to go through them."

"Could I take some of them with me to the hotel and work on them at night?"

"If it were up to me, I'd say yes, but I'm afraid our security system wouldn't allow it."

"Security system? Here?"

"It's a bit primitive but effective. The museum is guarded by a dragon." Celeste laughed. "What would I have to do, slay it?"

"Believe me, it wouldn't be easy. You haven't *met* Amanda Vuorisaari."

"Ah, I see." Celeste recognized the name.

"Amanda is a good soul, but she's territorial as a junkyard dog. She doesn't even like it that *I* have a key, but since I'm president of the Historical Society, she can't very well demand that I hand it over."

"What if I try groveling? I can approach submissively. Acknowledge her as the alpha female?"

"We'll save that as a last resort. It would be iffy. She hates outsiders and particularly outsiders who are doing pieces for magazines on Satama. There may be another way." Willie glanced at her watch. "It's nearly lunch time. How would you and Gabi like to join me at the New Broom?"

Gabrielle had been sitting on the floor, leafing through a copy of a Finnish schoolbook, the *Aapinen,* from which children learned their ABCs. School may have been conducted in English, but, back then, Finnish kids were taught to read Finnish at home, and, for Lutheran families, there was Confirmation School held in Finnish by visiting pastors. Celeste called to her, "Come on, Gabi. Time to go."

Gabrielle got up and threaded her way through the welter of museum exhibits. Suddenly she stopped and gasped, stared for a moment, then, as if frightened, hurried to where Celeste was dropping a bill into the donation box. "Mom, look! It's the big knife thing! Like the one in my dream. That's what the man was cutting hay with." Gabrielle made a sweeping motion. "Like this. And the black birds flew up and the man was laughing — and *that's his knife.*"

Celeste gaze followed Gabi's pointing finger. It was a scythe, an old-fashioned scythe with a bentwood handle with wooden hand pegs and a long, wide, curved blade.

* * *

"She's probably seen one on television," Celeste said to Willie as they were sitting, having lunch. "I can't think where else she could have come across a scythe. And you wonder, what would make a kid dream of such a thing!" Celeste looked at Gabi who was wolfing down a hamburger. "At least her appetite seems okay, although I don't approve of a steady diet of burgers." Celeste yawned and took a sip of coffee. "I needed this after last night."

"I'm sorry the foghorn kept you awake. It wouldn't have helped to warn you."

"It wasn't only that. There was an all-night card game going on, and some drunk came pounding on my door."

"*What?*"

"Oh, it wasn't really anything sinister. Gabi woke up screaming at one in the morning, and I guess the gentleman was being gallant as well as *borracho*. Anyway, between Gabi, the siren, the card game, the guy, and trying to sleep in a room that was either too hot or too cold, well, I *didn't.*"

"Okay, that does it," Willie said. "You're coming home with me. We'll get you checked out. Pack your things. You'll stay with me while you're on the island."

"Are you serious?"

"Absolutely. My place isn't the Taj Mahal either. Just one of those old houses on Kaunio Road, but there's plenty of room. Jeremy and I would enjoy a bit of company."

"But won't we be too much trouble? And Gabi's nightmares?"

"Don't you worry about Gabi. We'll all be fine. Besides, it'll be a way of slaying the dragon. She can't really object if *I* bring home some of the old records from the museum library, can she?"

"You don't know what a relief it is not to have to spend another night at the Inn! I'd offer you my firstborn, but I think you'd rather have a nice bottle of wine — if I can find one. Drink your milk, Gabi, we're going to stay with Willie and Jeremy."

Gabrielle smiled under her milk moustache. "Yay!"

CHAPTER 8

Although Willie Haapala's house on Kaunio Road was an easy walk from town, she preferred to drive her car because there was always shopping to do, and things to carry home, at least that's what she told herself. She hated to openly admit that to an octogenarian the walk to town was becoming a bit much, particularly since her left knee gave her the occasional twinge — and after a day of much walking she often found herself suffering from painful cramps in her calf muscles. When she'd moved to Broom Island, Willie had traded in her old car and bought the Jeep, hoping it would prove to be a reliable, all-purpose vehicle that wouldn't require too many trips to the dealership in Port Casper. Today she had Gabrielle, who had elected to ride with Willie, in the back seat. "Does this car have air bags?" Gabi had asked. When told that it did, Gabi said she'd ride in the back.

Willie mused that the children of today, especially the children of "outsiders" were of a different breed. They were more sophisticated, born to technology, socially aware, trained to avoid pitfalls such as cars with air bags. They were also, perhaps, more highly strung than the seemingly indestructible models of her own age. Even today's island children seemed more innocent, more childlike, yet less fragile. Or were they? Willie allowed that it had been some time since she'd taught school, and that she hadn't had much contact with kids lately. Still, it seemed that now every other child suffered from OCD or ADS or some acronym that kept them either on drugs or in therapy. She wondered how her own mother would have dealt with something like that.

Willie had grown up in an age where parenting consisted of: "Do that." "Stop that!" and "Go out and play." You fell and bumped your head, your mother would rub it and say, "That spot will be that much stronger from now on!" You complained of a pain, and Mother would say, "At your age, you shouldn't be having any. Wait till you get to mine!"

There was also much practical wisdom passed on by parents back then. Willie remembered that she had never been allowed to pretend that she was ill or crippled. One day when Willie had pretended to limp, her mother had delivered one of her lectures on how a little girl who had played that she was blind lost her sight forever. As a child, such admonitions had frightened Willie; as an adult she'd laughed at them as old wives' tales; in old age, she respected them. She'd come to understand that we each create our own reality, knowingly or unknowingly, and that what we picture comes to pass.

Celeste Ooms-Possum was following Willie's car, and thinking that things were looking up. Even Gabi was beginning to show an interest, and had actually asked Willie if she could ride in the Cherokee. *God, this island is beautiful!* Celeste was driving past homes and farms, some so obscured by a greenbelt of vegetation that she only caught glimpses of painted buildings and animals in pasture. (Odd-looking cattle, she noted, as if of some older, heritage breed.) Other houses faced the sea boldly, accepting the storms and winds as dues paid for the view. Most places had some evidence of the fishing industry — fishnets mounded on the lawn or draped to dry. Many had fences made of fishnet floats threaded onto wire. A typical house standing on the hill, would have a weathered wooden boathouse across the road at the water's edge. Some dwellings were virtual shacks, and looked to have been nailed together from discarded wood. They would be the "hippie" houses. Celeste would have to take photos of all this later.

On her right was the Strait of Georgia, dotted with islands, and with a view of snowcapped mountains across the way. And then there was the broom! It grew everywhere on the island, all along the roadsides — a drab green shrub that could grow to over six feet tall — a rather ugly, undisciplined, sprawling thing with bristles like long, flexible broom straws. The shrub had a woody stem, the tendency to fall prostrate, and the ability to propagate at an alarming rate. Over winter, a patch of it would sometimes die, leaving dead growth like old hay, not a pleasing sight. However, in early summer, the broom would bloom. Every wispy green stem would open, along its length, a profusion of bright yellow blossoms that resemble those of peas. The effect was that of an exuberant Mother Nature gone a little mad. Seen from an airplane, large areas of the island looked yellow. Viewed from the ground, the shrub was like perpetual sunshine, brightening a rainy day and gladdening the heart, even as it caused allergies to flare.

There wasn't much broom growing in the village of Satama itself; in fact, every year, there were sneezing, runny-eyed citizens who wanted to see it eradicated completely. Outside the village it held its ground tenaciously and afforded a glorious sights to the eye. It would be a while yet before the broom fully blossomed, but, here and there, an early smattering dotted the green like bright yellow popcorn.

Willie turned left at her driveway, drove through the open gate, up a gentle hill and parked next to Jeremy's station wagon. Celeste followed in her Volvo. As Willie had said, the house was old but sturdy, not built in the traditional stark Finnish style in that it had three stories and a widow's walk along the topmost. Willie's grandfather, who had built the house, had put it in so he could keep an eye on the sea. The outside was weathered, like old barn boards, although it had been painted red with white trim at one time. Huge spreading lilac bushes that had years ago escaped their original boundaries as foundation shrubs, framed and ennobled the building, which to Celeste's delight, reminded her now of a cross between a fairy castle in the woods and the Bates house in *Psycho*. She parked next to the Cherokee.

"This is beautiful, Willie. It's a wonderful old house."

"It's old all right. Jeremy and I have been having an argument whether to paint it. He thinks it would preserve the wood, and he's right, of course. But I kind of like the weathered look."

"What are those buildings over there?"

"Storage sheds, my father's workshop, greenhouse, and that building on the edge of the woods is the old sauna. It still works. We'll have to heat it for you."

"Living here must be heaven. That view! And it's so private. You can't even see your neighbors for the trees."

"It can get a bit brutal in winter when the wind blows, but we islanders are used to that. Right now let's get you settled. If I'd known this morning you were coming, I'd have had your room ready. But now if we all pitch in, we'll have you situated in no time."

* * *

Inside, the house was large with spacious rooms and well-kept hardwood floors. As with most houses Celeste had seen, there was a row of windows facing the ocean. A flight of stairs led to the second floor, where Willie situated Celeste and Gabrielle in a sunny room with twin beds. "You can use the small bath at the end of the hall. We used to have only one bathroom, but my parents put in another downstairs, and then when I moved back here, I had the east wing made into guest quarters with a bath of its own. That's Jeremy's room, across the hall from you."

"This place would be ideal for a bed and breakfast."

"I sort of had that in mind when I was remodeling."

"Why not start now? Let us be paying guests."

"Not this time, Celeste. You were invited. But if I should decide to go into business, I'd have the space."

"What's upstairs?" Gabrielle asked.

"It's more of an attic right now. Storage area. I'll show you later. Right now, let's go down and see if we can find Jeremy. He's probably out in back trying to figure out how to use the lawnmower with only one good arm."

As if in reply, they could hear the sound of a mower starting up, and as they approached, they saw Jeremy cutting a strip of lawn, guiding the self-propelled mower easily. Jeremy spotted them, let go of the handle and the mower automatically shut off. "See, no problem at all," he said to Willie. "Anyway, Dr. Swallow told me to exercise my wrist as much as possible."

"I can help you with that," Gabrielle said. Her mother looked at her in mild surprise.

"Well, I *can*. It doesn't look that hard. Want to see me try?" She reached for the handle.

"Why, thank you, Gabi," Jeremy said. "I'd be happy to have you help me. I can start the mower and we can take turns. And then you can help me lift out the bag and empty the clippings." He looked at Celeste. "If it's all right with your mother."

"Hey, I'd be glad to volunteer myself. If we're going to be house guests, its the least we can do," Celeste said.

"And so could I," Willie said. "But that's not the point. Jeremy is a man who doesn't let things stop him. It's best to let him do whatever he wants. Gabrielle will be fine here, if you want to go on down to the museum."

They left Jeremy and Gabi absorbed in their task. "We can look through some records, and if there are any you want to go over in more detail, I can bring them home. And we can both pray we don't run into Amanda." Willie looked at her watch. "Oh, wait a minute. We *can't.*

The Seniors are meeting at the museum this afternoon, and Amanda will almost certainly be there. I'd rather not confront the woman. It's always easier to apologize later than to get consensus. We'll either have to go tonight or tomorrow morning."

"In that case, I could take my camera and get some shots along Kaunio Road. Would you like to come?"

"No, you run along. I have things to do here. Why don't you walk down to the cemetery? There's a lot of island history buried there."

* * *

With camera slung on her shoulder, Celeste set off down Kaunio road. It felt good to be striding along the blacktop all on her own. There was little traffic on the island, and she met only a couple of cars. The drivers waved at her; Celeste waved back. She took photos of houses, the ocean, the Douglas firs that towered in the strip between the road and the shore — a couple of times stopping to pick up a piece of roadside trash, and deposit it into one of the containers that had been placed at intervals, thinking, as she did, what shame it was to spoil the natural beauty by littering. Once she spotted a pair of magnificent eagles perched on a rock by the water's edge, and took a photo. There were loons and ducks in the water, and a blue heron standing as still as a statue, except for the wind ruffling its neck feathers.

Brambles were in bloom along the roadside. She recognized thimbleberry, but there was a strange berry that was like a cross between thimble and raspberry — a rather *hairy* berry. Celeste was reminded of a poem from her childhood. How did that go?

A loaf or crusty bakers
Set out to bake a pie
A super hairy sour berry
Blackened tree bark pie.

She noticed that the bushes bore both berries and flowers at the same time. The month of May seemed a tad early for anything to be fruiting, and while some of the berries were red, others were yellow. She pushed her way into the shrubbery to get a better look. There seemed to be quite a lot of the berry bushes along the stretch of road. In sunnier spots a few of them looked ripe. She tasted a yellow one. It tasted bland.

They nailed the narrow nasty dough
Into a rusted pan
And baked it at 420
Till it reached a blackened tan.

She took a closeup of what she'd later learn were salmonberries, a shot of their thorny bushes, and a couple of long shots of the log-strewn shore — cobbled with stone and crusted with dried seaweed.

The hairy berries were squashed and squished,
(Their hairy sacks left in a dish)
While the super sour (simply awful)
Pulp was mashed and mixed.

Amazing! Those verses were still there in her memory banks, like something saved and stored in a computer, although she hadn't thought of it in years.

Add a dash of pickle juice,
Garlic roots and brine
Thicken with some sawdust
Or some powdered cones of pine.

What, she wondered, determines what information becomes stored in your mind forever, while other, more important things, are forgotten? Is there some coding in the brain cells? Does your mind do a "save-as" like her Macintosh computer? And what triggers such a command to begin with?

Scrape the hairies off the berries
To decorate the top
Then bake until they singe and flame
You'll know it's time to stop.

Man, if you could just harness that power! If you could consciously say, I shall remember this twenty years from now! But you never know which memories will become permanent and which will fade. Perhaps they're all permanent, coded genetically. Maybe it's the accessing of the memory that's the tricky part. It seems to take another trigger to unlock a memory. A sound, like piece of music, or a whiff of a fragrance, can instantly transport you into the past. In this case it was the hairy berries.

Plunge it in a snow bank
To squelch the searing heat
Slice it with a blunted axe
Voilà! It's time to eat.

And *voilà*, that must be the cemetery!

Celeste had come to a bend in the road and saw a tall privet hedge. She approached a small painted metal garden gate with no lock, just a spring latch, opened it and went inside to find the final resting place of Broom Islanders. The cemetery was well kept, neatly mown, with a motley assortment of tombstones. The location was beautiful, with tall trees on one side, the sea on the other, and the hedge serving to insulate the area from the bustle of the living.

Celeste was alone except for a raven or two on the grass. She found that she'd entered the old part of the cemetery. Farther up the gentle slope, it looked as if more land had been annexed, and there the headstones appeared to be newer. There was also a grave that looked to be so recent that the bare earth was covered with fading bouquets, and no marker had yet been put in place. In the old section, there were new stones as well — replacements for markers that had crumbled, and new graves in old family plots. She looked at the names. They were predominantly Finnish, and within a family plot, there might be variations in the family name, as members either modified difficult spellings or anglicized. In a plot that Celeste thought must be Willie's family, she found Haapalainen, Haapala, and Laine as surnames. In another, there was Järvinen, Järvi, and Lake. She guessed, correctly, that *järvi* was the

Finnish word for lake.

Some of the plots were so old that no trace remained of inscriptions. Others had tilted headstones or cracked concrete slabs, as earth had heaved and sunk, the undulations reminding Celeste of ski moguls. Some graves had become swallowed up by a shrub planted years ago. As markers, there were also natural stones, iron anchors, wooden crosses. In one, a square of ordinary wire yard fencing encircled an eroded pillar. Celeste saw that some of the graves had been decorated with seashells; a few, less fortunate, bore faded plastic flowers.

She walked about, shot her roll of film, reloaded her camera, and made her way down to a single pillar at the far end, snapped a photo of it, then read the inscription. The monument had been erected to the people who had died in the fire of May 19, 1927. Willie had mentioned a fire that had burned down the old town hall, and now Celeste saw that eight adults and six children had perished in it. She read down the list of names and, with a thrill, recognized one: Lemerriant.

Lemerriant! That had been her grandmother Fidelia's name. The name on the pillar was Elphique Lemerriant. He'd been just a boy of sixteen, born October 31, 1910. Had Fidelia Lemerriant had a brother? Would Elphique have been Celeste's grand-uncle? Celeste was startled out of her concentration by a flap of wings as a large raven came to rest on the pillar.

"Well, hello, 'ghastly grim and ancient raven,' can you tell me who Elphique Lemerriant was?" The raven said nothing.

"That's what I thought." As Celeste looked around, she noticed that there were now more ravens in the cemetery. A flock of them had flown in and they seemed to be surrounding her. Sitting on grass or on headstones, the birds were very still, regarding her solemnly. She realized that there must be dozens of them, just waiting. What *is* this? Then it occurred to her that people probably brought food for the ravens into the cemetery, and the birds were just checking to see if they'd get a handout. It reminded Celeste of a scene from that Hitchcock movie.

"Sorry, guys, I don't have anything for you."

Celeste took a closeup shot of the pillar inscription, walked away, turned and took a photo of the birds, then moved along. The ravens, one by one, silently followed. Celeste was beginning to feel the tiniest bit uncomfortable — but couldn't help being amused by her own discomfort. *It's just a bunch of birds, for god's sake.* The ravens weren't flying at her or threatening her in any way, but the sight of them was still a bit unnerving, particularly as they seemed to be focused on her and gradually coming closer. One was sitting almost at her feet on a flat stone marker partly overgrown with grass.

Celeste looked down and read the name: Lemerriant. Another Lemerriant! This was Brazeau Lemerriant, born May 15, 1872, died May 19, 1927. Next to his was a marker for Dauphine Lemerriant, his wife. Dauphine had been forty, born March 1, 1885 and had also died on May 19, 1927. Had they both died in the fire? If so, why weren't their names on the pillar? And what about Elphique? His name *was* on the pillar, but there was no stone for him in the plot. Where was *he* buried? Something about it was unsettling. Celeste was having what Gabrielle would have called "a bad feeling" about all this, and that included the dumb flock of birds. "Shoo! Get lost!" The ravens stood their ground. Celeste bent down and picked up the first thing she saw — a clamshell — and winged it at the birds. Silent till now, the birds sent up a collective scream as they rose in a body of beating wings, wheeled around her, then flew off into the topmost branches of a Douglas fir.

Celeste took a close-up photo of the tombstones. Tomorrow she'd see if there was any record of them at the museum. If they all died in the fire, the fire would also have burned their records. Still, there might be something. . . .

CHAPTER 9

Back at Willie's, Celeste smelled the heady fragrance of new-mown grass, and found Jeremy and Gabrielle sitting at an outdoor table, having a glass of lemonade. There was also the scent of wood smoke in the air. Gabi hopped up and ran toward her. "Guess what, Mom, I can run a lawnmower now. I know how to start it and run it, don't I, Jeremy?"

"Yes, Gabi, you certainly do. You were a big help to me, and I appreciate it."

"It was fun. We're going to do some more tomorrow."

"Sounds like you two had a good afternoon. Where's Willie?"

"Right behind you," Willie said. "Gangway, here come the cookies. Sit down, Celeste, and pour yourself a glass."

Gabi reached for a cookie. "I *love* chocolate chip."

"Just don't eat too many or you'll spoil your dinner," her mother said.

"I want to talk to you about that," said Willie. "If you haven't made other plans, Jeremy and I were thinking that perhaps you and Gabrielle would like to experience an old-fashioned Finnish sauna. It'll take another hour to heat, and afterwards we can barbecue a fresh salmon."

"Oh, that sounds heavenly. I hadn't really thought about dinner."

"Then it's settled. Did you get some good pictures?"

"I'm sure I did. I went to the cemetery. I think I found some of my own ancestors buried there."

"Really? I didn't realize you had family ties to Broom Island."

"Yes, I only recently found that out myself. My grandmother was Fidelia Lemerriant."

Willie's eyes widened in surprise and for a moment she said nothing. Celeste watched her intently. "You know something about my family, don't you?"

Willie spoke slowly and guardedly. "There was a Lemerriant family on the island when I was a little girl. There ... there was the fire, you see. Many died in that fire. It was a terrible shock to the whole community."

"Yes. I saw Elphique Lemerriant's name on the monument. Then I saw the graves of Brazeau and Dauphine. They'd all died on the day of the fire. Who were those people?"

"If Fidelia was your grandmother, then Brazeau and Dauphine are your great grandparents. Elphique was their son, Fidelia's brother." Willie seemed a bit abstracted. Jeremy was looking at her with interest. He knew her well enough to know that while she might not be hiding anything, she was obviously reluctant to tell all she knew.

"How did they come to die in the fire? How did it start? And where was Fidelia?"

"Oh, Celeste, it was all so long ago, and at the time things were so confused it's hard now to remember just how it was. The fire was an accident — a terrible tragedy. Fidelia was the only surviving Lemerriant, and she left the island right after it happened. We never knew what became of her."

"Is there some way I can get details of all this? I'd like to know about the Lemerriants: where they came from, where they lived, and what sort of people they were — and what happened to them. Are there any photographs? Can you help me?"

Willie sighed. "Of course, Celeste, I'll do what I can. We can go through the old museum photos tomorrow morning, although I don't hold out much hope for finding any. Tonight you should relax, enjoy a sauna and a nice dinner."

"We'd love that. I don't remember when I last had a sauna. I think it was in a motel once."

"Then you've never been in a *real* sauna. In that case, I'll go with you and show you what to do. Be prepared for a slice of authentic Finnish culture."

* * *

The log sauna had been built by Willie's grandfather in Finnish style with logs hewn square and fitted one on top of the other to form stout walls. It was heated by wood, and had been built at the forest's edge for that reason. The old roof had been replaced and was now of asphalt shingles, with a chimney from which issued the smell of wood smoke — the delicious smell of a sauna heating that every Finn recognizes and loves. On one outside wall, in line with the chimney, were two small, low, hinged iron doors opening into twin fireboxes within, so that more logs could be added from the woodpile without disturbing bathers inside.

One entered the sauna through a wooden door that led into a small dressing room furnished only with a narrow bench, a braided rug, and wooden pegs hammered into the wall to hang clothing and towels. There was no electricity; light came through a small paned window. Another tiny window had been built into the wall between the dressing room and the sauna so that, at night, a coal oil lantern could be placed on the sill to light both rooms.

The sauna itself was surprisingly large, suitable for groups of bathers. There were three bleachers tiered along the back wall, the topmost wide enough to lie upon. Beneath the window, a low bench held buckets, luffa sponges, brushes — and, normally, the sauna switches: bundles of leafy birch withes with which bathers could whack themselves to stimulate blood circulation. Today they would have to do without the switch (the *vasta*). Birch trees don't grow well on the west coast, and Willie normally substituted sour cherry tree clippings, sometimes even forsythia — but it was too early in the season; trees hadn't leafed out enough yet.

The dominant feature was the fireplace. In this sauna there were two, side by side, squares of bricks and mortar, each serving as a base. On one stood an oil drum full of water. The one next to it, the *kiuas*, was heaped with smooth, round stones held in place by its edging framework of bricks. The principle of the Finnish sauna is beautifully simple: a fire is built, the stones heat up, the bather throws water on the stones to create steam. Planks in the wood floor were spaced so that water escaped through cracks.

"You mean I have to take all my clothes off in front of Willie?" Gabrielle looked horrified.

"Pretend you're visiting a native tribe and the chief has prepared a sweat lodge in your honor. You take one or you die."

The two were in the dressing room, disrobing. Willie had gone out and around the corner to check the fire.

Celeste felt rather uncomfortable herself. She tended to be a private person, and the thought of communal bathing — or *sauna*ing — left her a bit undone. Willie came in and casually slipped out of her terrycloth robe. She looked at their faces and said, "Jeremy told me he *might* not be joining us what with the cast on his arm." Then, seeing their stricken expressions, she laughed. "Gotcha!"

Inside the sauna, Willie filled a bucket from a tap on the wall and sloshed water on the topmost bleacher to cool the wood. "We finally had water piped in here. Used to be we had to carry it in buckets from the well." She filled buckets for each of them, and handed each a wash-cloth. "You may need these when your ears catch fire." She grinned. "Gotcha again!

"We're not going to play who-can-stand-it-the-hottest. Men like to get into these macho chicken sauna games, but women usually prefer to just enjoy the experience. Climb up on top, Celeste. Gabi, you may want sit lower to stay cooler."

"I want to go on the top, too."

"As you wish." Willie took a dipper, scooped water from her bucket and tossed it onto the hot stones. There was a zapping hiss as the water vaporized instantly, sending up a waft of hot air.

"This isn't like any sauna I've been in. I expected we'd all be wrapped in towels or sheets and the place would be all steamed up."

"This is live steam. You won't see any fog." Willie tossed on more water. "You let me know if it gets too hot for you."

Celeste breathed deeply. Her sinuses, which had been a big clogged since she got to the island, opened up. "It feels good!" The hot air hitting every part of her body at once, was almost a caress, coaxing her pores to open, sweat to flow. It was almost erotic, like the touch of a lover. She glanced sideways at Gabi. "I don't know, you may be too young for this."

"My ears are getting hot," Gabi said.

"Dip your washcloth and cool them off."

Gabi dipped her cloth in the cool water and squeezed some out on her ears. Then she put the cloth in front of her nose and breathed through it. "I'm getting all sweaty," she said through the cloth.

"That's what happens in a sauna," Willie told her. "But maybe you'd be more comfortable on the next step down. If you feel too hot, just go into the dressing room and cool off a bit. In the old days we used to go out and roll in snow in winter."

"I don't think I'd ever be hardy enough for that," Celeste said.

Willie laughed. "That's one of those misconceptions. Rolling in snow after a hot sauna doesn't feel cold at all. Plunging into an icy lake after sauna feels like diving into dishwater."

"I think I want to go out," Gabi said.

"Okay, sweetie, but first wash."

"Just soap her down, then use warm water to rinse off," Willie climbed down, filled a bucket with cold water from the tap and with a dipper added hot water from the drum.

Celeste shampooed Gabi's hair, soaped her down with a sudsy wash-cloth, then poured water over her body. She rinsed her hair with a fresh bucketful, then finished by sloshing rinse water all over her. Gabrielle stood gasping, unsure whether this was fun or torture.

Celeste took Gabi into the dressing room and rubbed her down with a towel. The girl was rosy pink and squeaky clean. "You sit in here and have a cool drink." Celeste opened one of the cans of cold soda Willie had provided. "Then get dressed and go find Jeremy. Willie and I want to steam a bit more."

With Gabi gone, the mood of the sauna changed subtly. Celeste, who had been very careful to keep her gaze at eye level, glanced at Willie who seemed to be in a state of altered consciousness as she sat on the top bleacher, her arms clasping her knees, head tilted back against the log wall, eyes shut. To Celeste she looked like a marvelous old woodcut, rugged and eternal — an earth goddess, every sinew, every fold of aged flesh, a visual history not only of her own life but that of womankind.

The heat had mellowed from the first brash onslaught to a deep golden warmth. Celeste silently climbed back onto the bleacher, leaned back and also closed her eyes. *Yes!* A sauna was a world apart, like being on another planet. She felt she could stay forever.

"Was Gabi okay?" Willie asked languidly, eyes still closed.

"She's fine. She's having a cold drink."

"You want more heat?"

"No, this is wonderful."

"You should sleep well tonight. I'll bet Gabi does too."

"I hope so. I know I will if I'm *let*. It's been quite a day. Did I tell you I was accosted by a flock of ravens?"

"You'll see a lot of them here. This island has been a roosting place for ravens and crows since time began. Every night they fly in from neighboring islands, and they sometimes hold noisy parties."

"Where did they live? The Lemerriants?"

Willie opened her eyes and shot Celeste a sideways glance. "They had a farm not far from here, inland. It was more of a homestead farm. They had a horse, a cow. They grew hay and sold it. The old man did some logging."

"Tell me about Fidelia."

"Fidelia was three years older than I."

"Then you must have gone to school with her."

"No, the Lemerriant children didn't go to school. The Lemerriants didn't mix with other people."

"But wouldn't they have been required to go?"

"*Now* they would be. At that time things on this island weren't so cut and dried. The Lemerriants didn't want their children mixing with other kids, and nobody wanted to mix with the Lemerriants."

"Why was that?"

Willie took a moment to answer. Perhaps she was saying too much. The intimacy of sauna! "We were very ethnic in those days. The country was an amalgam of cultures, but not a melting pot. Each group clung to its own ways, its own language, and hated everybody else. If they didn't actually hate them, they certainly mistrusted them. When I was growing up, there were two kinds of people: Finns and non-Finns. A non-Finn was referred to as a *kielinen*. It literally means one with a tongue — or language. Usually it meant English, but the implication was that if the language you spoke was not Finnish, then you were on the periphery; communication with you would be difficult and perhaps undesirable."

"But this island is so small! And you say they lived nearby. What about Elphique?"

"Elphique Lemerriant was about a year older than his sister. He was a strange boy. We were all terrified of him. They say he was deranged. He may have been mentally retarded. He grew up half-wild, roaming the woods. People made up all kinds of stories about him. Half-truths .

..speculation ... superstition ... fear ... hatred. Poor Elphique was the target of it all. No wonder he went around frightening other children. He was in the town hall the night of the fire and that put an end to his tragic life."

"But what happened to his parents, Brazeau and Dauphine?"

"Dauphine died. We're not quite clear as to just how. Some say her husband killed her. Brazeau was found dead as well. Nobody knows what actually happened. Some say Elphique killed both his parents. Some say Brazeau killed his wife, then shot himself. Some even blame the mythical Loogy-Roo! Time, of course, has invested the event with a mystique out of all proportion."

"My *god!*"

"I'd rather not have told you any of this. Family history can be a can of worms. But you'll hear these stories anyway if you talk to islanders. Everyone, it seems, has a favorite Lemerriant story, each one more fantastic than the last. Some even say the ghosts of the Lemerriants still walk the island, and, of course, when anything unusual happens, the old legend is dredged up."

"You mean like the trouble yesterday?"

"Uh — yes, probably. We may be in the age of technology, but I think we treasure our superstitions all the more for it."

"I want to go there."

"Where?"

"The farm where they lived. Does anyone live there now?"

"No, nobody's lived there for years. I'm not even sure who owns it. Probably crown land by now. Anyway, there's not much there but a few crumbling buildings. One day it may be a heritage site, but now there's not much to see."

"I still want to see it."

"Well, we'll see what we can do tomorrow. We've baked enough. You want to go inside and shower properly or use the bucket method?"

"The bucket method, by all means."

"Fine. Then we'll go help Jeremy with dinner."

* * *

Gabrielle gulped down half a can of orange soda, left the rest in the dressing room. She pulled on clean socks, underwear, jeans, and shirt, then put on her sneakers and went out. Her mother and Willie were still in the sauna. Gabi had been told to find Jeremy, but he didn't seem to be out in the yard, so she decided to explore. She walked around the buildings, peering into shed windows, past the greenhouse, the vegetable garden, across the lawn that she and Jeremy had mowed, sniffing the fragrance of new cut grass. Idly she walked down the hill toward the road. The gate was open and a breeze from the water was making the fishnet float fence wobble. Gabrielle went over to it and found that if she gave the fence wire a tug it would snap back and cause the fence to bounce up and down for its full length. When it finally came to rest, another tug would send it flying again; Gabi became engrossed in the game.

"Are you a tourist?"

Gabrielle started. It was a kid, bigger than Gabi, but a boy about her own age. Gabi glanced at him sideways. *Dork.* "Yeah, so what?"

"My dad says tourists are ruining the island."

Gabi gave the fence another pull. The corks danced wildly.

"So what's your name?" the kid asked.

"Esmeralda."

"Nuh-aaa. Nobody's name is Esmeralda."

"Haven't you seen *The Hunchback of Notre Dame?*"

"No."

"Cheez, you guys are really out of it. Do you have television?"

"Yeah, of *course* we have television."

"Cable?"

"Uh, no."

"So what's *your* name?"

"Matt. Matt Weeks. What's your *real* name?"

"Gabi. Gabi Choate."

"Your hair's wet."

Gabi sighed. "I just took a sauna with my mom and Willie."

"What's a sowna?"

"Boy, you really are dumb. It's a steam bath."

"Oh, you mean a sawna."

"No, Willie calls it a sauna." Gabi pronounced it as in the word 'sound.' "Haven't you ever been in one?"

"No. We don't have one. You take a bath in steam? That's weird."

"Yeah, well, I thought it was too."

"You wanna see a dead seal?"

"Oh, yuck!"

"No, it's neat! I found it on the beach. Come on, I'll show you."

"Well, okay."

They crossed Kaunio Road and clambered over a barrier of piled-up logs. Matt, island native, hopped across them with the agility of an ibex. Gabi followed more cautiously.

"Careful," Matt said. "The rocks are slippery."

Gabi picked her way along the beach which was pebbled with rounded stones slick with seaweed.

Matt stopped and pointed. "There it is. See?"

At first Gabi saw nothing unusual. Matt seemed to be pointing at a stone. Then Gabi saw that it was, indeed, a small dead animal, as slate gray as the rocks around it, with a lightly dappled coat. It lay, as if sleeping, on the shore below the tide line, a few feet from the water.

"You want to touch it?" Matt was running his hand along the animal's coat. "It feels like a cat."

Gabi, fascinated but leery, came closer. "What happened to it?"

"Maybe got hit by a boat propeller. Washed up on the tide. It's just a little one. Harbor seal." Matt, exploring the carcass, lifted a flipper. "See, it's got nails like dog." Gabi now saw it also had cuts along its back.

"It's okay to touch it if you want to. It won't bite."

Gabi bent down and gingerly stroked the coat. It felt smooth, firm and solid. "Do we just leave it here?"

"It'll wash out again or something will eat it. Ravens will find it and peck out its eyes."

Just then a raven flew down from a Douglas fir to land in front of them. Matt picked up a stone and threw it. It missed the bird which flew away uttering loud caws. Matt cawed, imitating its call. "My sister has a pet raven. You want to come over and see it?"

"I don't like ravens," Gabi said. "They're scary. Let's go back. These rocks are hard to walk on. My mom will be looking for me." They made their way back over the pile of logs.

"Yeah, better not walk around by yourself or the Loogy-Roo might get you."

"What's a Loogy-Roo?"

"The Loogy-Roo always comes when the blackbirds show up. If you can scare the birds away, the Loogy-Roo won't come. But when there are lots of birds, the Loogy-Roo is coming to get *you*."

"You're full of it. There's no such thing."

"Oh yeah? The Loogy-Roo chased Dory Michaels yesterday. And he ate her dog too. And that's what the Loogy-Roo does. He eats kids and he pulls out their eyeballs and rips them open and yanks out their guts. My sister told me she saw it."

"She saw something ripping out somebody's guts?"

"No, but she saw *it*. She saw the Loogy-Roo. She says it's come back."

"Come back from where?"

"It used to be on the island a long time ago, and it killed kids. Then I guess it went away, but now it's back. My sister says she saw it."

"Matt, does your sister have black hair and a bird on her shoulder?"

"Yeah."

"Well she's blind, isn't she? So she can't see a thing, can she? I think your sister's been jerking your chain."

"Gabi! Gabrielle! Where are you?"

"Uh-oh. Gotta go."

"Me too. Hey, you gonna be here tomorrow after school?"

"Yeah, I guess."

"If you want, I can show you where we go swimming in summer. There's a lake in the woods out back."

"Aren't you afraid of the boogy-boo?"

"The Loogy-Roo? Nah! I've got this great big hunting knife and I'll slice its head off!" Matt made a sweeping gesture. "Don't worry. I'll protect you."

Gabi rolled her eyes. "Yeah, right."

CHAPTER 10

FRIDAY MORNING spilled sunshine onto the floor of Celeste's room. She came awake to its cheeriness and to the faint smell of fresh coffee. She'd been asleep for hours, had been sent to bed early by Willie who'd noticed that both mother and daughter were about to nod off in their chairs after dinner. Gabi was still sleeping, curled up and cuddly under a goosedown duvet. Last night there had been no nightmares, and Celeste guessed it had been the first uninterrupted night's sleep for either of them in she couldn't remember how long.

Celeste got up, made her bed, which only took a moment, since the bed was done in the European fashion, with one fitted bottom sheet and a goosedown comforter inside a duvet cover. No top sheet, no blankets. Fluff and toss, the bed was made. She looked out the window at greenery and a lawn white with English daisies, then put on a pair of faded jeans and a loose-fitting white nubbly knit cotton top. A glance into the vanity mirror gave her a start. After last night's sauna she'd just toweled her hair and let it dry without combing it. After dinner she'd been too sleepy to style it, so now her face was framed with a shaggy halo of crimped locks. She gave her head a shake. The "do" was quite fashionable. She's seen it everywhere — on teenagers. Hardly the look for a serious professional woman, but yes, it made her look younger. She decided to leave it alone. This was a different world and she might as well look the part. She left Gabi still asleep and went down the hall to the bathroom.

When she got back, Gabi was awake and pulling on clothing. Celeste smiled, watching her daughter. Beautiful child. Looking at her now, you wouldn't think she'd ever had a care in the world. "Good morning, love. Go brush your teeth and we'll go down and see what Willie and Jeremy are doing."

Willie and Jeremy were in the kitchen — a cheery room with a pine harvest table surrounded by graceful bowback Windsor chairs, cozier than the massive table in the *pirtti,* that would have served a number of hands at harvest time, or could have been used to butcher meat. The kitchen table was covered with a sky blue cloth patterned with a floral border worked in cross-stitch, and had been set for breakfast with cereal bowls, glasses of orange juice, and coffee cups. A glass of milk indicated Gabi's place. In the center was a large wooden bowl heaped high with golden popovers partially covered by a white tea towel.

Jeremy, as Celeste entered, rose from his chair — an old-fashioned, courtly gesture that made Celeste smile. "Good morning, ladies. I hope you slept well."

"We certainly did! Better than we have in a long time. Must have been the sauna and that delicious salmon."

"Come sit down and have breakfast," Willie said. There's oatmeal, but if anybody wants eggs . . . "

"Oh, Willie, thank you, but this looks wonderful. We don't usually have a big breakfast."

"Neither do we. Coffee and *pulla* most mornings, but now and then we like a bowl of porridge. Good for elderly innards." Willie was plopping spoonfuls into the bowls as she worked her way around the table. Gabi looked alarmed but said nothing when her turn came. "Gabi, you'll want a bit of milk and maple sugar on that."

Gabi glanced at her mother who gave her the "eat-it-or-die" look. As it turned out, the porridge was made from scratch, not an instant stir-into-hot-water variety, but creamy-textured and lump-free, not too thick, and with a pleasant grain flavor enhanced by milk and sugar. Gabi had no trouble polishing off her serving, and went on to sample the popovers with homemade blackberry jam, thinking that this was the best breakfast ever.

Jeremy had been reading the weekly island paper, the *Cormorant*. It contained Broom Island local news, ads from the Co-op, social items, and yet another editorial on the depressed state of the fishing industry. He handed the copy to Celeste. "You'll probably want to take a look at this. There's an article about the early settlers and the fire of 1927."

"*I* didn't see that," Willie said.

"This just came out yesterday. It's been seventy years ago this week, so I guess they did a historical piece on it. Not much detail, but it does list the names of those who died in the fire."

"Does it say what caused the fire?" Celeste asked.

"No, only that it was an accident," Jeremy said.

"Coal oil lamp," Willie said. "We didn't have electricity. People carried lamps at night to see their way. That's what started the fire."

Willie was thoughtfully stirring her coffee. "There was trouble that night. I was twelve years old. I only heard about it from the grown-ups. It was a strange time. People were more superstitious then, not as sophisticated as they think they are now. They tended to believe in witches and werewolves and trolls. Or maybe I should say that while they claimed *not* to, it didn't take much to strip away the veneer of civilized behavior."

Jeremy raised an eyebrow. "And you think things are different today? All you have to do is watch the six o'clock news."

"Oh yes, of course, man's inhumanity to man is very much with us.

I'm only saying that kids today aren't being raised, like I was, on tales of supernatural happenings."

"Have you been watching TV lately?"

"There's a difference, isn't there, between television shows and real life? My grandmother was a fount of stories about witches and how they could cast spells on cattle so cows wouldn't come home, and how if you went looking for them, you wouldn't be able to find them, because they'd been bewitched to look like rocks and trees. There was a woman who used to visit the island, said to be a witch. She was a gypsy. I remember that she made beautiful needlework shawls, and traveled around selling them. Whenever she came to our place, grandmother would throw salt in the fire. Don't ask me why, but she did. And the woman always left hurriedly."

Jeremy was laughing. "The woman probably thought your grand-mother was the witch and got out fast!"

Willie laughed too. "Mummo may have done that just to get rid of her, but that was the thinking of the times. Our dog, Ungo, was trained to lie on a plank set on a fence rail because everybody knows that you can't bewitch a dog if the wind passes beneath his body."

Celeste was listening to all this wished and she had her tape recorder running.

"Every culture has its lore," Jeremy was saying. "I had an aunt who used to leave food out for 'the little people.' We're not all that far away from the Dark Ages."

"Oh, there were spells and rituals for everything back then," Willie said, warming to her subject. "A girl might see the face of her future husband if she looked into a well on Midsummer Night's eve. And if she swept her floor with a broom made of field flowers, she was also sure to see his apparition. Of course she had to be in the nude while she did this."

"Apparition? I'll bet the young men of the village took full advantage of that one!"

"Wouldn't be surprised! Then on New Year's Eve, we peered into the magic mirror."

"Magic mirror?" Celeste asked.

"You prop up two mirrors facing each other, put lighted candles on each side so the mirrors reflect each other and the candles into infinity. Looking into it was supposed to be like gazing into a crystal ball. And on New Year's Eve we also melted tin."

"Tin?"

"It was lead or solder. You melt solder in a pan, pour it quickly into a bucket of cold water, and the resulting lump will foretell the coming year."

"Can we do that?" Gabi had been listening, wide-eyed.

"You mean on New Year's Eve? Sure, I guess so," Celeste said.

"Stuff like that is harmless enough, and we still do things like knock on wood, avoid walking under ladders, and throw salt over our shoulder," Willie said. "But back when I was a child, the superstitious atmosphere was thicker. Witchcraft has a long history among Finns, all the way back beyond the *Kalevala.* At one time, domestic spells were common and accepted, routinely performed by the woman of the house. They were meant to keep family and flocks protected, and to insure a good harvest. It was the men who were the shamans, and their spells involved commerce, healing, catching a thief, the return of stolen property. The graveyard was a busy place in those days, since many rituals were conducted there. Graveyard dirt was an important part of magic. So were human bones."

"Good heavens! Don't tell me they dug up bones of the dead."

"As a matter of fact, they *did.* Nails from coffins were used to cure things like a toothache. Picture digging around in an aching tooth with a nail or a splinter from either the coffin or the skeleton of dear departed Uncle Jukka. And then, of course, there was the *luutalo.* "

"What was that?"

"It was an ossuary. The custom started with the Swedish aristocracy during the time of Swedish rule in Finland. They buried their dead beneath the church building, and when they ran out of room, the bones were dug up, cleaned, labeled, and stored in a building in the cemetery — the *luutalo*, literally a bone house. In Finland the practice got a little distorted, in that the body was buried in the cemetery, but after a while it was dug up, usually by the family, and the bones were placed into the *luutalo*, and when the ossuary ran out of room, the older bones would be unceremoniously dumped on the floor. A shaman would have no trouble breaking into the *luutalo* to obtain bones or skulls for his magic spells."

"But that, of course, was *then*. Nobody would do that now!"

"Of course not, and we've never had an ossuary on the island. It wasn't a good idea anyway, because the dead generally don't like it, and, trust me, you don't want to upset the *Kirkkoväki*."

"What's *that*?"

"The restless dead that inhabit the cemetery."

Celeste was wondering to what degree Willie might be pulling her leg.

"Magic used to be just a part of life. Sometimes it *was* malevolent, used to settle old scores or inflict misfortune. Only later, under the weight of the church, did it become a crime punishable by death or, at least, a twenty-*taler* fine. There is no written record of magic spells ever having *worked*. But the point is that people believed in it, so it became ingrained in the national consciousness. When the imagination is aroused, it puts into motion forces more powerful than anyone can realize. People can be carried away."

"Is that what happened that night?" Celeste asked. "Did people go out of control?"

"According to the stories, yes, but there are many versions." She glanced at Gabi who seemed not to be paying attention, but Willie knew better. She changed the subject. "You're going to want to go to the museum. This morning would be a perfect time. Uh, Gabi could come with us." Willie's eyes met Celeste's. She didn't want to mention the incident of the scythe, but Celeste seemed to be thinking the same thing.

"Can I stay here with Jeremy?" Gabi asked.

"Jeremy may have plans for the day."

"Yes, I do! Big plans. And I could use a helper. We could start by chasing you two out of here so Gabi and I can do the dishes."

"Oh, we couldn't leave you with — "

"Yes, yes, of course you can. Gabi and I can take a walk to the village and pick up the mail, and later, maybe work in the garden."

Gabi was obviously delighted with the agenda, and Celeste gave Jeremy a grateful smile. She went upstairs to gather up camera, laptop computer, notepad and purse, and soon she and Willie were pulling into the empty museum parking lot.

"We can start by looking through the old books and photographs." Willie led Celeste into a small room next to the museum. "This used to be a cloakroom when the big room was used for meetings or plays. Unfortunately there isn't much left. Most family records were kept in the family Bible. We have a few here that have been donated by descendants who don't read Finnish, but most are kept by the families." She answered Celeste's unasked question. "I doubt we would have anything on the Lemerriants. They were outside the community by choice. I'd be surprised to even come across a photograph of any of them ... unless ... ." Willie had pulled out a large album of old photos and began thumbing through them. "Let's see if any of them were in any of the midsummer festival shots.

"Midsummer, *Mittumaari*, also called *Juhannus*, is a big Finnish festival held in June. We used to have bonfires and — okay, here we go. Here's a group shot June 20, 1915. I'm going to need a magnifying glass." Willie found a magnifier and began scanning the names written at the bottom. "Sorry, doesn't look like there are any Lemerriants in this one." The photo was old, cracked and splotched with yellow; it would have been difficult to identify anyone from it. Willie kept leafing forward, then saw a photo of a group of people gathered around the Co-op. Someone had written: Satama, June 30, 1918. There was nothing to identify who the people were, but Willie kept scanning with her magnifying glass.

"I'm not positive, of course, but this *could* be Dauphine Lemerriant."

Celeste took the glass. There, standing in front of the Co-op store, in a loose group of what looked to be shoppers, was a young woman in drab clothing. She was wearing a straw hat that obscured her features, and she had two children with her — a boy who looked to be seven or eight years old, and a girl who was younger. The boy was staring at the camera and leaning on his mother's leg, while the little girl hung on to her hand and faced away from the lens. All wore headwear that cast shadows over their faces.

Celeste studied the picture, trying to glean something — anything — from it, but it was of such poor quality and so impersonal in its *oldness* that it was as if all individuality had simply leached away through time.

"I'm not even sure that's her, but if it is, the children would have been Elphique and Fidelia. I'm going entirely by memory here; we didn't see the Lemerriants that often."

"Excuse me, but is there something *I* can help you find?"

Both Willie and Celeste turned to see a short, plump woman with thinning iron gray hair and rimless eyeglasses.

"Oh, hello Amanda," Willie said dryly. "What brings you here so early?"

"I was on my way to the Co-op when I saw a strange car in the lot. We don't usually open till one." (The last to Celeste.)

"Anyway, nice that you're here, Amanda. I'd like you to meet my friend, Celeste Ooms-Possum. Celeste, this is Amanda Vuorisaari, the museum curator."

"How do you do, Mrs. — uh — Very-sorry."

"Likewise, Miss Ooms — what?"

"With all respect, please call me Celeste and I'll call you Amanda; it'll be so much easier for both of us."

"*Hmph.* You're the writer."

"Well, yes."

"Celeste is doing a piece for a magazine on Broom Island and its history. We were just looking at some of the early photos."

"You're not the first. Happens all the time. Nobody ever gets it right."

"Then perhaps, Amanda, you'll help me," Celeste said smoothly, smiling her most engaging smile. "I was just wondering if there is anything here on the Lemerriant family that used to live here."

Amanda looked shocked. "The Lemerriants? Why on earth would you want to write about *them?*"

Willie started to say something but Celeste gave her arm a gentle pat. "Why, Amanda? Was there something unusual about them?"

"Spawn of the devil. All of them. Crazy as loons. None of them here anymore, and good riddance."

"You sound like you knew them personally."

"Nobody knew them. Nobody wanted know them."

"They kept to themselves, did they?"

"You could say that. The children never went to school. Ran wild like animals. The husband was a drunken brute. Everyone felt sorry for the wife, but there was nothing anybody could do for them."

Celeste was listening, wide-eyed, obviously hanging on to every word. Willie smiled inwardly and thought, *Celeste Ooms-Possum, you are good!*

Amanda, flattered by the attention, became more garrulous. "Yes, there were a lot of stories about the Lemerriants. 'Specially the boy. He was just like a wild animal, and all of us were scared of him. He used to stalk us like a cougar if we went in the woods, and some say he killed his prey and ate it just like one. It was said he could make animals and birds do whatever he wanted. They used to follow him everywhere. They say he killed three of the island children. Ripped them to pieces."

"*What?*"

"Oh, yes! Nobody ever proved it. Some said a cougar did it, but a lot of people thought it was Elphique Lemerriant. Some even said he could turn into an animal."

"You mean like a werewolf?"

"Yes! Some said they'd seen him do it — turn into a huge hairy snarling beast. Of course *I* don't believe that, but kids were scared of him, all right. And everywhere he went, the birds followed. We had a rhyme: *Beware the laughing blackbirds when you go out to play. If they don't stop laughing, throw a lump of clay.* Amanda chuckled. We all carried stones and clay and lumps of coal to throw at the ravens. If we scared them away, Elphique wouldn't come."

"How bizarre! Whatever happened to him?"

"They killed him."

"Who?"

"The townspeople."

"Didn't he die in the fire?"

"Yes. But it was townspeople who hunted him down and burned him out." Amanda glanced sharply at Celeste. "How did *you* know he died in the fire?"

"Uh, I remembered seeing the name on a cemetery marker. A lot of people died in that fire."

"It was tragic. Wasn't meant to happen that way. People got all worked up over the deaths of the children. The first child — Aake Jaakobsson was his name — had died a few years earlier, and they blamed it on a cougar. Then when two more children were killed, they blamed Elphique for all three. They stormed the Lemerriant farm. They didn't find Elphique but they found Brazeau shot through the heart."

"Dauphine, his wife, died too, didn't she?"

"They found her body in the barn. The story was that Elphique shot his father. Nobody really knows what happened because nobody was alive to tell it. Dauphine could have shot him herself. But others say that Brazeau killed Dauphine, and some say Elphique killed both of them.

"The story goes that the townspeople blamed Elphique for the deaths of the two boys. They went to the Lemerriant farm and found Brazeau and Dauphine dead and Elphique gone. They say they were hunting him with dogs, and somehow Elphique ended up hiding in the meeting house. Somebody saw him. There was a mob. A fire broke out and a lot of people died."

"What do *you* think happened, Amanda?"

Amanda Vuorisaari sighed, as if returning from a flight of fancy back to the land of common sense. "There are lots of versions, and I don't know for sure myself. But I think Brazeau killed his wife and then Elphique killed his father. He then ran away, probably panicked. Maybe there *were* men and dogs, and maybe that's why he headed for town, instead of the woods, and took refuge in the meeting house."

"What happened to the daughter?"

"Fidelia? They found her hiding in the root cellar. She left the island right afterwards. We never heard anything more about her."

"But she was just a child, wasn't she?"

"She'd have been fourteen or fifteen. They say she'd been sent off to live with some relative on the mainland."

Celeste was quietly doing the math in her head. Her mother's birthday had been January second. Madeline Lemerriant had been born in 1928. When Fidelia, at age 15, left the island, she'd have already been pregnant.

CHAPTER 11

"It's only about a fifteen minute walk to town," Jeremy told Gabi, but if you'd rather ride my bicycle, you're welcome to. I can trail behind."

"I'd rather walk with you," Gabi said.

Jeremy smiled. The girl seemed to pulsate with the electricity of youth. A walk into town would barely make a dent in her energy. *Was I ever that young?*

"In that case, we can hike to the post office, then stop off for a rest and a drink at Pearl's." He stopped when he saw Gabi's face darken. "Or maybe not Pearl's today. We can grab a soda pop at the Inn, or even have lunch at the New Broom. Would you like that?"

Gabi nodded. "I don't think I want to go to Pearl's. There was a scary woman in there."

"Yes, I heard about that. Her name is Sybil Weeks. She lives just over there." Jeremy pointed to an old weathered house on the hillside. "She's a little odd, but I don't think she means to hurt anyone."

"Her brother came over yesterday. He's okay. But she's weird. Her bird pulled my hair." Gabi looked pained at the memory.

"Well, let's just forget about her. It's a beautiful day. Would you like to see some stone birds?"

"Stone birds?"

They had come to a bend in the road, and, as they came around it, Jeremy pointed to a pile of boulders on the shore. On top of the rocks there looked to be birds of all sizes. When they got closer Gabi saw that they were just little heaps of stones. "How'd they get there?"

"Somebody started it just for fun. Now it's become a tradition. People who walk along the shore pick up stones and build birds. Sometimes kids knock them down. Last winter we had a storm that wiped the rocks clean, but they always come back."

"Can *we* build birds?"

"Sure. We'll have to climb over logs to get there. Just be careful."

Gabi had no trouble navigating the jam of huge logs that piled up as an obstruction between road and shore. Jeremy made a more stately crossing, careful of his balance and be-casted arm. "Why don't they get rid of some of these logs and make a path to the water?" Gabi asked.

"They sometimes do, but one good storm and they're all back again. They tell me they had a flood here once that sent all the logs out to sea. That was when they had an earthquake in Alaska. All the beaches were clean for a day or two. Then all the logs came back again."

"Where do they come from?"

"Everywhere, I guess. Some escape from log booms."

"What's a log boom?"

"It's a big raft of floating logs with a tugboat pulling it. You'll see one, I'm sure, while you're here."

Up close, the piles of stones were just piles of stones, although cleverly arranged to look like squatting seagulls. Jeremy and Gabi gathered smooth rounded rocks. Jeremy showed Gabi how to arrange them, and she, happily, added a couple of "birds" to the grouping. Jeremy then began building another figure: two pairs of flat stones with one long one on top like a bench, two more stacked in the center of that, another longer one balanced on top, and a round one in the center to top it off.

"It looks like a little man!" Gabi said.

"It's an *inukshuk*. Native people build them, particularly in the north. Some are really big."

"Neat! Why do they do that?"

"Oh, I guess it's a signal of some kind. Lets others know they've been there. A sort of 'Kilroy was here.'"

"Who?"

Jeremy grinned. Follow the path of a child's questions and you'll end up a long way from home. "A long time ago it was a popular expression. I don't even know how it began, but you used to see 'Kilroy was here' written everywhere as graffiti."

Jeremy expected to hear "What's graffiti?" but Gabi seemed to know. "You mean like 'fuck you'?"

"Oh, Gabrielle! You don't want to use *that* kind of language!"

"I only meant that you see it written everywhere."

Jeremy sighed. "We'd best be on our way. Tide's coming in."

They made their way back across the jumble of logs and onto the blacktop. Jeremy walked at a slower pace while Gabi, like a young puppy, zigzagged back and forth, digressing to look at a flower, a shell, an eagle in a tree. Jeremy, watching her, mused that being on the island seemed to be doing the child good. She seemed interested in everything, exhibiting the natural curiosity of kids. Yet, there was something a bit dark about the girl. Well, perhaps not *dark* exactly, but something hidden. Yes, that was it. Something beneath the surface. Something tightly wound. Perhaps there was something she wasn't telling anyone. Or had she formed the habit of secrecy and, if so, why, for god's sake?

"What's behind the hedge?" They were nearing the village.

"That's the cemetery, Gabi."

"Where they bury people?"

"That's right."

"Can we go look?"

"No reason why not. There's the gate."

"Man, look at all the stones! What's this one over here with just a pile of dirt?" Gabi was looking at the site of a recent burial with bare earth mounded over the grave and withering flowers lying on top.

"That was an elderly gentleman who died about a week ago." Jeremy had gone to the funeral although he didn't know the man. Longtime residents of the island customarily attended all funerals; Jeremy had gone with Willie.

Gabi lost interest and chased off in another direction. "What's *this*?"

She had come to a grave that looked like no other; in fact, at first it didn't look like a grave at all. She stood silently looking at it as Jeremy came up behind her. There was no monument, no stone with an inscription, nothing to indicate who was buried there or how long ago. Around it the grass was neatly mown, but the grave itself was a wild tangle of growth upon a cairn of large native boulders that had been piled waist high. What grew on it looked untended, and it was impossible to tell whether it had been planted, or whether it was the type of rampant vegetation that swallows temples in jungles.

Jeremy had been in the cemetery a number of times, but had never taken time to explore it completely. This grave stood alone in a corner; Jeremy must have seen it, but this was the first time he recognized it as a burial place. Now, looking closely at it, he noticed other things too. In among the greenery, there seemed to be rather crude figures fashioned of wood and stone. Pagan symbols of some sort? Or toys? They looked like toys that children of his own generation might have carved — or had had carved for them. A crude wooden horse. A doll with a decaying fabric shirt or skirt, the color long since bleached away. A rusted metal car or truck — something with wheels, at any rate. A small painted and peeling rubber ball. A child's tea set, the sort that these days would be made of plastic. There was a tiny teapot, one cup, and a saucer that had broken in two. These things, tucked into the grasses, made it look as if a group of children — playing a game called Cemetery — might have constructed such a marker. Jeremy's Irish aunt would have crossed herself and declared it the work of "the little people." Whose grave could this be? Willie would know. Jeremy would have to ask.

Gabi was staring as if entranced. She didn't seem to hear the flap of wings as a raven flew down from a fir tree and landed by her feet, then another and another. Jeremy looked at them apprehensively. They were just the cemetery ravens, of course, but Gabi didn't need another fright. He wanted to shoo them away, but feared their noisy exit might startle Gabi who was standing motionless, staring at the mound. She was so engrossed that she didn't even seem to notice the birds, although she had the attitude of listening to something. Jeremy gently touched her arm and she looked up at him, almost not seeming to recognize him. Jeremy felt a slight shock at the expression in her blue eyes. They weren't those of a child at all. The look was ageless, unfathomable, and seemed to say, who are you and why do you interrupt me?

"It's time we were going, Gabi," Jeremy almost whispered. The girl glanced around, nodded, as if acknowledging not only Jeremy, but also the presence of the birds. Jeremy took her hand, hoping to reassure her, but Gabi didn't appear at all frightened. She stood still, looking over the flock like a queen with her subjects. Then, as Jeremy gently led her away, the solemn, silent, ravens watched them go; their only movement was to edge out of the path as Gabi and Jeremy walked out through the cemetery gate.

* * *

The village was buzzing with morning activity, and the area around the ferry dock and the Co-op was the center of it. People were doing their grocery shopping, stopping to chat and exchange pleasantries. There was a line of cars parked along the road waiting for the next ferry to Port Casper. The *Island Empress* was large enough to accommodate a number of cars and trucks, but on busy days, if your car wasn't in the lineup early, you might have to wait for the next sailing. Some left their vehicles in the line overnight, while others would park, then spend an hour or two in the village. Whenever a ferry arrived, people would come straggling out of the Co-op, the New Broom, Pearl's, or The Sea Hole, get into their cars and prepare to drive on board. As the ferry unloaded, they would carry on last minute conversations with people on the road. "Goodbye, see you soon!" "Don't forget to pick up my cardamom seed." "Here, take this to your sister Hilda and say hello from me." — a jar of blackberry jam or home-smoked salmon thrust through an open car window.

Jeremy, with Gabi in tow, was making his way, nodding, waving, stopping to exchange a word here and there, as he and Gabi headed for the New Broom. He loved the casual informality of the island. There were few rules here. Traffic jockeyed and found its own level. There were no outlined parking spaces, no signs, no meters, and few posted speed limits. Vehicular accidents were rare, although, now and then, a tipsy patron of The Sea Hole might run his car off a road.

Still, there was one type of traffic accident that happened all too often on the island, mainly at night, to speeding teenaged joy riders. There was usually a funeral after one of those. Jeremy had speculated that it would be interesting to explore why, in a place that seemed safe and friendly, children, who should have had an idyllic childhood, grew, in their teens, to became a destructive force. Of course, not all of them, but a significant number. Was it boredom? Was it rebellion? Was it a lack of direction? Was it a sampling of the malaise of the world as manifest in a technological society? Or was it simply that every tortured teen has his or her own reasons, and it doesn't matter too much where they live. Broom Island was a microcosm.

Jeremy and Gabi left the busy square and went into the gloom of the restaurant. They found it nearly empty. A couple of tables hadn't yet been cleared after the diners had vacated to catch the ferry. Larry Nyquist was polishing a glass at the counter. He greeted Jeremy with a grin. "Hi, Professor, how's the arm?"

"It itches like the very — "Jeremy glanced at Gabi. "It *itches*, but I'm almost getting used to it. We're not too late for lunch, are we?"

"Nah! We'll be open till one. We're not doing much business, so all I have is soup and sandwiches." He pointed to a blackboard.

They settled on ordering ham sandwiches with a chocolate milk for Gabi and a cold beer for Jeremy.

"At least it isn't fish," Gabi said. She was wearing a baseball cap and a sweatshirt with a big seagull on the front, each emblazoned with the word "Satama."

Gabi wriggled into a chair at a table, placed the plastic shopping bag she'd been carrying on the seat next to her, took off her cap and put it on top. She leaned her elbows on the table and fixed Jeremy with an even gaze. "Jeremy, there really *is* a Loogy-Roo, isn't there?"

"Why, Gabi, what would make you think that?"

"Because it killed the children."

"What children, Gabrielle?"

"The long-ago children. The ones in the grave."

"You mean the one you were looking at in the cemetery? I don't know who's buried there — if anyone — there's no name on it."

Gabi raised her eyebrows and dropped her eyes, as she tried to recall exact details. "There were two children. Boys. They were about the same age as me."

"As I," Jeremy corrected absently. "How could you possibly know that?"

"The birds told me."

"The ravens in the cemetery?"

"Yes."

"How did they tell you?"

"They just told me."

Jeremy probed gently, "Did you hear them talk to you?"

Gabi sighed, as if exasperated. "They talked to me in my head."

Jeremy studied her keenly. A child's fantasy? Or the catchall diagnosis for the incomprehensible: a vivid imagination? "What did the birds tell you, Gabi?"

"They said the boys were playing in the woods and the Loogy-Roo chased them and found them and tore them to pieces. And the birds came and pecked out their eyes."

"But Gabi, you must know that's impossible. Even if the birds *could* tell you these things, all that happened a long time ago. Birds don't live as long as people. The birds you saw wouldn't have been around back then."

"But they *were*. They *saw* it. They were *there*. They were laughing and talking about how they pecked and tore the meat from the bones."

Jeremy felt disquieted, not so much by the story, but that the words were issuing from the mouth of this pretty little girl who should have been more concerned with Beanie Babies and Barbie dolls. Still, he mused wryly, children have a flair for the dramatic and a capacity for raw violence uncushioned by the packing noodles of civilization. They haven't yet learned euphemisms; they understand neither enormities nor consequences, which is what makes juvenile crime so vicious.

"Well, hello you two! I see somebody's been shopping!" It was Celeste. She and Willie had come in, unnoticed.

Gabi flashed a smile. "Jeremy took me to the Co-op and bought me a 'Satama' shirt. I have the hat too!"

"Really, Jeremy, this goes far above and beyond ... but how very kind of you. Thank you. Obviously Gabi has been having a wonderful time."

Jeremy had risen to his feet at the approach of the two women. "We've had an interesting morning. You'll join us for lunch, of course. We've already ordered." He courteously made a move to seat Willie, who quickly seated herself, as did Celeste, to prevent Jeremy from having to demonstrate that, arm or no arm, he was still a gentleman.

Gabi was now full of her day: "We went to the beach and built stone birds. Then we went to the cemetery — "

"And the post office," Jeremy smoothly cut in. "Gabi is toting your mail in her shopping bag." The mood had lightened, Jeremy preferred to keep it that way. He would ponder Gabi and her fantasies later, talk them over with Willie privately. "And did you ladies have a successful morning?"

"We did," Celeste said. I have all sorts of material in the back of the car that I want to go over and record on my laptop."

"Yes," Willie laughed. "We hope to get it back into the archives before Amanda Vuorisaari notices it's missing."

"I'll work as fast as I can. Maybe we can sneak it back by the light of the moon." Celeste glanced at her watch. "Of course I could go back after lunch and just work at the museum, couldn't I? She wouldn't object to that, would she?"

"Not today. Not unless you want to listen to three hours of accordion music. The island band is rehearsing. Besides, I have archives of my own that may be helpful, and you can use my scanner to record information on your computer. It'll be a lot more convenient than the photocopier in the museum, if it's even working. And I'll be there to translate."

Lunch over, Jeremy and Gabi rode home with Celeste and Willie. It was agreed that the two women would be spending the afternoon doing research. Jeremy volunteered (with Gabi's help) to take charge of dinner, but first he wanted to deal with his mail and read the latest issue of *Equinox*. This left Gabi with a couple of options. She rejected the nap her mother suggested, nor did she want to watch television — the thing she had so sorely missed at the Inn. Instead, she went outdoors.

"Go take a look at the hummingbird feeder," Willie called. "See if it needs refilling."

Hummingbird feeder? Gabi went out the door and onto the porch. There, by the living-room window, hung an upside-down glass bottle. It was one of the familiar waisted feeders common everywhere, with four tiny holes around its red base, each defined by a yellow-petaled plastic flower, and a small red plastic perch next to it. Gabi could see that it was half-full. As she watched, a tiny bird darted to it, hovered, wings a-blur, put its beak into a feeding hole and took a long drink. Gabi had never seen a hummingbird up close, and she noticed its iridescent green feathers, what looked like a black spot on its white throat, and the turkey markings as the bird fanned out its tiny tail. Soon another bird arrived. Now there were two, one hovering while the other perched. They didn't seem to be bothered by Gabi's presence, but both birds vanished in a hum of wings as yet another flew in. This one was different — rusty brown in color with a black throat, only it wasn't black at all. When the bird hovered and faced the sun, the gorget turned a fiery red, making the little creature look like a flying jewel.

"We got lots of them. They like to play in the water hose."

Gabi turned. It was Matt Weeks. "Yeah, when you water the garden they like to fly through the spray. And if their feeder goes empty, they come and get us."

"Yeah, I'll bet."

"They *do*!" Matt reached up and tilted the feeder, loosening several air bubbles. "See, sometimes air gets in there and if the birds can't reach the sugar water, they'll come looking for us."

"What do they do, whisper in your ear?"

"No, they just hover in the air and look you in the eye."

Gabi laughed. "They don't seem to be afraid of me."

"Sometimes when my mom's filling the feeder, they land on her arm."

"There are sure a lot of strange birds on this island."

"You want to go for a walk? I can show you the lake where we go swimmin'."

Gabi looked uncertain. "I'd have to ask my mom. She doesn't want me wandering off." She left Matt waiting on the porch while she darted into the house.

Celeste and Willie were deep into island history, and when Gabi came in to ask if she could go with Matt, Celeste cast a questioning glance at Willie.

"They should be fine. Matt's the little boy who lives next door. He's a bit mischievous, but a good kid. Where are you two going?"

Children have an instinct, a detector that warns them of imminent adult intervention. Gabi answered carefully: "Oh, just down to Matt's house. He said he wanted to show me something." She made no mention of a lake.

"Well, don't be long, and take your jacket. There's a cold wind off the water." Celeste frowned. "Gabi, isn't Matt the brother of the young woman we saw at Pearl's?"

"Yeah."

"I wouldn't want you to be frightened again."

Willie looked at her watch. "I don't think Sybil will even be at home today. She'll be working at Danielle's gift shop."

"Well, all right. Just make sure you're home soon. Jeremy will be expecting you to help cook dinner."

"Cool!" She was gone.

"How would a woman with Sybil Weeks' — uh — disability be working in a gift shop?"

Willie laughed. "Welcome to Satama, where everybody knows everybody's business. Danielle has a hair appointment in Port Casper, and she usually asks any one of a number of island women to keep an eye on the shop whenever she has errands to do. Today most of them are at band practice.

"Sybil Weeks is part of the community. We know her problems, but she's accepted by everyone. This is off-season. There won't be many customers in the shop. Locals are capable of helping themselves if Sybil has trouble. Mostly she'll just sit there and read her Braille Bible and answer the phone if it rings."

Celeste had a mental vision of Sybil spewing forth jeremiads at cowering sinners.

"And I'm sure she's back on her medication by now after the fracas at Pearl's."

Not entirely reassured, Celeste turned back to her work. She'd have been even less sanguine if she'd been able to see Gabi and Matt skirt the Weeks house and disappear into the forest.

CHAPTER 12

GABI FOLLOWED as Matt led the way through the Weeks property, past his house, and onto a footpath in the woods. Here they were surrounded by tall trees that gave way to an area that had been cleared at one time so that only stumps and brush remained. The trail went on, past frothy green stands of young hemlock, salal so tall it towered over them, then entered the deep woods again onto a more-traveled path. Gabi, big-eyed, looked around. "Are you sure you know where you're going?"

"I come here all the time."

Gabi had envisioned — well, she really didn't know *what* she'd envisioned, but a lake for swimming had sounded more like a park where there would be people, not just wilderness. The path itself was spongy with peat and last year's leaf mold. They were stepping over roots and skirting wet spots where mud showed the occasional marks of sneaker tread — evidence, to Gabi, that other human beings *had* been on the trail. Moss grew everywhere, and was of many textures, many shades of brown and green, and some of orange and deep red. There were a couple of places where a tree had fallen across the trail, a giant toppled in a storm. In each case a section had been sawn away to remove the blockage. A muddy patch had large rounds of wood laid across it like stepping stones. "Lily pads," Matt called them. Step on the pads and keep your sneakers dry.

It was cool, and Gabi was glad of her jacket, as she made her way through a woods unlike any she'd ever seen. Tall trees, some flocked with bright green moss, others hung with gray beard, towered on both sides. Some appeared to stand on tiptoe with a hole that would have been big enough for Gabi to crawl through at their roots.

"How come those trees grow out of the ground like that?" she asked.

"They grew on a log," Matt said. "The log rotted away and left the hole. See, there's one growing." Gabi looked at a stump of a tree that had been cut down. It must have been ten feet across, over six feet tall, and had holes cut into it like a pair of eyes. On top of it, growing from its center, was a good-sized evergreen tree. The whole thing looked like a Polynesian idol with a headdress.

"How come it has eyes?"

"Logger's cuts. Loggers used to stick a board into them to stand on so they could cut down the tree. Be another pair on the other side if you wanna take a look."

"No thanks." Gabi, feeling a bit spooked, had no wish to get off the trail even to check out a stump. "Maybe we shouldn't be out here."

"We won't be long. Too cold to go swimmin' yet. Anyway, we're almost there." He veered off the main trail to another leading to the left.

They continued on, then rounded a bend to see a small lake surrounded by trees and thickets of salal pink with bloom. Matt headed down a path to the water's edge where large quantities of sand had been spread to form a beach. It was patterned with footprints, but deserted.

"Where'd all the sand come from?" Gabi asked.

"They got that from the quarry." Matt pointed upward. "There's one on the other side of the lake, on the other side of the road." Gabi could see that there was a deeply rutted road heading up a hill farther on up the shore.

"What made these tracks?" Gabi asked, looking at large but mis-shapen marks in the damp sand at the water's edge.

Matt glanced down carelessly. "Dog, I guess."

Gabi stood looking at the lake. "Not very big, is it? What's it called?"

"Big Lake."

"What makes the water so dark? Like my mom's black coffee."

"I don't know. That's the way it's always been. Oh look, there's a goose with chicks." On the far side, a stately Canada goose was paddling along followed by a dozen little balls of gray fluff.

The lake was more of a pond, with yellow water lilies in bloom along the shallows. A small dinghy had been pulled on shore and tipped over on its side. In the middle of the pond someone had anchored a raft that was covered with canvas and floated by inflated inner tubes. Gabi saw that there was a long rope stretching all the way across the lake, tied high to trees on either shore. The tree with the rope — a large cedar — had a crude ladder of slats nailed to the trunk.

"There used to be a big fishnet we could climb, but it rotted and they took it down. Then some big kids put up the rope. You wanna climb up?"

Gabi shook her head. Matt clambered up the ladder like a monkey. "See? It's easy!" Gabi saw that the big rope had been securely tied around the tree, and that it had been threaded through a two-foot length of plastic pipe. Holding onto the pipe, a kid could slide down into the water or even onto the raft without getting his hands rope-burned. From around the pipe hung another length of rope, knotted for climbing, and long enough to reach the ground.

"If you swing from the rope you always hit the water, but if you hold onto the pipe, you can sometimes drop off on the raft. Want to see me do it?"

"Then how would you get back?"

"You could come get me in the boat."

"No way! You better come down."

Matt skittered down the rungs, let himself drop the last few feet and sprang upright. A raucous cry interrupted as a bird flew to the top of the tree where it balanced uncertainly on a topmost branch. It was joined by another, then more. As Gabi looked at the sky, she could see more birds arriving in straggly groups. They seemed to be landing in the tops of the tallest trees, their numbers growing so that the branches were becoming encrusted with black.

"Man, you sure have lots of birds here!"

"Yeah, they fly in every night. They come from other islands. You don't have to be scared of them unless the Loogy-Roo's around." Matt started to chant in a singsong voice:

Beware the laughing blackbirds
And the Loogy-Roo
If they don't stop laughing,
Then they've come for YOU!

He assumed a Frankenstein's monster pose, arms outstretched, and began lurching stiffly toward Gabi. Gabi stood her ground and eyed him evenly. "Then how come *you're* not scared of the Loogy-Roo?"

"Because there *is* no Loogy-Roo."

"But you just said — "

"Nah, that's just stuff."

"Your *sister* says there's a Loogy-Roo. You told me she's seen it."

"My sister's always talking weird. She sees things but they're never real. I just said that to scare you." Matt laughed. "Sometimes it's fun to scare girls just to see what they'll do. Hey, you wanna see a haunted house?"

"Are you still trying to scare me?"

"No, there's a real one."

"Well, where is it then?"

"On up a ways. Or are you sca-a-a-ared?"

"No, but it's getting late. We should be going back." Gabi had to raise her voice over the noise of the birds.

"Come on then." Gabi followed as Matt led the way, but then instead of continuing back the way they'd come, he turned left at the main trail.

"Are you sure we're not going to get lost?"

"Nah. This is the way to the haunted house. It's not far." Matt stopped. "You can see it from here."

They had come to a bend that opened up to a space that had once been a field but now, neglected, was growing broom, young hemlock, thickets of alder, and sparse grasses. In the distance Gabi could see wooden buildings.

"That's the old Lemerriant place. Nobody lives there."

"Is it really haunted?"

Matt shrugged. "I dunno. Nobody spends the night there. A year ago the graduating class was going to have a haunted house party, but they all got scared and went home. They say crazy old Lemerriant is still there, and if you spend the night in the house when there's a full moon, he comes after you with his scy-y-y-ythe."

"Is that that thing you cut hay with?" Gabi was remembering her nightmare, and the blade she'd seen in the museum.

"Yeah, my dad has one in the barn. They say Lemerriant chopped his wife into little bitty pieces with it."

"Yeah, I'm sure," Gabi murmured, although, right now, she *wasn't*.

"Well, it *coulda* happened. You want to go in and look around?"

Before Gabi could say yes or no, Matt was sprinting across the old hay field. Gabi followed at a trot.

The Lemerriant farm stood derelict in the late afternoon sun. Part of the barn roof had long since caved in, and the boards had buckled and spaced themselves to resemble ribs of a mastodon. A few smaller sheds were still standing but leaned at various angles. As Gabi approached, she saw that the house, more of a cabin, was still upright, but damaged. All the windows were broken, the targets of stone-throwing children. Blackberry bramble threatened to swallow the rickety porch, and the front door was partly off its hinges, propped permanently ajar.

"Let's go in," Matt said. Then, as Gabi hesitated, "I dare you. I *double-dog dare you!*"

Gabi made her way past brambles and squeezed through the door opening. The place was empty: Disappointing — plank floor, wooden table covered with dust, piles of old newspapers, faded and ragged pieces of curtain hung from a rusting rod on the window. A couple of metal gallon cans stood by the door. The floor was littered with trash. There was really nothing that spoke of the people who had once lived there. The room had once been a kitchen but now was bare except for an old mattress thrown in the corner, the relic of some teenage party or tryst.

"This is where they found old man Lemerriant shot through the heart," Matt said. "I think you can still see the blood."

Gabi looked but saw nothing but the dust and filth of ages. "Who shot him?"

"They say it was his crazy son, Elphique. He chopped his wife to pieces in the barn, and Elphique found him and shot him."

"Why did he chop up his wife?"

"I dunno."

"What happened to the guy who shot him?"

"He got burned in the fire."

"Well, it doesn't look scary to me. Now it's just a mess."

"It's okay in the daytime. But at night the Lemerriants come out."

"Were there lots of them?"

"Old man Lemerriant, the one with the scythe. Some say they've seen Elphique and his sister. And some people say you can still hear Lemerriant's wife screaming."

There was an eerie silence as both children stood in the gloom, illuminated only by a slanting sunbeam choked with dust motes. Then both Gabi and Matt started at the sound of wings. One of the ravens had lighted on the window sill and was looking at them. It took flight again and landed on the table top, puffing up a cloud of dust. Matt picked up a piece of broken window glass and shied it at the bird. "Get out of here!" The raven uttered *skra-a-a-k* and flew out again.

"Those birds seem to be following us," Gabi said.

"I've never seen so many. I think they're following *you*. Guess we better go. We don't want to be out here when it gets dark."

Twilight is long on a Pacific coast island in May. It wouldn't be dark for hours yet, although shadows were lengthening and the light would gradually lessen. Gabi and Matt left the house without exploring the rest of it. Outdoors the sun was shining and once again they found themselves surrounded by ravens that were hovering over a patch of field.

"They've found something to eat, that's why they're here," Matt said. "Let's go see."

At their approach the birds flew off to where they could continue their calling and squawking at a distance. The two children saw what they'd been feasting on: the carcass of a deer. It had obviously been killed by something that had eaten most of the meat. What was left were bloody bones, rags of skin, and a head. The birds had pecked out the eyes and cleaned some of the bones which, to Gabi, looked surprisingly small and delicate. Gabi felt a slight prickle down her spine. "What killed it?"

"Wolf. Maybe a cougar."

"Cougar?"

"Same as a mountain lion. Big cat. Might even have been a bear."

"You have wolves and cougars and bears?"

Matt sighed. "I haven't seen any myself. There are wolves up in the hills. Last summer a tourist said he'd seen a bear, but it might have just been somebody's dog. A long time ago there used to be cougars, but they were all shot. Maybe one swam in again from another island."

"Something killed this deer," Gabi said thoughtfully. And what about that kid who said something chased her in the woods? I heard them talking about it."

"That could've been a cougar. Cougars stalk kids. Follow them in the woods, then jump on'em and rip'em to pieces and eat'em." Matt shot Gabi a sly look.

"Matt, remember how you said you like to scare girls? Was it *you* who scared the kid on her way to school?"

"You mean Dory Michaels? Stuck-up little cow. Just because her folks own a nursery and lots of land and her father used to be a big-city lawyer."

"Well, *was* it you? Did you chase her? I promise I won't tell."

"No, it wasn't me."

Gabi looked at him narrowly. He wouldn't tell her if he'd done it. He didn't know her well enough. "Matt, let's just get out of here."

* * *

Getting back was now a matter of following the main trail until it finally reconnected with the one leading into the Weeks backyard. There was still plenty of light; the sun wouldn't actually go down until nine o'clock, but it was low enough to be hidden by trees. Gabi was worried that she'd been gone too long, and wanted to get back before it occurred to her mother to go looking for her.

Too late! As Gabi and Matt came out of the woods, they walked into a group of people that looked like a search party. Gabi's mother was there with Willie and a couple who could only have been Matt's parents. Even his sister, spooky Sybil, was there. Only Jeremy was missing. "Uh-oh," Gabi, the daughter of an attorney, said. "Better let me do the talking."

"Gabrielle Penelope Choate, where have you been?" Celeste rushed over and grabbed Gabi by the shoulders.

"Hi, Mom. Uh, were you looking for us?"

"Are you all right? Where on earth did you go? You were supposed to be here with Matt and all the time his parents thought he was at our place!"

"We were here, but we just took a little walk down the trail. We're sorry. We didn't know we weren't supposed to." Gabi's voice quavered and her eyes were huge, blue, and innocent.

Kirsti Weeks broke in. "Matt Weeks, you should know better than that. Strangers to the island should always stay out of the woods." Then, to Celeste, "I'm sorry, ma'am, if you were worried. Our boy grew up in these woods and plays there all the time."

"Please don't be mad at Matt," Gabi said. "I wanted to see what the woods were like and he was just showing me. Guess we kind of lost track of time." She turned to Willie, hoping to change the subject. "Where's Jeremy?"

"Well, when we began wondering where you were, your mom and I came to fetch you. Jeremy stayed home in case you got back before we did."

Celeste, by now, was visibly relieved. "I feel I should apologize to everyone. I'm sorry we caused a fuss. It's just that we're in a strange place, and yesterday we were warned not to go walking because there might be danger. When Gabi wasn't here, I'm afraid I panicked."

Rome Weeks spoke up. "Plenty of danger in the woods for the greenhorn. Easy to get lost in there, even on a small island. Could break a leg. Fall off a bluff."

"And the Loogy-Roo could get you."

Everyone turned to look at Sybil who, without her raven, was still cadaverous, though a little less menacing.

"Hush, Sybil," her mother said. "You know that's just a lot of nonsense."

"The birds foretold it and now the Loogy-Roo is back." She was looking hard at Gabi who wondered just how much she could actually see. "Blackjack magic bird of night proclaimed the evil at first sight! Sins of the fathers! *Sins of the fathers!*" She turned and walked toward the house, muttering as she went, then whipped around and shouted: *"Beware the laughing blackbirds and the Loogy-Roo!"*

She turned and ran into the house.

Rome sighed. "It's an old island legend. Many years ago some children were killed by cougars. Cougars sometimes swim to the island. Last one was shot, oh, must've been'bout five years back."

"But how did the Loogy-Roo legend get started?" Celeste was once again the inquiring journalist, pursuing her credo that you never have the whole story until you've heard it from a number of people.

"Family on the island. Name of Lemerriant. They were all peculiar and kept to themselves. They had a crazy son who used to go around scarin' folks. You know how people are. Stories began to circulate about how he was killin' animals, and livin' like one, and there was even stories goin' around that he could change into a wolf.' Course it was all bullshit."

"Loogy-Roo? Of course! *Loup garou*? That's French for werewolf!"

"Yeah, I guess that was it. One kid was killed by a cougar. When two more were killed, somebody got the idea that the Lemerriant boy had something to do with it."

"Why would they think that?"

"I think it was because of the birds. I guess the boy — Elphique was his name — had lived in the woods so long that the animals and birds all knew him. Anyway, ravens used to follow him everywhere. When they found the two dead kids, ravens were pecking — uh, sorry, ma'am — uh, there were ravens *there* and the boy, Elphique was at the scene. Now I don't hold with them stories, and the boy probably just happened on the two bodies that were already being scavenged by birds, but the word then was that the kid was some kind of a ghoul who was killin' children and eating human flesh."

"Rome!" Kirsti hissed. "The children! You're frightening the children."

"What happened to the boy, Elphique?" Celeste asked.

"He died in the fire. Nobody left of that family anymore. Nobody ever found out exactly what happened, but it ended up with the Lemerriants dead and their son killed in the fire."

"What became of Lemerriant's wife, Dauphine?"

"She was killed too. Did *I* mention that her name was Dauphine? Anyway, some say her husband killed her and then Elphique killed him. Some say Elphique killed both of them. There were so many stories goin' around that nobody seems to know anymore."

"Did old man Lemerriant really chop her to pieces with a scythe?" No one had noticed how closely Gabi had been following the conversation.

"Rome! You shouldn't be talking about stuff like that in front of kids," Kirsti said.

"Oh, it's all ancient history now. It was before my time. Not too many around anymore who remember. Those who do were kids at the time, and nobody would have told them anything. All kinds of wild stories got started. Got nothin' to do with anybody today."

"Mr. Weeks, we heard that a little girl was frightened by something that followed her in the woods. What do you think it was?" Celeste asked.

"Dory Michaels? Yeah, I heard about that. Her father used to be a big-time lawyer before he got disbarred. He's always crying wolf or threatening to sue somebody or orderin' people off his land. They moved here a few years ago with the idea of settin' up a bunch of greenhouses. They wangled some kind of silviculture contract from the government and put up fences and gates to keep the locals off their precious property. Now they want to build a golf course on the island and open a campground for tourists!" Rome spat out the word. "Chadwick Michaels. Who has a name like Cha-a-a-dwick? Story is that his last name used to be Shit Hill. Honest to god!"

"No, Rome, it was Schittle," Kirsti said.

"Yeah, whatever. They say he tried changing the pronunciation to Shuttle, but that didn't work so he legally changed it to Michaels. I wouldn't believe anything that man said. His kind will ruin the island. I wouldn't put it past him to make the whole thing up so he can print up Loogy-Roo T-shirts, you know, like they do Bigfoot. Something to sell to tourists. Coulda started that story about his kid being followed himself."

Gabi, standing next to Matt, saw that he was smiling faintly and a bit smugly. She nudged him and whispered, "The Loogy-Roo? I *know* it was you." Matt nudged back. "Shut up, *Penelope*."

"So you don't believe there's anything to be afraid of?" Celeste asked.

"Mind you, a cougar can be a real menace," Rome answered. "They don't usually attack adults. Most wild animals will run away if you just make some noise when you're in the woods. But a cougar will, if he's hungry, kill your dogs, cats, and they do stalk kids. Happens all over B.C. You see it on the news all the time."

"I think we'd better be getting back," Willie said. "Jeremy will be wondering why we're gone so long."

"Yes, thank you for your kindness, Mr. and Mrs. Weeks. It's been lovely meeting you and your . . . uh" — Celeste looked around for Sybil but she hadn't come back — "your daughter."

Kirsti extended her hand. "Nice meetin' you too. And call us Rome and Kirsti. We'll probably see you again before you go, since it looks like your little girl and my Matt are gettin' to be friends." Gabi and Matt seemed to be locked into some sort of jostling contest.

"And I'm Celeste. I'm glad Gabi has found someone her own age to play with. Come, Gabi."

Gabi gave Matt a last shove, then moved quickly out of range. Matt made as if to chase her, but stopped short. "See ya, I guess, *Penelope*."

"Don't call me that!"

"No school tomorrow. It's Saturday. You wanna ride bikes?"

"I don't have one."

"You can borrow my sister's."

"Can I, Mom?"

"We'll see. Right now, back to Willie's."

* * *

Upstairs, in her room, Sybil Weeks sat at her window. She could only see blurred shapes, and could only hear bits of the conversation drifting up from the group on the lawn. She sat quietly, stroking Blackjack, who, with keener vision, and perhaps keener hearing, stood motionless on the sill, seeming very interested in what was going on below.

"Sins of the fathers, Blackjack," she whispered. "Sins of the fathers. We must rid ourselves of this evil. Yaxagama, Ancient Mother, lend your power, lend your wisdom." She gently caressed the raven's glistening black feathers with her left hand, while, with her right, she twisted and twined, between thumb and two fingers, filaments of pale gold — strands of Gabi's hair.

CHAPTER 13

Elphique Lemerriant frowned in concentration as he walked through a thicket of tall salal and into the darkness of the forest. He was listening, trying to isolate a sound in the cacophony that played inside his head. Voices? The cries of birds and animals? They all sounded much the same to Elphique, who, it is doubtful ever experienced a moment of silence. If someone had asked him what he heard, he would have merely shrugged. Elphique didn't differentiate between the sounds of the world around him and those inside his own skull. The cries of the crows and ravens were full of meaning for him. The howl of a wolf, the grunt of a bear, were conversation, not much different from the voice of his sister, Fidelia, or his mother, or even his father, except that *his* voice was harsh and made Elphique's head hurt.

The voices of children made his head hurt too. He didn't see much of other children, as Elphique didn't go to school. Sometimes he would follow them as they walked through the woods. Sometimes he'd jump out of hiding and shriek, just to see them scatter and run. He knew they were afraid of him — now.

There had been a time when children tormented him, called him names, chased him, threw stones, lumps of coal and clay, and made up sing-song chants, as children have, throughout the ages, at anyone who was singled out as not of the herd. Elphique had been smaller then; it had been *he* who had to run into the woods to hide.

Elphique had spent his life hiding — hiding from his father, hiding from other children. His only human playmate had been Fidelia, but she had changed too. She hardly spoke anymore. And anyway, Elphique didn't spend much time at the Lemerriant farm, except the hours he spent at forced labor under the whip of Brazeau. Elphique had grown up terrified of his father, but he had been smaller then. Now, sometimes, it seemed to be the other way around, and Brazeau was not so quick to strike the hulking son who looked him in the eye. Even if he appeared dull-witted and slack-jawed, there was something in Elphique's gaze that caused Brazeau to look away.

Elphique had grown up living rough in the wild. He understood the ways of birds and animals, and they understood him. In the woods, he feared nothing, and often spent the night in a cave or under the stars. There were wolves on the island, and the occasional cougar that would swim in from the mainland, but since Elphique had no fear of them, he treated them as matter-of-factly as he treated other inhabitants of the forest. He didn't try to tame them or make pets of them, and they, in return, neither attacked nor ran away. The howl of wolves and the cry of the cougar were just part of Elphique's world of sound. And so were the ravens.

Elphique had not so much made pets of the ravens as they of him. The birds followed him almost everywhere. When Elphique caught a fish or a rabbit, they descended with clamor and beating of wings, knowing there would be scraps. Elphique had learned to imitate their calls which were many and varied — from the dry raspy *k-k-k-rk* to a melodious sound like a gong. To anyone within earshot, it would have been as impossible to distinguish Elphique's calls from those of the birds, as it would have been to understand the language that passed between them. It was partly the characteristic chatter, almost like laughter, that had led island children to make up the rhyme,

Beware the laughing blackbirds
When you're all alone
If they don't stop laughing,
Throw a hunk of stone.

Elphique Lemerriant, the young Elphique Lemerriant, had been pelted mercilessly whenever discovered, taunted and jeered at by island children, particularly gangs of rowdy boys who'd made it a sport to swarm into the woods and seek him out.

Over the years the game changed. Elphique grew like a mutant and became a menacing sight. He was still a target, but not as often, as the island young felt less inclined to harass him except in large groups. The groups grew smaller as some of his tormentors simply outgrew their vicious behavior; a couple left the island when their families moved away; and three did not survive.

Now Elphique was making his way up a slope, past a stand of young evergreen trees — hemlocks — full and lush with the new growth of spring, each with a feathery tip that curved downward gracefully like the extended hand of a languid southern belle. He climbed up a hill to where stunted mugo pines grew, where the view was of woods below and water and mountains in the distance. The sunlight felt warm on his back, and the air smelled of greenery. He stopped, looked around, and waited. The only motion was that of small clouds borne by a light wind.

He stood still and stared into the distance. Elphique related to nature more in the way that an animal does, and tended to live in the moment. While his body was morphing from child to man, the timber of his voice was changing and he was becoming taller and stronger. But there were other things as well. He had no basis for comparison, so he didn't question why it was that he could change things around him whenever he wanted. He could make it rain on a clear day. The rain wouldn't make him wet, but by just squinting his eyes a little, he could start to see it, first just a few drops, then harder and harder until he could hardly see anything else. He could also make things move. If he stared at a tree or a rock in a certain way, it would start to melt and flow and shimmer, as if his eyes had bored through what looked like a solid object to the dance of atoms within it. Here, on his hill, he could look at the sky and see shapes of things, flashing lights, even in the daytime, and huge, swirling forms that looked to be made of mist.

Sometimes he sat for hours, still as stone, watching, listening. The birds that usually accompanied him never followed him to the hilltop, and there, without their calls, it was quieter. Even the sounds that constantly played in Elphique's head were muted, then momentarily stilled so that he could tune in, first to silence, then to other sounds entirely. The pattern was always the same. First he would begin to hear familiar voices, the voices of his parents or his sister, as if he were overhearing muttered conversation. Then he would drift into a trance-like state and start hearing other things. Sometimes he would hear his name called. Sometimes he would hear a language that he didn't know. And then the shadow people might arrive. At first he'd only seen one or two, gotten a glimpse out of the corner of his eye, only to have them instantly vanish. Over time, however, here on his hill, they had begun to arrive in greater numbers. They never spoke to him, only silently stood watch. He knew they were different, not like the people in the village, and Elphique wasn't afraid of them. There was something comforting in their presence, and the experience was so extraordinary that he returned to the hill again and again.

Today Elphique found himself startled out of his reverie by the sharp cry of a raven from the top of a tall fir below him. As Elphique watched, the bird — a very large bird, much larger than the average raven, spread wings and flapped upwards. It described a wide arc, then made a circle above Elphique, its huge black wings making a sighing sound as it glided downward. As Elphique stared, the bird changed its path of flight, moving first in a straight line, then twisted to dip sideways, vocalizing, as it did, a bell-like note. The raven repeated the maneuver, first flying straight, then turning with wings spread, to perform a swooping bow toward Elphique, uttering its clear, sweet call.

Elphique watched impassively. The bird continued its deliberate, leisurely display, alternately flying and dipping as it circled above him three times; then, with a final pass so close to Elphique that he could feel the wind from its wings, the raven flew away, disappearing into the forest canopy below. The meeting was over. Elphique continued to stand on the hilltop for a few more moments, then turned and began to make his way back.

He headed for a clearing in the woods. The spot would later become a good-sized quarry, but now it was just a gradually widening pit where island people came to dig sand. It was a safe place to build a campfire, even in the dry summer, and a secure place to sleep. The Lemerriant farm was only a half mile away. If Elphique didn't come home for sup-per, his mother would leave food for him on a stump at the edge of the woods. Sometimes it was the Girl Who Watched who'd leave a loaf of bread or a bowl of stew. She didn't think Elphique could see her when she hid in the woods and spied on him. She'd called out to him once, but he hadn't replied. In any case, he hadn't seen her lately.

Tonight he wouldn't go home. Earlier, he'd snared a couple of rabbits and left them hanging on a branch of a tree. He would skin and roast them on a stick.

Elphique made a campfire. There was never any shortage of firewood on Broom Island, and the thick logs would burn well into the night. Sometimes Elphique would build his campfire on the shore where he could watch the sea and stars. Tonight he'd chosen the quarry. Night would soon fall and it would be cool; Elphique would sleep in a shel-tered spot.

The sky had taken on the deep tones of evening blue, and there was so little wind that sparks from the fire rose straight upwards. Elphique's fire gave off very little smoke, but did emit a heat that made him feel relaxed and drowsy. He would eat, then he would sleep, at least for a while. Animal-like, Elphique rarely slept through the night but would awaken to prowl every hour or two, listening for night sounds and peering into the darkness.

Birds were gathering. Crows and ravens were Elphique's companions during the day, but at night they flew off to their roosting trees. Elphique watched them go, in small groups, from different directions, toward the old-growth Douglas firs by the lake, twittering and chattering, their laugh-like calls gradually stilling as darkness fell.

Elphique had partly eaten one of the rabbits when he heard the sound. It was a cry in the distance that sounded like that of a baby — or a woman. Elphique had heard it before, knew what it was — a cougar.

Elphique imitated the call. It came again. Elphique answered. The call came again, and sounded closer. Each time the cougar called, Elphique replied, and it was clear that the big cat was approaching. Elphique waited. He sat still, his ears straining to catch every sound. All was silent except for the crackling of the campfire.

Then, like a change in the air, he could feel the cougar's presence. He knew the cat was there, watching him. Elphique had no fear of the animal. A slight noise above him caused him to look up. There, on the rim of the quarry, silhouetted against the darkening sky: a shape, and a gleam of eyes, that flash of phosphorescence that reflects only light but not the intelligence of the creature behind it. Elphique knew the animal was hesitant, uncertain. He knew it was hungry. He knew the cat was weighing its options, but knew it wouldn't attack him; even sitting down, he was too formidable, and there was the fire. He could feel the animal's mix of curiosity and wild impersonal hatred. He didn't have a gun. Elphique never carried one. He stared back at the cougar, matching look for look. Then, in one swift move he took the remains of the rabbit he'd been eating and threw it at the cat. The half-eaten carcass landed above him, caught in the coarse grass on the edge of the drop-off. The animal leapt back and vanished. Elphique waited. Slowly, the cougar advanced, grabbed the meat in its teeth and disappeared. Elphique laughed, and reached for the other rabbit, tore it apart with his hands and began to eat.

Meal over, he gathered a couple more logs and put them on the fire, then lay down next to it, leaving his hunting knife within easy reach. Cougar on the island! Wasn't the first time. It must have swum in from the mainland or one of the other islands. They sometimes did that, but didn't last long, because the villagers would hunt them down. The last one had killed a boy — one of the boys that used to torment Elphique. The body had been found half-eaten. Elphique had seen it, the body, that is. The ravens had told him where it was, and he'd followed them to the kill. He'd come upon it in the woods, ravens pecking at the flesh. Elphique hadn't been sorry. He'd gone away and left it to the birds, knowing the villagers would find it, and not wanting them to find *him*. Fresh blood, the bird had said, as it flew over his head on the hilltop today, *there will be fresh blood.*

CHAPTER 14

"How COME your sister has a bike when she's blind? I mean, she can't see to ride it, can she?"

Gabi and Matt were in the Weeks garage. Saturday had dawned sunny and mild, and when Gabi had pleaded to be allowed to go bike riding with Matt, her mother hadn't had the heart to say no. "Just make sure you stay on the roads. Don't go into the woods."

"She wasn't always blind," Matt said.

"So what made her go blind?"

"It was an accident. She got gasoline in her eyes."

"Oh, yuck! How did that happen?"

"Dad was taking the fuel pump out of the truck and she had her face stuck in to see what he was doing and got squirted right in the face with gas."

"Were you there?"

"Yeah, but I was just a little kid. I remember her screaming and yelling, and I went to get my mom and she came and they washed out her eyes but it was too late. Anyway, that's what the doctor said."

Matt had been moving cardboard boxes and pieces of lumber and plywood, to finally uncover a girl's bicycle.

"That old thing? You think it still works?" Gabi asked.

Matt was giving it a dust-wipe with a ragged terrycloth towel. "Maybe needs oiling. Tires seem okay. Need air. I'll check it out. It hasn't been used much. She only got it for Christmas that year. Gotta be in better condition than that junk at the gift shop. Those bikes are always falling apart."

"Well, do you think your sister will mind if I ride it? We never asked her."

"She won't care. She's probably forgotten it."

Gabi gladly left Matt to do the ritual boy-bicycle thing that would, in time, become the boy-car thing. Idly, Gabi walked around the barn. And there it was! A scythe. She stopped and looked at it thoughtfully. Matt *had* said that his father owned one. She remembered her dream. There were the pegs, the handles the man in her dream had held on to. *Swing, swish, swing, swish,* as the hay fell away noiselessly. There was the long, sharp, curved blade. *Had* old man Lemerriant chopped up his wife with one of those things? She tried to picture it. It seemed awkward. She pictured him swinging the blade the way she'd seen the man in her dream do. She, herself, could've jumped right over it. Gabi pictured Lemerriant's wife jumping as the blade swung at her feet, as if she were skipping rope. Maybe he swung higher. He could have kept on swinging and slicing her up, but she wouldn't have just stood there while he cut her up in rings like a salami. Maybe if he was able to swing it high enough, he could chop off her head. Or if he held it up over his head, and brought it straight down, maybe he could've sliced her in two like a cantaloupe.

Gabi pictured the blade dripping with blood. Maybe it would have hair stuck in it. Maybe, if he hit bone, it would get jammed like an axe in a log. Jeremy had been one-handedly chopping wood for the sauna, when he got the axe jammed. Gabi had seen him turned it over and hit the chopping block with the *back* of the axe and the log just fell away in two pieces. If old man Lemerriant got the scythe wedged in his wife's skull, how would he get it loose? Could he flip her over and whack her head on a block? Gabi didn't think so. Did they find Lemerriant's wife cut halfway in two with the blade wedged in her body? At any rate, it seemed unlikely he could have "cut her into bitty pieces" with that thing.

"All done. Works fine." Matt was on the bike, riding it in small circles on the barn floor. His own bike was leaning against a wall. "Let's go!"

"Where are we going?"

"Let's head for town. Have you seen the cemetery yet?"

"Yes, Jeremy showed it to me yesterday. We built stone birds too."

"Okay, we can ride into town and hang around the Co-op and watch the ferry come in. Or we can go to the playground."

"Is that all there is to do here? I mean isn't there a mall or someplace with computer games?" Gabi, who was accustomed to having her days structured, was having a problem with a Peter Pan existence where time is never planned. The idea of standing around waiting for a boat or chuting down a playground slide seemed boring and juvenile.

"I can show you where the Loogy-Roo chased Dory Michaels."

"Oh, I'll bet you can! But we're not supposed to go into the woods."

"We can take a logging road. Your mom only said to stay on the roads. A logging road is a road. I can show you a whole forest growing out of stumps. And I can show you the bluff where they found the dead kids."

"The kids who are buried in the cemetery? Let's stop there again." Gabi had been thinking about her experience there. It had been weird the way the birds seemed to be talking to her. Or maybe they weren't talking to her at all, but just talking among themselves.

"Remember? Remember? Remember how we flew that day. The wind was high. It was high."

"Remember the meat? It was fresh that day."

"Yes, it was fresh. Fresh. Torn."

"You pecked the eyes."

"No, remember? It was you pecked the eyes!"

"Ha-ha-ha! Yes, the eyes. They were fresh. We all pecked the eyes. Remember, we fought over the eyes."

"Two dead humans, remember?"

"Yes, dead. Dead children. The blood smelled fresh."

"Yes, the blood smelled fresh that day. A kill is always fresh. Two killed children with fresh blood and fresh meat and fresh eyes. Ha-ha-ha! Remember?"

Gabi had listened. Had she been older, she might have reacted with horror — horror at the pictures evoked and horror at her own sanity being assaulted. People don't hear voices in their heads, and birds don't talk.

But in Gabi's case the magical had not yet been banished by the conventional. Her focus was objective. If birds talked, she mused, why did they? How could they? She didn't question whether she heard them; she *knew* she did. She didn't wonder whether she was imagining things; she wondered how it was that she could understand their language. Then, too, having coped with nightmares, to her, the surreal was familiar territory, and the line between sleeping and waking not that firmly drawn.

The cemetery was as it had been yesterday. Gabi and Matt left their bikes leaning against the fence and went in the gate. The ravens were there, perched in trees, as Gabi headed for the strange wild grave. "This is where the children are buried, isn't it?" Matt looked a bit surprised. "Yeah, how did you know?"

"Has it always looked like this?"

"No, it changes all the time. Kids come and leave things here and take away stuff that's broken. Some old stuff has always been here, but you find new stuff from time to time."

"Why doesn't it have a proper stone like the other graves?"

"I dunno. It's always been like this. My dad says a long time ago this place was all overgrown with weeds. Nobody took care of it. Now they have a guy who mows the grass."

Gabi looked carefully at the cairn. The child's teacup was still there, but the broken saucer was nowhere in sight. Somebody must have moved it since yesterday. The birds were there, solemn and silent, not wheeling or calling. Nor were they talking. Gabi listened, but heard nothing except the sigh of wind in the Douglas firs. "Okay, Matt, let's go. You can show me your stumps and bluffs or whatever."

* * *

Celeste looked up from her computer and out the window. "I don't know whether I should have let her go. I don't like the idea of her riding a strange bike in a strange place."

"She'll be fine. She's with Matt. He can be a scamp, but he knows the island. There's not much traffic on Kaunio Road, and everybody looks out for kids on bikes."

"I hope you're right. I *am* glad she has a friend to play with. At least it gives Jeremy a break. He's been wonderful to her, and I can't help feeling we've been imposing on his time. And yours, Willie."

"Nonsense. But I think we could both use a break from this desk. I'm going cross-eyed with all these old records and photos." Willie had been translating old letters written in Finnish by early settlers, describing the conditions of the times, while Celeste had been typing the information into her laptop.

"I'm getting good stuff, and I hope my article won't get me tarred and feathered."

"Yours will probably be okay. You're digging a lot deeper than most, and you seem to be a stickler for getting your facts straight. What say you to a cup of tea?"

"Sounds good." Celeste got up and stretched. "And I could use a good hike."

"Well then, I'll put the kettle on and we can have a sandwich and then go for a walk."

Celeste looked at the clock. "Is it lunchtime already? Gabi should be getting back."

"Gabi and Matt will probably get a hamburger in town." Jeremy had come into the room, and was smiling at them. "My treat."

"Oh, Jeremy, did you give Gabi money?"

"Just enough so she could take Matt to lunch. You know kids. They'll ride till they get ravenous. They may have gone up Kaunio Road to see the herd of llamas at the lodge, then down again to the village. They may have gone to the schoolyard to play with other children. Either way they'll end up famished."

How different life on the island is, Celeste thought. Children here still roam free. The only danger is from some mythical Loogy-Roo, and now the whole idea sounded absurd. "Gabi isn't used to that sort of freedom. Back home I'd never be able to turn her loose. I guess the closest thing is when kids get dropped off at a mall where they meet their friends and 'hang out,' as they say, but Gabi is much too young for that yet, thank goodness."

Willie frowned. "It's a different time, even here. Accidents can happen anywhere, but here at least we all know each other. Every house is a safe house. Children here grow up with the sea, the woods, the wild country. They learn the dangers. It's the newcomers who get lost in the forest or break a leg crossing a log jam."

"Anyway, ladies, I thought both of you could use a break, so tea and sandwiches are being served in the kitchen."

"Bless you," Willie said. "I won't even ask how you keep managing."

* * *

Gabi and Matt threaded their way past cars parked in the ferry lineup, and stopped to buy candy bars at the gift shop. The place smelled nicely of chocolate, scented candles and coffee. There was an urn on the counter, with a stack of styrofoam cups, and next to it a tray of the ubiquitous *pulla*. Slices of the sweet, raised, braided loaf were individually wrapped in plastic and marked $1.25 each, but looked thick and unappetizing.

The proprietor, a short plump woman with bleached blond hair, asked "Did you children want some of that as well?"

"No, thanks." Matt said.

"Then run along." The woman had been watching their every move, as Gabi and Matt had paused briefly to look at a two-foot, hanging, painted tin man made of cans, with bottle caps for buttons and eyes. They edged out through the open door, past a rack of bicycles for rent.

"Bunch of junk," Matt said. "My cousin rented one and the handlebar came off. You wanna see my school?"

"Well, okay," Gabi said with little enthusiasm.

The school turned out to be a building not far from the Finnish museum. There was a playground and a number of children in it. "You wanna go in?" Matt asked. "I don't mind school on a Saturday!" He laughed.

Gabi didn't like playgrounds. She didn't like groups of children either. At her own school, she always seemed to get into trouble at recess. "They're all little kids," she told Matt.

Clearly, the children were all a couple of years younger, and boisterously wanton in their use of playground equipment. "What's your school like?" Matt asked.

"It's okay, I guess . . . sometimes."

"You make good grades?"

"We don't have grades."

"What do you mean? You get a report card, don't you?"

"No. I have an affirmation book."

"What's that?"

"I got it on Valentine's Day. Our school doesn't think we should send valentines because, you know, some kids get more than others, and then the ones who didn't get any feel bad, so we all got slips of paper for as many kids as there are in class, and we all had to write something nice about each kid, and then all the paper slips were put into affirmation books, and each kid got one, and I have Gabrielle's Affirmation Book."

"You mean instead of a report card all you get is a bunch of stuff other kids wrote?"

"Our school doesn't give out report cards 'cause some might be better than others and it would make the other kids feel bad so — "

"Wait a minute. So if you goof up in school, nobody tells your parents you're doing lousy?"

"They call your parents if you get in trouble. Like punching out another kid. Or throwing stuff in the cafeteria. Or breaking a window."

Matt raised an eyebrow. "You ever get in trouble?"

"Yeah. A few times."

"Okay, right! Let's head on up the logging road!

CHAPTER 15

"I DON'T know about you, but I could use a bit of exercise." Tea over, Celeste didn't feel like going back to transcribing records. "How about the two of us going for that walk?"

"It *is* too nice a day to stay indoors. Let's see, you've already been to the cemetery, we could go in the other direction on Kaunio Road."

"I *had* been hoping you'd show me the old Lemerriant farm. It's not very far, is it? Could we go there?"

Willie sighed. "Yes, I suppose so. It's a couple of miles away, but the path is apt to be muddy this time of year. I could lend you a pair of boots. Be a shame to mess up those designer sneakers." Willie produced a couple of pairs of rubber boots. "This footwear has a time-honored tradition both in Finland and on the island. The Finnish name for Finland is *Suomi. Suo* means swamp."

Celeste slipped hers on. Indeed, they were not just ordinary rubber boots. They were white, although stained a bit through use, beautifully crafted with delicate lines and a soft collar to keep the edge from chafing the calf. "These are lovely, and they feel lighter than the ones in the Co-op." Celeste had, in visiting the store, seen rows of thick-soled gum boots standing militaristically on shelves, as if waiting to be issued to a platoon.

"I bought these in Kajaani a few years ago." Willie had a similar pair in blue. "These are nicer than the ones you find here. More comfortable to walk in. You'll want to take your camera?"

"I'll get my camcorder."

Outside, in the yard, Celeste asked, "Which way do we go?"

"There's a path by the Weeks house. We can cut through the woods and connect with it."

"Lead on," Celeste made a mental note that the path to the Lemerriant farm sounded like the same one Gabi and Matt had been on. She wondered how far they'd gotten. Gabi had never elaborated.

They made their way through the woods, and as they entered the trail, Celeste could see the path patterned with the prints of small sneakers. Celeste was finding the walk delightful; she'd spent her time in cities, and life on the island, with nature crowding in on all sides, was very different. It was just a tiny bit spooky to be in what looked like primordial rain forest, and she remarked on that to Willie.

"Most of the island has been logged, but this section still has some old growth giants. There was a fire here, years ago, and you'll still see blackened trees."

Celeste had been stopping to film as she walked. "How come this tree seems to be burned inside instead of out?" She had trained her camcorder on a tall cedar, hollow, open and charred in the middle.

"It acted like a chimney. The flames swept up the center. You'll see a lot them like that."

As the footpath connected with the wider trail, Celeste, fascinated by the flora, filmed everything — mosses, stumps, twisted burls, tangles of roots of fallen giants. She was glad she'd brought extra batteries and tape; she didn't want to lose any of this. As they walked, making their way over roots, across wet patches, picking their way along wooden "lily pads," past stands of tall salal in bloom; Celeste tried to picture what life for her ancestors must have been like. Did Dauphine, her great-grandmother, make this trip to town on foot? Did she carry groceries? If this was the only path to the farm, it wouldn't have been wide enough for a horse and wagon — or perhaps it had been wider then, and the forest had swallowed it up, but that couldn't have been. The huge trees on either side must be hundreds of years old.

"Was this the only way to get to the farm? How did they bring in supplies? And why did they live so far out of town?" By today's standards, the distance was short but the hardship of traversing it might have put it on the moon. Other farms seemed to be right on Kaunio Road and within easy distance of the village.

"The Lemerriants didn't want anything to do with other people. There was another road, years ago, before Kaunio Road was even built, wide enough for a horse and hay wagon, on the other side. It was the road they used at the time. To get on it now, you'd have to take a road on the other side of the village and double back. It's seldom used and it's overgrown so if you value your paint job I wouldn't advise trying to drive there."

They were coming to the clearing, and Celeste narrowly eyed a wet area on the trail. The prints of children's sneakers were still there. *Gabi, did you come all the way here without telling me?*

"This is it, such as it is," Willie said. "We've talked about designating this as a heritage site, now that we have the trail, and doing something with the buildings, but it'll take a lot of work."

Celeste stopped and looked at the scene, feeling herself to be in the grip of some unfamiliar emotion. This, this *place* was of her history. The people here, whoever they were, had been her family. She would be carrying their DNA. And it was all so small, so primitive, as if she'd been transported through time to a cave, and been told it was the home of her great-to-the-umpteenth power grandparents.

"You can see some of the buildings are falling down, but the house could be cleaned up and restored — only the kids would probably vandalize it again," Willie was saying.

Celeste pointed her camcorder. "I didn't think island children would do that sort of thing," she said absently. She was panning over the partially roofless barn across to the house with its sagging porch.

"You can see they already have. Last time I was here there were a few window panes still intact. Oh yes, we have our mischief-makers. They burned the picnic table down at the lake last summer. When we replaced it, they burned that too."

Despite the rickety porch that now served as a trellis for blackberry brambles, and the door that hung crookedly ajar, Celeste saw that the house itself was architecturally more sophisticated than she had expected. No primitive rough-hewn cabin hastily thrown together, this one was sturdily built of squared-off logs, and the corners, instead of the typical notch-and-pass construction, were neatly dovetailed. As result, the walls were smooth, and although the logs were of irregular sizes, the wood fitted tightly to form a solid plane that needed little or no chinking. The roof, though covered with a thick, nubbly coating of bright green moss, was still in place.

"Did the Lemerriants build this place?"

"No, it was built by a Swede originally. He tried homesteading, but when his wife died, he sold the place and moved to the mainland. A lot of people have tried to make a go of living on Broom Island and had to give up. The Lemerriants must have added the porch after they moved in, and I think it was Brazeau who built the barn and outbuildings — some of which have vanished by now. I was too young to remember, but there's an old photo of this house before it had a porch. It was taken shortly after Gustav Wigren built it."

"Is it okay to go inside?"

"I suppose so, just be careful. There's probably broken glass everywhere."

Inside, Celeste shrewdly noted that someone had been there recently.

The dust had been disturbed. She filmed the dim interior, the trash on the floor, and the moldering mattress in the corner. The room had obviously been the heart of the house — kitchen, dining area, living room. All that was left was a wooden table, some shelves, and a pipe hole in the wall that showed where a stove had once stood. Oddly enough there was a wood box with logs still in it. The floor seemed sturdy, so Celeste walked through another doorway into a small bare room that might have been a pantry, except that there was a narrow wooden platform along one wall — a base for a bed?

There was only one other room that led off the main one — the master bedroom, Celeste surmised, with one window. It looked as though a curtain rod had once hung in the doorway. Not much privacy in the Lemerriant house, and Celeste idly wondered how a married couple managed to carry on normal conjugal relations — or if they did. Of course they must have. Maybe that's where the "roll-in-the-hay" expression came from.

The cabin didn't have a second story, but there was a small loft, probably accessible by a ladder which wasn't there anymore. That may have been where the children slept. There was no sign of a bathroom or any plumbing anywhere. She noted that there seemed to be no closets or storage spaces either. Nails driven into the log walls, she supposed, served as clothing hooks.

"What happened to the furniture? You'd think there'd be something left."

"Carried off by anyone who needed it. There are a few things outside, in a pile. When we started thinking of this as a heritage site, we began gathering up stuff to display, if and when we get the place cleaned up."

They had made their way back outside into the sunlight. "See, there's a pile of trash that's going to be burned, and that pile over there has a few artifacts we hope to restore."

Celeste filmed an old, dented aluminum kettle, a few things that looked like tin cans. "What's that thing that looks like part of a car muffler?"

"It's a stove grate, and here are the lids." Willie obligingly displayed them for Celeste's camcorder. "All that's left of the old kitchen stove. I guess someone made off with the body. It may have become a fireplace in somebody's sauna or it may be serving as part of a still."

"How did these people bathe? They had no bathrooms."

"Not that often, but in a tub. You carried water into the house. You heated it on the stove and then you filled the tub, and everybody took turns washing in the same water. That is, unless you were a Finn. Finns had saunas, and if they didn't, they knew someone who did."

"Where did they get water?"

"I'll show you. Follow me."

Celeste followed Willie to a spot a few yards away. "This is a sur-face well." There, almost hidden by a thicket of salal, Celeste saw what looked to be a hole in the ground, about four feet across, filled to the top with murky water. Someone had nailed up a wooden railing around it, but it had been knocked over and now was relatively useless, one end lying on the ground.

"We were afraid somebody might accidentally stumble into it, so Rome Weeks put up the railing. Looks like the kids have been at it. I'll have to mention it to Rome; he'll nail it back in place. Someone could trip over that."

Celeste was mentally trying to reconstruct life on the Lemerriant farm. According to Willie, the area that was now overgrown with broom and shrubs had all been hay fields. They had lived an insular and, Celeste thought darkly, incestuous life. Brazeau, the tyrant, Dauphine, his bat-tered wife, Fidelia, no doubt sexually abused by Brazeau — perhaps by Elphique — and Elphique, the wild child who became the Loogy-Roo, the island werewolf. Might make a good plot for a horror story.

As if in reply to her thoughts, Willie said "You have a colorful set of ancestors. I'm sorry we don't have any decent photographs of them."

Celeste chuckled as she did a 360-degree pan with her camcorder.

"Well, I *am* hoping they'll show up on this tape! 'What are those strange images, Ms. Ooms-Possum, a trick of the light, perhaps? It looks just like a man killing his wife.'"

Willie laughed. "You've heard the stories. Now here's the movie."

"Where did it happen? Where did they find the bodies?"

"Dauphine's was found inside the barn. Don't go in; it might be dangerous. You can see the spot from here."

"She'd been murdered? How?"

"I'm honestly not sure. Some reports say she'd been shot, others are more gruesome and maintain that she'd had her throat cut. That's how the scythe story started, but more likely it would have been a hunting knife."

"And Brazeau? Where did they find him, in the house?"

"Brazeau's body was found outside, by the barn door. He'd died of a gunshot wound."

"And Fidelia?"

"They found her in the root cellar, over there. It was just a hole dug in the hillside. She was hysterical and couldn't tell anyone what had happened. Later she said she couldn't remember. Perhaps she didn't see any of it."

"And Elphique?"

"Elphique died in the meetinghouse fire. They say that a group of men had been out looking for him, and that they may have followed him there. But I think Elphique started the fire himself."

"And then what happened to Fidelia? She was the only survivor."

"Fidelia stayed with us for a little while. We knew her. She'd come to us before when she needed help. The Lemerriants always came and took her home, and there was little we could do. There were no authorities or child welfare organizations in those days, at least not here.

"My parents would have let her stay. They'd have looked after her, but she wanted to go. I can't say I blame her. There was some relative on the mainland she was going to go to, but I never knew who it was.

I hope life was kinder to her however she ended up."

"Pregnant."

"What?"

"She was pregnant. By whom, I wonder. Elphique or Brazeau? My mother, Madeleine, was born January 2, 1928."

"Oh, my god!"

"Could there have been someone else in Fidelia's life, a boyfriend?"

Willie sighed. "I wish I could say yes, but the cold facts are that if there had been, Brazeau would have killed them both. He kept the women in his family prisoners."

"In that case, Brazeau Lemerriant is most likely to be my grandfather as well as my great-grandfather. And Gabi inherits all of this."

CHAPTER 16

GABI AND Matt had ridden through the village, then begun pumping their way up a hill toward a large green water tower. Matt was pedaling hard, but Gabi stopped, got off her bike, and began wheeling it. She was a little out of breath when she got to the top. "I'm not used to hills. All I ever do at home is ride around the block."

Matt laughed, then bragged: "We got much bigger hills than this one, but they don't stop *me*. Once we're past the water tower, Quarry Road isn't so steep."

They rounded the tower and there the road changed to dirt and gravel. The grade was easier, but it was harder to ride on. Gabi was beginning to wish they'd never come. She tried to guide her bike along the smoothest stretches, and to stay out of the ruts, some of which were puddled by recent rains. She also tried to stay back far enough, so that when Matt deliberately drove through wet spots, she wouldn't get splashed.

Around her was a section of clear-cut forest that had been replanted. It presented a dismal vista of stumps and debris, but among them bristled hundreds and hundreds of narrow plastic tubes as if they were growing out of the ground. "Hey, Matt, what are all those white things?"

"Vexar tubes. There's a new tree in each one."

"Why do they plant them that way?"

"Supposed to keep the deer from eating them. Doesn't always work. Sometimes they get knocked over."

"So what do they do, take them all off when the tree gets too big?"

"My dad says they're supposed to biodegrade, but that doesn't always work either."

"Where are we?" All Gabi saw was stumps and moss studded with the narrow, white, gently tapering three-foot tubes pointing skyward.

"Not far from Dory Michaels' place." They'd left the clear-cut behind and were biking through stands of hemlock. "Just keep going till you see a bus stop. There's a road there and you'll see a gate and a chain-link fence. Her dad put it up to keep people off his private road."

"I thought these were all logging roads."

"They are. Nobody's logging much anymore and now they're just roads. But when old man Michaels bought the property, he put a fence across his section. If he catches you anywhere near his place, he yells at you."

Gabi looked around at nothing but wilderness. "Why would he care if anyone walks on his road? There's nothing out here."

"Everybody thinks he's crazy. He hates everybody, and nobody likes him. Everybody's a bit scared of him because he knows all about how to sue people. He's always threatening to sue somebody."

After what seemed to be an endless stretch of trees, they came to a spot where a road formed a "T" with the one they were on. On the corner was a wooden bench with a roof on posts to cover it. "That's where the school bus picks up kids," Matt explained, as he took a left turn. The road now ran through an area of tall evergreens with pencil-straight trunks while the road edges were feathery with banks of young hemlock. And there, ahead of them, was a metal fence with a gate with a padlock. Gabi noticed that the lock hung open, and glanced at Matt.

"I've never seen it locked. Too much trouble to keep locking and unlocking, I guess. I never use it anyway. There's a gap between the fence and the gate you can squeeze through." Matt demonstrated, then squeezed back out again. Gabi noticed that the fence only extended a short distance on either side of the gate, so anyone could easily enter the property on foot.

"What if the old guy sees us? Anyway, is it safe to leave our bikes out here?"

"Oh sure," Matt said. "We can hide them in here." He wheeled his into the shelter of a thicket of hemlock, then parked Gabi's next to his. "Okay, come on." He went through the opening once more.

Gabi followed. She and Matt walked along the road, and down a little hill. Matt stopped. "See, there's the path Dory Michaels takes to catch the school bus. That's where the Loogy-Roo chased her." Matt was pointing to a footpath that ran through the trees and bypassed the road with its length of fence and its gate.

Gabi gave him a sidelong look. "Then we should both be really scared, shouldn't we?"

"Nah, there's nothin' to be scared of."

"I didn't think so." Still, Gabi was wondering how Matt had managed it. "How did you do it? I mean, this is a long way from your house, and you'd have been late for your school bus."

"I didn't say it was me. But I don't take the school bus. I ride my bike, and I don't always go to school."

They had been walking slowly down a hill toward the Michaels spread. There was a large greenhouse — a Quonset hut bubble covered with plastic. "What's in there?" Gabi asked.

"Uh — I'm not sure. But I think they grow vegetables to ship to the mainland. Cucumbers and tomatoes, stuff like that. My dad says Michaels is fixing up a campground for tourists. And he wants to build a golf course."

Gabi looked around. It didn't look like much of a place. "What's that, a shed?"

"That's his house."

Gabi stared, incredulously. The building was an A-frame covered entirely with cedar shakes. She couldn't see the front because it faced the other way, toward the water. The structure had an addition tacked onto it, covered irregularly with the same wooden shakes. It had an end wall that looked to be of stone or old cinder blocks with a small four-paned window. "You mean somebody actually lives there?"

"Yeah. I guess nobody's home. The truck's not here."

"Then I guess we'd better be going before anyone comes."

"Wait a minute," Matt picked up a stone off the road and threw it toward the house. It barely missed the window and bounced harmlessly off the shingles. Inside, a dog began barking frantically. Matt turned and ran. Gabi flashed a him a look, then raced after him.

As they approached the metal gate, they paused. There was a truck now parked on the other side, but nobody seemed to be in it. Matt and Gabi looked at each other, then quickly wiggled through the opening in the fence.

"What are you doing here?"

It had to be Chadwick Michaels. Short, bald, fat, and pink of skin, he looked, to Gabi, like Porky Pig. They hadn't seen him because he'd been lying in wait behind the hemlocks, right next to their bikes. Matt stood, momentarily speechless, then was able to come up with only a single mumbled word: "Nothin'!"

Gabi gave him a let-me-do-the-talking look. She raised guileless eyes at the man. "Oh, hi, I'm Gabi Choate. I'm a visitor on the island, and we were just out riding bikes. Matt was telling me you have a little girl my own age, and since I haven't had a chance to make many friends yet, I thought I'd come over and meet her. I guess she's not at home." Her ice-blue eyes seem to melt into pools of disappointment.

The man eyed her narrowly, then looked at Matt. "You're the Weeks boy, aren't you?"

"Yessir."

"Don't you know this is a private road and you're not supposed to be on it?"

Gabi broke in. "Oh, we're *so* sorry. It was all *my* fault. I was really looking forward to meeting your little girl. Dory? Isn't that her name?"

Michaels pressed his lips together, but looked a little uncertain. Gabi decided to push the envelope a little. "You have a lovely place here, Mr. Michaels. Matt said you'd be renting space to campers. My mother might like that. She *loves* the outdoors."

Michaels, by now, was chewing his lip, trying to decide whether to bellow or to fawn. The Weeks boy, he knew, was nothing but trouble, and his father was worse. Poised between belligerence and PR, he opened his mouth to say something, then stopped, his attention distracted by a raven that landed on the top rail of the gate. Gabi, startled, said "Oh!" as a couple more followed. She edged back toward her bike. Matt made a move to retrieve his as well, gearing for a quick getaway.

Michaels waved his hand at the birds sending them off wings flapping, then turned to Gabi. "Dory's in Port Casper today with her mother. Maybe you'll meet her later. Tell your mother she's welcome to visit here and see the place. Now you two better hightail it back to town. These woods can be dangerous to kids."

* * *

"I can't believe you nearly broke his window!" Gabi and Matt were biking back toward the "T" in the road.

"Woulda served him right."

"We're just lucky that dog was in the house instead of loose outside."

"They used to have two dogs. German shepherds. But one of them disappeared a while back, so I guess they're not taking any chances."

"What do you think happened to it, Matt? Did *you* have anything to do with that?"

Matt looked genuinely startled. "No! I don't know what happened to the dog. Maybe a cougar *did* get him."

This time Gabi believed him. "Then . . . then there really *is* a cougar loose on the island?"

"Could be. Or could be somebody had it in for Michaels. Lots of people want to get even with him."

"Oh, he didn't seem all that bad." Gabi smiled and glanced sideways at Matt. "You just have to know how to handle him."

They'd come to the road that led back to town. A raven was sitting on the bus bench. "If we went this way, where would we end up?" Gabi pointed in the opposite direction from which they'd come.

"You'd end up going around Tranquil Bay and then back on Kaunio Road, but there's a spot up ahead where you can go up a hill where you can see the whole island and all the way across the water."

"Let's go look."

Matt led the way to what looked like a turnaround from which a rough road led upwards, became narrower and more stony, and finally ended up as barely a footpath too steep for a bike. Gabi and Matt dismounted, leaving their bikes behind and started upwards on foot. The view, as they climbed, was of blue water, sky and white clouds, with mountains in the distance. Gabi could see, past a canopy of trees, the village below and a beautiful white ship making its way through the strait. "Wow! What's that?"

"Cruise ship," Matt said. "They come through here all the time. Probably coming from Alaska." Gabi tried, but wasn't able to make out the name on the prow. It looked a little unreal to see a pleasure cruise ship up close enough to be able to wave at the people.

Gabi kept climbing until she reached the top of the craggy hill. It was quiet up there, and rather chilly. The wind was stronger, and Gabi wished she'd put on the jacket in her bike basket. Matt was coming up behind her. "We better go back. That wind is cold." He started back down, then stopped to look back up at Gabi who hadn't moved.

She stood staring out over the water, as if she were waiting for something. Then, as both of them watched, a bird flew up from a tall Douglas fir growing in the forest below them. It was a very large black bird — a solitary raven. It circled the two children once, then came a little closer, turned in midair to present its chest and underbelly while it uttered a high-pitched note. It then straightened its flight, flew around them again, and once more repeated the winged salute and call. It circled yet another time, this time coming so close to Gabi that she could clearly see its merciless eye and long Roman beak. As it did, it made a chattering sound, like laughter, then lifted off and gracefully flew back down into the treetops.

"Jeez! I've never seen anything like that!" Matt said.

"Haven't you?" Gabi sounded dreamy, faraway. "I think *I* have."

CHAPTER 17

Sybil Weeks, in her black coat and black felt hat, made her way down
the driveway to Kaunio Road. With Blackjack balancing unsteadily on
her shoulder, and her Bible tucked under her arm, she walked the familiar
path, moving cautiously, tapping the terrain with the wooden walking
stick she carried. At Kaunio Road, she turned right, and headed toward
town. The road had been recently resurfaced, the crown raised, and the
bed banked wherever there was a bend. This made Sybil's progress more
awkward than usual, since she was no longer walking on a flat surface,
but navigating a hillside where, to walk comfortably, one leg would have
had to be shorter than the other. It made footing more precarious for
Blackjack as well, who hopped off her shoulder and accompanied her
by flitting from one roadside shrub to another.

Sybil moved off the blacktop, onto the weedy berm that was littered
with cans and styrofoam containers, residue of teenage night rides, fueled
by cokes, burgers, fries — and beer — usually brought over from Port
Casper on the last ferry. There was no nightlife on the island except for
The Sea Hole, the bar in the Broom Island Inn. Young people tended

to avoid it, and left it to loggers and fishermen. If you wanted to see a movie, you had to take the ferry to Port Casper, then make sure it let out in time for you to make it home. If you wanted fast food, except for Gisele's Burger Barn (which closed at six) there was none on the island. Yet mornings brought a dump of white litter along roadsides as surely as winter brings snow. Residents along Kaunio Road tried to keep things tidy. There were trash barrels placed at intervals, and anyone walking along the road made it a habit to pick up and deposit debris — just as most motorists made it a habit to stop and pick up Sybil, raven and all.

Normally Sybil had no trouble getting a ride to town. Everyone knew her. Islanders kept a wary but protective eye on her. Sybil, in turn, barely acknowledged most of the residents. Offered a lift, she would climb in wordlessly, stare straight ahead with whatever vision she had, then get out without a thank-you at the Co-op. Asked a question, she would answer, using the fewest words possible, but she seldom initiated a conversation. That, of course, was when she was taking her medication. Island residents also knew that when Sybil went off her meds, there could be dramatic personality changes until her parents managed to reestablish status quo.

This morning, so far, there seemed to be no traffic. Even the little yellow school buses were parked for the weekend. Sybil walked doggedly on, now and then flicking a paper cup or burger container out of her way with the tip of her cane. She seemed to be in deep concentration, her lips moving, muttering as she walked.

Satama was not Sybil's destination today; Sybil was headed for the Broom Island cemetery. She would find it deserted, as usual. On occasions, such as Decoration Day or someone's funeral, most of the islanders would turn out, but at other times it was rare to find any life there, except for the birds.

To any stranger, Sybil would have been a startling sight. In her gothic garb, with Blackjack on her shoulder, she might have been a version of the Grim Reaper, or a guide to the netherworld, as she opened the squeaky metal gate, and stepped into the corner of the island that belonged to the silent dead.

The grass had been neatly cut a few days ago, and now was studded with dandelions whose stems were short enough to have survived the blade, and with English daisies that open wide to the morning sun, but close their heads as the day wears on. There was no litter here, unless one regarded a few plastic flowers scattered by the wind as pollution. Sybil didn't see them in any case. She knew where she was going, and headed for the corner of the cemetery where the wild grave stood. She put down her Bible and her cane. Blackjack fluttered from her shoulder onto a tombstone. As if performing a temple ritual, Sybil circled the grave, stopping to touch the stones and the artifacts. Her touch was almost loving as she picked up and replaced objects: a small round stone painted with red spirals; a child's cap, once red, now old and faded. Her eyes may not have seen them, at least not clearly, but her fingers appeared to remember.

Sybil knelt next to the cairn, picked up her Bible and opened it. Her fingertips read the Braille while her lips mouthed words while Blackjack watched silently. She closed the book, put it down, and ran her hands over the feathery grasses that had grown tall enough to obscure the base, then pulled back sharply as something scratched her hand. Carefully, she reached in, found the root of a piece of bramble that had gotten a foothold in the dry soil, and yanked it out. Then from the pocket of her coat Sybil took a large plastic ZipLoc bag. She held it in her left hand, muttering what might have been an incantation, while, with her right, she grubbed around in the exposed dirt, scratching up handfuls of the sandy soil and putting them into the bag. Finally, when the bag was half-full, she raised it heavenward; Blackjack uttered a squawk and leapt on her shoulder. As he did, a raven flew down from a tall cedar tree and landed on the ground. It was followed by another and another. Silently the birds came, one by one, until the ground was nearly covered by the flock.

Then Sybil's voice rang out: "You've all seen it. You are my witnesses!" Her voice grew louder. "The sins of the fathers pass to the third and fourth generation." Then she was almost shouting: "You saw the evil! Ancient evil. Once again it walks the island. We must stop it spilling blood, send it back to fiery Hell! Smite it with our righteous fury, crush it into lifeless dust." She held the bag of soil aloft for a moment, as if trying to infuse it with some kind of cosmic energy: "Yaxagama, Ancient Mother, lend your power, lend your wisdom!" Then Sybil slid the bag into the pocket of her coat, picked up her Bible, and amid a flurry of wings as the birds took flight, she left the cemetery.

CHAPTER 18

Jeremy Banks glanced at the wall clock and saw it was nearly four. Willie and Celeste should be arriving soon, and *Gabi, where are you? Please get home before your mother arrives so she won't become alarmed!* Island children still roamed more freely than city kids, and Jeremy wasn't so old that he couldn't remember the endless afternoons of his own less-restricted childhood summers. Gabi and Matt. Jeremy and Jock. There was always one childhood friend who stood out in memory. Time, he mused, simply doesn't exist for children when they're off on some adventure in a world that grownups can no longer even find, let alone enter.

Jeremy went into the kitchen and put a kettle on to boil. In his childhood home, tea had been always served at four o'clock, but lifestyles were different now. He and Willie often had their evening meal between four and five. It seemed more benign to aging digestive systems to back away from dinner at eight — or even six — particularly since both of them were often tucked into their beds by ten.

Television, on the island, was limited to one reliable station; and as there was no cable service, islanders opted for satellite dishes, even though their operation bordered on the illegal. Providers were scrambling signals to block reception; the option was to purchase a descrambler and pay fees — but most islanders had become adept at circumvention. It had been only recently that Willie had acquired a dish, installed by a local, and nobody was really sure of its status — but it worked. Most of the time Willie and Jeremy were content to watch the news; perhaps play a movie on tape, rather than view the stream of mindless sitcoms and violent cop shows, with sex as the central theme of *everything*. Jeremy sometimes found it hard to stay awake after dinner, so to really see a movie, he would have had to sit through it a number of times, on the chance of filling in the parts he'd dozed through. He did like the old Charlie Chan black-and-white films. He and his childhood buddy, Jock, had biked to the movies on Saturday afternoons to see them, and nostalgia had led Jeremy to purchase the ten movies starring Warner Oland. Willie would patiently endure one, only occasionally looking up from her knitting or her counted cross-stitch. Sometimes she would excuse herself, mumble something about checking her e-mail, and close herself in her office for the rest of the evening.

Now, with guests in the house, things were livelier. Gabi brought a vitality that was almost like ozone. The very air seemed charged whenever she was around. There was, to Jeremy, something vaguely disturbing about the child, but also a vulnerability that stirred in him feelings that could only be described as grandfatherly. Celeste, too, was an interesting woman, but not easy to get to know. She was very pretty, even beautiful, in an understated way, but there was tension in her as well. Personable and articulate she was, but there still seemed to be a region within Celeste to which nobody had a passport. Or was it just that off-island people all seemed to be edgy, harassed by the pace of the modern world? Had he, himself, been that way when he was living his old life in Portland, Maine?

Teaching astronomy in a private college could hardly be called a "rat race," although, within the ivy walls, there had been seething jealousies, ruthless competition, and intrigue enough to rival the court of King Louis XIV. He sometimes felt they should have all been wearing powdered wigs.

Jeremy Banks had certainly learned to play the game, and he had endured, sought and won tenure, then retired gracefully with pretty speeches from colleagues and proper homage from the boys. His private life had been kept private, and although there had been some speculation about it among staff and students, it had flowed as a river does under a bridge, with little effect on those who stand upon it.

Now Jeremy could hear voices approaching — adult voices. *Damn! Where was Gabi?* In spite of himself, Jeremy was becoming a little anxious. Then, smiling affably, with a heartiness he didn't really feel, he greeted Willie and Celeste. "Ladies, I was just wondering if I should revive the old English custom of tea at four o'clock. I already put kettle on, as they say on *Coronation Street*." The kettle was beginning to sing.

"Where's Gabi?" Celeste asked.

"I'm . . . I'm afraid she's not back yet, but I'm sure she'll be arriving any minute. She and Matt probably lost track of time. You know how children are." Jeremy rinsed a china teapot with hot water, filed a metal tea ball with leaves, dropped it inside, then poured in boiling water and covered the pot with a quilted tea cozy.

"I certainly *do*. And I'm going to have to have a serious talk with mine about going off without our knowing where she is. I should never have let her go out unsupervised with that Weeks boy."

"Oh, Celeste, I'm sure she's fine," Willie said. "She may be at Matt's. Shall I call and ask?"

"Yes, please, Willie. When we're at home, I always know exactly where Gabi is. I drive her to play dates with her friends, then I drive her back. She's not used to being out alone, and doesn't know how to handle it. I don't either."

Willie had gone into her office to make her call. Jeremy tried to sound reassuring. "Gabi isn't alone if she's with Matt, and he's a native island boy who knows every inch of it. If anything unusual had happened, someone would have called us immediately."

"Not if she's out in the woods. Not if she's hurt and can't get back. Not if something's happened to both of them and nobody knows where they are."

"You *did* tell her not to go into the woods, Celeste. Is there any reason to believe she would go anyway?"

"No. Yes. She knows it could be dangerous, but she and Matt went all the way to the old Lemerriant farm yesterday. They didn't just walk a little way up the path, like Gabi said. They went the whole distance and they went inside the old cabin. Their sneaker prints were all over the trail, and it was clear someone had been there. I don't want my daughter roaming through the woods and into old buildings. That place is dangerous. There's a well that a child could fall into and drown. Some of the buildings look ready to topple over, and Willie and I saw the remains of a deer that had been killed and eaten by some predator."

Jeremy poured Celeste a cup of steaming tea. "The deer may have died a natural death and any number of animals could have eaten the carcass. Mother Nature's cleanup committee. That's why, despite a large deer population, you don't see their bodies stacked up like cordwood."

They both looked at Willie as she came into the room. "Is she there?"

"There was no answer. They may all be out in the yard and didn't hear the phone. I'll try again in a few minutes if Gabi isn't back by then."

Jeremy poured two more cups of tea, one for Willie, one for himself. The phone rang and Willie got up. "That's probably Gabi calling from Matt's." She stepped into her office. Celeste and Jeremy listened silently. At first they heard nothing, then Willie's voice: "Oh, my god! Where? How did it happen?" Then Willie quietly closed the office door.

Celeste had turned pale. Jeremy reached over and put his hand on hers, but he, too, looked grave. "Let's just wait and see what this is about. It may not have anything at all to do with Gabi."

Their eyes were riveted on the door when it opened and Willie stepped through. It was clear from her expression that something was horribly wrong, but Willie hastily held up a hand. "That was Kirsti Weeks. It's okay, it wasn't about Gabi; Gabi and Matt are fine. Gabi is on her way home." She caught Jeremy's eye, and sent him an agonized look. Celeste was visibly relieved, but also realized that something must have happened, and sat waiting to hear what it was.

Willie was fighting back tears. "It was bad news. The most *horrible* news. A child has been killed."

Jeremy stared in disbelief. "What? Who? How?" He was picturing a teenager in a car crash. Celeste just kept on staring at Willie but her whole body had gone tense.

"It was little Dory Michaels."

Celeste's eyes widened. "Isn't that the little girl who said somebody was chasing her?" Picturing an abduction by a sexual predator, she stood up. "I must go find Gabi."

Willie looked at them both, calmly now, her gray-green eyes anguished. "They say it was a cougar."

Celeste sat, only because her legs seemed to give way. Jeremy looked stunned. Then the kitchen door banged open and Gabi bounced into the room. She stood, panting, out of breath, disheveled. "Did you guys *hear* about the kid who was killed by a *cougar*?"

Celeste burst into tears, ran over and grabbed Gabi almost as if she were going to shake her, then pulled her into a hug so tight that Gabi squirmed to get free. She was full of her news: "Mrs. Weeks said it was Dory Michaels, the kid who was chased in the woods, but I know it wasn't a cougar that chased her, it was Matt, although he says it *wasn't* but I know it *was*. We didn't see her when Matt and I were riding bikes and we went over to her house and . . ." Gabi stopped, realizing that in her excitement, she was probably saying much too much. Seeing her mother's look, she tried to make it better: "When we were at Dory's house *our bikes never left the road*, just like you told me."

Willie flicked her eyes to Jeremy. They both knew that the island was crisscrossed with roads that led into the darkest depths of it.

Celeste spoke evenly, her voice low and intense: "Gabi, while we are on this island, you are never, ever, to be out of my sight. Not for a single moment. Do you understand?"

Gabi nodded.

"Now I want you to go upstairs and take a bath and change your clothes. You're filthy, and your pants look like you've been sliding down a hill on your backside. Later on, we'll have a long talk and you can tell me everything you did today and everywhere you've been. *Go.*" Gabi went.

At least some of the tension had lifted, and the three adults sat back down at the table. Willie mechanically emptied the untouched tea which was now cold and poured each of them a fresh hot cup from the pot — because she needed something for her hands to do. They all stared at the rising steam without making any move to drink.

"Did Mrs. Weeks tell you how it happened?" Jeremy asked.

"She didn't go into details, but Dory was found in the patch of woods next to her house. Kirsti said that Dory and her mother had been in Port Casper. They came back on the one o'clock ferry. Chad Michaels picked them up in his truck. Dory must have gone out to play in the woods." Willie paused, struck by a though. "I wonder if she had the dog with her. Kirsti didn't say, but the Michaels have a guard dog — a German shepherd. They used to have two, but one disappeared a few weeks ago." Willie was trying to picture how it could have happened, but there was something that was not quite adding up. "Why would Dory have been out alone in the very area where something chased her? How would her parents have allowed that? And surely she would have had the dog with her. He'd have at least tried to protect her."

"I don't know about the dog," Jeremy said, "but the day Dory was followed, the area was thoroughly searched. Michaels and several of the villagers went over it with a fine-toothed comb, according to Mrs. Westerlake at the post office. She said they found nothing."

"It could have been Gabi." Celeste said dully. "They were out there, the two of them. The sooner we leave here the better."

"And until you do leave, we will all keep close watch on Gabi," Willie said. "Every child on this island will be carefully guarded until that beast is killed. I'm sure there's already a hunting party being organized."

"How often does this sort of thing happen?" To Celeste it was like some twisted science-fiction tale of a paradise with some horrible *thing* routinely killing the inhabitants.

"In British Columbia, it's not uncommon, Willie said. "On the mainland and on Vancouver Island, cougars can be a threat as well as a nuisance. Usually they go for easy prey like dogs and cats. Sometimes they end up wandering around in a city like Victoria. There was one that even got into the Empress Hotel. The wildlife conservation people usually tranquilize them and transport them back into the wild. Now and then, though, you hear of one stalking and attacking a child, even an adult. It wasn't that long ago that one leapt on the back of a young man who was riding a dirt bike along a trail. We don't have a cougar population on Broom Island, but they're good swimmers. A cougar must have made his way across the strait. But it'll be found and destroyed."

Celeste felt a chill. Then, for no real reason she asked, "How do they know for sure it was a cougar?"

"I . . . I guess from the look of the remains." Willie answered without elaborating. "We have no bears — no history of bears, although now and then you hear of someone who thinks they've seen one."

"Yes, but there will be an autopsy, won't there?"

"I'm sure there will."

"To rule out a pedophile who might have wanted to make it look like a cougar attack?"

That hadn't even occurred to Willie. She looked thoughtfully at Celeste who obviously lived in a more complex world where such things happened. "I suppose they'll send the body to Port Casper for examination, then return it to the island for burial."

Nobody noticed that Gabi had come back into the room. She had changed her sweatshirt and put on fresh jeans. "Are they going to bury her next to the other kids who were killed by a cougar?"

Celeste looked startled. "What other kids?"

"The two kids in the funny grave in the cemetery. The ones that were ripped to pieces and the birds could smell the fresh blood and they came and pecked out their eyes."

"Gabi! Who told you such things?" Celeste was aghast.

Gabi opened her mouth, hesitated a moment while she caught Jeremy's eye in what, to his surprise, seemed to be a look of warning. "Matt. It was Matt who told me."

"That young man needs a good talking to."

"But that was such a long time ago, Gabi. I'm a little surprised that Matt even knows about it." Willie said.

"Oh, he knows. And his sister knows. She says it was the Loogy-Roo. She says the Loogy-Roo is back. Matt said so too, but I didn't believe him."

"Well, I hope it didn't frighten you, Gabi. The Loogy-Roo is just an old island story. But a cougar is very real, so you be sure to stay close to us."

"I knew there wasn't any *real* Loogy-Roo, and I'm not afraid of the cougar either. I'm not afraid of anything anymore. Can I go watch TV?"

"Yes, run along, Gabi," Celeste said, a bit absently.

"If there's nothing on TV that you want to see, Gabi, there might be something in that stack of VHS tapes on the shelf. You want me to show you how to work the VCR?" Willie called after her.

"Oh, I know how to work a VCR," Gabi called back.

"I suppose we should be grateful that Gabi isn't traumatized," Celeste said. "I thought she'd be terrified."

"Children can surprise you," Willie said. "Gabi didn't know Dory Michaels so she wouldn't feel grief, and she wouldn't realize the enormity. To her it's just a lot of excitement. I remember when I was a schoolteacher we always tried to protect children from anything frightening, but they were always capable of scaring *us*. We're appalled by their music, and often by their appearance, and yet every generation manages to make it to adulthood to produce the next generation which, in turn, will scare *them*. In my youth everybody worried that comic books were going to be our ruination."

"I'm worried that Gabi will start having nightmares again. She hasn't had any since that first night at the Inn."

"Has she been troubled by them for a long time?"

"For the better part of a year, ever since she turned ten." Celeste appeared reluctant to say anything more, but then went on: "She's .. . been having problems. Changes in behavior. Trouble in school. She always seemed to be such a happy child, but then the nightmares started." Celeste was nervously rubbing her thumb against her fingertips, wishing she had a cigarette. "It could all have been caused by my divorce from her father when she was five."

Willie nodded. "Yes, that certainly can affect a child. But perhaps it's just a stage she's going through. I've never had any children of my own, so I can't speak from experience, but Gabi is such a sweet child. Until this terrible day, I would have said that being on the island seems to agree with her. She was having fun exploring with Matt, and doing things she doesn't get to do in a city."

Jeremy had been quietly following the conversation, and did not add that among those was the act of talking to ravens in her head. Why didn't he just come out and say something about that? Gabi had asked him not to — with that look she'd given him — like a splash of cold water. Very well. Let it be a secret between the two of them, for now. He sensed that if he had said something, Gabi would have come up with some glib obfuscation, then never trusted him again. Jeremy might be the only one with a gateway into Gabi's mind, and it was possible that she might, at some point, need him to stride into it and rescue her. From what, Jeremy didn't know.

CHAPTER 19

THE VILLAGE reacted like a disturbed anthill. At first everyone was shocked, horrified and confused — the community abuzz with news that consisted of as much misinformation as fact: a cougar had carried off Dory Michaels. Her mother had seen it from the window. The cougar had fatally mauled her while her father had tried to fight off the beast. It had happened only a few feet from the Michaels house where the body had been found. The cougar was still at large, and it may not have been a cougar at all. It may have been a wolf. The body had been taken to the clinic, and there would be an autopsy. Phones rang. Party lines lay open to three- and four-way discussions. People came out of their houses to talk with neighbors over backyard fences, and knots of islanders stood in grave conversation in front of the Co-op and at the ferry dock.

Beneath it all, infrastructure was kicking in. Broom Island was one of the last single-man RCMP detachments in Canada. Constable Grant Hewett, and Dr. Medgar Swallow, who was also new to the island, were both dealing with their first crisis in Satama. Dr. Swallow and his wife,

Doris, a registered nurse, had arrived a couple of months earlier to take over the running of the clinic, allowing old Doc Swanson to retire, then die two weeks later, of a coronary thrombosis. The body of Dory Michaels had been transported to the clinic where Dr. Swallow was doing a preliminary forensic examination. A group of men, headed by Constable Hewett, and including Chad Michaels, had formed a hunting party and gone in search of the cougar.

Willie's phone was ringing wildly as friends called to ask how much she'd heard and to report what they thought they knew. Now the talk was about what gesture of sympathy might be appropriate, and that proved to be a little awkward.

Many islanders had had run-ins with the man who called himself Chadwick Michaels. His combative manner and bellicose demands, always accompanied by threats of legal action, had given him the reputation of being dangerous to know. As result, most islanders gave him and his family as wide a berth as possible in such a small place. They didn't invite them to their salmon barbecues, bonfires, or other socials — any more than they did, among themselves, ever refer to Chad by his newly-adopted name, Michaels. "Best not have any of 'em in your house," it was said, "If Schittle stubs his toe on your doorsill, he'll sue you." The name was pronounced "Schittle," or "Shit-hill" depending on how much the speaker disliked the man.

Willie felt a bit sorry for his wife, Weena. Rowena Michaels was a brittle, city-thin woman with a defensive manner, but Willie attributed that to her having lived with Chad. Dory, their little girl, hadn't been popular either, poor thing. She had tended to resemble her father with her pink skin, her piggy little nose and roly-poly shape, and she'd had his unfortunate habit of lording it over other children, parroting her father's threats of lawsuit. This had made her a target, particularly of Matt Weeks and his friends, who'd idly tormented her whenever the opportunity arose, while doing their best to stay under her father's radar. They knew that if Dory recognized them, she would "tell" and that would mean trouble. If Dory found a slimy banana slug in her lunch box or a dead weasel in her desk, it was usually a *coup de pied dans l'eau* — a maneuver so subtly executed that it left no more trace than a foot pulled out of water. Even when there were suspicions, there was no hard evidence.

But none of that mattered now. If Chadwick and Rowena permitted it, the village would reach out to them to offer whatever comfort and support they could. For the first time, the Michaels would be considered part of the community.

Danielle Herron, who ran the gift shop next to the ferry dock, was the nearest to a friend that Weena Michaels had. A couple of times, as a favor, Weena had done a stint of working in the shop when Danielle needed help — as had most of the women in Satama. To visitors, it was always mildly surprising to witness the musical chairs nature of island enterprise. The woman who had registered you at the Broom Island Inn might next be seen pumping gas at the tiny station next to the ferry dock, or working as a checker at the Co-op. The economy had undergone many setbacks that had prompted much of the population to move back to "the mainland" (which largely meant Vancouver Island). Those who had stayed juggled any number of jobs, and such was their love of the place that no honest work was looked down upon — whether it was going out into the woods to harvest salal to sell to the florist industry, or picking up trash along the highway. A few, like Butch Westerlake, the husband of the postmaster, were able to make a living by commuting to work at logging camps off-island, as did some of the women who signed on as camp cooks. One thing most residents seemed to agree upon: Broom Island was the best place in the world to live, and they were willing to do whatever allowed them to stay.

Weena Michaels hadn't needed to work outside her home, at least not at first. The Michaels had bought fifty acres of land with the windfall from one of Chad's successful lawsuits, and Weena had rather fancied herself as the *madrona* of an estate. There was a house on the property

— more of a shack — which the Michaels had barely made livable, with the idea that a larger, grander home would be built as soon as their planned campground, gift shop, and greenhouses began to pay off.

There was plenty for Weena to do. She found that it was her job to look after the plants, although she'd been shocked, at first, at how physical the labor was. A city woman with a part-time maid and a monthly yard man, she was unaccustomed to wheelbarrows and compost heaps and shoveling. But, to her own surprise, she found she really didn't mind the work, once she'd grooved into it.

When Chad had bullied them into moving to Broom Island, Weena had hoped that the change in lifestyle would have a calming effect. She felt that "going back to the land" might also be good for Dory, recalling her own small-town upbringing where life was free and not so fearful. Yes, Weena had thought it might be good for all of them, but she hadn't counted on the isolation being . . . well . . . so *isolating*.

Socially, Weena felt cut off. Townsfolk treated her with cordial wariness. If she approached a group of people chatting on the ferry dock, conversation wound down, and the group soon dispersed as each remembered they had to be getting home. Danielle's was the only place in town that Weena felt comfortable, because she and Danielle had a few things in common. Neither was a descendant of early settlers, nor had ties to the Finnish community.

Danielle, also a city woman who had moved to Satama five years ago, was still an outsider, not quite in the loop. The Finns tended to complain that her prices were too high. Others resented Danielle's political spirit. Many didn't appreciate her spearheading a movement to bring in more tourism, or to incorporate Satama officially as a village — a move that would bring new rules and regulations that most residents didn't welcome. Danielle was considered an upstart by the Old Guard.

And so it was, that now and then, when Danielle had a slow day, and Weena, feeling the need for human contact, made her way to town, the two of them would perch on long-legged stools and chat, balancing mugs of coffee and sometimes a slice of *pulla*, insulated by a welter of merchandise. There, surrounded by artwork, candles, rugs crocheted from fishnets, Chinese lanterns, baubles, bangles, and beads; Weena Michaels would hear the latest town gossip, and nod solemnly while Danielle ranted about the backwardness of a village that refused to keep up with the times. Sometimes, at more intimate moments, they exchanged confidences, giving cautious voice to personal problems. Danielle, by nature, tended to be more outgoing and bombastic; Rowena was more subdued and pragmatic. Danielle of the glad smile and the ringing voice was outgoing; Weena hoped for the best and prepared for the worst, which often made her the voice of doom.

And now that doom had fallen, Danielle was the only one who felt impelled to go at once to be at Weena's side. She needed someone to watch the store until closing time, called around, but nobody seemed to be available — except Sybil Weeks.

Danielle, of course, could have simply put up the "Closed" sign and left early, but Danielle really, *really* hated closing the shop. The previous owner, when the shop had been called Jacinthe's, had only kept it open five days a week, which allowed her, very sensibly, to have a personal day for hair appointments, visits to the dentist, and shopping in Port Casper. Danielle, an energetic and astute business woman, had realized that she would have to make an extra effort to fit into the tight little community of Satama. The best of her policies was to hire locals to keep the shop open whenever she was unable to be there herself. This meant that if she left Irja Suomela in charge, some of Irja's friends would stop by the shop to chat, have a cup of coffee, and maybe buy. It was brilliant, and Danielle's was becoming a social center. She made it a point to be visible, smiling and waving at the incoming ferry traffic, and her inventory was carefully calculated to appeal to tourists as well as local people. With her imported coffees, green cardamom seeds (so far, Danielle's was the only place on the island were you could buy the aromatic spice so prized by Finns in making *pulla*), and gift cards featuring photos of Broom

Island taken by local photographers, Satama people were finding their way into Danielle's, even if not yet beating a path to her door.

Danielle also offered local artists a place to display and possibly sell their work. She made it a point to stock a few high-ticket items, and had actually sold, to a wealthy tourist, two of the expensive Haida ceremonial masks made by carvers in Alert Bay. This had encouraged other artists, and she currently had a half dozen masks, varying in price from one thousand to a whopping fifteen thousand dollars each. Anywhere else, Danielle would have taken the masks home every night for security, but in Satama, she was comfortable about merely locking the door and the stout collapsible iron gate.

The worst crimes in Satama were littering and vandalism, always committed at night and always by kids. They weren't out to steal; they were simply out to destroy. The new metal signs on the Finnish museum had been torn off and bent. Boxes of donations left at the Seniors' Club for a charity sale had been ripped apart, and the clothing strewn all over the parking lot. Wooden picnic tables at the lake were set afire so routinely that the town council was vowing not to replace them. Whether from boredom or *diablerie*, a faction of youngsters was bent upon personifying the flaws of mankind. Sadly, they were equally wanton with their own lives, and all too often the community was shocked by their sudden deaths, either by accident or suicide by car. One never knew.

No, Danielle wouldn't close the shop even for an hour. She would pick up Sybil Weeks, although leaving Sybil in charge was like putting a plane on auto-pilot. It was okay as long as nothing unusual happened. Even with her limited vision, Sybil was capable of ringing up purchases and making change, and local customers were happy to assist her if she should need it.

It would never have occurred to Danielle to hire Sybil in the first place except for Kirsti Weeks, her mother. Danielle, that day, had an eye appointment in Port Casper, and asked Kirsti if she could keep the shop open for the afternoon. Kirsti had been busy, but suggested that

Sybil could do it. That had been, to Danielle, a moment — awkward and politically charged. If she refused, would that be snubbing a local family? Worse yet, would she be seen as unsympathetic to the handicapped? Hesitantly, she'd agreed.

To her surprise, Danielle had found Sybil to be surprisingly bright and willing. As long as she was taking her meds, her sight seemed to be her only handicap. Her fingers had a feel for coins, and whatever vision she had (plus Danielle's making sure bills in the cash register drawer were neatly segregated) allowed her to operate the till.

Sybil didn't appear to be mentally wanting, although, even medicated, she was *odd*. She rarely spoke, but when she did she seemed to prefer to speak in verse. Danielle had remarked to someone that it sounded like she was reciting *Beowulf*. She'd been told that it was probably the *Kalevala*, the Finnish epic, since every kid on the island had grown up hearing its cadences; *Kalevala* readings were part of every celebration: New Year's, Easter, Mayday (celebrated by Finns as *Vappu*), Mother's Day, Midsummer (*Juhannus* or *Mittumaari*), Independence Day, Memorial Day, and sometimes even weddings and funerals. The practice had begun with the early settlers, and had always been conducted in Finnish. As the old language declined, and by now pretty well had died out among the young, the text had changed to English — but the custom went on, despite criticism by seniors who resented hearing the *Kalevala* in a foreign tongue, as well as scholars who could never agree on which translation they should be using.

Sybil's appearance was odd as well. Her funereal garb and cadaverous appearance were something to be seen on a totem pole. And indeed, Sybil did have the blood of the First Nations coursing through her veins. Her great-grandmother on her father's side had been a full-blooded Haida — or was that Kwakiutl? Sybil might, at least theoretically, qualify for tribe membership, now that the Métis had been given official tribal status — whatever that meant. Legitimacy of some sort, Danielle mused, for the "ghost children who walk in two worlds."

Danielle had been only peripherally aware of the history of aboriginal peoples until she began buying native art. It was in Alert Bay that Danielle came face to face with a residential school — a huge, forbidding building with leprous paint — that overpowered the landscape and seemed totally out of place on the little island. She had stood looking at it, appalled at the thought of little children being forced out of their natural environment into this . . . this *thing* . . . forbidden to speak their native language, stripped of family ties, and subject to God knows what abuses and horrors within those walls. The Nimpkish Band had owned the building since 1973, but to Danielle it still loomed like the Gates of Hell.

Anyway, Danielle had decided to give Sybil a try. She persuaded her to leave Blackjack, her bird, at home, but had wondered if her strange appearance would spook customers. As it turned out, just the opposite happened. Visitors accepted her as part of local color, and the islanders suddenly became friendlier. Had Sybil, to Danielle, been some sort of initiation? Odd or not, Sybil was one of *them*, and *they* tended to look after their own. Danielle vaguely sensed that she'd dodged a bullet. Now, while Sybil was never her first choice, it was not unusual to see her minding the store; in fact, she'd just been there the day before, when Danielle had gone to Port Casper to get her hair done, and again on Thursday morning, when Danielle had to wait at home for the septic tank people. Three days of Sybil in one week seemed a bit much; she would have preferred someone else, but there seemed to be nobody.

Danielle picked up Sybil, left her with instructions to auto-dial her cell phone if anything came up that she couldn't handle, then drove on out to the Michaels place.

Despite their friendship, Danielle had never visited Weena Michaels, nor had she explored the tiny island with its network of logging roads. She'd never gone past the water tower where Quarry Road turned to dirt and gravel, and now her Volkswagen drove rather daintily across the rough terrain, as if trying to keep its petticoats out of the mud.

Danielle looked for landmarks, hoping she wouldn't take a wrong turn that would have her scrabbling across weed-grown ruts, with shrubbery clawing at the finish of her car. Common sense told her that it would be impossible to get permanently lost on an island the size of Broom. Still, it was she who routinely advised visitors to stay out of the interior, where you could wind up trying to find your way out of a series of dead ends, not unlike one of those paper place mat mazes in Pearl's Café.

Danielle was beginning to feel the tiniest stirrings of discomfort, as she drove through wilderness where the only sign of civilization seemed to be a stumpy clear-cut area toothed with white spikes. Past it lay nothing but the road in front of her, hemmed in by dense greenery that allowed no glimpse of surrounding landscape, and gave her a sense of traveling through an endless tunnel. She felt relief when she came to a landmark: a 'T' with a bus bench, where she gratefully turned left toward what she now knew would be the Michaels property.

The gate was open; Danielle drove on down the hill and pulled into the yard where there were several cars parked. She got out and knocked on the door. There was no answer. There was no sign of the Michaels dogs either — or dog. One had gone missing, but the other, Weena had said, was a good guard dog whose loud barking let her know when anyone arrived. They didn't usually let the dog run loose, and from the way Weena had spoken, Danielle had wondered if she weren't a little afraid of it herself. Chad had said that if it bit anyone, he could be sued, so the dog was only allowed to run free when it was with the family.

Apparently Weena wasn't at home, and Danielle realized she should have called first. Why hadn't she? She admitted to morbid curiosity as she slowly walked about the grounds. The woods were only a few feet from the house, and it looked as if someone had started clearing the underbrush and staking out areas as campsites. The setting was lovely with its view of water and the pebbly beach piled at the tide line with logs. Silent except for the soothing splash of waves, it was difficult to visualize terror and sudden death here. Danielle thoughtfully walked the path and noted that there was no sign of . . . whatever had happened. Then, realizing that she was alone in an area where there'd been a cougar attack, she backtracked, then walked on past the house to the large, plastic-covered greenhouse. She tried the door. It opened, and Danielle gasped as if she'd seen a ghost.

She'd come face to face with Rowena Michaels who was standing motionless, silently looking at her. Danielle put a hand to her heart. "Oh, God, Weena, you scared the stuffings out of me. I thought you weren't home. Are you here all by yourself? I saw all the cars."

Weena said nothing, just stared dully. Danielle glanced around and saw plants, bales of peat moss, bags of fertilizers. The ventilator fan hummed steadily, pumping air between the sheets or plastic covering, causing them to rustle softly. "Weena? Are you . . . all right?" She bit her tongue. Of course Weena *wasn't* all right. She'd be in shock. But what was she doing here all alone? Danielle gently put her hands on Weena's shoulders. "Why don't we go in the house and I'll make us a nice cup of coffee." Then, as Weena continued to stare, "Weena, you're scaring me. Where is everybody? How could they leave you here by yourself?" Not really knowing what to do next, Danielle put her arms around Rowena Michaels and gave her a hug, then just continued to hold on as she, herself, suddenly and uncontrollably, burst into tears. "Big help I am," she sobbed. She became aware then that Weena was crying too and clinging to her. And then it was somehow better. The two women, arms linked, made their way slowly back to the house where Danielle settled Weena into a chair and set about making coffee.

As the pot perked, they sat across from each other at the kitchen table. Danielle, not knowing what to say, said nothing. What *could* she say that wouldn't sound stupidly inadequate? Weena looked so . . . wounded. Inwardly, Danielle felt rage at Chad for not being with her, or at least making sure that someone was.

"They all went off to look for the cougar . . . the men."

"Weena, I want you to come back with me. I want you to stay at my place for awhile."

"No, I'm . . . I'm all right here. I needed to be by myself. I told them to go."

"Someone should be here with you. There's no way I'm going to leave you."

Weena gave a shuddering sigh and directed her gaze out the window. "We'd been to Port Casper, Dory and I. She had an appointment with the dentist. It was a good checkup. No cavities." Her voice broke; she took a deep breath and went on: "We came home on the one o'clock ferry. It was fifteen minutes late. Chad had been waiting in the truck. . . ." Her voice trailed off.

"You don't have to talk about this now, Weena."

Weena went on, her voice now flat and emotionless. "We came home and Chad said he had to go see Burt Strunk about getting some stakes cut for the camp area. Burt has that sawmill, you know, on Quarry Road. Chad said a couple of kids had been by to see Dory — or at least so they said. He thought they were just snooping around. He said one of them was the Weeks boy who's always trouble, and there was some little girl with him. Chad said she'd asked if Dory was home, but Chad didn't recognize her. Dory didn't know who she was either."

"I think I know who that was. She and the Weeks boy were in my shop this morning. I was keeping an eye on them to make sure they didn't touch anything. The girl is the daughter of that writer who's doing an article on Satama for some travel magazine."

"Writer? Chad would want to meet *her*. He'd want to make sure she mentions Michaels Acres," Weena said dryly.

"She's a city woman from Seattle, I hear. Has a funny name — Oops or Ooms something. She was staying at the Inn, but now she's ended up at Willie Haapala's house. She's been going through old records at the museum and asking questions. Her kid looks to be around ten years old, and I don't know why she's not in school. Maybe she goes to one of those ritzy-ditzy private schools where you don't have any rules, the kind where you have to enroll the kids when they show up on an ultrasound."

Weena frowned in concentration, momentarily distracted. "I think I did hear something about her. People were talking on the ferry. I heard she might be from here — or at least her family was."

"Oh?" Danielle leaned forward. "Who told you that?"

"Nobody, but I happened to overhear Grace Maddox talking to Goldie Slumber — you know they're both in the Senior's Club — and they said Amanda Vuorisaari had told them that the woman — oh, what was her name — Possum, they said — Possum? Could that be right? I guess it *was* Ooms-Possum. Anyway, she's been snooping around in the museum records, trying to get information on the Lemerriant family. They were wondering why she'd care about them just for a travel magazine article? It didn't mean much to me, but that's what I heard. They were wondering if she might be related in some way."

"Hmm. Interesting. Considering the stories about the Lemerriants."

"I know I've heard the name, but that's about all," Weena said.

"Of *course* you've heard the name: Lemerriant farm? Not far from here. There's a trail that leads past it now. Hiking trail. There's a falling-down barn and a cabin. I was on the committee to push the idea of restoring it as a tourist attraction."

"With a name like that, they couldn't have been early Finnish settlers. Seems like Finnish names all have too many vowels. Ooms-Possum wouldn't be Finnish either, would it?"

"No, if she's a Lemerriant, that must be a married name." Danielle giggled. "Would you marry a man named Ooms-Possum? Anyway, the Lemerriants were French, and there was a — " Danielle caught herself. She really didn't want to talk to Weena right now about past cougar attacks. "They're gone from the island now. There was a fire here years ago and most of the family died in it. But I think the daughter survived and went to the mainland. Nobody knows what became of her."

"That must be the monument in the cemetery," Weena said. "I remember seeing it when I went in there once."

Conversation stopped at the mention of the cemetery. Both women, briefly transported by gossip, returned to the moment; and for Weena, it was doubly painful as she realized with a jolt that for just a little while, she'd almost forgotten. *My god, I almost forgot that my child was brutally killed hours ago!* A wave of fresh grief washed over her; haltingly, she tried to talk her way through it. Danielle listened, pained by the playback of what had started out as such an ordinary afternoon in the Michaels household.

"When we got home, Chad got in the truck and left. Said he'd be back in half an hour." Dory and I went in the house. Turk had been inside all morning, so I told Dory to take him out. I had several flats of pepper plants to transplant, so I went in the greenhouse and took the radio with me. They say music helps plants grow, and the radio is a bit of company for me when I'm working. I guess I had it on too loud."

"Then you heard nothing?"

"I heard nothing. I saw nothing. It was Chad who found Dory — and it was too late." Weena took a breath that was more of a sob.

"Where was Turk?" Danielle asked. The dog should have been with Dory. Why hadn't he kicked up a fuss?

"I don't know. He's nowhere. I thought Dory would just take him out to do his business, then bring him back inside. After the scare she had, I didn't think she'd be going into the woods. I don't understand any of it."

"You mean the dog just disappeared? Like Bruno did?"

"I guess so. Nobody's found hide nor hair of either of them."

"Maybe Turk got frightened and ran away. He's probably hiding in the woods. He'll come back on his own."

Weena nodded, wiping her eyes. "It's getting late. The men will be coming back. They wouldn't be hunting cougar at night, would they? I guess I should see about dinner."

Danielle looked shocked. "You'll do no such thing! Nobody expects you to be cooking at a time like this. You can leave a note for that husband of yours, and then you're coming home with me. I left Sybil Weeks in charge. We'll swing by, close up the shop, drop off Sybil, then head for my place and a couple of double martinis."

Weena started to protest weakly, but the thought of having to deal with Chad and the hunting party — whether they'd shot the cougar or not — was suddenly something she didn't have the heart for. "I don't have to leave a note. I'll call him from your place."

CHAPTER 20

Sybil Weeks, left alone in Danielle's, sniffed the air and detected scented candles, a faint smell of coffee, and stillness. It wasn't the first time Sybil had been left in charge of the shop, but she didn't think there would be any customers. There rarely were. The shop was officially open, but locals tended to avoid it when they knew Sybil was on duty. One never quite knew about Sybil. One was always cordial to Sybil, and one hoped that Sybil would not have failed to take the medication that allowed her to lead a semi-normal life.

If anyone had come in, Sybil could have handled it. She had a basic knowledge of the shop's contents, so that on the rare occasion when she might be confronted by a tourist, she could point to the card rack, the book rack, the souvenir cases, and even answer questions about native art. In fact, the First Nations artwork, particularly the wooden masks, held a burning fascination for Sybil, and were the real reason Sybil consented to working in Danielle's. She didn't care about the money.

Sybil had her own agenda. In good weather, the shop door was usually propped open. Sybil shut it, but resisted the impulse to flip the

"Open" sign to "Closed." It wouldn't be necessary. Danielle's car was not parked outside, so everyone knew she wasn't there. There weren't any tourists on the island at this time of year. The ferry wouldn't be coming in for an hour, and it wouldn't be carrying visitors anyhow, just people in a hurry to get home. Nobody would be stopping in to browse or to grab a cup of coffee and chat. Sybil would have the place to herself until closing time or later, if Danielle was delayed getting back.

The wooden masks, intricately painted and carved, were kept in a separate alcove which also housed Danielle's desk, with only a curtain across the doorway to shield them from view. They were, by far, the most expensive items in the shop, and Danielle preferred to display them personally to anyone who might be a customer. They represented the output of various West Coast tribes, and some of the faces had moving parts cleverly devised to transform them at the touch of a panel. It was *not* permitted to play with the masks. Danielle was always quick to explain that it would have been considered a sacrilege to even try one on. This was less out of respect for native culture, than a precaution against anyone causing them wear and tear. Most of the masks in the shop had, after all, been carved specifically for tourist trade. Danielle made routine trips to various islands to find artwork for her shop, and native carvers were realizing higher and higher prices for their work.

There was only one authentic shaman transformation mask that had actually been used on ceremonial occasions. Not much was known of its origin, but Danielle had been told that it was the mask of a mythical or historical figure, and that, atypically, the shaman had been a woman. Possibly because of that, Danielle had been able to scoop it up at a bargain price. Research on the Internet proved the mask to be even more valuable than she thought, and it was now the jewel of her collection. The mask showed authenticating traces of leather and glue where some of the original trappings had been stripped away. The ties of cedar bark used to fasten the mask in place were still intact, but worn and fragile. The inside had been shaped to fit comfortably across the face without rubbing the nose, and the eyeholes, when the mask was open, were functional. The face on the mask was unusual in that it looked like it could have been an actual person — very pale, rubbed with white paint — though the wood grain of red cedar showed through the thin coating — with large, very full, bright red lips pressed together, the corners of the mouth drawn downward. (They had made Danielle think of the wax lips of childhood candy counters.) Piercing painted eyes stared straight ahead under thick black arching brows. A row of black upcurved horns jutted out of the forehead like a crown. There were still ragged locks of what must have been "hair" made of either wool or cedar bark, dyed jet black. The face exuded authority. If it were that of a real person, then she must have been someone of power and stature in the tribe.

The mask had a seam from hairline to chin, and by grasping the horns, the panels could be opened, like shutters, to reveal the interior. This transformed it into a more traditional piece of West Coast native art — the fierce and stylized face of a raven, painted in reds, blacks, and greens in bold, blunted geometric patterns. The red jutting beak and staring eyes echoed the face of the shaman, but the eyes had holes in them, allowing the wearer to look out. The insides of the swing-open panels were decorated with the large-eyed salmon motif often seen on artifacts and totem poles.

This was the mask that Sybil now held in her hands. Lightly she ran her fingers over the wood. She had learned about the masks the first time she'd worked in the shop, when Danielle had explained that they were not to be touched, particularly this one. This one, Danielle had told her, had been of a woman, a powerful shaman in her tribe, and hinted that it might even carry a curse to anyone who mishandled it.

Since the masks were not kept in plain view, normally no one would inquire about them. However, if anyone came in and asked specifically, Sybil was to either contact Danielle at once, ask the customer if they could come back later, or have them leave their name and telephone number. Sybil was not to show the masks herself or even indicate that there were any in stock. Did she understand that?

Yes. Sybil understood. During her times at Danielle's, nobody had ever made any inquiries about masks, but to Sybil they were a point of consuming fascination. That first day, as soon as she was alone, she had slipped behind the curtain and run her hands over the wooden faces. To her eyes they were a blur, but her fingers trembled as she "read" their features the way she read her Braille Bible. Then she gasped. *This* one was different. She felt a thrill of excitement — and recognition. *Yaxagama!* As she spoke the name, she could feel a tingling in her fingers. *Yaxagama, the Ancient Mother! The mother of all The People!* She remembered when she'd first heard the name whispered by Ernie, the man from Alert Bay. Ernie had always whispered the name, when he told stories of how The People were created, while the young Sybil had listened spellbound to tales of magic and wonder. Yaxagama *was* her Ancient Mother, and Sybil felt that their hearts were one. The mask had drawn her like a magnet, and there was nothing in the world she wanted so much as to have it for her own.

She had, with casual guile, asked Danielle about *all* the masks, and Danielle had seemed to enjoy chatting about their origins, perhaps relieved to find something she could carry on a conversation with Sybil *about*. Sybil's habitual silence made the chatty Danielle uncomfortable, because she couldn't tell whether Sybil was agreeing, disagreeing, mocking, or even listening.

Now, while the carved and painted faces of Haida, Coast Salish, Tsimshian, and Tlingit looked on, Sybil grasped the horns of the forbidden mask and opened the panels. She turned it over and raised it to her face. The cedar bark thongs were too fragile for her to fasten the mask on, so she held it in place with her hands. She was The Raven now. Raven the Trickster. She slid the mask smoothly down just a little, allowing the eye holes to line up with her own. Sybil smiled triumphantly.

With the mask on, Sybil Weeks could *see.*

* * *

The first time it happened, she'd lost her grip and almost sent the head of the shaman crashing to the floor. Heart pounding, she'd hastily put the mask back. But curiosity got the better of her, and she took it down again and carefully looked through the eyeholes. What was she seeing? It wasn't the shop, as she would have expected. It was sky and trees, and it was as if she were flying over a forest canopy, swooping down, then soaring up, banking to the left and to the right. It was making Sybil dizzy and she hadn't had time to experiment further; when she heard Danielle's car drive up, she quickly put the mask away.

Since then, Sybil had looked through the mask's eyes a number of times. She didn't always see the same thing, but it was as if she were, indeed, looking through the eyes of Raven the Trickster, a major totem in West Coast native mythology. Guided by Yaxagama, the Ancient Mother, Sybil was as free as a bird!

Holding her breath, she had asked about the price of the mask in an assumed offhand manner, so as not to reveal how desperately she wanted it. Danielle told her it was much too expensive, but that if Sybil really wanted a mask, she'd see if she could get one of the apprentice carvers to make one for her, although why the girl would want one, Danielle couldn't imagine. It wasn't as if she had enough vision to appreciate its artistry.

Of course Sybil didn't care about any other mask! She wanted *this* one. She had to be content to use the mask whenever she had the chance, and while she found the seldomness of it frustrating, she had been able, over a period of several months, to explore its properties.

She'd found that, at least to some degree, she could control her flight by picturing a destination. She had flown over her own house and seen her father in the yard. She had flown over the spine of the island, up along logging roads, and once, in late summer, over the lake, a place where Sybil had never been. Some boys were there, swimming and sliding down the rope to the raft. Some were climbing the dangling rope and swinging from it into the water. Sybil laughed when she saw one almost lose his trunks, then his grip as he tried to grab the waistband with one hand. As he ended up plummeting into the lake, Sybil recognized him as the kid who had nicknamed her "Sipuli," the Finnish word for onion. Served him right, the little snot!

Today, Sybil had a more compelling agenda. Today would not be a day of flying just for the fun of it. Today she had a task — a vital mission, entrusted to her by the Ancient Mother. She had to find the Loogy-Roo. She had seen the Loogy-Roo through the eyes of the raven mask twice before, and couldn't believe her good luck at having Danielle need her again so soon.

Now, once again, she had the mask. Through its eyes she had watched the Loogy-Roo arrive on the island, seen her on the deck of the ferry, and then, two days later, followed it to the Lemerriant farm and then to the lake. She had even come face to face with her in Pearl's coffee shop. Oh, the Loogy-Roo looked innocent enough! It looked like a little girl now, but Sybil knew. And the ravens knew. And the little girl knew. And Yaxagama, the Ancient Mother knew. Sybil was no longer the only one who could hear the ravens talking. The little girl could hear them too, of course she could! And the ravens could hear *her*. The ravens had foretold her coming. They'd left signs and messages for those who could interpret them. And they'd foretold that someone would die . . . and now Dory Michaels was dead. Everybody was looking for a cougar, but Sybil *knew*. But of course no one would believe *her*.

It would be up to Sybil alone to deal with the Loogy-Roo. Matt, her brother, had made friends with the girl and that might be a good thing. Sybil could sometimes make Matt *do things*. But she needed help. She needed the mask through which Yaxagama who could open up the world to her, show it to her through the eyes of the raven. It would be dangerous. Danielle would notice, but maybe not. Maybe if she just borrowed the mask for a day or two, perhaps she might even return it before Danielle realized it was gone. The shop would be closed on Sunday, and Sybil might figure out a way to put it back before it was missed.

Somehow, she would have to get it out of the shop without Danielle seeing it. Sybil always carried her Braille Bible, so an object on her lap wouldn't be unusual, but she had to disguise it. She needed a bag. A large plastic shopping bag was big enough to contain the mask, but it still wouldn't look like a book. Sybil put the bag on the counter, then laid her long black coat over it. If she picked up the coat *and* the bag, put them both across her knees, Danielle wouldn't see what she was carrying. Meanwhile, she would leave her Bible in the office. She could say she'd forgotten it, pick it up on Monday and make the switch. Besides, if she were caught, what was the worst that could happen? She'd be arrested? On Broom Island? Hardly! She'd get a talking-to from Danielle, maybe even her parents, but what could they do to her? She *knew* what they could do. They could make sure she never had access to the mask again! Well, it was a chance Sybil had to take.

Luck, or the perhaps the power of Yaxagama, was with her. Danielle pulled in and seemed to be in a hurry. She hardly noticed Sybil as she got out and hastily locked the shop and shut the gate. "Sorry I'm late. Hop in back, Sybil," she said. "I have Mrs. Michaels with me."

CHAPTER 21

WILLIE STARED out of her kitchen window, her eye caught by the brilliant color of the late afternoon sunshine on a clump of rhododendrons in the perennial bed. They were lush and red and beautiful, but now they seemed to be the color of blood. English daisies on the lawn were closing up, as the angle of the sun threw long shadows on the bright spring grass. Willie's hands were poised over the task of cutting up onions: ordinary work on such an extraordinarily terrible day.

The household was quiet. Jeremy was in the living room, leafing through a newspaper, although finding it hard to concentrate. He, too, was shaken. It seemed to Jeremy impossible that here, in his orderly world, violence would come, not through the agency of man, but of beast. It seemed raw and primitive compared with his old life in New England, a little like going back in time into a world populated by saber-toothed tigers, in which any journey might include running for your life. He reminded himself that, in the province of British Columbia, one was always surrounded by wilderness and whatever lived in it. There was a curiously disfigured clerk in a hardware store in Port Casper who had told him about surviving a grizzly bear attack in the Kootenays. In the city of Victoria there had been incidents of cougars having to be tranquilized, captured, and relocated. Wolves and cougars were so numerous on Vancouver Island that the hunting lobby routinely pressured for a cull in order to preserve the deer population for sports hunters. And the deer population made seven-foot fences necessary to anyone who tried to maintain a garden.

Jeremy, himself, had seen any number of black bears wandering along roadsides on Vancouver Island; and in the parking lot of the Wickaninnish Inn, he'd once seen a young bear hold a Volkswagen hostage by circling around it, while a group of watchers remained at a safe distance — until the bear tired of the game and lumbered off into the woods. Jeremy was also sure that he'd heard the howl of a wolf on Broom Island, although he'd never seen one. People here seemed to take such things in stride, although there was an increasing rancor between wildlife enthusiasts and the Old Guard who believed that the only good predator was a dead one.

If a cougar had come ashore on Broom Island, it would be hunted down and killed. Jeremy was rather glad that his injured wrist rendered him useless for the hunt. He found tracking down and killing animals distasteful; but yes, if there was a cougar endangering children, then of course it would have to be destroyed. He vowed that he would personally keep a sharp eye on Gabi, Willie, and Celeste; and provide whatever sense of security he could to the women he felt were entrusted to his care.

Celeste was in Willie's office, busy at her laptop computer, working on the article she was writing. Fidgety and distracted, she kept getting up to pace the room and peer out the window to make sure Gabi was within sight.

Gabi was sitting in the porch swing, one leg folded under her, the other extended, idly pushing with one sneakered foot to keep the swing moving, causing the rusting metal chain to creak rhythmically. She didn't seem bothered by the noise, although Celeste found the sound as annoying as it was reassuring. Gabi's Game Boy Pocket lay on the seat beside her, ignored on a day when real-world events were more riveting and terrifying. Or were they?

Gabi didn't feel terrified. If anything, it had all been exciting. After all, she didn't know Dory Michaels, and with the matter-of-factness of a child, she was more curious than scared. There, at the edge of the woods that marked the margin of the Haapala property, Gabi pictured a cougar lurking, watching, waiting. It made her spine tingle, but in the same way that a scary movie might. She didn't feel herself to be in danger, and was a little nettled at the restraints put upon her (don't leave the porch). Gabi wished she could go over to the Weeks' and talk it all over with Matt. She hadn't told him about the ravens, nor had she told him what the big raven on the hill had said, the one that flew close and dipped its wings: "More fresh blood!" Had Matt heard it too? She didn't think so, but she wanted to ask him — now. But he was probably grounded as well.

Inside, the phone had finally stopped ringing and Willie was going through the motions of preparing dinner. She would make a big pot of chicken and yellow rice, a favorite company offering that never failed to please. A simple one-dish meal, so fragrantly delicious that it would be hard for anyone to resist, in case anyone professed to be not hungry. The aroma of *arroz con pollo* would soon fill the house.

CHAPTER 22

BACK IN her upstairs bedroom Sybil Weeks latched her door. The old house didn't have locks on doors, but the room that had become Sybil's had been used as a guest room of sorts. The plank door never had hung quite squarely, and tended to swing open easily, so Rome Weeks had installed a hook and eye latch that afforded house guests more privacy. Later, when Sybil had taken over the room, she'd found the latch useful for barring her brother, and for keeping Blackjack, the raven, from flying freely through the house when he was out of his cage.

Her hands trembled with excitement as she carefully took the shaman mask out of the shopping bag and laid it on her bed. She could hardly believe her luck, and was having a bit of trouble breathing normally. "Look, Blackjack." She slid open the cage door to let the bird loose. With a squawk, the bird made a flapping leap and landed on the quilt.

Luckily no one had seen her bring the mask home — except Matt. Sybil had taken the shaman mask partly out of its bag, as if to make sure it was still there, when Matt had blundered in; Sybil had hastily taken it upstairs to her room, brushing off his inquiries.

Now, sensing that she stood on the verge of something vast, Sybil hesitated. She sat on the bed, ran her fingers over the wood, exploring the painted face for some sign. *Yaxagama, Ancient Mother, help me find the Loogy-Roo!* She leaned across to open the drawer in her nightstand, groped around and brought out a black object: a tuft of black feathers tied together with strands of hair — Gabi's hair. She fastened the tuft to the mask, knotting it loosely in place with one of the ties. *Yaxagama,* she murmured, then, swaying gently from side to side, she continued chanting: *Yaxagama, Yaxagama . . . bring your strength and bring your wisdom. Help me find the thing of evil.* To Sybil's blurred vision, the features of the big-eyed, thick-lipped shaman began to flow and streak like pigments being stirred into paint. She blinked and squinted as the expression on the face on the mask changed subtly. Now the eyes were more hooded, though still piercing, and the mouth twisted into what could have been a smile. The impression lasted only a moment, but it made Sybil gasp. She grasped the jutting horns on the forehead and opened the panels. Then, with a shuddering breath, she picked up the mask and raised it to her face.

CHAPTER 23

CHADWICK MICHAELS felt as if his head might explode. He needed an object for the rage that was coming up like acid reflux to burn his throat. He wanted to scream, to strike, to bellow — but at whom? At what? By god, he would find out who was responsible and yes, by god, he would make them pay and pay and pay! The government? It was the job of the government to keep its citizens safe. The RCMP? Wasn't it the job of the constable to keep them all protected? The town! The town had a lot of bleeding-heart animal lovers, didn't it? Yes, he could sue the community. It would be a safer bet than trying to take on Ottawa or the Mounties. He would find a way of suing the town. Dory. Poor Dory! But Dory was gone, and there was nothing to be done for that. So maybe he could formulate a lawsuit that would get them out of their financial difficulties. Something good could even come of this. He would have to try not to upset himself by dwelling on what had happened. He would have to force himself to move on. If only his head would stop aching. Had he taken his medication? He thought so, but maybe in all the excitement . . . had he taken his blood pressure pills? It was Weena's job to make sure he didn't forget, so it was her fault if he hadn't. A wave of emotion gripped him. Anger. Outrage. How dare this happen to *him!* How dare anything attack *his* family, *his* property, on *his* land!

Rifle in hand, he tramped through the bush. The gun felt heavy and awkward to carry. It was getting late. The men had fanned out into the woods but nobody had signaled a find of any kind. Constable Grant Hewett, Rome Weeks, Oliver Sylvester, Butch Westerlake, Veikko Kuusiniemi — armed with rifles — had volunteered for the search, combed the area, followed a few animal tracks, but found no cougar.

"Light's startin' to go. We might as well be getting back," Rome Weeks called to Oliver who was striding along few feet to the left of him.

Oliver Sylvester, a widower who lived on Kaunio Road, had been on similar hunts. "Yeah. With all of us trampin' around here, that animal's long gone. Probably holed up somewhere in them hills."

Butch Westerlake, a logger whose wife was the postmaster (she insisted she was *nobody's* mistress), walked out of the woods to join them. "See anything at all?"

"Nope. We was just sayin' there's no point going on with this anymore tonight." Oliver said. "Where's Schittle?"

Rome Weeks spat. "I dunno. 'Round here somewhere. Maybe he's with Veik."

Butch chuckled. "Don't think Veik would be hangin' out with him. Schittle's been making his life a misery. No love lost between those two."

"I can't say I've ever had any use for the man myself, but you gotta feel sorry for him now. Imagine losin' a kid like that." It was Oliver who spoke, a mild-mannered, white-haired worthy with the weathered skin of a lifelong fisherman.

"Yeah," Rome said, thinking of his own kids. "And until we find out what did this, nobody's safe. We need to organize a proper hunt. Make sure everybody stays out of the woods till we get that bastard. They say cougars won't attack an adult, but don't you believe it. A rogue cougar will attack anybody."

Another man emerged from the woods and joined the group — Veikko Kuusiniemi, the lighthouse keeper. The lighthouse stood on Windy Point, located on the tip of the left ear of the cat that was Broom Island. There deep water flowed through the narrows between the island and the mainland and served as a channel for cruise ships. Veik had manned the lighthouse for many years, but now he was thinking of retiring. With the children gone, his wife was finding it too lonely, particularly since Chadwick Michaels had bought the land adjacent, privatized the logging road that everyone had always used, and now denied access. Now visitors had to park outside his gate and walk along the cobbled beach in order to reach the lighthouse. Veik and his wife, Barb, had uneasy permission to use the road: they had to stop and open and close the gate; and if anyone wanted to visit them by car, they had to either get Chadwick's permission or take a chance on an unpleasant encounter with him.

"Guess you guys haven't found anything either," Veik said. "Constable Hewett just went back to radio his wife."

"Then it looks like we're all here except Michaels. " (Veik was the only one who always called him by his new name.) "Where is he, anyway?"

"We thought he was with you," Rome said. "Maybe he found the cougar — or vice versa."

"No such luck. I think I see him coming."

Chadwick Michaels was puffing, red-faced and out of breath. "So, here you all are. I thought you'd be out there tracking that cougar. What happened, you all get *tired?*"

The men exchanged glances as if to say, let's not react. Not now. Not today. "I think we pretty much covered the territory, and that cat ain't here," Oliver said. "I think we need to start fresh tomorrow."

"Cougars are cats, aren't they?" Michaels said. "They're nocturnal, aren't they? They hunt at night, don't they? So why can't we?"

"They do but *we* don't. Not legal to hunt after sunset."

"What the hell *is* this, some kind of a gentlemen's shooting party? We're out to destroy a killer cat, for Christ's sake!"

"Look," Rome Weeks said evenly, "A cougar's normal territory can be over a hundred square miles. On this island it could be anywhere. They're also good at staying out of sight. You hardly ever see one although we've got more of 'em here in B.C. than anywhere in the world. They hunt alone, day or night, and they see a hell of a lot better than we can. So unless you want eight feet and a hundred and fifty pounds of cougar jumping on your back in the dark and breaking your neck with a snap of its jaws, I think you should go home, get some food, get some rest."

"Yes," Oliver Sylvester agreed. "That cat's probably up in a cave in the hills or hiding in a thicket. Don't worry, we'll get him. But we need proper light. We'll go up past the quarry tomorrow mornin'; we're bound to find a sign. When we do we can track him."

"Well, if you pussies are afraid of the dark, then I guess there's nothing more I can do. But I'm going to remember this. And somebody, by god, is going to pay for all this. My rights and my property and my family have been violated and I expect compensation."

Veik Kuusiniemi had been looking at Michaels with open distaste. "Of course you do. But right now we *are* tired and I don't know about the rest of you, but I could sure use a drink before we all go home. What say we all meet at The Sea Hole? I'll buy the first round."

"You're on," said Butch Westerlake, then a bit reluctantly, "You coming, Michaels?"

"No." Michaels turned and stalked off ahead of them.

"City guy," Rome said. "Bet he's never hunted in his life."

"What the hell is that he's carrying — a .300 Winchester Magnum? He's loaded for bear." Oliver made a face.

"Yeah, but it looks brand new to me," Veik said. "Probably bought it when he moved here. Playing the country squire."

"Wonder if he's ever even fired it. Those things have hell of a kick."

They waited till Michaels was far ahead of them, then slowly followed.

"Poor bastard." Oliver said. "It's his wife I really feel sorry for. Hard to even imagine what she's feelin' right now."

* * *

At that moment, Rowena Michaels was feeling little pain. Danielle had made good on her promise of martinis, and a few stiff drinks had not only anesthetized Weena's grief, but loosed a dam of pent-up anger. She drained her glass and poured another from the pitcher. "None of this would have happened if it hadn't been for my crazy husband. Oh yes, crazy. *Crazy*. The man is a lunatic, Danielle. Oh, you don't know what I've had to put up with all these years. Him and his lawsuits and his symptoms and his medications. And *I'm* the one expected to see that he takes them. He's an alcoholic, you know. Takes Campral 666 three times a day. The Mark of the Beast! And fifty milligrams of Duh . . . Derysel. Derysel? *Desyrel*. Yeah. Once a day. And Toprol for his blood pressure. And Lami . . . Lamictal for his mood swings. And . . . and . . . . Effexor." Weena threw back her head and laughed. "Effexor. I don't even remember what the eff that one's for but he's supposed to take it once a day. The man needs a keeper and I'm sick and tired of being his nursemaid and his punching bag and bailing him out when he gets in trouble. Oh yes, Danielle, he can be abusive. When he's not medicated, I have to watch him like a hawk. And he's a liar and a crook and a f-f-f-financial drain. He was disbarred, you know. And it wasn't the first time he'd been in trouble. We've been moving around the country like reff . . . reff . . . refffugees."

Weena took a gulp from her glass and Danielle surreptitiously moved the martini pitcher out of her reach. "I think maybe we should have something to eat," she said. "How about scrambled eggs and toast? It'll only take a minute. And I'll make us a pot of good, strong coffee. I know *I* could use a good cup of coffee right now." As she chatted, Danielle picked up the martini pitcher and carried it into the kitchen. "You just sit there and relax a minute," she called through the open door. She eyed the near-empty pitcher. Danielle, herself, had had only one drink. "Or if you want to call Chad to let him know where you are, there's a phone on the hall table. You could tell him you're spending the night with me."

Rowena drained her glass, then put it down rather heavily. "I'm not calling that bastard. Let him stew. I don't think I'm ever going back there." Pause . . . no answer. "Danielle, did you hear me? I said I'm leaving that miserable sonofabitch once and for all. He can just go straight to Hell."

Danielle had been working with speed and precision. The coffee was perking. The nonstick frypan was on the stove ring with a pat of butter melting in it. She was vigorously beating eggs in a bowl. "We can talk about that after we've eaten," she called, chagrined by the turn of events. She'd hoped that a couple of drinks would allow Rowena a bit of respite, but Rowena was obviously unused to alcohol, and now Danielle was having to deal with a drunken, enraged woman babbling confidences that she knew Rowena would regret later — if, indeed, she remembered them at all. "Coffee and scrambled eggs are being served." Danielle stuck her head out the kitchen door, but Rowena had already fallen asleep on the couch.

"That's right, Weena, sleep it off. You're going to have a hell of a hangover tomorrow, but maybe it'll take your mind off the worst day of your life." She realized that now she would have the unpleasant task of calling Chadwick Michaels. She'd have to do it, of course. Maybe he wouldn't be home yet. Maybe Danielle could just leave a message on his answering machine. What would she say? "Hey, you sonofabitch, your wife is passed out on my couch and she says you can go to Hell." No, not that. She picked up the wall phone in the kitchen, then realized she needed to look up his number; she found it easily in the current Broom Island tourism brochure that listed campgrounds, B&Bs and an ever-changing roster of island businesses. She punched in the numbers, hoping for no answer.

"Hello!" The voice sounded angry.

"Chad, this is Danielle Herron, Weena's friend."

"She's not here," the voice cut in. "And I don't know where the hell she is. Call back later," he barked, and was about to hang up.

"Wait, Chad. She's here. Weena's with me."

"Well, what in the name of Holy Christ is she doing over there? You tell her to get her ass home right away. She's got no business running into town. How'd she get there anyway?"

Danielle fought the urge to hang up. "Chad, your wife is in a fragile emotional state right now. Surely you understand that. She should never have been left by herself. I brought her home with me, and she'll be spending the night here. I only called you so you wouldn't worry."

"The hell she will! What about *my* emotional state? She's *my* wife and her job is here, taking care of chores and fixing *my* dinner. Put her on the phone. I'll straighten her out."

"She's resting, Chad. I'm not going to disturb her."

"Then I'll tell you what you *will* do. You're going to tell her that her husband says to get her malingering ass back home, then you're going to get in your car and drive her back here. She better be coming through that gate in about twenty minutes or . . ."

"Or what, Chad? You'll sue me for kidnapping? Your wife is fine. She's staying here. Tomorrow she can decide when and *if* she wants to come back to you. You're a big boy, Chad. You can do your own chores and surely you can feed yourself by now." And then Danielle did hang up. I shouldn't have said that. The man must be overcome by grief. He just lost his only child. But, dammit. . . .

CHAPTER 24

GABI WAS idly watching hummingbirds at the feeder. They seemed a nervous bunch. One would fly in, perch, insert its long beak into a feeding hole and suck up a long draught. Another preferred to drink while hovering, voiding a squirt of warm clear liquid to splatter onto the wooden floor. They were females with greenish plumage and what looked to be a black dot on their white throats that would flash red when light hit it. They jockeyed around the feeder, sometimes occupying all the outlets, in a game of jittery musical chairs as they fluttered and fled and returned, yet seemed to be performing with a sense of cooperation. Enter a male, resplendently rust-colored, his gorget blazing, and all the females would flee. The male would settle in for a solitary, lordly drink — that is, until spotted by another male, who immediately bulleted in to give chase. Males gone, the females returned, and the pattern continued to repeat itself.

Gabi hadn't heard from Matt, and wished she could go see him. She thought of going down to the road to play with the cork fence, but if her mom didn't see her on the porch, she'd have a meltdown and make her come in the house. She had a momentary flash of resentment at the unmet Dory Michaels. Why did she have to pick today to get herself killed just when things here were starting to be fun! So many things had happened that Gabi felt as if she'd been turned inside out. Back home there were the nightmares, and days when all she did was get into trouble, as if someone inside her was trying to get out, and was beating against her skull from the inside. Here it was different. Here things were beating against her skull from the *outside*. Birds were following her and talking to her. Children were getting killed by cougars. And it was a magical, wild, place with different rules, and things to see and explore, not unlike a computer game in which you had to evade monsters that would gobble you up.

She hopped off the porch swing, leaving it to creak gradually to rest, went into the house and looked in the door at her mother who raised her head with a bit of a smile, relieved to see her daughter within the safety of walls. Gabi wandered into the living area where Jeremy was sitting in a leather recliner, reading a paper. As Gabi quietly curled up on the couch, Jeremy put down the paper and looked at her over the rims of his reading glasses. "Ah, Gabi. What have you been up to?"

"Nothing. I'm not allowed."

"Well, we'll have to think of something to do, won't we?"

"Can I see your telescope?"

Jeremy removed his reading glasses and tucked them into his shirt pocket. "Yes, I think so. Of course this isn't the best time to look through one, but I can show it to you. Later, when it gets dark, if the sky stays clear we might take a look at the moon." Jeremy got up with a bit of awkwardness. "Don't ever get old, Gabi, and don't go falling off roofs!" Then, loudly enough for both Willie and Celeste to hear, he announced, "Gabi and I will be upstairs. I'm going to show her my telescope." Celeste waved a hand in acknowledgment while Willie called okay from the kitchen.

Jeremy's telescope was a Meade LX10 Schmidt-Cassegrain, bought when he saw how little light pollution there was in the Broom Island night sky. It replaced his old Meade 8" SCT, and had a few more bells and whistles that would permit him to do slow motion astrophotography. Light enough to be comfortably portable (it only weighed 26 pounds), and powered by four AA batteries, the Meade boasted an equatorial wedge and control keypad to provide essentials for power-independent photography of the stars. Jeremy had already ordered the optional declination motor that would allow him automatic tracking. The secondary mirror in the reflector scope allowed a long focal length to be housed in a sixteen-inch tube. Sweet! He'd always wanted to photograph the heavens, and looked forward to fine-tuning the instrument, doing a precise polar alignment and collimation — as soon as he had the easy use of both hands. So far, the seeing conditions had been only fair. He had found a certain amount of turbulence in the atmosphere was causing distortion, but didn't know yet how these conditions would vary seasonally.

The telescope was set up pointing out the window in an unused room on the third floor from where Jeremy could easily take it outside and put it on the widow's walk. That gave him a vista of the sky above the ocean but was blocked by the house behind him — and that had caused what he thought of as Banks' folly.

"How did you fall off the roof? Did you try putting your telescope up there?" Gabi was studying the instrument, lightly running her fingertips over it.

"No, there wouldn't have been a level spot to set it up. I wanted to get a look at the Hale-Bopp comet, so I very foolishly tried climbing on the roof with my binoculars so I could see over the peak."

"Did you get to see it?"

"Briefly. I lost my footing and landed on the widow's walk. Luckily when I fell I missed hitting the telescope."

"Does your arm still hurt?"

"No. Not much. Mostly it just itches, and I'll be glad to get the cast off."

"How long do you still have to wear it?"

"Another week or so."

Gabi was looking into the eyepiece. "Can you see anything in the daytime?"

"Oh yes, when there's a planet in the sky you can often see it if the atmosphere is clear. And you can see things on the ground too. Here, let me focus in on that tree on the far shore." Jeremy looked through the viewfinder which presented an inverted image, then guided Gabi to look through the 25mm eyepiece in which the diagonal prism corrected the image but presented it left to right.

"Cool. I can see an eagle on a branch. Oops, he's gone now."

Jeremy adjusted the viewfinder again. "Now you can see Port Casper across the water."

Gabi looked through the eyepiece. "I can see the ferry with all the people. Can we look at the sun?"

"No, Gabi. That's something you never, *ever* do through a telescope. You never even point the telescope anywhere *near* the sun. The sun is so bright that it would permanently damage your eyes. You could go blind."

"Like Matt's sister?"

"Yes, or even worse."

"She can see a little. Matt tells me she's seen the Loogy-Roo."

Jeremy paused, then asked, "What do you think the Loogy-Roo is, Gabi?"

Gabi frowned, her smooth forehead puckering. "I'm not sure. First I thought it was just Matt. And I *know* it was Matt who chased that kid."

"Did he tell you that?"

"Not exactly, but I know it was him." Gabi raised her eyes to lock upon Jeremy's, and for awhile seemed to be taking his measure. Jeremy met her gaze and said nothing. She seemed to be trying to decide whether she could trust him. Then, apparently, she decided that she could, at least to some degree. "But I think maybe there *is* a Loogy-Roo."

"Why do you think so, Gabi?"

"The bird. He told me there would be more fresh blood."

Jeremy felt something akin to a pain near his heart. What could be so wrong with this pretty little girl that she'd have such morbid fantasies? He wondered if it could be just a game — perhaps a deliberate put-on — a practical joke played on an old man by a mischievous child. He hoped so! Well, if it *was* a game, he would continue playing: "How did that happen, Gabi? When did they tell you this? Was it when we were in the cemetery?"

"No, it was on the hill. Matt and I rode bikes. We went up the logging road to Dory Michaels' place. She wasn't home. Her dad caught us so I told him we had come to meet Dory, since she's my age."

"And that's why you went there?"

"No. But Matt said if Dory's dad saw us he'd yell at us so that's what I told him."

Jeremy smiled faintly. "Quick thinking."

"Anyway, a bunch of blackbirds showed up and Matt and I left. Then we went up the hill. There was a path to the top and Matt said you could see everything from up there. And we saw a big white ship. It was really cool!"

"And were there birds on the hill?"

"Just one. Big black bird. Huge. It flew up from the trees and circled over us. He told me about the fresh blood."

"Did Matt hear it too?"

"I don't think so. I think it kind of spooked him. He was in a hurry to come back down. I must have slipped. I got my jeans dirty. It's funny, but the place seemed different after that. We —" Gabi stopped, as if she thought better of what she was about to say. "I can't really remember what all we did, but I guess we got on our bikes and rode back." Gabi delicately ran a finger over her eyebrow. "Some of it was sort of like a dream."

"Do you have a lot of dreams?"

"I used to. But they were mostly bad ones."

"Can you tell me about them?"

"I remember the last one. It was about a man with a big knife thing who was cutting hay and there were lots of blackbirds in that dream too. Sometimes I dream of a fire. Everything's burning. I dream of birds a lot. And they're big and black and scary."

"A raven did give you a fright when you first got here. Could that be why?"

Gabi looked thoughtful, then sighed. "I've been dreaming of birds for a long time. They always used to scare me, but I'm not afraid of them anymore."

"Why do you think that is?"

"Because . . . I don't know. I just know I'm not. I can talk to them now and they can talk to me. I guess we know each other."

Jeremy was feeling that he'd come full circle. "Why do you think the birds are talking to you?"

Gabi chewed her lower lip. "I dunno. But it's sort of like they've *always* talked to me. Like I remember them."

"But you couldn't really remember them, could you?"

"No, I guess not. But I *do*."

***

Willie's call that dinner was ready brought them all into the kitchen. Although the atmosphere was subdued, the Spanish chicken and rice was so delicious that everyone except Celeste had a second helping. Of course the conversation, no matter how carefully they tried to avoid it, kept coming back to the tragedy. They were all harking back to the time frame of it, and Jeremy in particular, was listening carefully.

"It must have been around two o'clock or thereabouts," Willie was saying. "Weena and Dory didn't get back from Port Casper till the one o'clock ferry and it was late, as usual."

Celeste looked at Gabi. "And to think that you and Matt were out there. You realize that could have both been killed. You didn't get home till after four. Where were you all that time? At Matt's?"

Gabi nodded slowly.

"And you were filthy. What on earth were you doing?"

Gabi toyed with her fork. "We were just playing."

Jeremy was doing some mental calculations. Dory and her mother were not back yet when Gabi and Matt were at the Michaels' place. That must have before one o'clock, since Michaels hadn't yet gone to the ferry to pick them up. Gabi had said they'd ridden off, then climbed a hill to see the view. That couldn't have been any later than half past one, if that. "When did Mrs. Weeks get the news about Dory? You must have been at Matt's by then."

"I don't know. Matt and I were still out in the yard, putting the bikes away, and Mrs. Weeks came out and she was crying and told us something terrible had happened, and that she would call Willie and I should go right home. Matt asked his mom what was wrong and she said Dory had been attacked by a cougar, and that we had to stay out of the woods. Matt asked if Dory was dead and his mother just started to cry harder, so Matt said she must have been. That's when I came back here."

Jeremy was mentally reconstructing the afternoon: *It was about four o'clock when I was making tea and wondering where Gabi was, that Willie and Celeste arrived. Willie tried calling the Weeks and got no answer, because Kirsti was out in the yard with Matt and Gabi. And then Kirsti phoned and said Gabi was on her way.* There seemed to be a couple of hours of Gabi's day that were strangely unaccounted for. Where had she and Matt been between one-thirty and about three-thirty in the afternoon, allowing a half-hour for them to bike back? Had they come down the trail or had they biked along Kaunio Road? They evidently missed running into Willie and Celeste. Oh well, children lose track of time. They dawdle. Time is never of the essence to a kid. Or was there something else Gabi wasn't telling them?

CHAPTER 25

THEIR GUESTS tucked in for the night, Willie and Jeremy were spending a quiet moment together. After dinner Jeremy had kept his promise to show Gabi the rising half-moon as it came up over the water. Gabi had happily viewed craters through the telescope, but soon her eyelids had begun to droop, and it was clear that the little girl was ready for bed.

Celeste, who had seemed withdrawn and abstracted, begged off for an early night, whether to sleep or simply lie awake and think, she didn't know. Willie was rather glad to be able to connect privately with Jeremy. They were sitting at the kitchen table, nibbling slices of raw apple, a healthful bedtime snack. It was a scene of quiet domestic grace, but the troubles of the day hung over them like smog.

"What will be happening this week?" Jeremy asked. "Isn't there supposed to be a ceremony in remembrance of those who died in that fire? The article in the paper said that since the anniversary falls on Victoria Day, there would be an observance at the cemetery."

Willie sighed. "I don't know. I think Amanda Vuorisaari wanted to plan something, but I don't know if anyone will have the heart for it now. Everyone is much too upset, and piling one tragedy on another is the last thing anyone wants to do."

"I guess they'll be out tomorrow hunting the cougar. Is it legal to hunt here on a Sunday?"

"Yes, although the season is over. I suppose it would be proper to call in wildlife people from the mainland, but that's never the way it works here. There's too much emotion involved to rely on authorities. I hope Gabi is all right. Celeste tells me she's had problems, and I hope this doesn't make them worse. How did she seem to you?"

"Well, actually she didn't seem all that upset. She didn't know Dory Michaels so she doesn't have a personal connection. I guess I'd have to say Gabi is a strange child. She told me about her nightmares, and I've heard that many children do suffer from them. She also seems to live in a world of her own, and I don't think she lets anybody into it, at least not all the way."

"She seems very bright and poised for a child her age."

Jeremy laughed. "Yes. And she thinks on her feet. I understand she was able to handle Dory's father when he caught them on his property today."

Willie chuckled. "She might have a career in the diplomatic corps. She handled her mother pretty well too — the day she and Matt went exploring in the woods."

"Children seem to be more worldly and sophisticated these days. Should I make us a cup of tea? I'm not ready for bed yet."

"I'll do it," Willie said. "You sit." She got up to fill the kettle.

"Maybe that's why Gabi didn't seem to react the way I thought she would," Jeremy said. "I thought she'd be frightened, but I guess children today see violence and sudden death on the media all the time. They've probably become so desensitized that they don't even see a difference between the six o'clock news and a TV show."

Willie set out two china cups decorated with blue forget-me-nots and put a tea bag on each saucer. "Maybe to them, life is like a computer game. I just hope they find the cougar and put an end to all this. Right now nobody on the island feels safe, and we're not used to that."

"Do we positively know that it *was* a cougar that attacked Dory Michaels?"

"There's been no official word, and I don't know what the autopsy will show, assuming there'll be one. Dr. Swallow says it *was* an animal attack, although he said it could have been a wolf or even a dog. To my knowledge there are no bears on the island. There have been wolves and cougars from time to time. Technically, I guess the only thing we could maybe rule out is a Sasquatch."

"We'll have to keep close watch on Gabi. She tends to be adventurous, particularly when she and Matt are together, and she doesn't seem to have any sense of danger. I don't know what they were up to today, but we didn't hear all of it. She told me earlier, when we were looking through the telescope, that she and Matt went to the Michaels place, and after their encounter with Dory's father, they climbed to the top of a hill to look at the view."

"Oh, really? I know where that is. It's the highest spot on the island, and yes, there is a great view, but to get there, you have to take a logging road, then climb a path on foot. Her mother expressly told Gabi not to leave the road."

"Gabi said they saw a cruise ship and a big raven and then they came down and rode back home. But there's about a two-hour time discrepancy in her story. Those kids could have been running around in the woods all afternoon. We don't want that to happen again."

"It was probably all down to Matt Weeks. He's grown up in these woods and knows every inch of them the way kids always do. We'll have to make sure those two aren't left unsupervised until all this is over."

"How much longer will Celeste and Gabi be staying?"

"She hasn't said. Originally she was going to be here for a week, but now I get the feeling she'd like to leave as soon as possible. She's worried about Gabi. And she's also disturbed about her own family history. Too bad she had to dig all that up, but of course it's her right to know. Now I think she's wondering if the craziness of the Lemerriants is somehow surfacing in her daughter."

"Why would it? That was four generations ago, and every family has a potty relative or two somewhere."

"Yes, but family traits do get passed on. It's all in the genes."

The kettle was singing. Willie put tea bags into cups and poured boiling water on top. Jeremy watched silently, then asked, "Willie, do you think there is such a thing as genetic memory?"

"You mean like coded information in DNA that allows for the experiences of one generation to be passed directly on to another?"

"Yes. Normally the skills of a parent will be taught to a child, but could the child inherit such skills or knowledge in any other way?"

"It's an intriguing idea, and I'm sure we could all point to instances where it seems to be true, particularly with musical or mathematical savants. They seem to bypass the learning process and just instantly access information."

"I remember reading somewhere about experiments with flatworms and calves. They conditioned flatworms to curl up when exposed to a light. They cut them in two, each half grew into a new worm, and the bottom halves grew a new brain. Both halves reacted the same way to the light, even those with a different brain." Jeremy removed his tea bag and put in a lump of sugar.

"Flatworms would be a very simple life-form."

"They did an experiment with calves as well. They took calves born of stock that had been accustomed to cattle grids, but the calves had never actually seen one. Then they painted lines to simulate a cattle grid and the calves wouldn't cross them. How could the calves have known about grids?"

"There's a lot we don't know. It's always been magical to me how a tiny seed carries coded information to become a cabbage or a tomato or a tree. Memory is different. I can remember things clearly that happened fifty years ago, but I can easily forget what I was going to say in the middle of a sentence. I put it down to old-brain befuddlement, and I'd be a lot more worried about it if I hadn't always had that problem to some degree. I can forget your name — or my telephone number — or grope for a word that just keeps eluding me. As I grow older, it happens more often. And yet, there are things that are indelibly implanted. I can recite poetry that I learned in high school. But if I try to memorize a new poem now, I won't retain it for long."

"But what if genetic memory doesn't even involve the brain? If, say, a complete history of our lives is somehow coded in our DNA, we couldn't forget it, could we? And, as our DNA gets passed on to our descendants, wouldn't that information still be archived in there?"

"I would think so. But accessing it would be another thing. To do so, we'd still need to *use* the brain, wouldn't we? I was reading something recently about primitive tribes, hunter-gatherers, who would actually dream en masse, about where to find food. They were saying that what we call instinct played a greater part in the lives of early peoples who had no other form of communication. Even their language was rudimentary."

Jeremy looked thoughtful. "Animals are creatures of instinct. They don't have vocabulary as we know it. We call it instinct, but maybe they're acting on coded information when they migrate or return to spawning grounds or leave an area before an earthquake."

Willie silently sipped her Red Rose, then looked sharply at Jeremy. "What brought all this on?"

"Oh, I guess I was just wondering. Gabi and I were in the cemetery and a flock of ravens came in and they were wheeling around, you know how birds and fish do, all changing directions at the same time, and you wonder who gave the command?"

Willie was listening, half smiling. "And this has something to do with Gabi?"

"Uh . . . yes it does. I honestly didn't know whether to say anything because I'm sure what Gabi told me was in confidence, but I'm worried about her, too; she's too young to know what's best for her. Gabi is convinced that the ravens are talking to her, and that she can understand their language."

"*What?* Well, okay, what do you mean talking to her? Like a parrot would talk?"

"No, she says they're talking to her *in her head* and that the birds told her that there were two children buried in that unmarked grave in the cemetery. She said they'd been killed by a cougar and the birds saw it all."

Willie slowly put down her cup. "There *are* two children buried there, and they *were* killed by a cougar — a very long time ago — but you remember she said it was Matt who told her about that."

"It was the day we walked to town and stopped in the cemetery. Gabi walked over to a grave. It was the first time I'd even noticed that it *was* one. It's just a cairn of rocks overgrown now with grasses and weeds. She just stood there as if entranced and the ravens flocked around her. I thought after the incident in Pearl's that she'd be frightened of them, but she didn't seem to be. And, she told me the birds don't scare her anymore because, as she said, she *knows* them now. Later she told me that she could hear the birds and understand what they were saying. I don't think Matt told her anything, but when we started questioning her, she mentioned Matt just to put an end to it."

"And you believe her?"

"I don't think she's lying, although she may just be a child with a wild imagination. I was just looking around for some logical explanation. Gabi *is* a descendant of the Lemerriants. We've all heard the lore about their son who was supposedly able to communicate with animals. The ravens are probably descendants of those ravens. Could it possibly happen?"

"You mean the DNA of both ravens and Lemerriants is surfacing? Another question would be *why?* What possible purpose could it serve?"

"I have no idea, nor I think, does Gabi. She did say that the bird today told her someone would die."

"Good heavens! Where was this?"

"Up on the hill. She said a big raven flew past them and told her there would be fresh blood. And of course there was."

"That must have been terrifying!"

"I don't know. She and Matt were gone for a couple of hours after that. She was rather matter-of-fact about it when we spoke of it upstairs."

"Do you think we should mention this to Celeste?"

"At some point, I'm afraid we may have to. My inclination now is to just keep a close eye on Gabi, don't let her wander away, give her things to do, keep her focused. Maybe all of this will just sort itself out."

* * *

Willie lay awake a long time before sleep came, remembering that she, herself, had been about Gabi's age the night that Fidelia Brazeau had sought shelter in their home, and how Fidelia had cried and screamed and been so terribly frightened of things nobody else could see. Her father had said that Fidelia was drunk and suffering from delirium tremens. Willie's mother had insisted it was biblical: the sins of the father being visited upon the child. Genetic memory? Is that what the Bible meant? Could such a thing be possible?

And what of Gabi? Could she be carrying the Lemerriant history coded within every fiber? If so, could a drop of her blood or a strand of her hair contain not only that knowledge, but her own personal history tracing back to whatever her beginnings were at the very dawn of time? Do we all carry such genealogical records? Do we access them sometimes under hypnosis? That might explain memories of past lives, but if such records exist, they weren't readily available, were they? They would, Willie thought ruefully, be encoded in the DNA of brain *tissue*, but the functioning brain couldn't just call them forth. The brain, like a computer, could only access what was stored in its memory banks. Willie went on to extrapolate that then the tissue was smarter than the brain. And maybe, if all atoms and molecules are similarly coded, and if everything is made of the same basic stuff of the universe, composed, perhaps, of even finer particles than science has ever detected, then a computer wouldn't be a smart as the case that contains it! And (this was mind-boggling) if the minute building blocks keep combining and recombining to form all matter, each one would virtually not only carry our own history, but the history of the world, possibly the universe, stuffed into its tiny self. Knowledge, after all, takes up no space and has no mass.

Of course, a brain is not as limited as a computer. The brain has other connections, and *something* operates the brain. The mind? The part that survives? The part of us that is independent of the body? Willie thought of it as the divine connection. And through the divine connection, all knowledge is possible, if not always desirable. We have to focus on *this* life. If knowledge of all our past lives were constantly flooding in, it would be difficult, perhaps impossible, to function. Perhaps that's what madness is. Drugs can open floodgates that can engulf the user like a storm surge. Was some neurological agent, connection, or *glitch* causing Gabi to be assailed by information from the past? We balance rather precariously in our reality, and have little knowledge of what infrastructure lies beneath our Disneyland world. We don't even understand sleep. We think of it as repose. We fight against it. We resent the need of it and glorify the lack of it. It seems sort of lazy to us, and the alpha personality who manages to get by on four or five hours of sleep or less, is considered a real go-getter. If everyone in a position of authority would *simply get enough sleep*, the world might immediately notice a change for the better. And with that, Willie drifted off into hers.

* * *

Jeremy was wakeful too. He tried reading the *National Geographic*, but found it awkward to hold, so he turned out the light and closed his eyes — only to have them spring open again. His wrist twinged a bit — and would continue do so to some degree for the rest of his days in cold or rainy weather. The cast, thank god, was coming off next week. The first thing he would do is to take a good hot sauna and scour himself with soap and a wad of coarse nylon net — a curious ritual Willie claimed to follow, and which now sounded good. Meanwhile, he would try to think of other things. Focusing on the cast only made his skin itch.

Yes, indeed. Here he was, Professor Jeremy Banks, retired astronomy teacher, living on a remote island in the Pacific, a life totally different from his old one in Portland, Maine — one he had shared with his off-and-on companion of many years, Steven. Rest in peace, Steven. No, he didn't want to think about that now: his and Steven's life together — and Steven's death as result of AIDS. He wished he could just get to sleep, but thoughts kept intruding.

Gabi. Gabrielle Choate. He didn't know what to make of her. Jeremy hadn't had much experience with young children, particularly girls. Somehow this child had annexed him, and, albeit cautiously, made him her ally. Should he have told Willie about the ravens? Willie was a sensible woman who didn't overreact to things, and a good sounding board when he needed to work through an issue. She also had a quirky view of life that Jeremy found sometimes disconcerting, sometimes reassuring. He never really knew what to expect of Willie. She was into a lot of stuff — metaphysics, the study of dreams, meditation, even yoga. Since coming back to live on Broom Island, Willie had also embraced many forms of self-expression: gardening, handicrafts, art, and writing.

The only thing Willie was really tight-lipped about was her writing. She simply wouldn't discuss it. Not that she refused, but Jeremy had learned not to ask how the book was coming. He wondered idly whether she felt that talking about it might somehow jinx the project or scatter her focus. Whatever the reason, if asked, Willie would give a vague answer, change the subject, or zero in on some bit of technical detail that would send the conversation spiraling in an entirely different direction. "I'm glad you brought that up, Jeremy, because I've been meaning to ask you if you know anything about string theory. I need to research it." That, of course, would lead into one of their long discussions. Mind you, Willie hadn't said *why* she was researching it; she was just letting Jeremy assume it was for her book.

When it came to Willie's writing, Jeremy didn't know whether she would one day emerge with a thousand-page novel; or whether she simply didn't want to admit that she was suffering from the world's worst case of writer's block, and was spending her time playing thousands of games of Solitaire Till Dawn on her Mac. No matter, she didn't need to justify anything to Jeremy, or anybody. The woman was — and that was another thing — Jeremy didn't know just *how* old she was, but she had to be at least as old as he, and entitled to do whatever she damned well pleased in her golden years.

Confiding in Willie had been good. Jeremy might need her input when it came to Gabi, and he was more willing to accept the idea of genetic memory than to think that Gabrielle Choate, age ten, had gone mad.

* * *

Although Gabi had fallen asleep easily, Celeste had not. In the old days she would have gotten up and had a cigarette, but that was no longer an option. She didn't want to turn on the light for fear of waking Gabi, so she just lay in the darkness, thinking. She was not focusing on the tragedy, at least not the one that had just happened. She was, in fact, digesting some information that she'd come across in researching the Lemerriants.

Using Willie's Internet connection, she had put the name through search engines. At first the name brought forth nothing, but, in poking through genealogy sites, she'd come across other variations that had dead-ended her in a place in Bretagne with a family named LaMarianne. She tried "Meriant" and found a number of entries, but nothing that seemed to fit. In the process, Celeste began idly trolling through a site of early

French family coats of arms. There, in a succession of traditional lions and fleur-de-lis designs, one had caught her eye because it was atypical. The family crest was a black bird — raven or crow — rampant, a bit like the American eagle, a sickle clutched in one claw, the other holding a sheaf of wheat. At first it looked rather jolly, almost cartoonish, since the bird's beak was open and it looked to be laughing. But as Celeste studied it, it took on a more sinister appearance. The sickle was raised menacingly, as if it were a weapon, and the yellow heads of wheat were mottled with black. Now, was it her imagination, but was the laughter of the bird touched by madness? Beneath it, on a red ribbon were the words *Le Merle Riant.* The laughing blackbird. Celeste's high school French was sketchy, but could the name Lemerriant be a shortening and corruption? Interesting! She tried putting it through a search engine to see if it would bring up any information on the family, but lost her Internet connection. She reconnected, waited for the Turkey-in-the-Straw notes, then the buzzing whistle, got her connection back, only to have it fail again. (Willie later told her that that often happens, particularly in peak hours, when a lot of people are at their machines.)

But what was the rhyme that Sybil Weeks had shouted out? Something about laughing blackbirds and the Loogy-Roo. *Loup garou.* Was all this a coincidence? Celeste had supposed so, but it continued to intrigue her enough to try again later. Further research that evening brought up a period in early French history when a whole village had gone mad by ergot poisoning. Ergot was a disease of grain, particularly rye, but it also occurred in wheat and other cereal grasses. It was caused by a fungus, *claviceps purpurea*, that contains lysergic acid — LSD. It thrived in damp, cold climates. Bread flour, contaminated by ergot, caused vomiting, diarrhea, and hallucinations. It was connected with the Salem witch trials.

The black mottling on the wheat in the crest? Was that, perhaps, to symbolize infected grain? There was another related case in which a young boy, who suffered from ergotism, was convinced that he was a werewolf, and admitted to killed other children and eating their flesh. He ended up being imprisoned for life in a monastery, although no proof of his claims had emerged. She wondered what strange circumstances could have actually prompted anyone to consign such symbols (if that's what they were) to a family coat of arms, and vowed that once she got home to a more stable computer connection, she would do more research on the laughing blackbirds, whoever they were. She also idly wondered about her own ancestors whom everyone seemed to have considered to be mad. Could ergot have been a factor? It would be reassuring to think so! Better that than to conclude that her forbears had all been nuttier than trail mix.

It wouldn't be easy to unravel the past, and except for the tantalizing similarity in names, there was no evidence that there was any connection between her family and the family with the coat of arms. There would be a lot of digging to do, and she might run into a dead end, but it might even be worth a trip to France to poke through old church records. Meanwhile, as much as she now wished to remove herself and Gabi from this eldritch island, she was *here*. And if there was more information on *her* Lemerriants, it would have to be here as well. She looked over at Gabi, a small lump under the covers in the darkened room, sleeping peacefully (thank goodness!) — a sweet little flower on the Lemerriant family tree? Or a toadstool springing up from the mycelium that had also brought forth Brazeau and Fidelia and Elphique — and her mother, Madeleine, and herself. Celeste drifted off into a fitful sleep.

CHAPTER 26

Sᴜɴᴅᴀʏ ᴍᴏʀɴɪɴɢ dawned rainy with a blustery wind that peppered the roof with fir cones and littered Kaunio Road with leaves and bristly bits of evergreen. Willie, an early riser, was up before seven to check the seedlings in her greenhouse, and to make sure the plastic cover was still secure. One day she hoped to replace the old structure with a new one made of twin-walled polycarbonate, with a heater and a fan, and panels that open automatically for ventilation. Willie was picturing this as she opened the top half of a wooden Dutch door and propped it open by looping the waistband from a pair of old pantyhose over the handle and stretching it so that the other end caught on a nail on the outer wall.

The greenhouse had been built years ago by her father, and the fact that it was still standing was a tribute to his workmanship. The Dutch doors at both ends could be opened on hot days to provide a fresh current of air, or closed for warmth. The bottom half of the doors, when latched shut, barred most wildlife and wandering pets. The rounded, corrugated fiberglass roof, that had withstood wind and weather, leaked now, so Willie and Jeremy (before he injured his arm) had covered it with a sheet of plastic that would only be good for a single season. They'd anchored it with twelve-foot long two-by-fours laid lengthwise along the sides, but winter winds would rip it to shreds. No matter. The greenhouse wasn't heated; Willie didn't use it year-round. Next year she'd at least have a new roof put on it, if she didn't replace it entirely.

To Willie, her greenhouse was a place to meditate and chat with her plants. (Jeremy made gentle fun of her, saying that if Willie ever went away on vacation, she'd be sending them postcards.) Most of her seedlings were in the garden patch by now, and in another week or two she would plant the tomatoes that were growing tall and robust in their gallon pots. That would leave only the eggplant, green pepper, and basil — heat-loving plants that would remain inside and do their growing under plastic.

Willie checked to see whether anything needed water. Like everything else in her life, her irrigation system was freestyle: There were plants in five-gallon pots, in an organic medium — her own formula: peat moss, compost, vermiculite, greensand, blood meal, and phosphate rock. In the bottom of each pot were burrs from her chestnut tree (for drainage), a generous layer of horse manure (from a neighboring farm), with a wick threaded through the drainage hole — once again, a strip cut from the leg of the ubiquitous pantyhose — the fiber of a thousand gardening uses. The pot sat, on two wooden blocks in a dishpan of water, so that the wick could suck up moisture, while the blocks held the plant high enough so it wouldn't develop "wet feet." The eggplant and peppers seemed happy with the arrangement, and seasonally provided her with plump, delicious vegetables.

"Good morning, Hector," Willie said, this time not to a plant, but to the tiny greenhouse frog that was poised on a leaf, so nicely camouflaged, that it would have been easy not to spot its bright eyes looking back at her from under its little dark "eyebrow" stripes. There was also a resident garter snake that Willie would sometimes encounter on the wooden walkway; more than once it had slithered across her boot before disappearing through a crack between the boards. To Willie, these creatures were old friends, gardening buddies that kept harmful insects and rodents in check.

Everything seemed to be fine this morning. Later, in summer, when the weather dried and sea winds blew, watering would become a daily task, but not yet. The island climate was a good one for gardening — except for the forceful winds. The salmon wind, as the fishermen called it, the one they claimed brought a large catch, could stir the ocean to such murkiness that scuba divers, who normally found the waters clear and the sea life beautiful, had to make other plans. In winter, while the island rarely had snow, the winds whipped and bit; vicious storms could knock down whole sections of forest. Last winter, a mighty *whoosh* had actually blown the campground outhouse off its moorings and sent it toppling down an embankment onto the pebbled beach, and the hanging sign in front of the Co-op had come off its post and stopped just short of crashing through the store window. No sheet of polyethylene could live through that, even though Willie's greenhouse had some protection from the trees in front.

Time to go in and start breakfast. Willie headed for the house, walking briskly through the sprinkling rain, but noticing how lovely the air smelled, perfumed by lilacs that were just coming into bloom. She went in through the kitchen entrance, stepped out of her Wellingtons, left them on the boot tray in the mudroom, and slipped into a pair of comfortable slides. She could smell coffee!

Jeremy was up. The pot was perking, the table was set, and there was the smell of *pulla* toast. "I brought in a jar of your strawberry jam from the freezer, but I'm afraid it's still frozen."

"There's an open jar of lingonberry in the refrigerator," Willie said. I'll put that out too."

"Do you think Celeste and Gabi would like cereal — or bacon and eggs?"

"Why don't we just wait till they come down and ask them. Let them sleep in if they want to. They can probably use a bit of a lie-in. I thought I heard Gabi in the night. The coffee's done. You sit down and I'll pour." She took four slices of browned *pulla* out of the toaster oven, put them on a plate and left the rest to keep warm. "Kind of a nasty morning out there, but the plastic on the greenhouse is okay." She poured coffee.

"Not a good day for the cougar hunt." A rattle of rain blowing onto the window seemed to underline Jeremy's observation.

"It's coming down harder, but you know how the weather is on the island. It can change by afternoon."

"Well, anyway, we won't have to worry about the kids. They won't be roaming around on a day like this. If Matt wants to come over and play with Gabi, they'll be indoors."

Willie smiled faintly. Somehow the picture of Matt and Gabi playing sounded old-fashioned. Play. Play nice, don't fight. Go out and play. Can Willie come out and play? It sounded so innocent and so young. And, of course Gabi and Matt *were* innocent and young. And yes, of course they played, she supposed, but play nowadays seemed to involve technology. She wondered if kids played board games anymore: Monopoly, Parcheesi, Chinese Checkers — and made a mental note to see if she still had any of them in the house. There was always television (if the picture held in a storm) and movie tapes. Oh dear! How many movies did she have that would be suitable for children? She didn't think they'd want to sit through Jeremy's Charlie Chans. She'd have to check what, in her library, might be right for a couple of ten-year-olds. She wasn't used to children anymore. To be honest, she'd never been used to them *loose*. In a classroom situation everything was structured, and she hadn't raised any of her own.

Willie had gotten up to pour a second cup of coffee when Celeste and Gabi came into the room. "Good morning, you two. You're just in time for breakfast. Who wants scrambled eggs?"

"Thank you, Willie, nothing for me," Celeste said. "Just coffee, please."

"How about orange juice?"

Celeste looked pale and a bit frowsy. "I just need black coffee to jump start my brain."

"How about you, Gabi? Juice for you? Toast? And maybe some cereal. We have Corn Flakes or Rice Krispies."

Gabi had nodded at the juice and toast. "Rice Krispies, please," she said. Willie poured a cup of coffee for Celeste, set out Gabi's juice and cereal, then brought the mound of toasted *pulla* from the warming oven and set it in the center of the table.

"It looks like you didn't sleep well last night," Jeremy said to Celeste. "Was it the rain?"

Celeste took a swallow of hot coffee wishing she had a cigarette to go with it. "Oh, maybe it was. I kept waking up, and then Gabi had a nightmare, and afterwards I don't think I slept at all."

"I thought I heard something last night," Willie said.

"I'm so sorry if we woke you. I tried to be as quiet as possible."

"Oh, you didn't disturb us at all. I doubt Jeremy even heard you, and I was still awake, otherwise I don't think I'd have heard anything either," Willie fibbed. "It's a terrible day out there, and there's not much to do indoors. You could go back to bed for a couple of hours. So could Gabi, or if she's not sleepy, we'll look after her while you do."

"Thank you, Willie, but I'll be fine once the coffee kicks in. I never can sleep during the day." The fragrance of the *pulla* toast was tantalizing. Celeste reached for a slice.

"Try my uncooked strawberry jam with that," Willie said. "I think it's defrosted enough on top so you can spoon it out."

"So, Gabi, you had another one of your bad dreams?" Jeremy asked.

Gabi toyed with her cereal. "It was the girl singing. I couldn't sleep because she kept singing."

"What?" This came from all three of them.

"The little girl. She kept singing about a rainy day. Stuff that happens on a rainy day."

"That doesn't sound like a bad dream," Willie said.

"No. I was awake. I was going to get up and go look for her."

Celeste, who had been looking thoughtfully at her daughter, closed her eyes and shook her head as if to say, I have no idea what this is all about, but we've had so many disturbed nights, that this is just the latest spin on a long line of crazy stuff. "Willie, do you have any Ibuprofen in the house?"

"I'm sure I do."

"Thank god."

"Speaking of which," Willie said, as she came back with a bottle of caplets, "This is Sunday. The island pretty much closes on Sunday. I should mention that there are religious observances for those who would like to attend."

Celeste looked surprised. "Really? I thought the island was — well, you know."

"Communistic? Hedonistic? Atheistic? Actually it's quite complicated. In our little community there are three congregations. Mind you, they're all rather small, but they do exist. There's a group of Catholics, a few Lutherans who adhere to the conservative Missouri Synod, and then there's Circle of Light Evangelical Church, a rather loose group — loose only in that they're hard to define. They don't seem to adhere to any hard-line dogma. They welcome everyone. They love everybody. There's lots of singing and praising His name, and the witnessing is often done by various members of the group. The different groups hold meetings at ten o'clock on Sunday morning in various places. The Circle of Light meets in the town hall across from the museum. Charlie Peterman, who is a commercial fisherman, is the closest thing they have to a pastor, and his sermons, as you'd expect, involve a lot of sea metaphor. You want to go?"

Celeste pondered. She didn't, really, but wondered if it was expected. "Uh, are you and Jeremy going?"

Jeremy shook his head. Willie said, "I can't. I don't want to give

Charlie Peterman cardiac arrest."

Celeste laughed, relieved

"I have to live here," Willie went on. "If I go, it will establish a precedent. I'm not a Catholic so I don't have to worry about *them*. As a Finn I have roots in the Lutheran church, so technically that's the one I should be going to. If I were a religious woman, I'd probably opt for the Circle of Light because they seem the most benign. I can only sit in one pew at a time, so I've recused myself. However, as a visitor, if you'd like to experience the spiritual side of the island, you'd be a welcome guest. The Circle is the jolliest although their services tend to run long. And they serve coffee afterwards."

Celeste thought it over, but the Ibuprofen hadn't started working yet, and she really didn't feel up to it. "Maybe on another visit," she said. "I suppose the museum will closed today."

"Not as long as I have a key. Is there something specific you want to try to find?"

Celeste had quietly helped herself to another *pulla* toast and was putting strawberry jam on it. "This is delicious," she murmured. "No, nothing specific — because I don't know what to look for. Just anything at all on the Lemerriants. I'd like to know where they came from, and when they arrived on the island, and if they have relatives elsewhere from whom I might get genealogical data. I came across a strange coat of arms on the Internet that might even be a possible link to a family in France."

"Their name was Lemerriant?"

"It was *Le Merle Riant* on the family crest, which translates to the laughing blackbird. The crest was a black bird holding a sheaf of wheat and a sickle. I bookmarked the link; I can show it to you later."

"Interesting," Willie said. "Bit of a reach, genealogically speaking, but you never know. Tracing your roots can be more intriguing than a mystery story. We can poke around in the archives, but I don't know if we'd find more on the Lemerriants than we already have.

"We might have better luck talking to people who were here during their time. There aren't many of us left, and, as you know, the Lemerriants kept to themselves. But there are a couple of seniors who might remember something. There was a family that lived on the far side of their property along that old road that the Lemerriants used to transport logs and hay. Nobody lives there anymore. The road is overgrown. But one member of the family still lives in the village. She's in her late eighties. Her name is Ulla Kampsula. Mind you, I can't vouch for her memory, but sometimes we old people remember the past more clearly than the present. Of course I can't promise that she'll even want to talk to you. She suffers from rheumatism and can be a bit crotchety when her leg is acting up."

"Where would I find this worthy?"

Willie giggled. "Well, she'll probably be at the town hall attending the Circle of Light church service. Your best bet would be to go, be totally devout, sing every hymn, recite every prayer, and listen with rapt attention to anything Charlie or whoever may be speaking today has to say."

Celeste looked alarmed. "You'll go with me, won't you?"

Willie sighed. "Oh, yes, of course, I'll have to introduce you to Ulla. If we can all chat over a cup of coffee, maybe she'll have some reminiscences, particularly if I may tell her you're a descendant of the family. More coffee?"

"Yes, please. I think I'm going to need a large dose of caffeine in my system."

CHAPTER 27

DANIELLE HERRON was up early. She'd been awakened by a shutter banging in the wind and had gotten up to secure it. In her small bungalow on Kaunio Road, Danielle seldom had house guests; but this morning Rowena Michaels was still asleep in her tiny guest bedroom. It was Sunday, so Danielle wouldn't be opening the shop. She quickly showered and dressed, then made a big pot of coffee, knowing that it would be needed, although not knowing just what condition Weena would be in once she awakened. Hangover? Oh, yes, she'd have one of those! Better have the aspirin ready.

Danielle hadn't heard anything more from Chad, although she'd half expected him to arrive in her driveway to drag his wife back home. *Overbearing sonofabitch.* While most of the town was afraid of him, Danielle wasn't one to be easily cowed. Even so, she preferred to avoid the man simply because the very sight of him annoyed her. Rowena would be better off without him, and if she was serious about leaving him, Danielle would offer practical support in giving her a place to stay until she got her bearings. Of course, last night, it had probably been the gin talking. In the clear light of day, Rowena might regret the things she'd said, *if* she even remembered saying them. Danielle went to look in on Weena, thinking that if she found her asleep, she'd let her go on snoozing. If awake, well, she'd be needing that black coffee.

Weena Michaels was lying with her eyes closed, the back of her hand resting on her brow. She let out a low groan when Danielle approached.

"Good morning, Weena," Danielle whispered. "I brought you some strong black coffee. It'll help."

"I feel like I'd have to get better to *die*."

"Haven't you ever had a gin hangover?"

"No. Nor any other kind either." Weena's voice was hollow, and when she opened her eyes, she quickly closed them again.

"In a few hours you'll be just fine. It takes about twenty-four hours to detox. Now try to sit up and drink this coffee. I brought you some aspirin."

"Oy!" Weena carefully pulled herself up into a sitting position. "What did you put in those drinks?"

"It wasn't what I put into them, it's how many you had. Just keep drinking coffee, it *will* help. Trust me on this. Later you can take a shower. That will help too."

Weena was slowly making her way back to a reality that now seemed infinitely more painful than the hangover. *Dory!* She stifled a sob, then, looking startled, she asked "Does Chad know where I am?"

"Yes, he does. I called him last night so he wouldn't worry."

Weena stirred, as if to get up. "I've got to get back home. He'll need me. He never gets his medications straight without me, and he must be terribly upset."

Danielle put gentle hands on Weena's shoulders and pressed her back against the pillows propped behind her. "Now you just give yourself a little time. Chad is fine. He's a big boy. He can take care of himself. Besides, he may not even be home right now."

Weena leaned back gratefully and took another swallow of coffee.

Her hands were shaking, making the cup and saucer rattle. "Yes, they may be out hunting the cougar. They didn't find it and kill it did they?"

Danielle gently reached to remove the saucer, leaving Weena to grasp the cup more securely. "I don't think so. I'd have heard. You just take your time, let the coffee work, and if you think you can eat something, I'll fix you some dry toast. There's no hurry to rush home. I'm sure we'll get a call from Chad, and I'll be glad to drive you back when you're ready to go."

* * *

Chad, meanwhile, was cursing the weather — Rowena — the cougar — the townspeople — and the fact that he didn't know how to work the coffeemaker. He ended up with a lukewarm cup of instant as he made an attempt to sort out his medications. Goddam Rowena anyway, going off and leaving him at a time like this! Was he going to have to drive to town and drag her back by the hair? Was it two caplets a day or a caplet every two days? He tossed them aside. Let Rowena take care of it. If he suffered an attack it would serve her right. Yes, that bitch Danielle seemed to be in no hurry to bring her back, so now he'd have to go over there. He'd get even with Danielle Herron, by god. He'd drag her ass into court so fast on a charge of . . . of . . . well, he'd think of a charge. Right now he'd just have to go out in the downpour and — no, he'd *call* and demand that his wife be returned immediately . . . but who was that coming into his driveway? Rowena? It was damn well time . . . but no, it was somebody else — someone he didn't know in a Ford pickup truck. Annoyed, Chad opened the door and, from the shelter of the small porch, bawled out, "You looking for something?"

The man had gotten out and was walking towards Chad. "Mornin'! Guess I'm the first one here." He extended his hand. "Smithson. Eddie Smithson. And you'd be Chad Michaels."

Chad shook hands a bit gingerly, then stood back to allow the stranger to step in out of the rain. "I'm Michaels. What can I do for you?"

"Sorry for your loss," Smithson said. "The boys asked me to help with the cougar hunt. I understand it was you who found your daughter."

"Yes," Chad said uneasily.

"You want to show me where that was?"

"Now? Shouldn't we wait for the others?"

"Probably won't make much difference since this rain is washing away tracks and sign, but there might be something. I understand you had a dog, and he's missing as well, is that right?"

"Second dog we've lost in the past few weeks." Chad was wondering just who, exactly, this Smithson fellow was. He didn't look like a cop. In fact, with his somewhat misshapen cowboy hat and fringed jacket, he reminded Chad of an Indian scout — except for the neatly trimmed gray beard and moustache which made him look like a judge. And now that he looked more closely, there was something about the eyes that looked a little Asian; and the man either had a suntan or naturally dark skin. Maybe he *was* an Indian.

Reluctantly Chad pulled on a rain slicker and boots, then led the way past a campsite marker into the woods. "It was here. She wasn't far from the house."

There was nothing about the area, now trampled, that gave Eddie any clues. "Did she usually play in the woods?"

"No. There's a path she took to the school bus, but that's on up along the road. She'd had a scare. Said something chased her. I don't think she'd have gone in the woods."

"You think an animal attacked her and dragged her in here?" Smithson was watching Chad closely, trying to determine how much Michaels, as the bereaved parent, would be able to talk about all this.

"She was here, just laying out in the open."

"Was she covered at all with leaves or brush?"

"No. Would an animal do that?"

"A cougar would." Cougars cover their kill. When a cougar kills a deer, it will feed on it, then partially cover the carcass. Sometimes it leaves it for a few hours, maybe a day, then returns to feed again — if other scavengers haven't already devoured it." He couldn't bring himself to ask about the condition of the body, not directly of the father of the victim. "Did anyone hear anything?"

"My wife was home but she was in the greenhouse with the music on. She says she didn't."

"Cougars can kill silently. If it's any consolation, your daughter must have died instantly. But where was the dog? He must've been making a racket."

"I don't know. Turk would have tried to protect Dory. Maybe he ran off the cougar before it had time . . . time to . . ."

"Yes. That could be the case. And if your dog had an encounter with the cougar, it may have been killed as well. He may have tracked the cougar some distance. We'll look for signs."

The sound of vehicles in the driveway announced the arrival of more of the hunting party. Rome Weeks and Oliver Sylvester had ridden together in Rome's truck. They both got out, armed themselves with their rifles, then greeted Eddie Smithson as an old friend. "Hey there, Two Feathers, glad you could make it. I guess by now you know each other. Two Feathers here has been trackin' cats for most of his life."

Chad looked puzzled. "Two Feathers?"

"Yeah, that's Eddie's Indian name. He's Métis. When they made him a member of the tribe they gave him the name."

Eddie laughed. "It shoulda been Three Feathers but the bottle was empty."

Veikko Kuusiniemi rode in on his motorbike, and Butch Westerlake arrived in his Jeep. Chad saw that the men all seemed to know Eddie Smithson well.

"Have you had a chance to look around yet," Veikko asked.

"A bit, but the rain's washing everything away."

"It's lettin' up a little," Rome said. "Maybe we should fan out and look for tracks. What should we be looking for?"

"Tracks, scrapes, scent posts, scratches on tree bark, scat," Eddie said. "Although I don't think the cat will be around here. We should also look for traces of the dog. Track of a big dog and the track of a cougar can look a lot alike when the ground's been rained on, so if you find a print, try to cover it with something to protect it, and I'll take a look at it. Either way it'll tell us what's been out there."

"What's a scrape?" Chad asked.

"If you find a spot where the earth has been scraped into a pile — you know how a housecat will cover its scat with dirt. Cougars do it too but it's more of a territory marking for them. Means he's been around long enough to stake out an area. Cougar scat can be out in the open as well, and it looks about the size of dog scat."

"Then how the hell are we going to know the difference?" Chad asked. He didn't like being lectured, and he didn't like Eddie Smithson or Two Feathers or whatever he was supposed to be. He didn't like any of the others either. It was the first time that Chadwick Schittle Michaels had actually been in a group of men in which he could technically have qualified as being "one of the boys." His life had been one of one-up-manship and legal maneuvering, and being convinced that everyone was out to get him. He had no friends, only uneasy associations. Now here was a real threat, not from man but from animal — how elemental was that! — and here he was in a hunting party that was composed of men of a different stripe. They didn't like him either. Chad knew that. How could they? Nobody liked him. He wasn't in the business of being liked.

It crossed his mind that Veik, or even Rome or Butch (with whom he'd had altercations over the use of his road to move logs), might be tempted to settle a score. Hunting accidents happen all the time; he'd have to watch his back. He was tempted to pull out of the hunt or call it off — or just wait and go out by himself later. By god, he'd find that cat and blow its fucking head off. He didn't need a two-bit Two Feathers to tell him what to do. He, Chad Michaels, was the one supposed to be in charge of this hunt. He didn't need any of them. Bunch of pansies. He should have gone out last night before it rained. He'd have found that mountain lion and it would be dead by now instead of all of them standing here in the wet nattering about scat and scrape piles.

"It's usually dark if it's fresh, and full of hair and bone. It's more segmented than dog scat," Eddie was saying. "Old cougar scat turns white. A scent post is like a scrape except it's bigger and higher, built up with leaves and brush. Cat shits and pisses in it. Smells terrible.

"If we fan out, check for tracks and whatever else we may find, we may get an idea of which way it went. If we find nothing here, then I think we should drive over to the quarry. Every time there's been a cougar on this island, it's always been in that area. That and the lakeside. Be a good place to look for prints in the sand."

"Isn't Constable Hewett supposed to be here?" Chad asked. He felt he'd be safer in the arms of the law.

The men looked at each other. "I guess so," Rome Weeks said. "Did he say he'd be here?"

Butch shrugged, "He'll probably show up. I don't think we should wait for him, though. He'll find us."

"Did anybody actually tell him we'd all be here?" Chad asked.

"Oh, I'm sure he knows." Rome said, a bit too smoothly.

"Seems to me there should be some kind of procedure in place for this sort of thing," Chad persisted. "Shouldn't we be notifying Animal Control?"

"Of course, and I'm sure Constable Hewett will be doing that if he hasn't already." Eddie Smithson said. "Meanwhile, we'll see what we can find. Right now nobody knows for sure whether there even *was* a cougar. We're just going out on a fact-finding mission." Chad noted that Eddie was the only one not carrying a firearm.

"If you want to wait for Constable Hewett, it's okay by me," Butch said. "Go back where it's warm and dry. Get yourself a hot cup of coffee. Then when Hewett shows up you can show him which way we went."

Chad chewed his under lip. That might not be a bad idea. The eyes of the men were all upon him, and he just *knew* the minute he left they'd all be laughing at him. By god, he wasn't going to give them the satisfaction. Besides, this was *his* land, under *his* control, and damned if he'd let a bunch of strangers go tramping all over it unsupervised. He'd be keeping an eye on them, and if any of them did anything to infringe on his rights as the owner, there would be legal hell to pay. Besides, he wasn't going to be sent back to his room like a kid. "Hell, no," Chad said, and spat on the ground. "Just let me get my gun."

Butch Westerlake was smiling faintly as he watched Chad go into the house. "Sorry, guys, looks like we'll have Big White Hunter with us."

"Did anyone really tell Hewett about this hunting party?" Veik asked.

"Don't think so," Rome said.

"But the cougar, if we find it, we're going to shoot it, aren't we?" Oliver Sylvester asked.

"Only if it resists arrest," Rome said, and everybody laughed.

* * *

Willie parked her Cherokee, then she and Celeste got out and walked up the hill to the town hall. Celeste had hastily put on a denim skirt and blazer, the nearest thing she had to Sunday-go-meeting clothes, and wondered if she should be wearing a hat. Willie, who was also hatless, clad in a blue polyester pantsuit had assured her that there was no dress code.

The door was open and there was a small group inside, abuzz with conversation. As they entered, every head turned and every eye was upon them. Celeste felt as if she'd been pinned by a searchlight. Willie seemed to rather enjoy making a grand entrance, bowing, smiling, nodding, waving, as if she were royalty on a walkabout. They sat down on a couple of folding chairs, and Willie devoutly closed her eyes and bowed her head for a few seconds. Celeste, with her eye forever on the gatekeeper in unfamiliar social situations, did likewise. A sweet-faced, middle-aged woman with hair so wonderfully long, thick, and luxurious, and so tightly curled that it had to be natural, approached to greet them.

"How nice to see you here, Willie. Welcome to the Circle of Light." She reached out her hand.

Willie executed a warm handshake. "Hello, Hilda. I'd like you to meet my friend, Celeste Ooms-Possum. Celeste is visiting me for a few days. Celeste, this is Hilda Widjescoog. She lives in the village and runs Bloomers, the plants and seeds shop across from the ferry dock. You must stop in there before you leave."

"Oh, of course. You must be the writer who is doing an article on our little island." Hilda extended her hand but sounded just the tiniest bit guarded.

"I really feel privileged," Celeste said. "This island is so beautiful, and you must be the person responsible for all the lovely flowers and gardens I see everywhere."

Hilda smiled broadly. "Oh, yes, we do have a lot of enthusiastic gardeners on Broom Island. Mind you, we have our challenges with the strong winds and the deer, but otherwise it's a gardener's paradise."

"I would love to visit your shop," Celeste said. "I'd like to find a nice plant that I could take back with me as a souvenir. Something to remind me of all the delightful people I've met here. Possibly you could help me choose one and give me advice on the best way to care for it."

Hilda was beaming. "Of course! Of course! We open at ten-thirty, Monday through Saturday, and we're open till two. I'll look forward to seeing you."

Conversation had stopped as a tall spare man made his way to a lectern. Hilda handed Willie a couple of hymn books and quickly returned to her seat. Celeste assumed that this must be Charlie Peterman. Would it be *Pastor* Peterman? The man took his place in front of the group and Celeste found it difficult to look at him. Despite the rainy day, the light from the large windows behind him cast his face in shadow and caused a glare that was already producing eyestrain. Celeste blinked, then looked down at her lap. Willie passed her a hymn book.

Pastor Peterman seemed in no hurry to start the service. He stood, pausing perhaps for effect, then finally spoke in a low voice, greeting them all on "this sad occasion." Celeste realized that today, in any church, the service would be about the tragedy that was Dory Michaels. To begin with, there were a few announcements. The Sweet Notes, the island band, had canceled practice this week. The hazardous materials ferry sailing had been changed to Wednesday. And, due to the threat of cougar attack, it was important to remind all islanders stay out of the woods, and make sure that their children and pets were not allowed to wander freely until the situation has been resolved.

At that point, Pastor Peterman left the lectern and sat down. Two young women with guitars took his place and began to sing. They played well and their voices were sweet. The hymns of praise were unfamiliar to Celeste, and, as she listened, she allowed her eyes to wander around the group. There were only about twenty people present, and she wondered which one might be Ulla, the woman she had come to meet. Ulla Kampsula, Willie had said, and corrected her pronunciation when Celeste had given it a rhyming sound: *Oola Campsoola*. The correct pronunciation didn't rhyme at all, since the stress was on the first syllable, and came out more like *Kampsla*. There were four or five elderly women, any of whom might have been she. One had a cane by her chair and appeared to be weeping. Celeste was touched by the sight of the careworn old matriarch, who had led an exemplary life of hard work and family responsibility, staunchly adhering to the faith that had sustained her through life's tribulations — or so Celeste mentally cast her as a character in a story — a woman of patience, dignity, accepting the will of the Lord — weeping, perhaps, for Dory Michaels, or because she was affected by the beauty of the hymns, or in a larger sense, allowing her tears to fall for the sins of all mankind.

The girls had stopped singing and one was announcing that they would all now join in hymn number 19, "Let Us All Praise Him." The congregation burst into song, accompanied by the guitars. This was followed by another hymn, "Come to the Cross," then another, "The Sunshine of His Love," and yet another, "Blessed Message from Above" and . . . and . . . and. . . . The singing went on and on. Celeste, who had made a valiant attempt to join in, found herself becoming a bit muddled as the hymns, by now, were all sounding alike to her. Not a religious woman, Celeste had only been in church a few times in her life; usually when some well-meaning friend had invited her to go and it would have been rude to refuse. She'd usually found the experience bewildering.

Celeste surreptitiously glanced at her watch; they'd been sitting there for nearly an hour. She looked at Willie whose eyes were riveted on the hymnal, herself looking every inch the proper church-going matriarch. Well, Willie had said there would be a lot of singing, and Celeste had just about concluded that the service would be conducted in song. It was, after all, rather sweet and innocent: the little flock praising its creator with the same joy and spontaneity of birds greeting the dawn, with no threats of hellfire or eternal damnation. One more hymn, "Thy Day Is Ended, Thy Soul Flies Home" finally concluded the service — Celeste hoped.

She was beginning to feel uncomfortable, and wished heartily that she'd never had that third cup of coffee. Her eyes roamed the room, looking for a reassuring door with the word, "Ladies," but didn't see one. Well, church services usually last an hour, and Celeste hoped she could stick it out — but she'd have to find a washroom before she met with Ulla.

Pastor Peterman was returning to the lectern. Celeste awaited the closing prayer; but instead, the good pastor proceeded to offer a sermon. He talked at length about the tragedy of Dory Michaels being cut down before her life had even begun to flower, and that we cannot always know the ways of the Lord, or why He would have needed to call her home at such a tender age, but that we must trust in His plan for us all, for none of us knows which day may be his last, anymore than a fisherman knows what storms may beset him at sea. He followed that with a lengthy anecdote of one of his own experiences, when God delivered him from dangers of the deep — and then another — and another. Celeste suddenly realized who Pastor Peterman reminded her of: Ben Stein. He spoke in a school slide-projectionist's monotone, rarely changing inflection, and since Celeste couldn't see his face because of the glaring light behind him, she pictured him as the comedian who had appeared as Mr. Cantwell on the TV series, *The Wonder Years*.

She shifted in her chair and glanced again at her watch. And now, unbelievably, she was even beginning to *smell* coffee — and even hear the sound of a percolator — which only made her plight more desperate. Glancing around, she could see that behind her, in a corner of the room, a table had been set with a white cloth, cups, paper plates, cakes, cookies, and the ubiquitous *pulla*. Of course, Willie *had* said there would be a fellowship period afterwards at which coffee would be served. The service must nearly be over, but could she wait any longer? She gave Willie a slight nudge. "Is there a ladies' room?" she whispered.

Willie gave a nod in the direction of a side door and murmured, "Through there and down the hall on your right." Celeste gave her a questioning look. Willie nodded: "It's okay. Go." Celeste tried her best to leave unnoticed, glad she'd been sitting in the back row. Pastor Peterman and the flock had just closed their eyes for the final prayer as Celeste slipped away, doing her best to open and shut the door without making a sound. Nobody seemed to be paying her any attention, so why did she still feel that everyone was watching her?

By time Celeste returned, the congregation was singing a closing hymn, once again accompanied by the girls with guitars. Were they sisters? They looked alike with their long, strawberry blond hair, full lips, and big blue eyes. The women on Broom Island, Celeste had noted, were remarkably good-looking. She had seen some truly stunning long-legged blondes, and everyone seemed to have a beautiful head of hair.

She'd idly wondered it the fish diet had anything to do with that.

Celeste seated herself gratefully. Now they could go on singing until their voices were hoarse as far as she was concerned, but the service had finally come to an end. People were getting up, drifting toward the coffee table; some, with more pressing matters to attend to, headed for the door, waving cheerfully to friends, exchanging parting comments. Willie steered her to a woman seated next to the wall, near the coffee maker. It was the old woman with the cane — the one who had been weeping. Indeed, she was still drying her eyes with a large white handkerchief. "That's Ulla Kampsula," Willie murmured. "We should just meet her now, and ask if we might drop by and visit her at her home later."

"Isn't she in the Seniors' home?" The woman had seemed to have trouble walking.

"No, Ulla lives in the village. She still has a house there, and if she's willing to talk to us, it'll be better to do it without the distraction of people around."

Willie approached the woman, smiling, "Ulla, how nice to see you. How have you been? You're looking well."

"Uh, Villie, I'm okay I guess. It's just mine ice. Dey keeps vatering all the time, specially de left one. Drives me crazy." Celeste noted that while she certainly spoke English, it obviously wasn't her first language. The flattening of "th" into a "d" and transmuting "w's" into "v's" was typical of a Finnish accent.

"I'd like you to meet my friend, Celeste. She's visiting me for a few days."

"Oh, de vriter. Yes, I heard you vas here. I hope you didn't have any trouble vit the toilet. It sometimes don't flush."

"Uh . . . no, it was fine." What in the world could she say next? Should she call her Ulla or struggle with the name, Kampsula, which she knew she'd still mispronounce. "It's nice to meet you, Ulla," she said, shortening the "u" and lingering over the "l" sound, as Willie had done to make it rhyme with *pulla*. "Willie told me you've lived here a long time. She said I should talk with you because you are really the most important person in the village, and everyone considers you to be the mother of the community."

Willie gave Celeste a glance that said, nice going! Ulla smiled, pleased but a bit surprised. "Really? De mother of de community. Vell, I suppose in a vay I am. I been here a lot of years. Seen lots happen. Sit down and let's have a cup of coffee." She moved her cane and leaned it against the wall, freeing two folding chairs. Willie filled styrofoam cups and met requirements for cream and sugar.

Ulla fixed Celeste with a look. "So, you are one of the Lemerriant family, huh? I thought dey vas all dead."

Now it was Celeste who was surprised. Apparently the whole village knew who she was, why she was here, and when she had to go to the bathroom. "My grandmother was Fidelia. I didn't even know that, myself, until recently, so I don't know much about my family."

"Hmph. Nobody knew much about *dat* family," Ulla said. "Dey vas the neighbors ven ve had the farm, but not friendly. Not friendly at all."

"I was hoping you might be able to give me some information about them, anything at all would help. Anything at all that you might remember."

"You have a little girl," Ulla said. "Is she crazy too?"

"What?"

Ulla shrugged, "Vell, I hope not. And you seem okay. The Lemerriants vas all *hullu,* crazy as loons, at least that's vat everyone said." She dabbed at her watering eye.

"Why *was* that?" Celeste asked. "What did they do that made people think they were crazy?"

"Vell, for one ting — " Ulla stopped talking as an elderly woman approached. The woman nodded at Willie and Celeste, then addressed Ulla. "You about ready to go? I have to get home to fix lunch. My daughter is coming."

Ulla shifted her bulk and reached for her cane. "I gotta be going now. Grace, you know Villie, of course, and dis is her friend, Celeste. Grace Maddox, mine neighbor. She gives me ride to church. Can't valk as vell as I used to." Grace looked curious, and for a moment was torn between having to leave and wanting to stay.

"Oh, please," Willie said, "*We* can give Ulla a ride home." She turned to Ulla. "You can sit and enjoy your coffee, then we'll drive you back."

"Oh, okay," Ulla said. "I go vit them. Tanks, Grace. I see you later." This was working out better than Willie had expected.

"So you were saying, about the Lemerriants," Celeste prompted.

"I vas saying dey vas a bunch of cuckoos. I vas just a kid back den, but dat old man vas terrible. Used to drink like a fish and, drunk or sober, he vas a mean old sonofabitch."

Celeste half-smiled, thinking she'd have to revise her devout matri-arch impression. "Have you any idea of where they came from, or when they arrived on the island?"

"I dunno much about dat. Only ting I might have is old pictures. I vas about a year older dan Elphique. I had camera. If you like, you come to mine house and ve look."

* * *

Gabi had been left at home with Jeremy who had assured Celeste that he wouldn't let her out of his sight. But Gabi had seemed edgy, even a tad unruly, nervously pacing and quickly bored by any activity Jeremy suggested. No, she didn't want to watch television. No, she didn't want to play games. All she seemed to want to do was look out the window at the rain and hum a little tune. Jeremy ruefully realized that he was experiencing the frustration of a parent whose child was housebound by weather, and wished he could think of something that would keep her cheerfully occupied.

Gabi, herself, finally came up with the answer: "I wish I could go see Matt. Can't I go over to Matt's house? I'm sure my mom would say it's okay."

Jeremy knew that Celeste would say no such thing. "Why don't we call the Weeks and see if Matt can over here for a while. We can invite him to lunch."

Within the half-hour, Matt arrived, looking a bit disgruntled at being accompanied by his rained-upon but relieved mother. "They get so restless when they can't go out and play," she said, giving Matt's hair a swipe to slick back his wet forelock. "You be a good boy, now," and then, to Jeremy, "Call me when he's ready to come home. I'll come pick him up." Matt rolled his eyes.

"Please come in, Mrs. Weeks, and have a cup of tea," Jeremy offered.

"Another time, Professor Banks. Sybil is by herself, and I'm going to fix her lunch. Rome is out with the men, hunting the cougar."

"I guess they haven't found it yet?"

"No word from anybody so far. This weather would make it hard. Anyway, thank you; it's good to get Matt out from under my feet for a while. He can still be a handful in rainy weather."

Gabi and Matt had already settled themselves in the living area, and seemed to be having a quiet conversation. Jeremy left them to it and went into the kitchen to see about lunch.

"I hate rainy days," Gabi said. "I wish the sun would come out."

"That would be even worse, because they *still* wouldn't let us go outside."

"Do you think they'll kill the cougar?"

"My dad says if there's a cougar on the island, they'll find it and kill it."

"I'm sort of glad we didn't run into it yesterday," Gabi said, for the first time acknowledging that yes, they could have met with danger. "Did you tell your folks what all we did?"

"No. Did you?"

"No. Well, I did tell them about going up the hill and seeing the ship and the raven."

"And that's all?"

"I said we came back down and rode our bikes home."

"You didn't say anything about going to the lake or the quarry? Or coming home on the trail instead of the road?"

"No. My mom would kill me."

"It was shorter even if we had to push our bikes most of the way."

"And you were all wet."

"It was your fault I fell in the lake. You knocked me over. You're not supposed to stand up in a boat."

"*You* were standing up."

"You're not supposed to stand up when anybody else is standing up."

"You looked pretty funny falling over the side."

"And you looked pretty funny rowing around in circles."

"And you looked pretty funny shivering and turning blue. What did your mom say?"

"She didn't notice. I guess she was all upset about Dory. I sneaked up to my room and changed clothes. Sybil looked right at me but she can't see that well."

"My mom made me take a shower."

"You didn't say anything about . . . anything else, did you?"

"You mean about all the birds following us?"

"Yeah. That was kind of creepy."

"Yeah." Gabi lapsed into silence. It had been weird, the way she'd wandered through the woods with Matt trailing behind her, like she'd been showing him the way. And everywhere they went, the birds followed. It had been kind of fun, like visiting an old playground, but it had also been . . . she wasn't sure what. And then they'd decided to try out the dingy. It had been Matt's idea. Gabi sighed. It had been a strange afternoon. . . .

Matt sat quietly, looking thoughtful, then shrugged. "You got any good tapes? We can watch a movie."

Gabi went over to the shelf of movie tapes and began looking through them. As she flipped through the titles, she was, again, humming to herself.

"What's that you're singing?"

"Oh, some song about a rainy day. Some kid was singing it last night and keeping me awake. On a rainy daaay, on a rainy daaay."

"It's a school song. All about stuff you can do on a rainy day. Matt started singing: *On a rainy day*

When the skies are gray

There is a lot that you can do

On a rainy day.

"Yeah, something like that."

Matt resumed: *You can play a game of darts.*

You can cut out paper hearts

You can bake some cherry tarts

On a rainy day.

"That's not what she was singing last night."

"There's lots more to it, but it's just a song we sing in school. Dory Michaels used to sing it all the time."

CHAPTER 28

Celeste had used her cell phone to check on Gabi, and had been told that she and Matt were busy watching *Charlie Chan in the Feathered Serpent* while Jeremy was making pancakes for lunch. All seemed well.

She and Willie had eased Ulla Kampsula into the Cherokee, Willie making mental note that her next car would be lower to the ground. The SUV had been great for moving her stuff to the island, but it seemed like too much car now, especially since she rarely traveled.

The village only had three streets: First, Second, and Third; and Ulla's house was nestled into the middle of the block on Second. Willie parked, helped Ulla disembark, then waited for her to open her gate which was kept shut by a wire looped over the fencepost. The house was surrounded by tall wire fencing, and the height of the gate had been extended by an additional piece of fence wire in order to bar the island deer.

Ulla's was one of the earliest homes in Satama, a small wooden frame building that had been repaired and added to. A short flight of wooden steps led to the front door that opened on a small porch, with its row of windows crowded with faces of flowering houseplants, looking out. Ulla, however, led them past a bank of tall rhododendrons — a wall of red — around to the back, where a longer flight of wooden steps led up to a porch that had a roof and railing but was otherwise open. It overlooked the back yard which, in itself, was a showplace of trees, plants, and blossoms. The area under the porch sheltered a woodpile, and a rough wooden door gave entry to what must have been the cellar.

"This is beautiful," Celeste said, looking at the masses of flowers, their colors heightened and brightened by the rainy day.

"I don't keep it up like I used to," Ulla said. "Gettin' old, I guess. Kid next door cuts my grass now. Haven't been able to reach de rhodos to deadhead them."

"Doesn't seem to matter. I've never seen anything like them."

"Ven I moved here, I didn't know nuttin' about rhododendrons. I put dem all too close. And after mine husband died, and the boys vas grown, I vorked as a cook in logging camps. Not alvays home to look after flowers."

"They're magnificent." Celeste watched as Ulla started up the steps with aid of her cane, and wondered why she didn't use the front door.

As if in answer, Ulla said, "Gotta exercise dis leg. Can't baby it. Needs to last as long as I do."

They entered a tiny living room with a kitchen alcove. It was cheery and spotless, with the clutter of a lifetime in family photos, knickknacks, arts and crafts. There were also a number of framed photographs on the walls — seascapes, a pair of eagles, lovely close-ups of flowers. A small black iron stove with a stack of wood next to it offered the promise of heat when needed. A wall clock ticked. There was a television ("Mine kids seem to tink I need TV set.") but the crocheted linen cloth on top with one lacy corner overhanging the screen gave the impression that it was rarely turned on.

"You have a lovely place here, Ulla," Celeste said. "So peaceful."

"Yah, I just like to sit here in de evenings and look at de vater. I can see ferries from here. Kids keep telling me I should move to Vancouver and live vit dem, but I don't vant to. Dis is home to me. I hope God takes me before I have to move. Sit, sit, you two. I'll go get my albums. Probably dusty. Haven't looked at dem in years."

Ulla returned with an armload of albums, shuffled through them to find the beginnings. "Ve came from Finland 1921. I vas eleven. Older brother and sister both died of Spanish flu. Just our parents and younger sister left. Ve got a piece of land and Papa built, first, a sauna, and ve lived in it vile he built de house. All gone now in forest fire."

"Were the Lemerriants already here when you came?"

"Not sure if dey vas already on de island or not, but I remember ven they moved next to our place."

"Were they a French-speaking family? Did they speak any English?"

"I guess dey spoke both. Yes, I know Lemerriant spoke English but vit heavy French accent. He sold hay to English and to Finns. His vife spoke some English too."

"Do you have any idea where they came from? Were they originally from France?"

"I don't know. But I tink dey moved here from Northern Ontario. Place named Looteri."

Celeste was scribbling notes. "How do you spell that?"

Ulla chuckled. "That's vat Finns call it. Looteri, but it's L-o-w-t-h-e-r. In Ontario. Mind you, vas lifetime ago. I only remember it because dere vas Finnish family here from Kapuskasing, dat lived in Looteri. Dey tried homesteading, but it's too damn cold up dere. Maybe dat's vat the Lemerriants did too. Dere vas talk dat dey came from Looteri."

"So they came here and moved into that place in the woods?"

"At de start dey lived in town, and seemed pretty much like anybody else. I tink the boy even started school, but den ven they moved into de voods, de father decided he shouldn't go no more."

"But that would have been against the law, wouldn't it?"

"Oho, de law. Yes, of course, *law*. Law didn't go near Brazeau

Lemerriant. Anyvay, tings got vorse. Dere vas stories. Brazeau beat de kids, beat his vife. Nobody could go near de place. He'd shoot you as quick as look at you." Ulla dabbed her watering eye with a Kleenex.

"Did you get to meet Fidelia and Elphique?"

Ulla's expression was enigmatic. "I vas probably de only one. Elphique, poor kid, he had terrible life vit that father of his, and other kids used to tease him. A boy vas killed by cougar, and de story got around that Elphique had something to do vit dat. Kids chased him, trew rocks, called him names. And, after a vile, he just started acting like a vild animal. Mama felt sorry for him so she vould sometimes leave food for him on a stump. I used to put it dere, den hide and vait for him to come, and try to get picture vit my camera. Dat vas de year I got de Kodak Box Brownie for Christmas." Ulla chuckled. "You know, I still have dat camera." She got up and left the room, then came back with a small black box.

"Here it is! It vas my pride and joy. It took roll of film, number 124. Original price vas four dollars, a lot of money, but Papa got it used, made a trade for it. Pictures of Elphique didn't usually turn out. Not enough light in de voods, or he moved too fast." Ulla laid the camera on the table, and began leafing through her album.

Celeste looked at the camera. Primitive technology! The film winder was slightly discolored by rust; the coarse grained leatherette cover was worn through on the corners and seams. A short, shabby carrying strap lay snug against the top, held on by a couple of pins, each flattened on top to keep the strap from popping off, but the elongated holes in the leather allowed enough play so you could get your fingers under it. Two viewfinders let you take a vertical or horizontal photo. The shutter was a small bar that moved in a slit, and the lens was a round opening. A couple of tiny latches could be unfastened in order to pull the cover off the camera. However, given a roll of number 124 film, it would probably still work as well as it did in the 1920s. Cost? Four bucks, new. And here were the pictures, still viewable. Celeste thought ruefully of how the slides taken at her own wedding had already deteriorated and been discarded.

"Dere," Ulla said, "dat's Elphique." She pushed the album over to Celeste.

Celeste eagerly looked at the black and white print with white border and ragged edges. It was only about four inches high and two wide, but in it a young boy was standing by a stump and looking into the camera as if in defiance. He was dressed in misshapen clothing that he seemed to be growing out of — the pants and sleeves were too short — and he had a knife in a sheath on his belt.

"Did he ever talk to you? Did he know it was you who left the food?"

"I tink he knew. I tried to talk to him once. He didn't say notting, but he vasn't scared of me and I vasn't scared of him neither — not *den*. After vhile he grew big and den everybody vas scared of him. Den ven two more boys vas killed, people started saying it vas Elphique, and dey started calling him Loogy-Roo and making up stories about how he vas eating raw meat and drinking blood. Dey vas saying he could turn into a volf or a bear or anyting he vanted. Kids carried coal and rocks to trow at him. And dey had their chant:

Bevare de laughing blackbirds
Ven you're in the vood
If dey don't stop laughing,
Trow a lump of mud! I remember kids used to skip rope to it in schoolyard at recess."

"Do you believe Elphique did any of those things?"

"No. I don't tink so. It vas just crazy talk. Elphique just tried to survive best he could. Dey said he could talk to animals — and vhy not? I talk to animals all de time. Dey said birds used to follow him. Vhy not? Dey knew vhere food is. Birds aren't stupid."

"Did you get to know his sister?"

"I don't have picture of her. She vas kept home. Once or tvice she came to our place trying to run avay. Dey always came and took her back. It must have been hell for dem kids."

Willie, who had been silently following the conversation, nodded. "Yes, I remember Fidelia came to our place once, although we lived farther away."

Ulla sighed. "Didn't do no good to run. Dey always brought her back and den Brazeau beat her. She told us he said he vould to kill her if she came back to our place. Maybe dat's vhy she vent to yours."

"What about Brazeau and Dauphine? Did you ever talk with them?"

"No. I vas a kid. They vas grownups. Grownups live in one vorld, kids live in other. But I tink I got a picture once." Ulla thumbed through the album again. "It vas haying season, and dey vas on edge of de field, and I vas in voods vit my camera like alvays . . . here it is . . . no, dat's not it. I vas hiding because I didn't vant them to see me. Brazeau didn't vant anybody snooping. It vasn't safe for any voman around Brazeau Lemerriant." She peered down, dabbing at her eye with a tissue. "Here! Dat's the only picture I ever took of Brazeau and Dauphine."

Celeste's hand was shaking as she reached for it. At first it was a bit of a shock. What had she expected? They were an *ordinary* looking couple. Brazeau was bearded, wore a tattered hat, and was holding a scythe. He was a muscular man, not particularly tall, but with powerful arms and shoulders. Dauphine, wearing a cotton dress with the sleeves rolled up, was bareheaded, squinting in the sun. She would have been pretty, Celeste thought, but her life had stamped her features with an impassive hopelessness. The thing that made the picture interesting was the wind. It had been blowing on that long ago day, stroking the hay like an invisible hand, loosening wisps of Dauphine's hair and molding her dress to her thin body in front while the long skirt billowed out in back. It pushed up the rim of Brazeau's hat, threatening to peel it off his head.

"This is wonderful picture, Ulla," Celeste said. "I'm so grateful to you for letting me see it. Would it be possible for me to have this photocopied while I'm here? Would it be asking too much to let me borrow it for a while?"

"No. Photocopies not vorth the powder to blow dem to hell. But you can keep it. It's your family. You can have Elphique's, too."

"Oh, Ulla. These are part of the history of the island. How could I possibly . . ."

"I'm an old voman. Ven I die pictures vill end up in *garbitsa*. Kids don't know who dese people are, and dey'll toss them avay. You can have dem vit mine blessing."

"Are you sure? Wouldn't the Historical Society want them?"

"Maybe, but de boys von't bother. One's a trucker, de other vorks for a plumbing and heating company. They von't be interested in old pictures of strangers. Dey'll dump the lot, I know. Dey belong to you by right anyvay."

"In that case, thank you. I'll take them home, scan them to my computer, and then I'll enlarge them and I'll send you copies that you can give to the island museum if you wish. You're a good photographer, Ulla. Did you take all the photographs I see on your walls?"

"Oh yes, I take. I like to take pictures all my life. I don't anymore because I don't see so good as I used to, and mine damn ice alvays vatering."

Celeste was holding the snapshot of Brazeau and Dauphine, gazing into it. "Ulla, what do you think happened on the night of the fire?"

"I may be one of few left who remembers someting. It vas terrible. People can act crazy. De town had been like de storm coming on, ever since de two boys vas found dead. Brothers. Sons of Eesti Linna. He vas Estonian. His vife was dead. Boys grew up kind of vild. Maybe it vas accident. Dey vas out in de woods. Maybe one fell off de bluff and de other tried to help, but both vas found at de foot of de cliff. Looked like cougar kill. De father, Eesti, vas strange after his vife died, and he put up dat grave of rocks. No inscriptions. Didn't vant the devil to know vhere his sons vas buried. Soon after, he shot himself in de quarry. But dere was dis . . . dis fear and hate bubbling like stew. Poor Elphique. Nobody vanted to come out and say he's de killer, because it vould make dem look foolish. But in back of people's minds . . . *in back of people's minds* . . . all de old fears and superstitions from de Old Country can still fester. Nobody admits, but I tell you dat people are no different today.

"Papa vas one of de first to go to the Lemerriant farm dat night. He said Dauphine vas killed in de barn. Stabbed in de throat vit de pitchfork. Brazeau vas shot in de back. Elphique vasn't there, because he vas already dead in de fire. Dey found Fidelia hiding in de root cellar."

"What about the fire? Who started the fire?"

"It must have been Elphique. Or maybe it vas accident."

"So did Elphique kill both his parents?"

"I don't tink so. I tink Brazeau killed his vife."

"Did Elphique then come home to find his mother dead — and did he shoot his father?"

"Dat's vat everyone tinks. Elphique ran into de village, I guess to get help or maybe he just panicked. He ran into de town hall. There vas meeting going on, and he busted in on it. He probably vasn't making any sense, yelling and screaming, and looking scary. People tought he vas crazy, and started to chase him. He ran, like he alvays did, for safety, and it must have been to de kitchen. There vas vomen in dere making coffee, and kids running around. Dey say it vas de coal oil lamp. Maybe Elphique knocked it over, or maybe he trew it. De building vas made of raw logs and dey had shrunk enough to leave spaces in betveen so air could blow. It vent up like a campfire. There vas no firefighting equipment handy."

Celeste was trying to picture the events. Elphique did not run away from a mob that was chasing him; he ran *into* the mob at the meeting house. Elphique happened to come home at the precise moment that his father had killed his mother, and shot his father through the back. Then, instead of hiding in the woods, he ran into town. Why would he do that? Was he overcome by remorse? Was he just being wild and crazy? Was he in a state of shock and hysteria?"

"Ulla, did Elphique often go into the village?"

"No. Ve never saw him in de village."

"Did Elphique carry a gun?"

"Brazeau vould never let Elphique have gun. Elphique hunted, but he set snares. He used hunting knife."

"So if he shot his father, he must have been at home already, and he must have used his father's gun. Why would he go rampaging into the village?"

"I don't tink he shot Brazeau. I tink he found both parents dead and, like kids now say, he freaked out."

"So then you think Elphique *didn't* shoot his father?"

"No. I alvays tought it vas Fidelia."

CHAPTER 29

Back at the house, Celeste and Willie walked past Gabi and Matt who were sitting on the floor in front of the television set and laughing uproariously. They found Jeremy in the kitchen, reading a paper.

"What on earth are those kids watching?" Celeste asked.

"Right now they're watching *The Gods Must Be Crazy* on tape. They *were* watching Charlie Chan. They seemed to be enjoying it, although they were finding it funnier than I remember. At first they thought there was something wrong with the color on the TV set. I had to explain that old movies were made in black and white. Have you two had lunch? I could make you something."

"Oh, no thank you," Celeste said. "We had coffee at the church after the service."

"I'm fine too," Willie said. "They had sandwiches and cake and *pulla*." Not that she or Celeste had actually eaten anything, but she didn't feel hungry, and apparently Celeste didn't either.

"Celeste, I *do* have a scanner. If you like, we can use it to enter those photos on computer. I know you're eager to see them enlarged. You'll want to see these too, Jeremy. Ulla Kampsula actually had a couple of pictures that she took of the Lemerriants years ago. I didn't think any existed."

Jeremy folded the newspaper and got up. Willie noted with a bit of amusement that Jeremy was becoming more relaxed. There had been a time when he'd have leapt courteously to his feet when a woman entered the room.

"The children seem to be occupied," Willie said, at another burst of laughter from the *pirtti.* "We'll take the photos into my office and get them on screen."

The picture appeared on the monitor about four times its size and was clear and distinct. Enlarged to full screen size, it began to pixelate a bit but still retained surprising definition.

"What kind of camera was she using?" Jeremy was studying the photo.

"Box Brownie," Willie said. "Remember them?"

"Oh yes, I used to have one."

"To me, it's just so ... well, I guess I'm blown away at seeing my own great-grandparents on a computer screen. And now I have to digest this latest information. What Ulla told us makes more sense than the other stories we've been hearing."

"What did she tell you?"

"She thinks that Brazeau killed his wife, and that it wasn't Elphique, but Fidelia, who shot him in the back. She thinks Elphique came home to find both his parents dead, and that he just lost it and went ranting into the village. He ran into the town hall. There was a meeting going on. They must have thought Elphique had gone raving mad, and there were some, at least, who blamed him for the deaths of the children. They chased him into the kitchen where a lamp got broken and started the fire."

"Did she have any idea of why Lemerriant would have killed his wife in the first place?"

"No, she didn't. But I think I might guess."

Both Willie and Jeremy looked at Celeste in surprise.

"Fidelia was pregnant. Dauphine probably found out, and she knew that Brazeau had to be the father. She confronted him. He probably didn't know about Fidelia's pregnancy until his wife told him. He flew into a rage and stabbed her with a pitchfork. Fidelia could have heard the scream, picked up her father's gun, and gone into the barn. She may have witnessed Brazeau standing over Dauphine's body — and fired. She then dropped the gun and ran away and hid in the root cellar. I would bet that the root cellar was a familiar hiding spot for Fidelia."

"But everyone thought Elphique killed his father." Willie said.

"Yes, and since he was dead, there was no need to investigate further. If anyone knew better, they weren't saying."

Willie looked thoughtful. "If that's what happened, it was probably self-defense. At that point Brazeau might have killed Fidelia as well. She could have fired a shot, then run away, not knowing whether Brazeau was still capable of coming after her. Perhaps he tried, since his body was found outside."

They were now looking at Elphique's photo onscreen. He looked a little like an animal at bay, glaring into the camera, his hand hovering over the hilt of his knife.

"It was rather brave of Ulla to take these photos," Jeremy said.

"She's quite a lady," Willie said. "She had very little formal education, only a couple of weeks of nomad school in Finland. She married and was widowed young, left with two boys to raise and no money. By then her parents were dead, and her younger sister had married and moved off the island. She turned her hand to any work she could find, and managed to keep a roof over her head and feed her sons. She did washing and ironing, took any part-time job that was available, grew vegetables for sale in her garden, picked salal in the woods, harvested mushrooms, cooked for loggers."

"She never remarried?"

"No." Willie laughed. "We talked about it once. You know, she was a stunningly beautiful woman in her youth, and she certainly had her offers when she was widowed. I always thought she looked like Marlene Dietrich. But she told me that she really didn't want any more men in her life. She'd had a husband, raised two boys, and she said it made her *tired* to love, honor, and obey. Men, she said, always need something from you. She had to cook for them, clean up after them, and on top of that they seemed to need to be adored. She said she'd rather go it alone, and that it was nice now, not to have to worship and admire anybody."

Celeste laughed. "When I first saw her, I thought she was the poster woman of proper religious devotion. Then, in that wonderful accent of hers, out slipped a few words that labeled her more as a woman of the world."

"Oh, Ulla can speak fluent logging-camp if you get her riled."

"But she *is* religious, isn't she? Circle of Light?"

"Ulla Kampsula is one of the most spiritual women I've met," Willie said. "But although it's become a cliché, there *is* a big difference between religion and spirituality. She once told me she likes the Circle of Light because they're not always rattling the keys to heaven in her face. And now that she doesn't get out as much anymore, she likes the fellowship after the service. She said it's a good place to get a cup of coffee and catch up on gossip — and she said she likes to look at the pretty girls and listen to them sing."

"They certainly are pretty! I've noticed that there are a lot of really beautiful women on this island. Must be the gene pool. I saw a tall blonde going into the Co-op who could easily be Miss Finland. And everyone has wonderful hair — and some rather startling hairdos."

"Ah, you must have seen Pauliina Ukkonen. She wears it pulled up on top of her head, caught in a rubber band so it sprays down like a fern."

"Yes, and it looks great that way — on her! And there's a very lithe older woman who jogs along Kaunio Road. She has long, thick, white hair that streams behind her. She wears a jogging suit and looks like a superheroine."

"That's Rosemary Gray. She's heavily into fitness. She used to have a little health food shop on the island, but it's closed now." Willie was about to turn off her Mac, then hesitated. "If you like, you could print these pictures up for Ulla on my Hewlett-Packard."

"Thanks, Willie, I may do that, although I think I'd like to use my PhotoShop application to clean them up, adjust the brightness and contrast. You don't happen to have PhotoShop do you?"

"No, but I do have GraphicConverter, if that's enough."

Celeste paused, listening. "You know, it's gone awfully quiet out there. I wonder what the kids are up to."

Willie turned off her computer and they all went into the living area where they found Gabi by herself, sitting cross-legged on the couch.

"Where's Matt?" Willie asked.

Gabi looked up sullenly. "He went home."

"Did his mother come for him?" Jeremy asked.

"No, he just went."

"Why?" Celeste asked.

" 'Cause I told him to."

Jeremy was already on his way to the door. "He's not supposed to go anywhere by himself. He knows that. I'm going after him to make sure he got home all right." He shot Gabi a reproachful look; Gabi guiltily dropped her eyes.

"So what happened,?" Celeste asked. "Did you two have a fight?"

"Uh . . . sort of," Gabi mumbled.

"What on earth about?"

"He thinks he knows everything."

"What does he think he knows that would make you send him home, Gabi? He's not supposed to be out by himself anymore than you are."

"It's not far. He'll be okay."

"Nevertheless, when you are the hostess, you should not be rude to your guest and tell him to leave. That is not acceptable behavior. You need to call Matt and apologize."

Gabi sighed theatrically and rolled her eyes. "Okay, Mom, I will."

"So what was the fight about?"

"I told him somebody was going to get killed."

"What?"

"He didn't believe me. He just got mad and told me to shut up."

"Is that all you said? That somebody would be killed?"

"Well, maybe I did say it could be his dad."

Celeste was shocked almost speechless. "Gabi, how could you say such a thing? That was horrible. It was vicious and mean and hurtful — don't you realize that? How would you like it if somebody told you *I* was going to be killed?"

"But you're not."

"And I'm sure neither will Mr. Weeks, but it was just a terrible thing to say to Matt. I just don't understand you, Gabi. I . . . I . . . don't know what to say to you."

Willie had been listening to the exchange and watching Gabi closely. "Gabi, what made you think Mr. Weeks is any danger?"

"He's out hunting the cougar, isn't he?"

"Yes, I suppose so, but that doesn't mean he's going to be killed. In fact he's with a group of his friends. I'm sure the only one in danger is the cougar, if they find it."

"That's not what *she* said."

"Who?" Celeste's voice was beginning to crack. "Who said it, Gabi?"

"The singing girl."

"*What* singing girl?"

"The girl who woke me up singing about a rainy day."

"You mean the nightmare you had?"

"I wasn't asleep."

"Be that as it may," Celeste said, exasperated now, "but can you tell us exactly what you thought you heard?"

"Well, she was singing softly at first. All I could hear her say was "On a rainy day." Gabi sang the line. "And then she was singing louder and I couldn't really understand the words except for the rainy day part.

And then She sang, "And a man with a gun will be shot on a rainy day."

Celeste was struggling between incredulity and relief. "Gabi, listen to me. Even if you actually heard what you thought you did, it means *nothing*. You never should have said what you did to Matt. There's no reason to think for one moment that it has anything to do with Matt's father. If you heard the song at all, you probably didn't hear it correctly."

"Matt said it was a school song. All about things to do on a rainy day. Stuff about baking tarts and paper hearts."

"There, you see, Gabi. You probably heard someone sing it somewhere and it stuck in your mind, and when you had the nightmare, you only thought you heard it."

"Matt said it was Dory Michaels' song. She sang it all the time."

"Well, it couldn't have been Dory singing because she's . . . well, just think about it Gabi. A man with a gun will be shot on a rainy day? That's only what it sounded like to you, but it could have been something else, like how it *can* be *fun* to be *out* on a rainy day. Don't you see, Gabi, that *couldn't* have been a line from a school song! You *couldn't* have heard it right."

Gabi was staring at her sneakers. "You think you know everything, too."

"No, Gabi. If I knew everything, maybe I would know what to say to you. I was hoping that things would be better. Right now I think you need time out to give some thought to what you've done and how hurtful it was. Then you need to call Matt and say you're sorry. When you're ready, I'll get him on the phone for you."

"I know how to use the phone."

"The one in my office has the number on speed dial under Weeks." Willie gave Gabi a reassuring smile.

Gabi went. Celeste shook her head. "I'm at my wits' end with her. At first it seemed she was so much better — here — on the island. But now it's starting all over again."

"Would it help to talk about it?" Willie asked gently.

"It seems to come from nowhere. She seems like a normal ten-year-old and then, out of the blue, I get a call from her school that she's attacked another child, or she's had a screaming fit. Once she even broke a window — threw a chair through one, in the cafeteria."

"Did she ever say why?"

"It always started with her getting into a fight with another child. Okay, kids get into fights, I suppose, but this behavior wasn't typical of Gabi. She'd never been violent; she never even threw tantrums. I took her to a doctor to see if there was anything organically wrong with her, but they found nothing abnormal. Of course they suggested a child psychologist, then a shrink. Best they could do is prescribe medication. We tried that, out of desperation, but I don't think that's the answer. The idea of drugging a child into docility seems monstrous."

"And you think there might be something in your family background that might shed light on Gabi's behavior?"

"It was worth looking into. Now, of course, I find that we're both descended from a family that was so unbalanced that they killed each other off. It's not reassuring. And the things Gabi said to Matt were just — well — demonic. She obviously didn't care how hurtful that must have been."

"You know, that may be a clue. Gabi is too young to understand the meaning of the word 'edit.' A child blurts. Is it possible that Gabi may have been telling the absolute truth about the singing she heard? I mean, just entertain that idea for a moment. What she actually heard or didn't hear doesn't matter right now. She *thinks* she heard a girl's voice singing, and the line she heard was that a man with a gun would be shot on a rainy day.

"Okay, she tells us that, and of course we do our best to talk her out of it. We try to convince her she didn't hear it. But Gabi knows, or thinks she knows, what she heard. And maybe this isn't the first time. Is it possible that something similar may have started her school fights? Did she go over to some other child and utter some terrible prophecy?

Did that start the brouhaha?"

"I don't know. She never exactly told me."

"I'm not a doctor or a psychiatrist, nor do I even necessarily believe either would be helpful here. However, there are thousands of people who have paranormal experiences — too many to ignore or pooh-pooh. They often appear more vividly in childhood, when the young mind is unprejudiced, but usually they are either ignored or suppressed as the child grows older."

"You think Gabi might be psychic?"

"I don't know. I do know that there are cultures in which psychic ability is not only recognized, but welcomed and honored. In ours it isn't. Among the Plains Indians they had their place in society, as they often do in so-called primitive tribes. In early Finland, psychic ability was well-known, and sometimes regarded as an affliction, like any illness, and that it could be cured by witchcraft. It's nothing new. We, on the other hand, live in a materialistic age in which any deviation is unacceptable. In Tibet, when a lama dies, a search is made for an incarnation. A child is found, and if he meets the tests, he then becomes accepted as the new incarnation of the lama. To us this sounds charmingly deluded because, in our arrogance, we assume it to be impossible."

"Do you think Gabi could be a reincarnation of one of her ancestors?"

"I think that the theory of reincarnation is more complicated than just being reborn into another body, but I do believe that Gabi is being assailed by *something*. There may be open pathways in her brain that are normally closed. In some people this happens naturally, others follow a discipline that develops it, and some have it thrust upon them when they use hallucinogenic drugs. We tend to dismiss 'hallucinations' by labeling them as such, but there hasn't been much actual study done except categorizing them as good and bad trips. Drugs can destabilize the personality. Gabi's ability, if that's what it is, seems to be natural to her."

"But why would that make her lash out the way she does?"

"Think Helen Keller. There was a woman of remarkable intellectual gifts trapped in a body that closed her off from the world. How frustrating that must have been! Before her teacher took her in hand, Helen Keller raged too. At ten years old, a child takes life as she finds it. She has no yardstick to measure against. If she sees visions, she assumes everyone does. Then when she finds out that that's not true, and then is told that *she* doesn't see them either, it must seem an outrage. A young kid doesn't question her own sanity they way we might; she questions *yours*. And if she finds that you overreact, or disapprove, or negate, she either defends her position or goes underground."

"And you think that's happening to Gabi?"

"Maybe she's learned it's not safe to talk about it."

"So what would that mean? Is she going to become a crystal ball reader? Does her future lie in a circus tent?"

"She may simply outgrow it. Most of us do. We vaguely recall the imaginary friends of our childhood, or we rewrite our own history to exclude any such experiences."

"And if she doesn't outgrow it?"

"Then she will learn to direct and control what may be an enriching gift. We are sent into this world with tools for living. That may be one of hers."

"Well, right now she's driving me crazy."

Willie laughed. "I'm sure Annie Sullivan said the same thing about Helen Keller."

* * *

Jeremy rang the Weeks doorbell. He hadn't seen Matt, but the boy had had a head start. Kirsti opened the door. "Professor Banks, come on in. Has the rain stopped?"

"Thank you." Jeremy stepped inside and took off his shoes, as he'd learned was the custom in Canadian houses. Unfamiliar to him, as an

American, was the Canadian worship of floors, that made you either tote a pair of slippers or walk around in socks. Neither he nor Willie observed the practice in Willie's house (unless they'd been walking through mud), but on a day like today it made perfect sense. "It's letting up. Now we're getting intermittent drizzle. Did Matt get home all right?"

"Oh yes, thank you. He's upstairs."

"I'm sorry, Mrs. Weeks, I should have kept a closer eye on him. He and Gabi were watching a movie and seemed to be having a good time. Then they must have had a tiff because Gabi said Matt had suddenly gone home. I followed as soon as I found out."

Kirsti sighed. "Kids, eh? It's the weather. They always get antsy when it rains. It's like there's something in the air. Sybil has locked herself in her room. I couldn't even get her to come out and eat lunch. Now Matt has done the same thing. I guess they're both upset about Dory and the cougar and, well, we all are, aren't we? Would you like a cup of coffee, Professor Banks. I just made a pot in case the hunters get back early."

"Please call me Jeremy. And yes, I'd love one."

"And you call me Kirsti. No need to be formal with neighbors."

"Have you had any word from your husband yet?"

"No. They're probably still out in the woods. I made sandwiches and coffee for them so I hope they found a dry place to eat lunch. Rome doesn't have a cell phone so he can't call. We'll just have to wait to see if they had any luck."

"How many are out there?"

"Half a dozen, I guess. There's Rome, and Oliver Sylvester, Veik from the lighthouse, Butch Westerlake — and Chad Schit — uh — Michaels, of course. And Rome said they'd invited Eddie Smithson to come along. He's a Métis from Alert Bay, and he's tracked cougar all over BC."

"Sounds like they'll be able to handle it."

"Except for the rain. Rain messes up tracks and makes hunting a misery. More coffee?"

Jeremy opened his mouth to say, "No thanks, Kirsti, I should be getting back," when both of them were transfixed by a piercing scream.

Kirsti gasped "Sybil!" and ran out of the room. Jeremy followed her up the stairs where Kirsti tried Sybil's door to find it latched on the inside. "Sybil! Open the door!" No answer. "Sybil, it's mama. Are you all right? Open the door."

"Should I try to break it down?" Jeremy asked.

Kirsti shook her head. She reached up over the doorframe and grasped an ordinary kitchen knife. Pushing slightly on the door, she inserted the blade into the crack and shoved it upwards. The hook slipped out of the eye and the door flew open. Matt had heard the commotion and appeared in the hall.

They all trooped inside and found Sybil in a heap on the floor. She seemed to be having convulsions. Blackjack, the raven, flew up at their approach and landed on the dresser. There was a carved and painted Indian mask lying on the floor, as if dropped or thrown. Kirsti knelt by her daughter. "It's all right. It will pass. She'll be fine."

To Jeremy it was clear that everything was not fine, and he waited to see if he'd be asked to call the doctor. Kirsti gave no such command, but just continued to observe her daughter until the shaking subsided. He watched as she and Matt then lifted Sybil up and laid her on the bed.

"Will she be all right?" Jeremy asked.

"Yeah," Matt said. "She gets these sometimes."

Apparently this was not an isolated incident. Sybil lay with her eyes shut, her face pale, almost as if dead.

Kirsti picked up the mask. The outer panels were open, exposing the face of a raven with two eyeholes. "What's that?" Jeremy asked.

"I don't know. I haven't seen it before, but it looks like one of those wooden masks Danielle Herron has in her shop. She buys them cheap from local carvers and tries to sell them to tourists. I don't know what Sybil is doing with it. Maybe she borrowed it, though I can't imagine why. Anyway, I'll see that Danielle gets it back tomorrow." She laid it on the dresser. A cedar bark thong with something tied to it had come off the mask and was lying on the floor at her feet. Kirsti unceremoniously picked it up and tossed it on the dresser as well. Blackjack hopped over to it as if to stand guard.

Kirsti was ushering them out. "Are you sure she'll be okay?" Jeremy asked her.

"If she can sleep for a while, she'll be fine when she wakes up. It may be that her medication needs to be adjusted again. I'll make an appointment with her doctor in Port Casper."

Downstairs the phone in the hall was ringing. Kirsti hurried to answer it, then handed it to Matt. "It's your little girlfriend."

Matt held the receiver to his ear. "Hello," he said sullenly. "Yeah . . . No . . . It *was* stupid. Yeah . . . Okay . . . See ya." He hung up.

Jeremy, getting into his shoes, smiled faintly. Childhood reconciliations, unencumbered by protocol, were quick and uncomplicated.

CHAPTER 30

THE DRIZZLE had let up, but water dripping from branches formed a secondary rain that made the woods poor shelter. The men had parked their vehicles at the lip of the quarry, glad to be out in the open.

"Before we start, would anyone like a sandwich and hot coffee? Kirsti packed us a lunch."

Butch Westerlake grinned broadly. "Rome, your wife is a wonderful woman. You're a lucky man."

"Oh yeah!" Veik leaned his rifle against a tree. "I didn't think to bring food. I guess I thought we'd be back early."

"There's a picnic table down by the lake unless the kids have burned it down again," Oliver said.

"We should check the beach for tracks first," Eddie Smithson cautioned. "If we go tramping all over the sand we'll mess 'em up. Same with the quarry. We have to go slow and careful."

"We can tailgate it," Rome said, bringing out a large insulated carrier. He opened it. "Hey, the bar's open. Kirsti put in a sixpack of Molson's too. You guys gotta tough decision here — hot coffee or cold beer."

"I'll start with the coffee," Butch said. "I need something warm in my gut."

There were "me-toos" from Oliver and Eddie and Veik. They found that the hamper not only contained sandwiches but also a plastic bag of *pulla* slices. "How about you, Michaels, beer or coffee?"

"Nothing for me."

"Oh, come on Chad, you must be as cold and wet as the rest of us. At least have some hot coffee." Rome filled a styrofoam cup from the thermos.

"No thanks." Chad seemed edgy and irritated by the delay. "I came here to hunt cougar, not a kaffeeklatsch."

"Dude, you better eat something," Eddie said. "We all sympathize, but you're going to need to try to lighten up. We're a bunch of guys with guns, out in the woods on a miserable day, trying to track down a killer cat. This is not the time for anyone to have a hissy fit because his blood sugar is low."

Chad reluctantly accepted the cup, took one swallow, threw the rest away. "There, you happy now? And where's Constable Hewett? I thought he was supposed to be here."

"I don't know. Maybe he got called somewhere else." Rome said. "So, does anybody want a beer before I pack everything away?"

Butch looked longingly at the Molson's, then shook his head. "Maybe later. We can save it to toast our success. What should we do, split up and check out the quarry and the lake?"

"It would save time," Eddie said. "How be it you and Veik and Oliver go down into the quarry. Mark any tracks or sign you find. Rome and I can look around the lake. Michaels, you're with us."

"You don't need me," Chad said. "I'll follow the road. You guys can catch up with me later."

"That cat could have gone off in any direction if he was here at all. So far we haven't found any sign. Tracks might tell us which way it went. If you go wandering off in the wrong direction, then we'll have to waste precious time looking for you."

"What, you're worried I might find the cougar and kill it myself?"

"No, I'm worried that *it* might find *you*. It could be a female with cubs, and if you blunder into its territory by yourself, it could ambush you. It's killed before; it won't hesitate a second time."

Chad looked surly but stayed with the group as they made their way to the lake. The sandy beach was pockmarked with rain-blunted dents — footprints, both human and animal — deer, mostly. The lake's dark reflection, studded with colonies of water lilies, was calm except for the occasional rain ring as a drop hit the surface. So far, the new picnic table had survived, but there were marks along the shore showing that someone had dragged the dinghy into the water, then left it sitting on the edge of the pond. "Somebody's been here recently," Eddie said.

"Kids. Too early for swimming. Wonder what they were up to." Rome was walking along the wooded side of the beach next to the growth of greenery. "Here's something. Looks like a paw print. It's quite clear. Guess the salal sheltered it."

Eddie made his way over to it. "It's a dog. See the nail marks? Cougars have retractable claws so they don't leave a nail print. Could that be your dog, Michaels?"

Chad approached, looked, then shook his head. "How the hell would I know! Could be. I guess the size would be about right." The prints followed a line, growing less distinct, then stopped as if the animal had gone off into the shrubbery. "I think we're wasting time here."

Eddie pushed back his hat and scratched his balding pate. "Yeah, I don't see anything except dogs and kids and deer. Just about what you'd expect. Let's go see if the quarry gang has had any luck."

Over the years the quarry had deepened and widened to where it was now a broad area surrounded by high banks of sandy soil and shale. The island young used it as a dirt bike track; others as a target range; and although it was discouraged, some insisted on using it as a dump for such things as old, broken wooden pallets and rusting cans. Animals and birds found it attractive. Deer and occasional wolves patrolled it. A pair of eagles nested in an overlooking snag. Gulls fed there, leaving heaps of shells; and bank swallows had studded the far slope with burrows excavated from the soft sandy soil, their openings making a target for rock-throwing kids who liked to try for a hole in one.

The quarry had become an unofficial, and sometimes unsavory, social center. It was a site for bonfire picnics, teenage trysts, and occasional fights when a pair of combative young men needed a place to settle their differences. It was an outlaw area where rules didn't matter — a no-man's land, a wilderness in a wilderness. At least two people had committed suicide in that quarry, and there had been one unsolved murder. The sandy bottom, marked by tire tracks, dipped and duned, so that walking along it, one was often climbing or descending, slipping and sliding. In some places the underfoot was a litter of wood chips, bleached to a driftwood gray, as over the years, dried saplings became detached from above, either by wind or erosion, and made their way downwards into the bowl and there gradually disintegrated. To rock collectors, the quarry offered stones in many sizes and colors, prized by tourists looking for mementos, as well as deep blue, heat-holding granite for islanders who needed rocks for their saunas.

A road, of sorts, bisected the quarry. Earth, sand, and stones had been bulldozed up to the edge to make it possible for vehicles to drive in for a load of whatever was needed. Tufts of scrub grass, stunted wildflowers, and tenacious little hemlock trees scrabbled for a foothold on the floor and on the embankments which, under their fringe of salal and grasses, were steep slopes washed with grays, blues, pale browns, and white — depending on which mineral deposit had come loose and begun to slide. There were always the remains of a campfire and wood enough to build another.

Today the sand was wet and clung to the feet of the hunters. They had fanned out to circle the area by walking along the edge of the embankment, and would then close in toward the middle so as not to miss any possible sign or tracks.

"Hey, here's something!" Veikko Kuusiniemi called from the farthest wall, the one studded with bank swallow nests. He was quickly joined by Oliver and Butch. "I'll bet that sonofabitch is a cougar track!"

"Looks like he jumped down from the top of the bank," Oliver said. "We need to get the rest of the guys over here. Eddie would know for sure."

Eddie, himself, was just arriving with Rome and Chad. "Find anything?"

"Yeah, come on down."

Eddie studied the markings in the sand. "Seems to have jumped down, then continued across the quarry to the other side. See that dog track over there? You can tell the difference. Cougar track has a bigger pad." The print they were looking at was about four inches wide, and within it, the size of the palm was as large as the mark made by the digits. "Notice how one toe is longer and points inward. This is a front right footprint."

"Still looks like it could be a dog track to me," Chad said.

"Notice the little dimple in the top of the palm under the toes. That's cat," Eddie said. "And there are no nail marks. See the dog track over here? You can see the nails. This is a cougar, all right. I think it's a young female. It jumped down into the soft sand, then went across to the road. It was moving fast. See how the hind feet overreach the front ones. And these tracks are recent, made after the rain. So she may still be around here."

"Looks like it was headed for the road," Chad said. "I knew I should have gone that way. I'd have had him by now. But you guys wanted to waste time farting around the lake."

Rome looked at Chad coldly. "Yeah, might have been a good thing if you had," was all he said.

"From here on in, that cat might be anywhere." Eddie was studying the road surface where there was more gravel, and where tracks would be less distinct or washed away." He walked along the edge of the road, then paused. "Looks like she might have gone into the woods here. We'll have to follow her."

"Oh shit," Oliver said, looking with dismay at the dense growth. They were in high country where the trees were smaller — mugo pine and hemlock — and as more sunlight hit the forest floor, undergrowth was thicker. Farther on down the hill they would enter the mossy, dimly lit tall woods.

"If we follow and cut through here," Veik said, "we'll connect up with the trail to the old Lemerriant farm. If the cat went that way, we may see prints in the soft mud."

"Should we try to be quiet?" Butch asked. "We don't want to scare it away."

"We'll walk single file and try not to make too much noise, although if she's around she already knows we're here. I'll go first. Rome, you can stay close since you have your rifle. I may come back later and make a plaster cast of that print," Eddie said.

"I'll go last," Chad said. He didn't want anyone with a gun behind him.

"Okay then," Eddie grinned. "If the cougar is stalking us, she'll jump the last man."

Without comment, Chad stepped in behind Butch, leaving Veikko Kuusiniemi to bring up the rear.

The terrain was hard to traverse at first. Evergreens and salal made for slow going and the greenery was still be-sogged with rainwater. "Wish we'd brought machetes," Oliver said, holding a branch so it wouldn't whack Butch who was coming up behind him."

"We're coming to a clear spot." Eddie broke through the vegetation and stepped onto a trail. "Some of us should follow this path in case there are tracks. Rome and I will circle to the left. How about you, Butch, and Chad going to the right. That way we can cover a wider area. Oliver and Veik can take the trail. Stay within hailing distance. And I guess I don't have to warn you guys not to fire unless you know what you're shooting at."

Veik and Oliver found the trail preferable to fighting wild growth. They'd been traveling downward and now the trees towered above them and the ground was wetter. They'd entered the trail at a spot where the path had been partially laid with rounds of wood placed in a row in muddier areas. "You reckon Eddie put us on the trail because he thinks we're gettin' too old to go blazin' through the woods?" Oliver mumbled.

"Speak for yourself," Veik said, laughing. "I'm still in my prime."

"Oh yeah, you're still ridin' that Harley."

"I've been thinkin' of trading it in for a GoldWing."

"That's an old man's bike, ain't it?"

"A *rich* old man's bike," Veik said. "That's why I haven't got one. You gotta be a millionaire to own one and keep it up. I'd like to find a used one, though. You can go cross-country in comfort on those things. If I could talk Barb into it, her and I could go all the way to PEI to see the kids."

"Has she ever ridden on your motorcycle?"

"No, but maybe if I had a Wing. I keep telling her they're comfortable. Like sittin' in your favorite rocking chair. I keep telling her GoldWing clubs aren't like the Hell's Angels. A lot of 'em are retired people in their sixties — and they go on *ice cream rides*, for chrissakes."

Oliver laughed, picturing the rather proper Barb Kuusiniemi as a motorcycle mama riding as part of a gang — to a Dairy Queen. "Maybe it's the image she doesn't like. Hey, what are we coming to here?" They'd come to a spot where the lily pads ended and the wet soil showed marks of bicycle tires. "I thought bikes weren't allowed on this trail."

"Kids, you can't stop 'em. Looks like they had a dog with 'em. At least there are dog tracks as well. Hard to say when they were made, but the dog went through first. Tire tracks go over them. Dog tracks go off into the woods; tire marks keep on going. Looks like a couple of kids might have been pushin' their bikes. I don't see anything that looks like cougar. We should be able to see paw prints in here. Rain wouldn't have washed them away under the trees. See how clear the tire marks are? God, I hope no kids are on this trail today! Wasn't that long ago that a biker was killed on the mainland by a cat that jumped him."

"I don't mind saying that this is givin' me the willies," Oliver was looking around. "I don't hear the other guys."

"They're out there, and they'll show up soon. I think they just wanted to cover the area, make sure we weren't being stalked. Flush out the cat if she's here."

"We should be gettin' to the Lemerriant farm pretty soon, shouldn't we?"

"Oliver, don't tell me you've never hiked this trail!"

"No, I haven't. Have you?"

"Well, no. Been meaning to, though, ever since they opened her up."

Oliver laughed. "Yeah, just about everybody on the island has been meanin' to hike it, but so far, I think only tourists and kids have done it. Must say, though, that the guys who laid it out did a nice job. But we could use some benches along the way. My hip's startin' to grumble. There's a fallen tree over there. Let's take a load off our feet for a few minutes. Now I wish we'd brought the beer."

"I wish someone had thought to park one of the trucks at the other end of the trail. We could've ridden back to the quarry. This way we have to hike all the way back again." Veik propped his Winchester against the log and sat.

"What do you care, you're still in your prime! Anyway, ain't it just as far to the other road?" Oliver, shorter of leg, had to pull himself up to sit on the giant length of fallen Douglas fir.

"From here it is. The Lemerriant place is just about in the middle of the trail. But if we track that cat all the way, we'll be stuck out there with our vehicles back at the quarry."

"Oh, Jesus. Maybe somebody has a cell phone. We could call for a ride."

"I don't, do you?"

"No."

"Bet nobody thought of that either. Phone might not even work out here. Guess we're not really the best organized hunting party."

"Be different if we were headin' for the Rockies." Oliver said. "We'd all be outfitted with pack frames and survival gear up the Yazoo."

"This is a small place. Nobody thinks anything of just going off into the woods, but I've known people to get lost up here. If you don't live here, you can get really fucked up on some these logging roads."

"Well, I guess we better be goin'. Don't want the rest of them to get way ahead of us. This log looked more comfortable than it is." Oliver slid off painfully. "Ever been on a cougar hunt before?"

"Can't say I have, have you? There hasn't been one on the island for a long time, has there?"

"Been at least five years, maybe longer. Now and then one swims over, and it gets shot. Last time Les Dahlquist shot it. It didn't get a chance to kill anybody, but with the history of cougars on this island, nobody wants one around."

"It was before my time, but we've all heard the stories. You wonder though, what really happened way back then. Three dead kids killed by cougars."

"And a fire that wiped out eight adults and five children — six counting the Lemerriant boy. I was just a little kid," Oliver said. "But I'd have never thought to see the day the Lemerriant farm would be a heritage site, for god's sake!"

"They say it's still haunted, but I don't hold with that crap."

"I think they should've burned it down long ago."

"Well, Oliver, old buddy, there she still stands!"

* * *

"How come you don't carry a rifle, Eddie?" Rome asked.

"Sometimes I do. If I'm off by myself in the mountains on the mainland. Most of the time I pack a camera and plaster of Paris for making molds of the tracks I find. Gun gets in the way. I'm not out to shoot anything, although I do have a .44 Magnum Blackhawk in my backpack for emergencies. You guys all have guns so I didn't think I'd need one today."

"My trusty .270 Winchester is at your service. If we find the cat, I'll shoot it dead."

"Yup. It's a rogue. Once a cougar has attacked a human being, it has to be killed."

"These days you always wonder, I mean what with all them animal rights people. Maybe they'd want to catch it alive and try to rehabilitate it. Seems like every time you turn around there's some new bullshit about the environment or political correctness. Hard not to get in trouble. Maybe we should have checked with Hewett."

"Rest assured, Rome. RCMP policy is clear. Killer cat gets blown away."

"What happens if we don't find it?"

"It can't hide forever. If we can't find it, then we will get help from the RCMP. That animal is dead cougar walkin'."

They were in the deep woods where the trees were tall and the light was dim. Rome paused to look at a tree trunk. "Look at this!"

"Whatcha got?" Eddie approached.

"Take a look at those marks. They look like scratches."

"Yeah, those could be marks made by a cat. And they're recent. They'll use a tree as a scratching post. A bear will claw mark a tree too. Are there any bears here?"

"I haven't heard of any recently," Rome said. "But you can never be sure. People — usually tourists — think they see things. One even says he sighted a Sasquatch. Ever see one *them* in your travels, Eddie?"

"Nope, but I'll tell ya. One time, up on the mainland, I swear I was stalked by one."

"No kidding!"

"Nope. My truck broke down and I was walking along a logging road and I kept feeling I was being watched. And I heard something. Whooping sound like I never heard. Made my scalp tingle and the hair stood right up on the back of my neck. And there was this smell. I'll tell you, in all my years of tracking, I've never had an experience like it."

"Well, my sister-in-law swears that this actually happened on Vancouver Island. She said a couple of good friends of hers — one was a Cowichan woman — were driving to Tofino, and they saw this huge guy all covered with hair standing right in the middle of the road. They screeched on the brakes — he wasn't moving — they didn't want to hit him — and came to a stop just a few feet of him. He just stood there with his arms out and stared at 'em. Scared 'em shitless! They didn't know what to do. They couldn't go forward, and they thought maybe they should just back the car away from it, but just then another car came along from the other direction, and the thing jumped and disappeared in the woods. They said it moved like lightning. They was really shook up and said they'd never drive that road again. People say Bigfoot's just a myth, but I kind of think they're out there."

"Yeah, me too." Eddie was studying the ground. It was mostly moss that had been disturbed. "Looks like something came through here and went on that way. Let's follow and see what we find."

* * *

Chad strode through the woods like a man in a hurry making his way through a crowded mall, lurching through underbrush with his long-barreled rifle held awkwardly in his hands, his footing uncertain. Butch Westerlake walked alongside, but kept a distance. "Hey, slow down. We're supposed to be looking for cougar sign."

"Have you seen any sign of anything? I think this is all just a big pile of crap. Don't think I'm not on to the game you jokers are playing."

"Yeah, lots of fun, this! But it's never a good idea to go blundering through these woods. If you trip and break a leg we'll have to carry you back. You got the safety on that cannon?"

"What, you think I don't know how to use a gun? This just happens to be one of the finest hunting rifles made."

"Oh yeah, Winchester Magnum. You planning on going after elephant?"

"If you're going to need a gun, then get one that'll do the job."

"Isn't it kind of heavy? Wouldn't it be easier to sling it over your shoulder?"

"Wouldn't it be easier for you to just shut the hell up and mind your own business?"

"Accidents happen."

"Yeah, I'll *bet* they do."

"What's that supposed to mean?"

"I mean you'd really like to take a shot at me, wouldn't you?"

"*What?*"

"Well, if you do, you better kill me outright because if you don't, I'm comin' after you with everything I've got."

Butch stopped in his tracks and looked at Chad. "Hey, where's all this comin' from? What've I ever done to you?"

"Everybody seems to think Chad Michaels is fair game. Don't think I don't know how you're all plotting against me."

"And how would we be doing that?"

"Oh, you *know* how. It all started the minute I got here. You. Everybody. The whole town. The whole island. You all stick together, don't you?"

"Well, yeah, I suppose. But you've never gone out of your way to be exactly friendly, have you?"

"I just want what's rightfully mine. I have a campground, but you let people camp free in the park just to undercut me."

"That park's been free for a long time before you got here."

"And when that storm blew down all those trees by the lighthouse, it was you who had them helicoptered out, wasn't it?"

"You didn't want anybody using your private road."

"You could have *paid* me for the use of it. But you, all of you, never lose an opportunity to stick it to me or my family, do you? I know the names you call me behind my back. You want me out of here, don't you, and you don't care how you do it."

Butch didn't like the way this was going. Chad was not looking well. He was red in the face, sweating, and his eyes were rolling wildly. He seemed to be hyperventilating, and Butch wondered if he'd overexerted himself and might suddenly have an attack. Being confrontational was normal for Michaels, but it would be a hell of a note to have to drag him all the way back down the trail. "Hey, buddy, maybe we need to sit down and rest for a while."

Chad looked as though he wanted to flee, then seemed to struggle for control of himself. "Don't worry about me. Worry about your own ass."

"Michaels, you don't look so good. Maybe we should just go back. I'll go with you. I'll go tell the guys we're going."

"No! I'm all right. Just back off." Chad resumed walking.

Butch sighed. This man was obviously teetering on the edge. Wasn't he supposed to be on some sort of medication? Had he forgotten to take it? They should take that rifle away from him — but then, of course, they'd be sued for assault to remove a deadly weapon, or kidnapping a Winchester. Well, they'd soon be coming to the Lemerriant clearing and the rest of the party would be there. Maybe they could just call it a day and try to get Michaels back home — and leave him there. His wife would probably know what to do with him.

Chad's thoughts were gerbil-wheeling inside his skull. *I almost lost it back there. I have to be more careful. Can't let them see I know their plan. They all hate me and they're going to try to kill me and call it a hunting accident. But I'm too smart for them. They say they're hunting cougar, but I'm the one they're really after. I should have known Hewett wouldn't show up. They planned this very carefully, but I'm not going to fall into their trap even if I have to kill all of them myself.*

Logic had long since fled. There was always a small part of Chad Michaels that recognized the slide into irrationality, but that part was no longer able to get through. It stood, like a man stranded on an island, watching the boat that could have carried him to safety come loose from its moorings and drift away. Without his medication, Chad's world was becoming surreal and terrifying. Every sound was ominous; every contact fraught with deceit and danger. He had the guile to partially mask this, but only for a limited time. Ultimately he would become more and more agitated and unstable.

"Hey, Michaels, let's go this way. We're at the Lemerriant place."

Chad turned, looked at Butch blankly. "Huh? Oh. Yeah." They moved from the woods into a sizeable clearing free of trees but covered with wild vegetation and grass. A tumbledown barn stood near a small log cabin with broken windows and a bramble-choked porch.

"I see Oliver and Veik are already here."

The two men were standing side by side, solemnly looking down at something. As Butch and Chad approached, they saw it was the body of a dead dog. The carcass had been partially eaten, then covered over with twigs, leaves and dirt.

All four stood silent. It was one thing to hunt a cougar by looking for tracks; but standing next to a kill made the cougar very real, and possibly close-by.

"Maybe it's out there watching us," Oliver said. "It won't come back as long as we're all standing here. We need to take up stations. If we wait, it's bound to return to its kill."

"Birds were pecking at it when we got here," Veik Kuusiniemi told them. "We scared 'em off. The barn might make a good blind. We could go in there."

"Might get a better shot from the porch," Butch said. "Why don't we split up and surround the area. I guess that's your dog, isn't it, Michaels?"

"Yes, that's Turk." Chad was staring dully at the remains of the dead animal.

"Looks like he followed the cougar and lost the fight." Oliver said.

"Where's Eddie and Rome?" Butch asked.

"They shoulda been here by now." Veik scanned the edge of the woods.

Oliver looked around. "Maybe we should wait till they get here."

"They might have gone around and on past us. They could be back on the trail heading for Tranquil Bay Road." Veik said.

"One of us should go look for them." Butch offered. "I'll do it."

"With that cougar out there? We need to stay together, don't you think?" Oliver asked. "We don't know where that cat is. They might find it before we do."

"Well, the kill is here, so the cat should be back. It's worth watching and waiting," Veik said. "I'll be in the barn."

"Me too." Oliver prepared to follow.

"In that case, I'll be on the porch," Butch said. "You guys be careful in there. That roof looks like it could easily fall down the rest of the way."

Chad looked confused. He'd been investing all his fear and hatred on the men, but now there really *was* an animal that might be a danger as well. This was the animal that had killed his daughter. This was the animal that he was going to blow to hell. It was almost as if he'd forgotten. Why was it getting to be so hard to focus? He looked around at the men as if he'd never seen any of them before. Who were these people? It didn't matter. He'd deal with them later. Right now he was going to shoot a cougar. Yes, he was going to kill the cougar that had attacked his child. But he wasn't going to hide in the barn or in the house with any of *them*. He needed to be closer. "I'll stay here and hide in that bush," he said. There was a thicket of salal that had grown up to partially surround what looked like a puddle,

"All right, but you'd be more comfortable up here with me," Butch told him.

"Fuck off," Chad said under his breath as he took up his position in among the greenery, aimed his rifle and looked through the scope. *First I'll kill the cougar, then I'll shoot any man who makes so much as a false move.*

CHAPTER 31

BACK AT Willie's, Gabi was once more watching a taped movie — another of the Charlie Chans — but it wasn't as much fun alone. She wished Matt were there to join her in mocking the stilted dialogue that had seemed so uproariously funny. Kids of their times, they were used to a faster pace, and Gabi had been pretending to be Servo and Crow, doing a *Mystery Science Theater 3000* critique of the movie.

She'd called Matt and said she was sorry. But was she? Well, yes, she *was* sorry that she'd made Matt feel bad. She wouldn't have said anything about his father if he hadn't called her stupid. And maybe she *had* been wrong, but she knew what she'd heard. It was nagging at her now: she'd heard the girl's voice singing about a rainy day; she's gotten out of bed to see who it was; and her mother had thought she was having a nightmare.

Gabi sighed in a much too grownup way. It wasn't the first time she'd wondered if she should just never to tell anybody anything. That time in school when she'd told Jenny Aldrich that she'd never see her grandmother again — and Jenny got upset and Gabi got in trouble.

And then, a couple of days later, when Jenny's grandmother died, Jenny said it was Gabi's fault, and they'd gotten into a fight. Just like that time in the cafeteria when a bunch of boys had surrounded her, and kept saying she was of the devil. They just kept chanting it and coming toward her. *Of the devil, of the devil, of the devil.* Gabi had picked up a chair and swung it around and it flew into the window and broke it. Her mother had been called, and there had been a lot said about "behavioral problems," and "not relating well to other children," and "the need for professional counseling." All she'd done is tell Doug Gateman that his dog had been run over by a truck. How had she known that? She just *had.* Sometimes she heard it, like a little voice. Sometimes she would see a picture flash in front of her eyes. She thought everybody did. Then when she realized she was different, *that* was scary. And it always got her in trouble — like with Matt. She hoped Mr. Weeks would be all right. Maybe her mother was right. The voice hadn't said *which* man with a gun. It could also be on another rainy day, couldn't it? This made Gabi feel a bit better. Number One Son was acting smart again and Charlie Chan was talking funny. Gabi managed a smile.

* * *

"And I thought we should have called the doctor," Jeremy was saying to Willie and Celeste, "But Kirsti seemed to think she'd be all right. We left her asleep."

The three of them were congregated in Willie's kitchen. The polished harvest table and Windsor chairs with their comfortable cushions were an invitation to sit and chat, and offered an air of intimacy that the *pirtti* furniture grouping never could.

"I know Sybil has had her problems," Willie said. "I didn't realize she was still having seizures. I wonder what could have brought it on."

"I've no idea. Apparently it's happened before. She's a strange girl, isn't she? She had a pet crow hopping around free in her room."

Willie chuckled. "That's Blackjack, the raven. He can talk, you know. Or at least so Sybil says. I've never heard him myself."

"I did hear him say hello, but that was all," Celeste put in.

"Oh, that's right, you met the bird at Pearl's Café."

"Goths," Jeremy said. "That's what they call themselves — those kids who dress in black and try to look as funereal as they can. The ones I remember in Maine had a lot of piercings as well."

"I don't think Sybil has had anything pierced. She can't see much, poor thing, but she's a Cassandra spouting prophecies. I don't know how much of it is just affectation. She likes to surround herself with black — black clothing, black bird, black Bible."

"She had some kind of an Indian mask in her room. One of those painted masks that opens up. It was lying on the floor."

"That sounds like something Danielle has in the back of her shop. She buys them cheap and sells them to tourists."

"That's what Kirsti said."

"Actually, she has a couple that are supposed to be quite valuable, but nobody here would have any interest in them. I'm surprised Sybil has one. I didn't think she could see well enough to be interested in native art."

Celeste had been following the conversation with mild curiosity. "Speaking of art, I was noticing, at the New Broom, that there must be a number of local artists on the island. There were several paintings on the walls that were tagged for sale. I'd like to feature some of them in my article."

"Oh yes, we have quite an art community here. Painters, sculptors, and some really fine woodcarvers. They usually have an art fair once a year, but it's not until July. I could arrange to have you meet some of them while you're here, and I'm sure they'd be happy to have their work in your magazine. You could photograph the paintings in the restaurant."

"And speaking of restaurants," Celeste said, "Gabi and I would love to invite you to dine with us at the New Broom tonight. Oh wait — will they be open on a Sunday?"

"Uh — I think so, by now. During the season they stay open seven days a week. Let me give June Nyquist a call."

"This is kind of you, Celeste," Jeremy said, "But I feel it should be my treat. After all, you're our guest."

"And that's why it must be mine. You and Willie have been wonderful to both of us, and this is just my small way of saying thank you."

"Good news," Willie announced. "June says they started opening on Sundays last week, so I told her we'd be there. Take your camera, Celeste, and get some shots of the paintings. If any of the artists happen to be there, I'll introduce you."

* * *

Danielle Herron was driving back from the Michaels' property. There had been no call from Chad, and Rowena had become increasingly uneasy about his being home alone. After Weena phoned several times and got no answer, Danielle drove her back to Michaels Acres. They found nobody there, and Danielle would have brought Rowena back again, but Weena said she had to check the greenhouse, and that she wanted to be at home when Chad arrived. They correctly guessed that he must be off with the men hunting cougar, but that he wouldn't be gone much longer. Weena said she'd wait for Chad and fix him dinner — and that she was feeling much better now, and yes, she'd be okay there all by herself and not to worry.

Danielle was rather relieved to be on her own again. Weena with all her troubles had been a bit of a strain, and now Danielle just wanted a nice quiet evening to herself. She'd go home, make a sandwich and a nice pot of coffee, then watch the evening news on television — maybe treat herself to some of those Godiva chocolates she'd just imported. They were expensive, but it was her responsibility to at least *try* each batch before she put them up for sale. Yes, she'd stop by the shop and pick up a box to take home.

She parked her car, opened the metal gate, unlocked the door and went inside. Everything looked fine. Sybil had remembered to unplug the coffee maker, as instructed. The boxes of chocolates were in her office, still in their carton. Danielle pulled back the curtain and was surprised to find a large book on her desk; she recognized it as Sybil's Bible. Odd that she'd leave it behind. Oh well, she would put it on the shelf and give it to Sybil next time she came in. It was then Danielle gasped and stared, horrified. *The mask was gone!* Not just any mask, but *the* mask — the mask of masks — the most valuable mask in her shop — was *gone.* Danielle reached up to touch the empty wall almost as if she hoped her eyes were tricking her and that somehow her hand would close over it. It simply wasn't there. Who? How? Sybil? Could Sybil have taken it? What possible use could it be to a blind girl? She *had* asked about it once, quite a while ago, but how could she have taken it? Danielle herself had driven Sybil home last night and she certainly hadn't been carrying it, had she? Could she?

Now Danielle couldn't remember when she'd last looked at the mask. How long had it been missing? Had she failed to notice? People came into the shop all the time. Had someone planned this? Could someone who knew its value have made off with it? Unless it was a kid's prank. There was no shortage of young vandals on the island. It wasn't that long ago that someone had stolen the carved eagle from Oliver Sylvester's fence. She could picture the scenario: I dare you to steal a mask from Danielle's shop! Might even be a treasure hunt object. She hoped it was still on the island, because, yes, a tourist could certainly have taken it away on the ferry.

Danielle dialed the phone. "Constable Hewett? This is Danielle Herron. I've been burglarized." She realized she was talking to an answering machine. Where was *he?* She glanced at the clock. He and his wife might be in the New Broom having dinner. Danielle hung up without leaving a message and left the shop.

CHAPTER 32

It was early evening, and there were few people in the New Broom. Islanders didn't dine out much; word may not even have gotten around that they had started opening on Sundays. Off season, Larry and June Nyquist's restaurant depended on non-island-based workers, mostly loggers — take-out contracts with companies that didn't want to set up camp kitchens for the short periods of time they'd be working on the island. Recently logging, like fishing, had declined, and Larry and June had joined the ranks of those who were quietly considering selling out and moving to the mainland.

Only four tables were filled, a couple by elderly gentlemen who looked to be bachelors or widowers, reduced to restaurant fare; and one by a family with young children who were wolfing down burgers and fries as they giggled and squirmed and jostled each other.

Willie's table was an island of animated chatter. Everyone but Gabi had opted for fish (the halibut at the New Broom was freshly-caught and excellent), so Celeste had ordered white wine — a Riesling from the Gehringer Brothers Estate Winery in Oliver, BC — and the group was discussing the fledgling wine industry in British Columbia, and how new vineyards were springing up on Vancouver Island.

Celeste was offering a toast to her hosts when Danielle Herron burst in. She looked around anxiously, then approached Willie's table. "Have you seen Constable Hewett? I thought he and his wife might be having dinner here. I tried calling the station but got an answering machine. You'd think there'd be someone there! It's the RCMP, for god's sake!"

Willie smiled. "We all have to remember that this is Satama." Then, seeing that Danielle was visibly upset, "Is anything wrong?"

"I've been burglarized; that's what's wrong. The most valuable piece of native art in my collection has been stolen."

"Please join us, Miss Herron." Jeremy, who had risen politely, pulled up a chair and seated Danielle. He sat next to her. "Now, what did the artwork look like?"

"It was a mask — a very rare Haida transformation mask. It's worth at least fifteen thousand dollars."

"Did it have a face with big red lips and a couple of panels that open up?"

Danielle looked astounded. "Yes, have you seen it?"

"I believe I have. Sybil Weeks has it."

"So! Sybil *was* the one who stole it. I just hope she hasn't damaged it."

"It looked to be fine. Mrs. Weeks told me she was planning to give it back to you tomorrow. Somehow I don't think Sybil intended to steal it. I'm sure she was just borrowing the mask. She probably doesn't realize how valuable it is."

"I must go over there right away and pick it up."

"It might be just as well to wait till tomorrow," Jeremy said. "Sybil isn't well today. She had a seizure this afternoon, so she's either still sleeping or possibly disoriented, and her mother will be busy caring for her. It's possible they may need to get her to a doctor. I'm sure the mask will be perfectly all right overnight. Won't you have glass of wine with us?" He poured the rest of the Riesling into the empty wine glass that had been part of Gabi's place setting. Danielle picked it up and took a distracted sip. Yes, perhaps she could wait till morning — now that she knew the mask was safe. She'd been looking forward to a quiet evening, and perhaps she could still salvage that.

Jerry Nyquist had spotted Danielle and approached. "Hi, Danielle. I see you've joined the party. What can I get you?"

"Oh, nothing, Jerry, thanks. I'm just leaving. I only came in looking for Constable Hewett. I thought maybe he and his wife would be here. I don't suppose they've had a chance to properly unpack their kitchen yet."

"Oh, then you haven't heard?"

Jerry was instantly the focus of five pairs of eyes. "Heard what?" Danielle asked.

"The Hewetts were here but they had to leave. There's been a hunting accident out at the old Lemerriant place."

"Did Matt's dad get shot?"

In the dead silence everyone turned to look at Gabi.

Jerry spoke slowly. "Yes, as matter of fact, it *was* Rome Weeks who was shot. But how did you know that?"

"Is he dead?" Gabi asked.

"No, but he's injured."

"Do you know how it happened?" Celeste had laid a restraining hand on Gabi's arm.

"Well, I don't know the particulars, but the guys were hunting cougar, and I guess there was some kind of accident. Rome was shot in the shoulder. Eddie Smithson called here, and the Hewetts took off. Peg Hewett's a paramedic, you know. They asked me to call Dr. Swallow to tell him they'd be bringing Rome in."

"Did they say anything about how the gun went off?" Willie asked.

"Rome is an experienced hunter."

"It wasn't Rome's gun. It was that greenhorn who calls himself Michaels." Clearly Jerry Nyquist was another islander who had no liking for Chad, formerly known as Schittle.

"Do you know how seriously hurt Rome is?"

"No. Eddie said it was a shoulder wound, but it was a big gun. I guess we'll be hearing more about it. Excuse me, I gotta go." A couple of people had come into the restaurant, and Jerry left to see to their table, casting a last, thoughtful sideways look at Gabi.

Gabi sat silent. She had a funny feeling in the pit of her stomach. Matt's dad had been shot by Dory's dad, just like the singing girl had said. "The man with the gun will be shot on a rainy day." She stared at her plate. Was she in trouble again?

* * *

Back at Michaels Acres, Rowena was helping her husband strip off sodden clothing. "What did you do, fall in a lake? I'll get you a towel and you can dry off properly."

Veik Kuusiniemi, who had left his Harley parked in the Michaels driveway and ridden to the hunt with Butch and Oliver, had been the logical one to give Chad a ride home. Chad had grumbled that he was perfectly capable of driving his own truck, but was trembling so violently that he could hardly get the words out. Veik, relieved to see that Rowena was there, left as quickly as possible after giving her only the sketchiest account of what had happened.

Chad, now dry and wrapped in a blanket, was sipping a cup of hot tea. Weena was eyeing her husband sharply, wondering what new trouble had come their way — and what the consequences might be. "I want you to tell me exactly what happened out there."

"It wasn't my f-fault." Chad's teeth were still chattering. "That d-damn Rome Weeks walked right into my sights. I thought he was the cougar."

"If you'd had him in your sights, you'd have *known* he wasn't the cougar."

"Goddammit, it all happened so fast. The gun just went off. I don't know how. I was holding it in position. We were waiting for the cougar. Then all I remember is the bang and I was knocked over and into the well."

"Well? Where *were* you?"

"The old L-Lemerriant place. There's a well there. It's just a hole in the ground and the water comes right up to the top. It has a thicket of brush growing around it and I was hiding in the shrubbery. Westerlake was on the porch and Sylvester and Kuusiniemi were just inside the barn. We all had our guns trained over the dead dog."

"Dead dog?"

"It was Turk. Cougar got him. We were waiting for the cougar to come back to the kill. We were going to shoot it. Then this damn Weeks comes busting out of the woods like a cannon. He was lucky he didn't get shot four times. Maybe he did. Maybe it wasn't even me. Could have just as easy been one of the other guys who shot him, but of course they blame *me*. They're all out to get me. They've always hated me."

"How badly was Rome Weeks hurt?"

"I dunno. He's still alive. That guy Smithson — Eddie — or Two Feathers — or whatever the hell they call him — had a cell phone and was able to get through to the RCMP station. Hewett wasn't there but he finally got hold of him. Hewett should have been with us all along. Anyway, we had to wait for him and his wife to show up. Smithson managed to stop the bleeding, and Hewett's wife is some kind of a field nurse or whatever. Anyway, the Hewetts came in with a stretcher and then we had to hike all the way back to where we'd left the vehicles."

"Is Rome going to be all right?"

"Probably, more's the pity. Better if he died. If he lives, he'll sue my ass. He'll get all his cronies to testify it was all my fault and make it look like I did it on purpose."

Rowena looked pained. "Is that all you're thinking about? Our daughter has been killed. A man nearly died, and you're the one who shot him, and all you're worried about is *lawsuits*?"

"And you're *not*? Listen, they could sue me for everything I own, and that means everything *you* own as well. I wish I'd shot the sonofabitch through the heart."

Rowena sighed and shook her head. "Chad, I'm sure everyone knows it was an accident. That stupid rifle. I always knew it was dangerous. What do you know about guns anyway? You never should have bought that thing, at least not until you'd taken a course in gun safety."

"Hey, I know about guns, all right?"

"Yes. That's how you ended up in the well."

"I was just a little off balance, that's all."

"And that Winchester kicked you in the chest like a mule."

"I must've stepped back and tripped over the broken railing. Hey, I could have drowned in that well. Bet you never thought of that? I could sue them for negligence."

Rowena said nothing, just paused briefly, then picked up Chad's wet clothing and headed for the clothes dryer. "Have you been taking your medication?"

"What do you think I am, a kid? Of course I've been taking it." In truth, Chad couldn't remember whether he had or hadn't, but he wasn't going to give Rowena the satisfaction. "It's a bit late to be worrying about *me*, isn't it? You weren't worrying about *my* welfare when you decided to go off and spend the night in town with that Herron woman. Come to think of it, you two have been thick as thieves lately. I'm beginning to wonder just what kind of relationship you're having. What kind of wool are trying to pull over my eyes? Don't think I can't figure out what's going on. She's a lesbo if there ever was one. She's mouthy and she hates men."

Rowena put clothes into the dryer and turned it on. Its soothing hum and the gentle tick-tick of clothing tumbling in the drum buffered Chad's voice and allowed her mind to wander. She mused at how quickly everything could change. Was it only yesterday that her world turned over? Rowena still had a bit of a headache that blunted the emotional pain but increased her irritability. She was starting to feel like a stranger in her own house. Or maybe it was the house that had suddenly gone strange. Chad was there, still endlessly talking, talking, talking. But Dory wasn't. Even Turk, whose dark presence had been part of the household, was gone.

The very room looked different, somehow smaller, and disconnected from the world, as if she'd stumbled onto a stage set. There was no sense of belonging anymore. She felt as though she could walk off the stage into another world, away from the troubles that choked this kitchen, this life. Freedom? Was it really an option? She'd always felt the pull of responsibility. She stood still and waited for her little voice to prompt her — the voice that had always reminded her of Things That Must Be Done. There had always been a mental list of chores, and most of them revolved around Chad — his needs, his medication, his tantrums, his problems, his insecurities, his delusions. Whatever it was that had anchored her to this place, to this man, was vanishing. Now she seemed to be drifting like a balloon with a broken string — but to where? She didn't know, but it didn't even seem to matter.

"And as far as I'm concerned, *I'm* the one who's been wronged here. *I'm* the one who should be compensated for all the persecution I've been subjected to ever since we moved to this island. And as *my* wife, I expect your loyalty, and I'm telling you, Weena, I don't ever want you talking to that Herron woman again. You understand me?"

Rowena looked calmly at her husband and uttered three little words she'd never said to him before: "Shut up, Chad."

* * *

Upstairs, in her bedroom, Sybil awakened. The house was quiet. She got up feeling shaky and needing to go to the bathroom. The raven flew from the window sill and landed on her shoulder; she brushed him off, "Not now, Blackjack." She made her way to the lavatory at the end of the hall, emptied her bladder, thankful that this time she hadn't wet herself, then dampened a washcloth and ran it over her face. The house sounded empty. She called downstairs for her mother, then for Matt, but got no reply. Good. She was alone.

Back in her room, Sybil looked around for the mask, then, with her clouded vision, saw its blurred colors on her dresser. *Yaxagama*. She picked it up, carried it over to her bed, sat down and stared into the wooden face. *Help me, Yaxagama*. While she'd been wearing the mask, Sybil had seen it all: She had flown over a trail patterned with footprints — footprints of animals, men, and children — and among them those that belonged to the Loogy-Roo. She had swooped through the woods over the heads of the hunters to the clearing where the old house stood, the house she'd never visited, but she'd seen it clearly through the eyes of the mask. It was an evil place — the lair of the Loogy-Roo — and the Loogy-Roo had been there, and would go there again, because it couldn't help it. It would always keep going back there until someone killed it. *Beware the laughing blackbirds and the Loogy-Roo*. Then the men with guns had come to stand watch over the dead dog. And then she'd seen her father come out of the woods. She'd heard the shot and seen him fall — and she'd screamed. And then Yaxagama had entered her body and taken possession of her, and Sybil remembered nothing more. But now she knew what she had to do.

And she shrewdly guessed that she would have time to do it. By now, her mother and brother had most likely heard of her father's . . . accident. Sybil didn't want to think of him as dead, but she'd seen it, hadn't she? — and heard it: the horrible sound of the gun and her father crumpling to the ground.

Sybil knew that her mother and Matt would have gone to wherever her father had been taken, and nobody would be even thinking about her right now. When they got back, they probably would be careful not to tell her anything in any case. They sometimes acted as she were half-witted, and often it served Sybil's purpose to let them think that.

Yes, she'd have time.

The Loogy-Roo had killed her father, and it was up to her to avenge him. Sybil gathered up a number of items, then made her way downstairs and into the kitchen. There her movements became more assured and precise, as if she were either performing a practiced task, or her impaired vision no longer hampered her. Into an iron fry pan on the stove, she laid out a coil of jet-black fiber — a lock of "hair" from the shaman mask. She also had in her hand the cedar bark thong that had fallen off with the tuft of feathers still tied to it. *Ancient Mother, Yaxagama, lend your wisdom, lend your power. Blackjack, Blackjack, bird of vengeance, bring the keenness of your vision, lend your wings to aid the seeking.*

Sybil ceremonially laid the thong and the feather tuft tied with human hair into the pan. *Now to fight the evil forces we will need the Word of God.* She remembered that her Braille Bible was still in Danielle's shop. Never mind. She left the kitchen and went to a bookshelf in the living room. There she let her fingers run along the row of books until she found what she needed — the family Bible. She couldn't read it, of course, but that didn't matter either. She held the book between her palms, and carried it back into the kitchen. There she set the spine on the counter and let go. The book opened. Sybil tore out the page that faced her and laid it in the pan. *God will smite thee, Loogy-Roo!* Sybil groped for matches, struck one, and tossed it in lit, then added a few more. The matches flared and flames shot up while the room filled with the acrid smell of sulfur and burning feathers and wool. The pile consumed, the fire quickly died, leaving a heap of gray ash.

Next, Sybil emptied the plastic bag of graveyard dirt that she'd brought back from the cemetery into a bowl, added a handful of salt, then stirred in the ashes. Carefully, so as not to spill any of the precious substance, Sybil spooned the mixture back into the plastic bag, tapping out the last bit, then zipped the bag shut, washed and put away the pan, and went back upstairs.

Yes, Sybil knew exactly what she had to do, and now she needed

Blackjack to help her.

CHAPTER 33

Willie, Jeremy, Celeste, and Gabi had returned home in near silence, and once again the group had gathered at the kitchen table — except for Gabi who had quietly gone into the living room to sit on the couch. Celeste kept glancing at her through the kitchen door, as if in disbelief — or denial. But there was no denying that Gabi *had* predicted that Rome Weeks would be shot . . . on a rainy day.

Gabi, relieved that nobody, at least for the moment, was yelling at her, was lying low, idly playing with the Game Boy that had lain neglected since she got to the island. She wished Matt were with her, but of course Matt would be at the hospital with his dad. Matt would be mad at her in any case. People always got mad at her twice, once when she told them things, and then again later when the thing really happened, as if it were somehow all her fault. And it wasn't just kids; it was grownups too. There had been that time when her music teacher, Mrs. Golding, had told the class they'd be starting a Christmas choir the following week, and Gabi had told her that they'd be having a substitute teacher then. Mrs. Golding had looked surprised and asked whatever would make Gabi say such a thing. When Gabi had told her it was because Mrs. Golding would be in the hospital, Mrs. Golding had laughed — at first — then told Gabi she shouldn't be making up nasty things to tell people. Then, after Mrs. Golding's appendix had burst, and they'd had a substitute teacher for over a month, Mrs. Golding hardly ever spoke to Gabi, just kept eyeing her in a strange way, as if she found Gabi's presence threatening. Gabi had found it creepy too.

The grownups were talking about the Weeks family. Willie had tried calling Kirsti but got no answer. "They'll be at the clinic," Jeremy said, "except maybe for Sybil. She was asleep when I left. If she's still sleeping she wouldn't have heard the phone."

"She shouldn't be left alone," Willie said. "Maybe I should go over there and see if she's all right."

"I'll do that," Jeremy offered. "Unless you think it would frighten her to have me show up. Of course if Sybil is still sleeping, she may not hear the doorbell either."

"Kirsti never locks her door," Willie said.

Celeste raised an eyebrow. "Really?"

"Welcome to Satama. Back in the old days, nobody on the island ever locked a door. Mind you, it's different now. People, particularly those in the village, are becoming more cautious. Anyway, I have Kirsti's key — just as she has mine. I'll nip on out there. For all I know, Matt might be at home too, and just didn't happen hear the phone ring. I'll either bring them both back with me, or stay with them and see that they get dinner. I'm half-expecting Kirsti to call and ask me to check on them. If she does, please tell her I'm already over there."

Gabi pricked up her ears. Matt might be coming? But so might his weird sister! Would she be bringing her bird? Gabi picked up her Game Boy and quietly went upstairs.

The movement caught Celeste's attention and she watched her daughter through narrowed eyes. Who *was* this child? Who was it that lived inside the body of her beautiful little girl, the babe she had birthed and raised, and for whom she would gladly give up any body organ — or her life — and who now seemed to be slipping out of her grasp, moving to some alien place where Celeste couldn't follow? Celeste, worried, frightened, and most of all frustrated, blinked back tears, then noticed that Jeremy had been silently watching her.

"She'll be all right, you know."

Celeste met his gaze. "That's just it, I *don't* know. And how can you or anybody know?"

Jeremy opened his mouth to speak, hesitated, then said, "No matter what she's going through right now, and no matter what lies ahead for her, she will emerge into adulthood as a lovely, vibrant young woman. I just know it. Put it down to an old man's intuition."

"Well, I hope you're right. It's just that I'm at my wits' end. She was always such a normal child — until this past year. Then she started having nightmares and getting into trouble at school. I told myself it was just another phase. Kids go through phases. But it just seems to be one thing after another, and I don't know how to deal with it. I don't have much faith in psychiatrists. We tried that. But the bottom line is that Gabi *did* predict that Rome Weeks would get shot. She called it, didn't she?"

"Yes, she did."

"But that's impossible, isn't it?"

"Obviously not, but it doesn't mean there's anything wrong with her. The very young, and we, the old, I think, are in closer touch with our spiritual roots. Whether it's because the young are newly emerged and the old are close to departure, we tend to have a closer tie with our origins."

"But it's not normal for a child to go around hearing voices singing about people getting shot."

"Normal? No. Unheard of? No. Gabi may be tapping into her so-called subconscious mind through auditory means. It's not any different from looking into a crystal ball or using Tarot cards. Some people see visions. In fact, there is a condition called synesthesia in which people who are normal in every other way can *hear* or *feel* colors or *see* music. Life is full of unofficial pathways."

"Oh, sure. 'There are more things in heaven and earth, Horatio. . . .' But it's a lot different when it's your own kid. I worry about what will become of her."

"She may simply outgrow it."

"Willie said the same thing."

"I'm sure that all of us, if we can remember our childhoods, will find incidents that now seem odd. How many children have invisible playmates, even pets, who talk to them? As adults we look back and say, of course they weren't real. Gabi, when she realizes that she's not supposed to have these experiences, may block them out like the rest of us." Jeremy added dryly, "And then she'll be normal, won't she?"

"And if she doesn't?"

"Then she'll be needing love, support, and understanding, particularly from you. If she can trust you not to overreact, she'll talk to you. You can be a safe haven in a bewildering world."

Celeste looked at Jeremy sharply. "She's talked to *you*, hasn't she?" Jeremy averted his gaze. "She *has*, hasn't she?"

"Not an awful lot, but there was that time in the cemetery." Jeremy, when faced with the possibility of emotional encounter, automatically shifted into professorial mode: "I got the impression that Gabi is somehow able to access historical data. She correctly identified a grave as that of two children who had died on the island many years ago. There's no inscription, just a cairn of rocks, but she went right to it, and appeared to be connecting to something. There was a flock of ravens in the cemetery and I thought they might frighten her, after that incident with the bird at Pearl's."

"Somebody must be feeding those birds. I saw them when I was taking photos. They were all over the place."

"Gabi didn't seem at all bothered, and later she told me that there were two children buried in the grave, and that they'd been killed by the Loogy-Roo. I asked who had told her that and she said it was the birds. She heard them talking about it."

"I thought she said Matt Weeks told her about the children in the grave."

"I think she said that because she didn't want to be questioned. She told me it was the birds."

"But that's insane," Celeste almost whispered.

"No, I think it's symbolic. If Gabi is, indeed, gifted psychically, her avenue may be more auditory than visual, or it could be both. The birds were a point of focus, just like a crystal ball. The ball doesn't foretell the future, it merely allows the reader a tool by which he can connect to his inner self, and I believe that to be a place where all information resides and nothing is hidden. I did ask her how the birds were able to talk to her. Did she understand their language? She told me the birds talked to her *in her head*."

"So you think she really *did* hear someone singing about a rainy day?"

"I think she did, but it may have been a subjective experience. You and I wouldn't have heard it. It's her way of translating information that's she's picking up on — perhaps like radio waves. Many people have noticed, for instance, that when they find themselves humming a tune, if they turn on the radio, that tune will be playing. Back in the days when radios were everywhere, I've done it myself. If someone can pick up police calls with the filling in a tooth, why couldn't we receive sound waves in the atmosphere?"

"But there wouldn't have been actual sound waves, would there?"

"I don't know. There are people who claim they've actually been able to record voices in a so-called haunted room. We're being bombarded by all sorts of waves — sound waves and light waves that are above and below our range of perception, magnetic waves, gravity waves, ionized solar winds, protons and electrons — all sorts of atmospheric disturbances that we're generally not aware of pass through our bodies."

"But not birds talking, surely."

"If I'm correct, the birds talking would be a translation of a psychic experience, Gabi's effort to convert a paranormal phenomenon into everyday language. The results are usually distorted or incomplete. It's probably like dreams we have. Willie is a student of dreams, and she says she believes all our dreams are purposeful and have continuity; but that many of them come from such a deep level of consciousness that we can't translate them, and if we remember them at all, we end up with something chaotic or silly."

"Then you clearly believe in psychic ability."

"I suppose I do. It seems to be on the rise, doesn't it? A few decades ago anyone admitting to it would have been considered a crackpot. It's possible that we are slowly approaching a time when we'll all be developing abilities that are now regarded as paranormal. There's a biblical quote in the book of Joel: ... *I will pour out my Spirit on all people. Your sons and daughters will prophesy, your old men will dream dreams, your young men will see visions.* It may be a natural next step in the cycle of human development."

"I'm curious about one thing, Jeremy. Why didn't you mention any of this to me earlier?"

Jeremy had been afraid she might ask that. "Well," he said slowly, "Perhaps I should have, but I didn't know either of you well enough. I'm afraid, at first, that I put it down to a child's imagination. Children are dramatic. They *do* tell wild stories sometimes. And, after many years in the school system, it also ran through my mind that Gabi might just be teasing an old man — 'putting me on' — or, I guess now they'd say 'freaking me out.' So I thought I'd just wait and see. And I still think that may be the best approach: just keep an eye on Gabi, make her feel accepted and safe, then wait and see what happens."

Before Celeste could reply, Willie came into the kitchen. "There was nobody home. Sybil must have gone with her mother after all. I could use a cup of tea, how about you?"

"I think I'll make an early night of it," Celeste said. "I didn't sleep much after Gabi had her nightmare."

"It's still early. Do you think a cup of chamomile tea would relax you? Or even a small glass of wine before bed? You could take it up with you, if you like."

"Thank you, Willie, but I think I'll go up and spend a little time with Gabi, and then I hope we'll both sleep well. I had wine with dinner, so that should help me doze off. Gabi is probably exhausted too."

"Then we'll see you in the morning," Willie said cheerfully, and put the kettle on. "Orange Pekoe, Lapsang Souchong, or chamomile?

"Chamomile sounds good. How's the weather? Is it still drizzling?"

"No, it's clearing up. Big gibbous moon coming up over the water. Quite lovely."

"So nobody answered the bell at the Weeks house?"

"Nobody was there. As I expected, the door was unlocked and I went inside. I thought Sybil might be sleeping, so I went upstairs and peeked in her room. It was empty. I checked the rest of the house but nobody was around. There was a strange smell in the air, though, and I wondered if something was burning. They probably left in a hurry, so I went in the kitchen to see if Kirsti had forgotten to turn off the stove, but I didn't find anything on fire or even out of place. Whatever Kirsti had been cooking smelled like burning feathers. I don't think I'll be asking her for the recipe."

Jeremy sat watching Willie as she chatted away and set out tea cups. "I told Celeste about Gabi and the birds."

Willie sat down. "How did she take it?"

"I don't know how much of it she believes, but she has to admit that Gabi was correct about the shooting. I didn't go into great detail. I only told her about the incident in the cemetery, when Gabi said the ravens had told her where the two children were buried."

"Did you tell her about the raven at the lookout?"

"No. I'd have had to tell her that Gabi and Matt had been up there against her instructions, and — I guess I didn't want to be a tattletale. Besides, I think Celeste has enough to deal with for the moment. The children got back safely, and they're not going to get the chance to go off by themselves again, so I didn't mention it. Celeste is very worried about her daughter."

"I'm uneasy about her myself. She's so young."

"I tried reassuring Celeste, but I don't know if it worked."

Willie grinned. "Did you go into our genetic memory theory?"

"No. There are things I only discuss with you. She'd have probably thought it was harebrained. I did go into *your* dream theory — that dreams are legitimate experiences but that we can't always translate them. I compared it with psychic experiences, in that we need to translate those into something we can understand. I suggested that if Gabi is psychically gifted, her avenue might be that she hears things, that the birds talking to her was not a form of dementia, but instead symbolic. I don't know if it made her feel any better or even made much sense."

"I think I said something along those lines myself. Back in 18th century Finland they would have diagnosed Gabi as being afflicted by the *Kirkkoväki.*"

"You mentioned that before; just what *is* that?"

"*Kirkko* means church; *väki* is a group, so it sounds like the congregation of a church. However, in the past, *Kirkkoväki* had a darker meaning, and actually referred to the dead in the churchyard. It was believed that those who died continued their existence where their bodies were buried. There were many abodes of the dead, but the first was always the churchyard. The soul was believed to follow the body to its burial place, and reside there for a length of time before it migrated on to a place called *Tuonela.* So, back then, the cemetery was literally a village of the dead, hence the fear of graveyards. However, the dead had power, and their mojo was called upon in magic rituals. That's why bones and coffins and graveyard dirt were prized by shamans who would recite incantations in an effort to tap into it."

"And the dead just hung around, waiting to be called on?"

"Not always. Sometimes the dead resented being disturbed, and then they could *attach* themselves to you. And *then* you would actually start *seeing* them, singly or en masse!"

"Like the Nightmarchers in Hawaii? I saw in a documentary that if you see them you die."

"Yes, I think many cultures have versions in their mythology. A number of Finnish magic charms had to do with just trying to get the dead to stay in their graves. One ritual involved digging up the coffin, crawling into the empty grave and rolling around in the dirt, while exhorting the dead one to stay buried once the body was put back."

"Sounds grisly."

"In the transcripts of witch trials of the day, all this is documented. Of course there is no documentation of any of the magic having *worked*, but there is always a gulf between historical events and myths. Myths become part of national consciousness and gain a power all their own. But you can't scientifically measure it."

"So if the churchyard dead became attached to you, you'd be haunted by them?"

"Yes. At best they'd follow you around. At worst, they could afflict you with illnesses — mental or physical. You would certainly demonstrate psychic ability, but you could also become unstable or even go mad. My own take on that is that *if* the dead have some reason for hanging around, they might seek out those who *are able* see them or hear them. But that could be terrifying if it happened to you."

Jeremy was trying to picture the era: uneducated, superstitious peasants attributing the inexplicable to magic spells and curses. Death had always loomed as the mysterious unknowable, giving rise to speculation and myth as to what lay beyond it. Interesting, indeed, but why did he feel a wee bit uncomfortable with what Willie was telling him — like having your psychiatrist suddenly confide in you that he's controlled by space aliens. Was this another Finn thing? Anyone who lives in a

Finnish community will encounter Finn things that leave them wondering just how much the times really *have* changed! After this, was he ever going to be able to shake the image that Satama cemetery could be populated by hoards of dead islanders? Did *Willie* take any of this seriously? No, of course not. That would be ridiculous. "Well, of all the possible explanations, I guess we can at least discount that one. I hardly think Gabi is being possessed by the island dead."

Willie smiled enigmatically. "Possibly so, but suddenly it seems like all hell *is* breaking loose: Dory Michaels dead, Rome Weeks shot, all the old stuff about the Lemerriants being dredged up, Sybil having seizures again. And then there's the business of the mask."

"I guess you saw that in Sybil's room. Kind of a monstrous thing, isn't it?"

"I didn't see it. Maybe Danielle picked it up after all. Or I just didn't happen to notice it. Come to think of it, I didn't see Blackjack either." Willie yawned. "It's not really time for bed yet, but I'm feeling a bit sleepy myself. Maybe I'll turn in early and read for a while." She reached for the empty cups.

"You run on up. Leave those. I think I'll have another cup and take a look at the news before I go to bed."

* * *

Celeste had found Gabi stretched out on her bed, fast asleep, the Game Boy beside her. She was sleeping so soundly that she didn't fully awaken when Celeste gently undressed her, put her into her pink cotton knit pajamas, and tucked her in. If only her sleep were always this sweet and undisturbed!

Celeste, on the other hand, found herself clamorously awake, her thoughts swirling, her mind rejecting any notion of winding down. Should she go back downstairs? No, she decided to take a relaxing shower, then, while Gabi continued to sleep, she took out her laptop and looked again at the photos of the Lemerriants that she'd copied to her computer. There they were in all their immediacy — and yet so inaccessible. She would do more research on the family when she could connect to a modem. Tonight she couldn't concentrate. She kept replaying the conversation with Jeremy, feeling a twinge of resentment that Gabi would have found it easier to talk to him than to her own mother. Still, wasn't it true that it was always easier to talk to strangers? Perhaps that's why people sought out psychologists and priests. Tell your troubles to friends or family and they'll keep them alive long after you might have found a way to banish them. She'd never discussed her marital problems with anyone. There had been no parental shoulder to cry on, and no best friend to offer advice. Her mother, Madeleine, always seemed too fragile to burden with family problems, and her father had been a rather shadowy figure, too abstracted to be approachable. He was not an unkind man, but he carried an air of melancholy, and tended to withdraw into brooding silences, so deep and so remote, that Celeste was convinced that he didn't always quite realize who she was — even when she was standing right in front of him.

Obviously, Celeste did not want to be that sort of parent, but how does one manage to be a *good* one? What are the guidelines, if any? We're all human. We make mistakes. Children don't come with a book of instructions. Is it the destiny of all of us to be judged by our children? If not by them, then through them? This was no good. She needed to clear her mind and try to doze off. She looked at Gabi again: rosy cheeks, sweet lips, blond hair, long sweeping lashes, quiet breathing, snuggled under a duvet. Surely she would sleep peacefully through the night! Celeste got up, went to her bag and took out a bottle of sleeping pills, shook out one, and swallowed it. She didn't like taking pills, but tonight a mild sedative might gentle the galloping horses in her mind.

CHAPTER 34

Sybil Weeks, with Blackjack accompanying her, walked the Lemerriant trail. Dressed in her voluminous black coat, she carried her stick and tapped the ground to disclose raised tree roots, rocks or fallen branches. There was little light in the deep woods even in the daytime; Sybil's vision was already so limited that she normally depended on other senses to navigate, but tonight she had help. She was carrying the shaman mask, and, from time to time, paused to raise it to her face. At such moments, Blackjack took flight and flew low over the trail as if searching; then when Sybil lowered the mask, the bird would glide back to travel from branch to branch in her wake.

Sybil *was* searching, seeing through the eyes of the mask what Blackjack could see. The woods were rain-soaked although the sky had begun to clear; if the forest hadn't obscured them, both the sun and moon would have been visible on that evening, one setting, the other rising. Her walking stick told her that she was approaching a muddy place, and once again, she paused to look through the eyeholes in the mask while Blackjack flew over the area. Yes, this was a good spot. The trail was patterned with footprints, and for a moment Sybil stood confused. There were many footprints, but only some of them made by the Loogy-Roo. How was she going to distinguish the ones she wanted? *Yaxagama, Yaxagama, help me find the trail of evil!* Then, realizing that it would make no difference, since her mixture would only work on the ones it was created for, she reached into the plastic bag in the pocket of her coat, brought out a handful of dust, and broadcast it high into the air, letting it sift down over all the prints. *Yaxagama, Yaxagama, raise her, bring her to this spot. Guide her feet into these footsteps.* She continued to walk through the mud. *Keep her walking, walking, walking, straight on up this forest trail.* Gracefully, she tossed another handful of dust. *And let her sleep and keep on dreaming as she goes toward her doom.*

Single-mindedly, Sybil continued up the path. She would have to go the whole distance, she realized, or at least until she ran out of dust. She felt the bag. Good! There was plenty of the graveyard dirt mix left, as long as she conserved it. She couldn't risk having her plan go wrong, and would have to cover the entire trail to make sure the Loogy-Roo would be sent back to its lair. *Guard her closely, Yaxagama, let her footsteps never stray.* She let fly more dust. *Let no word or cry escape her, send the moon to light her way. Whoosh*, more dust.

Sybil was coming to the clearing where, in pale light, stood the Lemerriant farm, still and shadowed. *Bring her to this place tonight, let her death await her here.* She tossed the last of the dust, then, suddenly exhausted, she sat down on the porch step of the Lemerriant cabin. Once again she placed the mask to her face. "Fly, Blackjack, fly and find the Loogy-Roo." The bird lifted off and vanished into the trees.

Raise her softly, Yaxagama, make her silent steal away, so no one will see or follow, let her move just like a shadow, guided by the bird of night to where her glowing footprints lie. Guide her feet into the footprints, while she sleeps the sleep enchanted. Send her where her doom awaits her, bind her here to never leave it, as the others, also bound, walk the night in anguished torment, hounded by their earthly sins.

Sybil, a little out of breath, stopped chanting, and lowered the mask. The sudden quiet seemed menacing. She felt cut off, unsure of what would happen next. Up until then she'd been operating with purpose. The chanting had kept her focused, but now, in the still darkness, she was beginning to feel small and afraid. Should she go back? Had she done all she needed to do? At that moment Sybil wanted nothing more than to be at home, safe in her own room. She shivered in the chill of the night. Would the Loogy-Roo come? Without Blackjack Sybil felt vulnerable. She raised the mask to her eyes but saw nothing but darkness. *Yaxagama, help me*, she whispered, but there was only silence. What was going to happen now? Would Blackjack bring the Loogy-Roo? And then what? Would the ghosts of the Lemerriants come and claim her? Surely nobody expected Sybil alone to battle all the forces of evil. Or did they? Or would there be some other way? Would the cougar come? In the stories of the Loogy-Roo, the beast was always there. But would it attack and kill the Loogy-Roo? Or was the cougar a creature of Satan who *served* the Loogy-Roo and did her bidding? Perhaps the cougar *was* the Loogy-Roo. If the Loogy-Roo could take the shape of a child, it could also appear as a cougar. In any case, Sybil did not want to be found there, in the lair of the Loogy-Roo, by either the living or the dead.

It was then she heard a soft growl.

CHAPTER 35

Danielle Herron was back at home in her cozy, though drafty, house on Kaunio Road with its unobstructed view of the sea. She had purchased both shop and house — cheap — from Jacinthe Bellavance, and realized later why Jacinthe had been eager to sell. The house needed renovation; and business was spotty. Poor economic times had convinced many that there would never be a way to make a living on Broom Island.

Danielle felt otherwise. She'd seen the island as a potential jewel. Had it been across the border, in the U.S., it would have been a French Riviera — a Monaco — and in the increasingly computerized age, it would only be a matter of time before it became peopled by the wealthy.

Danielle, needing a place to live, had shrewdly assessed the location as being an excellent investment. She'd made an offer on the house as well as the shop, and once hers, she'd had new windows put in and a new roof installed to replace the leaky moss-encrusted wooden shingles. Then (possibly as a way of marking her territory) she had, herself, painted the house purple so that it now stood out as a landmark, serving as a reference to any stranger seeking directions. As she could afford to funnel more money into it, she planned to have the house properly insulated, and also toyed with the idea of adding on a closed-in porch, possibly one of those bubble-type conservatories that might serve as a sunroom and a place for plants.

To Danielle, although the house was small, it had become an oasis. There were no visible neighbors, as the houses along Kaunio Road were either spaced like farms, or at least screened by vegetation. Living alone was not a problem; Danielle was used to it. She'd never married, and she found the solitude soothing after a day of keeping shop, interacting with suppliers and dealers, involving herself in island social and political issues, and generally immersing herself in the swirling life of Satama.

Tonight, Danielle had come home, stripped off her working clothes, put on a pair of comfortable "fat" pants, then made herself a sardine and onion sandwich which she ate while sipping beer out of a bottle and watching the evening news. Later she would tune in one of her favorite TV shows, make a cup of tea and open that box of Godiva truffles. It should have been a relaxing evening, but Danielle couldn't get her mind off the day's happenings. Poor Rowena! And she felt that she should, after all, have gone over to the Weeks' and retrieved that transformation mask. What could Sybil possibly have been thinking? And what with that scamp, Matt, in the house, how could she be sure the mask would be safe? Danielle looked at the clock. Maybe the family would be home by now. She wondered about Rome and how seriously injured he might be. She could ask about him, couldn't she? She should call to see if anyone was at home.

But then, Jeremy Banks had mentioned that Sybil had had a seizure. Danielle hadn't realized she was subject to them. She could even possibly have had one when she was minding the shop! No, it wouldn't do to have Sybil there anymore. Not after she'd taken the mask, and certainly not if she were likely to have epileptic fits! Did Danielle really want to confront Sybil right now? No, Danielle decided; better to wait until morning. As she settled comfortably in her recliner, the doorbell rang. With a look of annoyance, Danielle lowered the footrest, got up and padded to the door.

It was Rowena Michaels. "I'm sorry to bother you again, but — "

"Nonsense! Come in!" Danielle ushered her friend inside. "Has something happened?" She seated Rowena on the couch and switched off the television. "Tell me what's wrong. I can see that something is."

"I've left him."

"Chad?"

"Yes." Rowena sat staring straight ahead.

"Uh, well, it's probably a good thing, but how — uh — what did he do to you?" All this was too much of a switch from the Weena she'd left at Michaels Acres a few hours ago — the one whose main concern seemed to be feeding and medicating her husband.

"I just couldn't spend another night under the same roof with that man."

Danielle waited silently to hear the rest of it.

"He just never stops talking."

So what had happened? Had something snapped? "Well . . . uh, Weena . . . was that *all?*"

Weena turned and pinned Danielle with eyes bright with indignation. "All? *All?* Have you any idea what that's *like?* Twelve years of listening to someone complain and carp and threaten and whine and yell and criticize and brag. The man has never had a good thing to say about anyone or anything. And he wants everyone to fall to their knees and adore the Great God Chadwick. He really thinks he is a god, you know, when goes off on one of his toots. And he just *never . . . ever . . . shuts . . . up.*"

Danielle was trying to picture it — and found that she could, sort of. But why now? "Isn't this a bit sudden? You didn't say anything about leaving when I took you home." (Danielle had been relieved that Rowena appeared to have no memory of the night before.)

Weena gave a bitter laugh. "Call it an epiphany. You know, it's not the big things that break up a marriage. An affair? Piece of cake! Spouse is a drunk? Help him kick the habit. Husband ends up in jail? Stand by your man! But one annoying thing that goes on and on and on and *on*. . . ." Weena was speaking through gritted teeth.

"How did you get here?"

"I took the truck."

"Chad's truck?"

"*My* truck. Why the hell should it be Chad's truck? It was paid for with my money."

"So then I guess we can assume that Chad won't be coming over here to drag you back by the hair."

"Not unless he does it on foot! Although he probably will be calling as soon as he finds out."

"If he does, we won't answer — or I'll unplug the phone. But what do you mean by when he finds out? Doesn't he know you've gone?"

"He was in the shower. After he shot Rome Weeks, he arrived home soaking wet — something about falling in a well — and he was going on and on about how everyone including me was out to get him. And I just suddenly realized that I didn't have to be there! And for the first time in our marriage I told him to shut up. If he had, I might have stayed. I finally got him to go take a hot shower. When he did, I got in the truck and drove away."

"Just like that?"

"After all these years, yes. Just like that."

Danielle studied Weena's face. She looked tired and a little empty, but she certainly hadn't been drinking, nor did she seems emotionally overwrought. Most of all, there seemed to be no ambivalence, no sign of remorse or inner conflict. Yet, Danielle realized that decisions made impulsively are not always written in stone: "Tomorrow might put a different face on things."

"If I show any signs of going back to him, I'm counting on you to stick out a foot and trip me."

"You sound serious."

"I *am* serious. It penetrated my skull that there's no reason for me to stay — not anymore. When Dory ..." Weena's eyes filled with tears. "When I had Dory it was different. I could never have left *her*, and Chad wouldn't have let me have her. He'd have found some legal way of twisting things to make me look like an unfit mother. He's good at using the law as a club."

"Have you thought about what you're going to do?"

"I won't stay on the island, at least not as long as Chad is here. I want to put a lot of distance between us. He'll make it difficult, I know. He's an expert at screwing people over, but I don't care if I don't get a penny. I just want to be able to breathe. I blame him for Dory, you know."

"Oh, Weena, you know he'd have never hurt Dory!"

"No, he wouldn't. But if he hadn't been such an asshole and if we'd had a normal life we'd never have come here. I now realize that in our family the craziest person made all the decisions."

Danielle said nothing.

"And, of course, I have to blame myself as well. Where was *I*? Why did I let Chad run things? I was a coward. It was easier to appease and to go along than to deal with his hysterics. I told myself I was keeping the peace, and kept dangling the carrot in front of my nose that things would someday change."

Danielle shrugged. "I think ... I think you did the right thing."

"Right or wrong doesn't seem to matter. I'm doing it. I realize that a man like Chad needs someone to look after him, and I'm a bit sorry to leave him on his own, but I think I'm up for parole. He'll manage. If I dropped dead, he'd *have* to manage. I'm sure he'll find some woman to replace me. He'll probably be remarried within a year."

Danielle was processing all this with surprise and new respect. This wasn't the Rowena she knew. If anything, the old Rowena had often sounded helpless and hang-dog. Now she seemed ready to fight city hall — or at least walk away from it. "It sounds like you've thought this through."

"No, I haven't really had time yet. I don't know where I'm going or how soon. I'll have to get in touch with a few people and make plans. I didn't even bring anything with me."

"Well, you'll stay here, of course, as long as you like. You probably haven't had any dinner. Why don't I make you a sandwich and a cup of tea. Then we can watch *The X Files* and open up one of those new boxes of Godiva chocolates." Danielle smiled. "Rx for a troubled day: tea and chocolate."

* * *

"Weena!" Chad Michaels was shouting. "Weena, where the hell's my shampoo? The bottle in here is empty. Goddammit, Weena, can't you tell when a bottle is empty? Weena! Can't you hear me calling you? Woman must be going deaf. Dammit, Weena!" Red-faced from the hot water as well as from simmering rage, Chad stepped out of the shower as water sloshed onto the bathmat and floor. He grabbed a towel and swabbed his face, then opened a cabinet to find various bath items but still no shampoo. "Weena! What am I supposed to do? Wash my hair with toothpaste?" he bawled. There was no answer. *Damned woman must have gone out into the greenhouse again. She can't hear anything when she's in there — but why would she go out at this time of night?* Realizing nobody would be rushing to his aid, Chad stepped back into the shower, opened the shampoo bottle and held it under the stream of water, gave it a shake, then upended the contents into his palm, whereupon he had a handful of shampoo — certainly more than was needed for his balding pate. "Why do *I* always get the dregs?" he muttered. He shampooed his head, rinsed, then sloshed out of the stall to dry off, leaving a puddle of water and towels in a heap on the floor. He wet-footed into the bedroom and considered putting on a pair of pajamas. Too early to go to bed. He opted for a polyester jogging suit and slippers. All at once he realized that he was hungry. No wonder! He hadn't eaten anything all day. He'd go see what Weena had made for his dinner. But something wasn't right. There was no smell of anything cooking, and the house was too quiet.

Chad made his way into the kitchen. It was clean and empty. He opened the refrigerator, expecting to find a meal on a plate, but there was none. "Weena!" he bellowed, then when this was greeted with nothing but silence, "Now I suppose I'll have to go out and find her and tell her to get her lazy ass in here." He listened. The quiet seemed a bit spooky. He poured himself a glass of milk and downed it, abandoning both the milk carton and the empty glass on the counter. "You'd think the least she could do is have dinner on the table on time. It shouldn't be too much to ask, considering all the things *I* do for *her*." He rooted around in the refrigerator, found a package of sliced ham, and wolfed it down. "Weena! Where the hell are you!" He opened the door and looked out, expecting to see a light on in the greenhouse, but there was none. He stepped outside. The rain had stopped, the sky was clearing, and the moon was shedding its light, forming a mottling of shadows.

"Weena?" It was more of a whisper now, and then Chad noticed that there was something different about the driveway. The truck was gone! He blinked and looked again, at first disbelieving. Then he felt the anger welling up. He screamed his rage at the unconcerned moon, then rushed back into the house and picked up the phone. He knew where she'd gone. She'd taken his truck and gone off to see that Herron woman, her lesbian lover. What was her number? Didn't he have it? He'd recently called her, hadn't he? Or was it *she* who had called him? *Goddammit.* His hands shaking, he found the phone book and leafed through it to find the number for Danielle's shop — and under it, the listing for her home phone. Yes, he would call and straighten those two broads out once and for all. He punched in the wrong number and waited. There was no answer.

Now that the routine of his life had been dealt another blow, Chad was shaken. While for periods of time he could go along on a familiar track, any bowling ball of an event could knock him into a panic that his muddled mind couldn't process: Where was he? What was it he had to do? He stared at the kitchen counter at an array of small prescription bottles. Medication. Yes, he'd have to take his medication to make the panic go away, but which one? He'd get a glass of water. By time he'd found the glass and filled it, he no longer remembered why. He felt himself in danger, and no one could have reassured him, because at such times he exuded aggression like a cloud of squid ink, hurling accusations at anyone who happened to be in range. Only now, to his horror, there was no one to blame, no one to order about, no one to *care*.

Oh yes, he remembered now what he had to do. He had to kill the cougar. He needed his gun. Where had he put it? Oh yes, it was by the door where Veikko Kuusiniemi had left it leaning against the wall. He should clean it, shouldn't he? He'd shot Rome Weeks with it. Why was it here? Wasn't it evidence? How did he come to still have it? No matter. He'd clean it after he killed the cougar. Blew that bastard to kingdom come. But first he had to find Weena. She was in on it, wasn't she. She'd always been in on it. They'd all been against him from the start, and his bitch of a wife had been the ringleader.

She was the one who wanted him dead! She and that cunt who owned the gift shop. He'd have to settle the score with her. Oh yes, they thought they could get away with stealing his truck, but he had a surprise for *them*. He'd follow them in Weena's car. But Weena no longer owned a car. He'd told her they couldn't afford one until she made a go of the greenhouses. It didn't matter. Nothing mattered. He would track them down all the way to Hell if he had to. Nothing would stop him, and then they'd see what happens to people who try to outsmart Chadwick Michaels! Hell, he could walk to town. He could do anything. He had superhuman strength, didn't he? He was smarter than all of them put together, wasn't he? Chad Michaels laughed. All those poor little people crawling around like ants, just waiting for him to step on them. They were only there for his convenience, created only to serve him, and it was up to him to decide which of them would be allowed to live. And, by god, a couple of them would never see the morning!

CHAPTER 36

JEREMY TURNED on the gas under the kettle to give it a jag, then poured boiling water into his cup over the old teabag. Chamomile was a bit bland to his taste, but it would probably not keep him awake. In their senior years, both he and Willie occasionally experienced sleepless nights, although never as Willie ruefully said, the *same* night, when they might have gotten up and kept each other company. At such times Willie usually turned on her light and read for an hour or two. Jeremy tended to wander, and would sometimes go upstairs to stargaze through his telescope if the skies were clear; or he'd watch old movies on TV, keeping the sound turned down so as not to disturb Willie. There was now plenty of variety since they'd installed the satellite dish.

Jeremy carried the cup into the *pirtti*, where he switched on the TV and settled into his recliner. Normally this was a favorite time of day for him, and if Willie had gone to bed (she tended to retire earlier than he) Jeremy would seek out a stateside news channel just to get the feel of what was going on across the border. Any major news event made it to all channels, but there was familiarity to the sound of the Seattle station, a subtle difference in approach that Jeremy, now that he was straddling both countries, could detect.

In the slant of U.S. news there seemed to be an increasing ethno-centricity, if not an outright xenophobia that lurked like a weed in the American culture. Had it always been there, or had he just not noticed it? It seemed to be a running gag that the average American knew nothing about Canada, and pictured Canadians as hockey-crazed people living in igloos. (They were wrong about the igloos.) The perception was also that Canadians were "polite" but inconsequential, their health care was better, and that the country was more law-abiding and tolerant of minorities. Jeremy had found these things true but only to a degree. Canada, to Jeremy, seemed more yin while America was yang to the point of macho.

He rather fancied the United States and Canada as a dysfunctional married couple: Canada nagging and complaining that her husband paid no attention to her — while Uncle Sam hid behind his newspaper and grunted in order to at least appear to be listening, then made some patronizing remark or demand. They'd been together a long time, and they couldn't really divorce, but they never seemed to let up in their game of tit for tat.

Tonight's news wasn't particularly interesting, centering on the Whitewater investigation, which Jeremy found tiresome and political. Delta II launch had been postponed due to bad weather; a tornado in Illinois had caused minor damage. Jeremy clicked off the set, quaffed the last of his tea, then went on to secure the house. Before retiring, either he or Willie would make the rounds, seeing to it that nothing had been left turned on in the kitchen, that the lights were out, and that the doors were locked. Whoever did it would intone, like a town crier, "The house is secure!" This was a ritual peculiar to them, as both were American citizens and former American residents. Most of the people on Broom Island didn't bother to lock anything.

Jeremy headed for the kitchen to wash the cups. But what was this?

The back door, that opened onto the mudroom off the kitchen, was not only unlocked but ajar! The mudroom door to the yard was open as well. Could the wind have blown it? Winds on Broom Island could be gusty. Jeremy peeked outside. The night was calm, the rain had stopped, the moon had risen, and there were only a few drifting clouds. Odd! Jeremy closed both doors and flipped the bolt, but something bothered him. He stood, for a moment, idly rubbing his wrist just under the cast (it always seemed to itch in that spot). Had someone gone out? If so, who? Willie had gone to bed, or had she remembered some last-minute errand? In that case Jeremy might be locking her out! He undid the bolt, stuck his head through the outside door, and called her name softly. No answer.

What should he do? Go upstairs and count heads? He couldn't just go barging into Celeste's room, or Willie's either, and if he knocked on either door he might awaken all of them. He didn't want to alarm the household, when it was probably nothing. Perhaps the latch had failed to engage, and an air current simply caused the door to drift open. But, just in case, he would go upstairs and see if anyone's light was still on. He could then ask if anyone had been out, make sure that everyone was inside, and then stop worrying about it and go to bed. If anyone had left the building, she would have had to come downstairs and cross over into the kitchen. Jeremy should have noticed — or would he? He'd had his back to the area and the TV turned on.

Willie's bedroom, the master bedroom that her parents had occupied, lay toward the front of the house and faced the sea. Jeremy climbed the stairs and saw no light under her door. Willie was either asleep, or for some unfathomable reason, outdoors. His own room and the guest rooms, one now occupied by Celeste and Gabi, were set apart, to the right at the stairway. No light showed there either. *Damn.* He walked to the end of the hall and checked the bathroom. The door was open, the room was empty, and the light was off. He returned to Willie's door and knocked softly. No reply. He very quietly turned the knob and cracked the door just enough to be able to peer in. There, partly bathed in moonlight, he could see a lump in the four-poster bed — a lump with a nightcap! A nightcap! Did Willie really wear a nightcap? Who wore nightcaps anymore? This one appeared to be white with flaps that framed the face like the ears of a beagle. Jeremy suppressed a smile and softly closed the door. He promised himself that he would never, ever, mention it.

But now, with a tiny sense of foreboding, he went down the hall and approached Celeste's room. There was no light on there either. Did he dare? He had to. If there were two sleeping figures, then all was well. The door was unlocked and swung silently on its hinges. There he could make out Celeste, asleep, making a graceful figure "S" under her duvet. The bed next to hers was palely illuminated by the moonlit night, and it was empty.

Long afterwards, Jeremy wondered why he didn't raise the alarm, awaken both Willie and Celeste at that moment. It would have made perfect sense, but it was almost as though it didn't even occur to him, and he did later wonder what he'd been thinking as he turned and ran, with the agility of a much younger man, down the stairs. Maybe he realized he'd wasted too much time already. Maybe he envisioned Gabi sleepwalking aimlessly in the yard, and knew he had to find her at once. He only knew that Gabi was out there, somewhere, and that she could be in danger. Stopping only long enough to grab his jacket and a flashlight from a hook on the mudroom wall, Jeremy rushed out into the night.

CHAPTER 37

CHAD MICHAELS was breathing hard as he toiled up the road toward his gate. He was awkwardly carrying his Winchester rifle, with nothing but the moon to light his way. He hadn't taken time to change clothes, and the bedroom slippers on his feet were poor protection — although he didn't appear to notice. He was taking the gravel road rather than the shortcut path that Dory used to catch her bus; when he got to his chain link gate, he pushed it open and went on up the road to the "T" where the bus bench stood. He paused, for a moment, to catch his breath and now felt a chill through his polyester knit, as the perspiration he'd been generating began to evaporate in the cool night air. He shivered. He had to keep moving. For a moment he stood on the road. Either direction would take him into town, but which was shorter? He always went to the right, but he wasn't going into town, was he? To get to the house on Kaunio Road, he'd have to go through the village, past the cemetery and up the road to Danielle's cottage.

It would probably be shorter to go left on Quarry, then turn right on Tranquil Bay Road which would lead to the far end of Kaunio. He was a bit hazy on exactly where along that stretch Danielle's house was, but he calculated that it should be a shorter distance to travel. He wasn't as familiar with that route, and he vaguely sensed that it would still be a very long way; but by now the need to get even with Weena had become less important than the need to simply find his way *to* Weena, and he began to fancy that he heard her calling him. Dragging his gun, he lurched onward. The air grew cooler as he climbed the ridge of the hill to the spine of the island, and his feet were beginning to hurt, then grow numb with cold.

Maybe he should turn back after all. He should go back and try calling again, demand that Weena come home. Where was she? He could *swear* he heard her voice just now! Was she telling him to go back and take his medication? Was that it? Or was she telling him to keep going? "Weena? Is that you, Weena? Goddammit, where the hell *are* you?" The road was rougher and his slippers were beginning to disintegrate. He moved to the berm so he could walk along the wet grass. There seemed to be a lot of trees, suddenly, and less visibility. The way didn't seem at all familiar anymore, but at least it wasn't as stony, and now he seemed to be moving downhill. Maybe he'd reached the end, and would soon find himself on Kaunio Road. Yes, that must be it. He'd made it on foot and now, by god, he would find that wife of his and that miserable bitch who was probably holding her captive — but what was that? He was stepping into mud. Where was he? This couldn't be the connecting road. His foot sank into deeper mud and he lost a slipper, then stubbed his toe on a block of wood and dropped his gun. *Damn!* He couldn't see a thing and wished he had a flashlight. He felt around for his slipper but by now he'd moved away from the spot and couldn't find it. He groped the ground. There seemed to be rounds of wood on the road ranged like stepping stones. This couldn't be a road traveled by car, so it wasn't even a logging road. He must have veered off into the woods onto a hiking path!

Chad wasn't a hiker, and except for the few on his own acreage, wasn't familiar with the various walking trails on the island. *Shit!* Where was he? Chad's eyes glinted as a moonbeam made its way through the foliage. The hair on the back of his neck prickled. He felt himself in danger. *They tricked me. They're out to get me. They think Chad Michaels is a fool. They think I'm a greenhorn. They're probably all around me, watching me. But I'm too smart for them.* He backtracked and nearly stepped on his gun, picked it up, then hesitated a moment as to which way to go. Once again he thought he heard Weena. Was that Weena? It sounded like a woman's voice! Was it coming from up ahead? He began to walk toward it, dragging his gun, his feet bare, muddy, and cold. He couldn't see the wooden "lily pads" along the trail and kept slipping, either stepping between them into the mud or stubbing his toes on them. "Weena? Is that you? Where are you, Weena?" It was somewhere between a sob and a cry. "Weeeenaaaa!" And he thought he heard an answer. Yes, it was a woman's voice. Was it calling his name? It sounded almost like a baby crying — or a woman crying. He answered back, calling for Weena. He had to find her. He had to keep going. One painful step at a time, but he had to keep moving. "I'm coming, Weena."

CHAPTER 38

Jeremy stood still on the flagstone walk outside the kitchen door, listening, straining for any sound of Gabi, his mind racing: *You're not supposed to awaken a sleepwalker. Why? For god's sake, why not?* It made no sense, particularly if the sleepwalker happened to be in danger. Was Gabi sleepwalking? If not, why would she have slipped out the house in the dark of night? All right, there was a moon, and a moonlit island night could tempt anyone out to enjoy it; but Gabi knew better than to go wandering around when everyone was under cougar alert. He trained his flashlight out over the area, swept it in an arc to reveal no sign of her, and softly called her name. She could have circled around the house or she could be on the front porch. She might have just slipped out to sit in the swing, even fallen asleep there. He would go see, but first he shone his flashlight onto the walkway. It was wet. No way of knowing if anyone had crossed it. Carefully, he aimed the beam along the lawn he'd cut the day before. The grass was neatly trimmed and wet from rain, bejeweled uniformly by drops of water. And then, to both his relief and consternation, he saw that there were small irregularities in it, spots in which the raindrop pattern had been disturbed, and that there was a faint, yet unmistakable trail of prints that led across the wet lawn and — *oh, god, no!* — into the woods.

Jeremy followed the track, inch by inch, in the beam of his light, fearful that the fragile trail would become invisible where the smooth lawn ended — which it did at the edge of the forest. With keen senses born of desperation, if not experience, Jeremy continued to follow, noticing such indicators as a bent stem or trodden weed. Where was she going? Well, of course that was a pointless question; a sleepwalker moves in a different realm. She could be traveling anywhere in her dreams while she made her way into the woods. Then it occurred to Jeremy that maybe Gabi was not sleepwalking at all. Maybe she was on her way to see Matt Weeks! She was headed in that direction. He felt momentarily almost jubilant. Maybe those two little scamps had cooked up some escapade, some bit of mischief, and he'd find Gabi safe and sound.

But, as Jeremy made his way through the wooded area that separated the two houses, he could see that the Weeks house was dark. There was no sign of anyone's being home. He opened the door, helloed the house, but nobody answered. Apparently the whole family must still be at the clinic. Still, was it possible that Gabi might have gone inside anyway? The door was unlocked. She could have gotten in, and maybe he'd find her asleep in there, somewhere. Jeremy went back inside and searched the house: the upstairs bedrooms, the big country kitchen that served also as dining room (strange smell in there!) and the living room with its old overstuffed furniture. He even went down the cellar steps, all the while calling Gabi's name and becoming more and more anxious, knowing that she could still be outdoors, and in gravest danger.

But where? Back in the yard, with the aid of his flashlight, Jeremy began searching the grounds for any sign — anything at all. He wasn't familiar with the surround of the Weeks house, but he circled it carefully and checked the outbuildings. As he rounded the corner at the back of the house, he spotted an opening into the forest: the entrance to a trail.

Was this the trail the kids had been on the day Celeste and Willie had gone looking for them? Could it possibly be that Gabi, and perhaps even Matt, were somewhere on that trail tonight?

Jeremy entered it. The way was partly lit by the moon, and the beam of his torch showed the trail bed to be much traveled. There were all kinds of footprints on it, some made by Gabi and Matt, judging by the size of the sneakers, but many were so distorted by rain that it was hard to tell which way they were going. There were prints in the soft mud made by adult feet as well. How could he possibly know whether any of the prints were made by Gabi tonight? The marks only showed where the ground was muddy; there were stretches covered with wood chips that showed no tracks at all. Was he wasting his time looking in the wrong place, going the wrong way? He came to another muddy spot and saw tracks presumably made by Matt and Gabi and their bicycle wheels. These, protected by foliage, were clear enough to show that they were headed out, not in, so Jeremy judged them to be the old ones. He had almost decided to turn back when his beam hit something: it was clearly a footprint going up the trail, deeper into the woods, and distinct enough to have been freshly made — the print of a small bare foot in soft mud.

* * *

Kirsti Weeks and her son were driving home in Rome's rattly *Chrysler* pickup truck. Peg Hewett had brought the terrible news that Rome had been shot — *by that miserable bastard*, Kirsti thought darkly. She and Matt had ridden to the clinic with Peg, where they'd held a vigil until it seemed that Rome was in stable condition and asleep. There had been talk of ambulancing him to a hospital on the mainland, but Dr. Swallow seemed to feel he'd be better off resting quietly at least until morning. Peg had offered to give Kirsti and Matt a ride, promising to come get them if there was any change, but Rome's truck had been left in the parking lot with the keys in it. Kirsti opted to drive it home, so it would be there if they needed to get back in a hurry.

Kirsti felt worn and tired. It was late. She now had to check on Sybil, and guiltily realized she'd scarcely given her a thought. When the news came, Sybil had been asleep, and Kirsti hadn't wanted to awaken her, much less alarm her about her father at that moment. She belatedly realized she should have called Willie to go over to make sure her daughter was all right — not that Sybil was normally incapable of taking care of herself, but she *had* suffered a seizure.

Kirsti hadn't eaten anything all day, nor was she hungry. Peg Hewett had brought them sandwiches (Matt had devoured a couple), but all Kirsti had had was a number of cups of black coffee, and she was feeling shaky and light-headed. Regardless of the hour, she'd see to it that everyone had a snack before bedtime, Sybil as well, if she hadn't already fed herself.

She pulled into her driveway. The house was dark, so perhaps Sybil was sleeping and still unaware of what had happened. Matt was quiet and thoughtful, not at all his usual rambunctious self. She reached over and gave him a pat on the knee. "Papa's going to be fine. He just needs time to heal up."

Matt looked at his mother and started to say something, then seemed to think better of it. He frowned, forming one deep line between his brows in his otherwise child-smooth face.

"He will be fine, Matt," Kirsti repeated. "You believe that, don't you?"

Matt nodded, rather absently.

"We'll say a prayer for Papa tonight. And tomorrow he'll be much better, yes?"

Matt nodded again. They got out of the truck and went inside. Kirsti turned on the kitchen light. "What in the world is that awful smell? Like something was burning in here. Sybil, are you in the house? What were you cooking?" There was no answer from Sybil, so Kirsti went upstairs to check on her — and found her room empty. "Now where did that girl get to? Matt, is your sister downstairs?"

"No."

"Well, where on earth could she — oh, of course, she'll be at Willie's." Willie would have heard about Sybil's seizure as well as Rome's accident. She would naturally have come over to make sure everything was all right. She'd have found Sybil alone, and no doubt took her home, gave her dinner, and Sybil would be — Kirsti looked at the clock — fast asleep by now. No need to call and awaken the household at this hour.

Kirsti busied herself in the kitchen, "Matt, here's a glass of milk and a peanut butter sandwich. Get those down and then go to bed." But what *was* that terrible smell that kept hanging in the air? Burning wool? Feathers? She opened both the window and the door to let the cross breeze air out the room. She'd have to ask Sybil what in heaven's name she'd been doing.

* * *

Willie Haapala came awake realizing she had to go to the bathroom, and made a mental note not to drink tea late at night. She got up and used the en suite bath; then, aware that she wouldn't be able to get back to sleep anytime soon, she put on her robe and slippers, a formality that both she and Jeremy observed as part of civilized living, should they happen upon each other in the hall. She pulled off her nightcap — silly-looking old thing she'd bought at a charity bazaar held for the benefit of the island seniors. It was a hat worn by Lapp women, not the jaunty "hat of the four winds" that Lapp men sported, but a woebegone tube with a bit of a chef's puff and rickrack-edged ear flaps that made her look like Snoopy. She had bought it — and actually paid twenty-five dollars for the hideous thing (in a guilt-induced attempt to be supportive) from her nemesis, Amanda Vuorisaari, who had been manning a booth selling cultural handcrafted items. Willie had arrived late when most of the "good stuff" was gone and, under Amanda's implacable stare, had picked up the hat with no idea of what she'd ever do with it. After trying it on at home, she had vowed to tuck it into a Salvation Army box in Port Casper ASAP.

Then, later, on her first winter back on Broom Island, as she lay in bed, she noticed that there seemed to be a draft on her scalp. She ruefully concluded that her once-thick hair was beginning to thin; and, worse yet, when her head got cold, she started sneezing. Now she kept the cap under her pillow and only put it on after her lights were out, vowing that if she ever felt herself having a heart attack, the first thing she'd do is yank it off, not wanting to be caught dead in it.

Stepping into the hall, Willie could see, by the night light, that while Celeste's door was slightly ajar, Jeremy's was wide open. She walked over and looked in, saw that the room was empty, and snapped on the light to see that the bed hadn't been slept in. So, Jeremy must be having one of his "nights" as well! She'd find him watching some ancient movie, barely able to hear the sound. Willie had told him it was okay to leave the volume at normal level, that her hearing was no longer so sharp that she could even hear the TV set from upstairs, but he still insisted on straining his ears. Willie intended to gift him with a set of earphones on his birthday.

When Willie couldn't sleep, she would sometimes spend time at her computer. There were always e-mails to answer, surfing to do, research for her book — even online shopping that Willie had recently begun to explore. She went into the kitchen, thinking she might make a cup of cocoa to take into her office. There was no sign of Jeremy downstairs, and now Willie wondered if he'd gone up to peer through his telescope. It was a clear night, now that the rain had stopped. She went to the kitchen door and opened it in order to get a look at the night sky. The door, to her surprise, was unlocked. *That* was odd. Jeremy would have certainly bolted it before going to bed — but he hadn't gone to bed yet, had he? But he'd still have made sure the house was secure before going upstairs. So where was he? Had something happened? Had some noise or disturbance sent him into the yard? She stuck her head out the door and called his name but got no answer.

Willie closed the door but left it unlocked just in case Jeremy might still be out there. She would go upstairs to see if he'd gone up to the third floor to stargaze. Once again, Willie walked through the downstairs rooms, making doubly sure that they were all empty. Then, as she began to climb the stairs to the second floor, she looked up and almost lost her balance. Celeste was standing in front of her, dressed in a pair of knitted exercise pants and sweatshirt, her feet bare, her eyes wide with alarm. "Have you seen Gabi?"

Confused, Willie shook her head. "Why no, isn't she asleep?"

"She's gone. I woke up and her bed was empty. I thought she'd gotten up to go to the bathroom, but she's not there so she must be downstairs!" Celeste's voice betrayed her rising anxiety.

"I don't think so, Celeste. I just walked through the house and there's no one down there. I can't find Jeremy either. What we should do is go up and see if they're looking at the night sky."

That slim hope died when they found the upstairs rooms dark and unoccupied. "Where could she be?" Celeste cried, "I didn't hear her get up. You know she sometimes sleepwalks. Where could she have gone?"

Willie was apprehensive now as well, and puzzled. "Jeremy doesn't seem to be anywhere in the house either. I left him downstairs. He was going to watch the news before bed, but he wasn't there. The TV was turned off, but his door was open and his bed hasn't been slept in. The kitchen door was unlocked as well, so I think someone must have gone out."

"Gabi! Oh my god!"

"If Gabi had gone out, Jeremy might have heard her and gone after her."

Celeste gave Willie a look of anguish. "But he'd have found her right away and brought her right back, wouldn't he?"

The two women locked eyes, neither wanting to say the word *cougar*.

Then Celeste's expression changed subtly and became darker. "We have to call the police, Willie. I think Jeremy may have kidnapped my daughter, and god only knows what he's done with her."

"*What?*"

"If she's been kidnapped, she may still be alive, and we've got to find her right away." Celeste saw Willie's stricken look. "Oh come *on*, what else could it be? If Jeremy saw her leave the house why didn't he yell? What do I really know about Jeremy Banks? How much do *you* know about him?"

Willie took a deep breath. "Celeste, that's impossible. I know you don't know us very well, but please be assured that Jeremy would never, ever, do anything to harm your child or anyone else's. Right now all we know is that neither of them seems to be in the house.

"When I woke up, I came down and saw the lights still on, and the kitchen door unlocked. Normally, Jeremy always closes up the house, locks the doors and turns off the lights if he's the last to go upstairs. Someone must have gone out the kitchen door. If Gabi slipped out, she must have done it quietly, because otherwise Jeremy would have seen her and stopped her. I don't know what happened, but there has to be a logical sequence here. If Gabi went out, she either did it in her sleep, or she deliberately slipped out behind Jeremy's back."

"She wouldn't do that! Why would she do that?"

"I don't know, but if she did, then she didn't want Jeremy to find her. She may be leading him a chase out there. I know it sounds unlikely, but I'm wondering if Matt Weeks could be involved in this somehow. You'll need a jacket — socks and boots — you'll find them in the mudroom. I'll throw on some clothes and get a couple of flashlights. We *will* find your daughter."

"Oh my god, she's out there somewhere. She could be lost. She could injure herself a hundred ways out there in the dark. She could be attacked by the cougar! We don't even know how long she's been gone. If I hadn't taken that damned sleeping pill, I might have heard her get up. Something woke me . . . maybe the light in the hall."

"Never mind that now. We have to hurry."

Moments later Willie had changed into jeans, gum boots, and a thick oversized sweatshirt. Celeste had found a flannel jacket and boots. Armed with flashlights, they went out into the night. Calling Gabi's name, they circled the grounds.

"I think we should go over and see if she could have gone to the Weekses," Willie said.

"But they weren't even home when you went over there. It doesn't make any sense that Gabi would get up in the middle of the night and go there."

"Right now nothing is making any sense, but where else could she possibly be going? She doesn't know anyone else."

"If she's walking in her sleep she could be anywhere," Celeste wailed.

"We'll cut through the woods. If nobody's there, I'll go inside and call Constable Hewett and tell him Gabi's missing. We'll need all the help we can get."

They were making their way through wet vegetation and Willie was noticing that it looked like someone had recently taken the same route. Had Jeremy already come this way looking for Gabi? And what wildly freakish set of circumstances could have led to any of this? At any rate, as they approached the clearing, they could see lights on in the Weeks house.

"Look, Celeste. Someone's home," Willie sounded relieved.

"Do you think she's there? Do you think she's all right?"

Willie went to the kitchen door — the one everyone used — and knocked. The lights that were on seemed to be upstairs, and that wasn't necessarily a good sign. There was no answer and Willie pounded more loudly. She saw the kitchen light go on and then Kirsti opened the door: "Willie? What's the matter? Come in, come in."

"Is Gabi here?" Celeste asked.

"No. Matt and I just got back from the clinic. We haven't been home, so if Gabi came by — but wait a minute. Isn't Sybil over at your place?"

"Sybil? No. I thought she was at the clinic with you and Matt. I came by to look in on her when I heard about Rome's accident. How is Rome?"

"Oh, we hope he'll be all right. But if Sybil isn't with you, then where is she? I thought you might have taken her home with you."

"I would have, but the house was empty, so I assumed she was with *you*."

"Gabi's missing. We have to find *Gabi*!" Celeste was near tears.

"Apparently everybody's missing tonight," Willie said. "I don't suppose you've seen Jeremy either. We thought Gabi might have slipped out of the house and come to see Matt — and that Jeremy might have gone to look for her. And now you say Sybil is missing as well? Where's Matt? Could we ask him if he has any idea where Gabi might have gone?"

"Matt should be asleep by now, but I'll go up and ask him to come down."

But Matt was already down. He hadn't been asleep; he'd heard voices and made his way into the kitchen, and now stood frowning his one-wrinkle frown, puzzled by the commotion.

"Matt," Celeste said, "We can't find Gabi. Have you any idea where she might have gone?"

Matt's eyes widened in surprise. He shook his head, then looked at his mother. "Sybil is missing too," Kirsti said. "We don't know how long she's been gone or where she went. If you have any notion of what's going on, please tell us."

"I thought you said Sybil was at Willie's."

"I thought so too, but Willie hasn't seen her. It's the middle of the night. Did Sybil say anything to you about what she may have been planning to do?"

"No, but she's been talking about the Loogy-Roo."

Kirsti gave an impatient snort. "You know there's no such thing, don't you Matt?"

"Oh sure. *I* know. But I'm not sure Sybil knows. She was saying she had to kill it."

"When did she say this?"

"Oh, I dunno. She's been talking a lot about the Loogy-Roo. I guess it was maybe after she got home from the shop and she had that Indian thing. I asked her what she was carrying and she said it was none of my business and that if I told anybody she'd make me sorry. She locked herself in her room and told me to stay out and keep my mouth shut."

"Is there any chance that Sybil might have taken Gabi with her?" Celeste asked, increasingly alarmed at what might now be a kidnapping by a deranged woman.

"I dunno," Matt said. "But she took Blackjack. He's not here either."

Kirsti looked narrowly at her son. "Matt, I want you to try to remember exactly what your sister said."

"When?"

"About the Loogy-Roo nonsense."

"She's been saying stuff about it for quite a while, but when she came home from the shop she had that Indian face with her. I asked her what it was, and she told me to mind my own business. I asked what she was going to do with it, and that's when she said it would help her get rid of the Loogy-Roo."

Kirsti nodded. "And then what?"

"I told her the Loogy-Roo was just dumb and there was no such thing. She said yes there was, and I said no there wasn't, and she said yes there was, and she knew where it lived. And I said that's stupid because there is no Loogy-Roo and she said she could prove it and I said, oh yeah, well prove it then, and she said it lived in the old house on the trail, and I said okay, then show me."

"And did she show you?"

"No, she just got mad and told me to get out and stay out of her way."

Kirsti, Willie and Celeste all looked at each other. "You don't think . . ." Celeste began. ". . . Sybil could be out at the Lemerriant house . . ."

Kirsti said. "... At this hour of the night?" Willie added.

"Oh, my god! Could Gabi be with her?"

"Apparently anything is possible tonight," Willie said. "We'll have to go there! Now."

"I'll go too, Mom, I know the trail."

"I'll get my coat," Kirsti said.

"Shouldn't we have a gun or something?" Celeste asked, wide-eyed. "There's a wild beast out there killing children!"

"Do you know how to shoot?" Willie asked.

"No."

"Does anyone here know how to handle a gun?"

"I do," Matt said. "Pop showed me."

Willie looked at Matt as if to say, oh great, a kid with a rifle for protection! "Anyway, we don't have a gun."

"There's Rome's rifle in the truck," Kirsti said.

"Do you know how to use it?"

"Can't say I do. Never liked guns, and I've never fired that one."

"I really *do* know how to shoot, Mom. I could take it. Even if I couldn't hit a cougar, I could scare it away." Matt looked from one dubious face to another.

"I don't think so, Matt. You're too young."

"I'm almost twelve. Marvin Seiden had his bar mitzvah when he was thirteen and he said that made him a man."

"We're not Jewish, Matt." Kirsti sounded just irresolute enough for Matt to feel he could push on.

"And Mom, maybe you should stay home in case anything happens with Pop and they need you."

Kirsti, a bit taken aback by her son's sudden manliness, continued to look uncertain.

"Perhaps Matt is right," Willie said. "And you could also get hold of Constable Hewett and tell him the situation. We'll go on ahead. I'm sure the constable will follow us, possibly with a search party. He'll be qualified to deal with this, but we can't just wait for him. Matt knows the trail so — "Willie looked around, "Now where did that boy get to?"

Matt reappeared. He had gone up to change out of his pajamas and was now fully dressed and heading out the door. "Just a minute, young man," Kirsti called. "Put your jacket on. It's cold and wet out there." She helped Matt into a jacket, then, to his embarrassment, took a scarf off a peg and wrapped it around his neck. "And wear this. It'll keep your neck warm."

"Aw, Mom! You're strangling me. I don't need that."

"Just do it. And you can forget about taking your father's gun. There's already been one too many hunting accidents in this family today."

"But, Mom, I know how to use it. I've fired it lots of times."

"Only when your papa was with you. No. No gun."

Matt sighed. "Well, okay. I have my hunting knife."

Kirsti sighed as Matt opened his jacket to display a leather belt with a knife in a sheath. It was a large, Finnish *puukko*, given to Matt on his eleventh birthday by Kirsti's father over mild objections from Kirsti. Country kids grew up knowing how to use knives and guns, and since Rome seemed to think it was all right for Matt to have it, Kirsti said nothing more. It *was* good to have a knife with you when you went into the woods. "And be sure to take a flashlight; there's one in the truck."

Matt darted out the door and the women found him waiting in the yard, flashlight in hand.

"Okay, which way?" Celeste turned on her light, then followed Matt to the opening into the woods, hoping Constable Hewett would be along quickly to take charge of their ad hoc expedition. But right now they had to find Gabi. She glanced nervously at Matt who was striding along the trail. Matt was tall for his age, and a bit chubby, but he was still only a child who should be home, tucked into bed for the night. She looked at Willie who seemed to be studying the path.

"Looks like the Riverdance troupe has been all over this trail," Willie remarked dryly. What do we have here — a party going on at the old

Lemerriant place? Seems like a lot of people have been headed that way."
They'd come to a muddy patch and Willie was studying the indentations.

"Could any of them be Gabi's?" Celeste trained her beam downwards.

"Oh, I'm sure hers are here as well, since she and Matt were on this trail couple of days ago. Some of these could be Jeremy's." Willie's beam had picked up a large man's print. "Maybe he's already found her."

"Look at this!" Matt had come to a halt and waited for Willie to shine her light more brightly on the spot. And there it was, a short series of small prints made by bare feet. Celeste hurried over "Oh, my god! It's Gabi. She's not even wearing shoes! She could die of hypothermia!"

"We're on the right track," Willie said. "Let's move on."

CHAPTER 39

Sybil sat, frozen by the sound she'd heard, her hands pale in the moonlight as she gripped the transformation mask. Partly hidden by the canopy of blackberry bramble over the doorway, Sybil could feel a prickling as the hair on the back of her neck shifted position. She strained to listen but heard nothing. What *had* she heard? An animal? Sybil shivered, suddenly cold to the bone. Every one of her senses was on alert, but her body felt paralyzed as if made of stone. She could hear faint rustling, as if someone were moving through the darkness. The Loogy-Roo? Was it the Loogy-Roo? She heard the growl again, more like a cough, and it seemed to be closer. She couldn't see, but the sense of danger was like a bitter smell in her nostrils.

Acting more from reflex than reason, she slowly stood up, and reached for the walking stick she'd left leaning against the porch rail. Brandishing it, she tried to peer into the area studded with silvered shrubs and moon shadows to see if she could make out any movement, but her vision was too blurry. A twig snapped. The sound galvanized Sybil into action. She shouted out at the top of her lungs, swung the stick blindly and hurled it into the darkness like a javelin at whatever might be out there. Quickly she backed up to the cabin until her hand met the sagging door, squeezed through it, then backed into a corner where her knees gave way and she slowly slid down the wall to sink into a heap on the floor. She couldn't stop shaking. She sat, clutching the mask she still held to her bosom, trying to breathe normally. Would the beast follow and find her there? She heard nothing. Maybe she'd frightened it away. Did she dare leave? Could she make her way back home through the night without Blackjack and without her walking stick? She realized that she was too shaky even to stand up. She would have to wait — wait here in the old Lemerriant cabin — the home of the Loogy-Roo — wait and pray that she would live through whatever followed. She hugged the mask to her chest and pulled her coat tightly around her, becoming, in the beam of light that fell upon her through the broken window, just another dark shadow in the corner of the old deserted house.

* * *

Jeremy trudged through the night, his flashlight trained on the forest path, his eyes anxiously looking for footprints. He made his way uncertainly along the trail marked by mud, ambushing tree roots, and in the wettest spots, studded with wooden rounds that made footing easier, but in the darkness became stumbling blocks. He had time to wonder just what the hell he'd been thinking. Why hadn't he alerted the household and formed a posse? Although he was still an agile man, barely past his prime (he reflected), was it really wise for a retired schoolteacher to be tramping through a rainforest in the dead of night with a cougar on the loose? All he needed to do is break a leg. Who would find him? And when? Each time he was close to deciding that perhaps he should turn back, that perhaps Gabi hadn't gotten this far, he'd find another print in the mud. As he traveled, he kept calling Gabi's name. *Damn*, he thought.

It wasn't as if she were *his* daughter — or granddaughter. Why was he taking it upon himself to be her guardian? He didn't expect a reply to that one. It didn't matter who she was. She was a child in danger; he was an adult. Of *course* he had no choice in the matter.

"Gabi! Gabi, where are you?" You'd think she would hear him. How much farther could she have gone? "Gabi!" Could she be sleepwalking? If so, maybe she *couldn't* hear him. Can sleepwalkers hear you? She might even be close-by, maybe just a little farther on up the trail. The night was colder than it had first seemed, and Gabi didn't even have her shoes on. She'd be freezing! Jeremy was sorry he hadn't thought to bring a blanket. He was also sorry he hadn't thought to bring a couple of fresh batteries. Was his flashlight losing power? Maybe it just seemed dimmer under the canopy of trees. Perhaps he should conserve the batteries by turning it off wherever there was enough moonlight to navigate by. "Gabiiii! It's me, Jeremy. Please answer." His wrist under the cast, was beginning to ache from the cold.

"Gab-beee!" He wished he had brought his cell phone so he could call Willie. Jeremy so seldom used his cell phone that he rarely remembered to take it with him. Nobody ever called him on it, and it was mostly just a way of contacting help if he ever had car trouble. Why hadn't he come upon Gabi by now? Could she have veered off the trail into the woods? Now *there* was a frightening thought! He hadn't seen a footprint recently, but they wouldn't show where there were fir needles. He didn't want to even think that she could have been dragged away by the cougar, but the thought lay in his mind like a layer of quicksand.

Jeremy had never hiked the trail but he knew it led to the old Lemerriant homestead. There was no logical reason for Gabi to be going there, but since she and Matt had been there before, maybe she was following some dream connection. If so, then he would find her. If, however, she'd wandered off into the woods . . . but what was he seeing? The forest around him was giving way to a moonlit clearing, or at least what once must have been a clearing, possibly a field, but now was covered with shrubbery and brush. And there, in the distance, in the illumination, a small figure was moving — Gabi! *Thank God!* He called to her, but she didn't seem to hear him. As she was making her way toward the dark shape of the cabin, Jeremy put on a burst of speed and caught up with her. His hand on her shoulder caused her to stop, but otherwise she gave no sign of even seeing him. Dressed only in a pair of pink cotton-knit pajamas, her feet bare, she nevertheless didn't appear to be feeling the cold.

"Gabi?" Jeremy spoke her name softly, slipped off his jacket and put it around her shoulders. "Gabi, it's me, Jeremy. It's time to go home."

Gabi turned to look at him, her eyes wide and glassy, her face impassive. There was no recognition, no reaction of any kind. She didn't protest when he picked her up, nor did she cling to him the way a child usually would. It was almost like hoisting a lifeless mannequin. Jeremy hugged her to warm her, although she wasn't shivering — which Jeremy certainly *was*. He glanced around. There was no sound, no movement. Everything lay still and derelict. He awkwardly shifted her weight in his arms, wishing he weren't wearing the cast on his wrist, and started to head back down the trail.

He was frozen in his tracks by the sound of a woman's scream. Jeremy stopped, turned, but saw nothing. Had it come from the cabin? He started to call out but his voice didn't seem to be working on the first try. His mouth was dry; he swallowed a couple of times, then managed a rather quavery "Who's there?" No answer, and no further sound. Cursing himself for a fool and a coward, and still carrying Gabi, he headed for the cabin. "Is anyone in there?" No response. He stepped onto the porch. "Does someone need help?" He thought he heard a rustling inside. Carefully he sat Gabi down on the porch step and wrapped his jacket tightly around her. "I'll be right back, Gabi."

He went to the door which was jammed ajar and pushed against it so that it gave enough to allow his larger male body to squeeze through. "Hello? Is anyone in here?" Jeremy's flashlight clattered to the floor and he staggered backwards as, with a loud beating of wings, a large black bird flew at him, grazing his head. Jeremy flailed his arms as the bird flew past him and out the broken window. A crow? A raven? It couldn't have been the bird that screamed, could it? Breathing hard, Jeremy groped for his flashlight and trained it around the room, then gasped as the beam lit on a face looking up at him from the corner — a face with large black eyes that looked to be utterly mad: Sybil Weeks!

"Good god," Jeremy murmured. "Sybil?" He realized that she couldn't see well enough to recognize him, and was probably frightened to the point of being deranged. Jeremy tried to make his own shaky voice sound reasonable. "Sybil, it's me, Jeremy — Professor Banks. What are you doing here?"

"Go away." Sybil's eyes were wide and unfocused.

"I can't just go away, Sybil. I can't leave you here. I heard you cry out. Did something frighten you?"

"Just leave me alone. It was nothing. It was only Blackjack. He flew in the window."

"Sybil, I think you should come home. Your mother will be worried about you. I'll walk back with you."

"No!" It was a shout. "Just go away, *go away*, GO AWAY!" Sybil was rocking back and forth, her knees drawn up, her arms clutching the wooden mask to her chest. Her eyes were shut and her lips were form-ing words Jeremy couldn't quite hear or understand. She seemed to be chanting, slipping into a some kind of trance. Suddenly she turned her head and screamed again, sending a chill down Jeremy's spine. She was staring past him, blindly, and Jeremy turned to see Gabi standing in the doorway. Jeremy's jacket had fallen off her shoulders to the floor, and Gabi was just standing there in her pajamas, eyes fixed straight ahead. Next to her, at her feet, stood Blackjack. Sybil struggled to get up. The mask slipped from her grasp and thudded to the floor as she raised her arm to point at Gabi. She screamed again, then pitched forward and fell prone, her body twitching and jerking. Blackjack hopped over to stand by her.

Oh, my god, she's having another seizure. Jeremy set his flashlight on the table and bent over the girl. She was thrashing about, her eyes rolled back in her head, spittle drooling from her mouth. He looked around for something he could use as a pillow but there was only a torn and filthy mattress shoved up against a wall. Awkwardly he managed to move her bodily onto it. "Better than hitting your head on the floor." He turned her on her side, and would have inserted a rolled-up handkerchief into her mouth, but Sybil's teeth were tightly clenched and he knew he might injure her if he tried. There was nothing more he could do except wait for the spell to pass.

Jeremy realized that he couldn't take Gabi home and leave Sybil there alone. He certainly couldn't carry both of them. It would be difficult enough to get them both out of there even after Sybil regained consciousness. He turned his attention to Gabi who still seemed to be living in trance.

But now something was happening with Gabi. The girl, moving like a zombie in the pale beam of Jeremy's flashlight, had begun to walk. Jeremy saw her step through a doorway into a small dark alcove, then out again, and slowly walk toward the window. Jeremy made a move to grab her, fearing she might cut her bare foot on a piece of broken glass, but before he could reach her, Gabi had climbed onto the sill and knelt there, looking out, her face smooth and flawless in the soft moonlight. Jeremy couldn't help noticing how very pretty she was; her hair was lighter in color, but Gabi would one day look very much like her mother — then suddenly he noticed a change in her expression. No longer impassive, her eyes were widening and her face contorting as if she were facing something terrifying. As Jeremy reached out for her, she began to scream and scream and scream.

Jeremy picked her up and held her tightly. "Gabi, it's okay. Try to wake up, Gabi. You're safe here," he said, hoping that that was true. "Wake up, Gabi. It's Jeremy. Nothing's going to hurt you." As he spoke, Gabi's body, which had been rigid as iron, relaxed and her screams turned into soft whimpering sobs. Jeremy carried her away from the window and picked up his jacket. By now Gabi was clinging to him, her wet, and somewhat slimy little face nestled in his neck. Jeremy brushed away debris with his be-casted arm, sat Gabi on the wooden table and once again wrapped his coat around her. Gabi was looking around wildly. She glanced at the window and Jeremy thought she was going to start screaming again. "It's him. He's out there," she whimpered.

"There's no one out there, Gabi. You're perfectly safe."

"I saw him. The man with the big knife thing. He came to the window and he tapped on the glass. Didn't you see him?"

"No, Gabi. I didn't see anyone. You were dreaming. You've been walking in your sleep."

"But I could see him and I could hear him laughing — but he wasn't happy, he was *mean*. He wanted to chop me up with the knife thing. He kept tapping on the window."

"It was just a bad dream. See, there isn't even any *glass* in the window. You were just having a nightmare."

"Noooo," Gabi wailed. "He had that big sharp thing and he was cutting the hay, and then he came to the window and he wanted to chop me up."

"THE VENGEANCE OF GOD WILL STRIKE YOU DOWN!" The voice rang out like a car alarm. "THE SINS OF THE FATHERS WILL PASS ON TO THE CHILDREN!"

Startled, Jeremy turned. *Oh, good lord — Sybil.*

Sybil had awakened. Disheveled and filthy, she was trying to crawl up off the mattress which was now stained with her urine. She tried to stand but fell back down. Jeremy moved to help her, but she jerked back and made a gesture for him not to touch her. She crouched, like an animal about to spring. "They're *coming*," she shouted. "They're *all coming*."

Should I try to humor this poor girl? Can I talk reason to her at all?

"Who's coming? Who are you expecting, Sybil?"

Sybil laughed, and her laughter only made her appear more demented. "They're all coming. The Lemerriants. And all the ghosts."

"Ghosts?"

"This is where they live. This is where *it* lives. The Loogy-Roo."

"But the Lemerriants are all dead, Sybil. They died years ago, long before you were even born. How could they hurt anyone now?"

"Dead? They're not dead. They're waiting. As long as the Loogy-Roo is alive, they all have to stay here. They're all part of it."

"Part of what, Sybil?" Jeremy asked wearily. "It's all just a story. The Loogy-Roo doesn't exist. It never existed. It's just an old legend. Sybil, you have to be able to tell the difference between what's real and what isn't."

"And you think you know what's real?" Sybil hissed. "The killings were real *then* and they're real *now*. They won't stop until the Loogy-Roo is dead — until she's bound."

"What do you mean *bound*?"

"The ghosts, the shadow people, were all part of the Loogy-Roo, and now they can't leave. The Loogy-Roo has come back in flesh. Don't you see, we have to kill it. Then it will be bound too and the killings will stop." Sybil pointed at Gabi. "She's using their power. The Loogy-Roo always uses their power."

"Sybil, that's nonsense." Jeremy realized he'd never be able to reach this babbling young woman with anything resembling reason. "What we have to do is get out of here and go home. Do you think you'll be able to walk?"

"It's too late," Sybil said. "They're coming."

Jeremy sighed. "Well, I don't see anyone."

"You won't, but *I* will, and" — Sybil pointed at Gabi — "*she* will."

Jeremy put a reassuring arm around Gabi who, faced with Sybil's fiery persona, was shrinking back. "Sybil, I want you to try to listen to me. There won't be any ghosts or Loogy-Roos. The only real danger out there tonight may be from a cougar. It was the cougar that killed

Dory Michaels, *not* any Loogy-Roo. As far as I know, it's still loose, so yes, there is that danger. But a cougar is just a wild animal, and it will be killed. And then it will be *gone*. Do you understand me?"

"You don't know anything," Sybil spat out.

"All right, then Sybil. Why don't you try to explain it to me. Why are you here? And what does any of this have to do with Gabi?"

"She's the Loogy-Roo!"

"She's just a little girl. Surely you don't think Gabi killed Dory Michaels!"

"She's the host. While she's alive, the Loogy-Roo is alive and it will go on killing. Elphique Lemerriant was the host and when he died the killing stopped. But now the Loogy-Roo is back!" Sybil pointed a finger at Gabi. "She killed my father."

Shocked, then realizing, Jeremy said, "Sybil, your father isn't dead! He was hurt, but he's going to be all right. I thought you knew."

"No, he's dead. I saw it."

"How is that possible?"

Sybil reached for the mask. "Yaxagama showed me." She held the mask up. "Yaxagama shows me things."

"If you saw it, then you know it was a hunting accident. Your father was shot in the shoulder by Dory's father, not the Loogy-Roo. Dory's father didn't mean to do it."

Sybil mouth writhed into a twisted smile. "The Loogy-Roo can make you do anything." She looked long at Gabi. "And it's not over yet. The vengeance of God will strike and there will be more blood."

"Yes," Gabi said, her eyes wide and dark. "There will be fresh blood."

CHAPTER 40

"I DON'T remember it being this far," Celeste said. They were trudging along the trail trying to pick their way over the uneven terrain.

"Distances always seem different in the dark and when you're in a hurry. Shouldn't be much farther, though," Willie said. "Matt, how are you doing up there?"

Matt had moved on ahead of them. "I'm not seeing any footprints," he called. "Maybe she went off the trail."

"Oh my god," Celeste said. "You think she went into the woods?"

"No, I don't think so," Willie quickly said, although the thought had occurred to her as well. "You can't see prints right here. It's all needles and mulch."

"Gabi, where are you?" Celeste had been calling her daughter's name all the way, as had Willie and Matt. Not only were they hoping to get an answer, but to make enough noise to scare off any wild animals that might be around. Now the thought that Gabi might have veered off into the woods was making Celeste frantic. She kept training her flashlight beam into the forest, peering in to see if there might be a sign of her.

All she could see was a phalanx of huge tree trunks and deep engulfing shadows that could hide horrible things. She was coming to a spot where the needles gave way to mud, took a step and landed partly on the edge of a wooden lily pad, slid off sideways, twisting her foot. She lost her balance, fell hard onto the trail, then yelled as a sharp pain, like an electric shock, hit her in the ankle. She lay rolling in mud, clutching her leg and moaning.

Willie rushed over to her. "What happened? Are you all right?" Matt heard the commotion and came running.

"I think I broke my ankle." Celeste was wearing the white gum boots Willie had lent her, and they were loose enough for Willie to carefully pull one off. While Matt shone a light, Willie peeled back the sock and looked to see that the ankle was already swelling. She took hold of it. "It may not be broken, but it's certainly a sprain. It'll be blue tomorrow! You won't be able to walk on it."

"Oh for the love of Christ, what the hell else can happen?" Celeste was crying tears of pain, anger and frustration. "God, it hurts!" She hit the ground with her fist. "Shit! God *damn* it! Fuck, fuck, FUCK!"

Matt looked at Willie with the faintest of smiles and a raised eyebrow. Willie met his gaze evenly. "She went to college in the eighties." she whispered. "We need to try to wrap this to brace it. If we can do that, we can put the boot back on, but you still won't be able to put your weight on it. Matt, give me your scarf."

Matt gave it up gratefully. He'd been wearing it unwound and flapping, not daring just to discard it outright. Celeste winced as Willie wrapped the scarf around her ankle firmly but not so tightly as to impede blood flow. Willie eased the boot back on, and was satisfied to see that the bulk of the scarf formed an effective brace. "You really need to elevate that foot. When we get back we'll put ice on it."

Celeste was trying to struggle to her feet. "Help me up. We have to find Gabi."

Willie and Matt sprang to help her, but as Celeste put her foot down she howled in pain. "It's no use, Willie said, we'll have to get help." They managed to limp Celeste over to a fallen tree on the side of the trail and seated her on it. "Matt, one of us will have to stay with Celeste while the other goes back to get help."

"No! You have to find Gabi. Leave me here and you go on ahead. Constable Hewett will be coming soon, won't he?"

"I'm sure someone will. If Kirsti couldn't reach Constable Hewett, she'd have called someone else. I'm sure help is on the way, but we can't just leave you here alone. Matt, you stay with Celeste while I go on and check out the old cabin."

"No, Willie. *You* stay. I'll go. You might fall and break your hip."

"Thanks a lot, Matt," Willie said dryly, but she had to admit that an eleven-year-old boy, who traveled the distance routinely, would cover it faster and more easily than a woman in her eighties. "Okay, but just make a lot of noise so you'll scare off — "

" — the cougar. Yeah, I know."

"And if — uh — *when* you find Gabi and your sister, I want you all to go into the cabin and stay there. You should be safe there until we come get you." Willie glanced toward Celeste, and said, a little louder, "That is, unless Jeremy has already found them and they're safely on their way back — which is probably what will happen. You have your flashlight?"

"Yup," Matt picked it up from where he'd set it. "And I have my knife."

Willie sighed and rolled her eyes. "Fine. Be careful." She went over to sit by Celeste while Matt strode up the path with a bit of a swagger.

Matt's bravado lessened when a bend in the trail made him lose sight of Willie's light. He'd been over the trail dozens of times, but not in the dead of night, and not with a cougar on the loose. He tried to whistle, but his lips were dry and the whistle was weak. He called for Gabi a couple of times, then decided he'd sing, and found that the only song he could think of was the one Dory Michaels always sang:

On a rainy day

When the skies are gray
There's a lot that you can do on a rainy day.
You can whittle on a stick
You can do a magic trick
You can have a lot of fun on a rainy day!

Matt stopped singing. Stupid song. And the thought that Dory Michaels had always been singing it was spooky. Now that Matt had gone silent, everything around him was deathly quiet too. All he could hear was his own soft footfall. What if something came out of the darkness and attacked him? Matt pulled out his knife and clutched it in his hand. Did his flashlight make him a target? He didn't really need it. He was coming to a moonlit clearing and could see without it. What if the cougar was stalking him? What if there really *were* ghosts in the Lemerriant house? Matt didn't believe in such things, but on a night like this the idea didn't seem quite so far-fetched.

He could see the cabin up ahead but it looked empty and scary. "Gabi? Sybil?" He couldn't seem to make his voice work properly. If he called louder, would the cougar hear him? Would the ghosts come out? And what if there really *was* a Loogy-Roo after all? He was tempted to turn and run back, but then he'd just be a scared little kid, wouldn't he? He began to walk warily across the clearing. Then he gasped. Something was moving in the shadows of the old house. He couldn't make out what, but he was suddenly terrified. Matt clutched his knife and ducked down, hiding behind a shrub of broom. Was it the Lemerriants? Breathing hard, Matt waited.

* * *

Jeremy looked from Gabi's solemn face to Sybil's mocking one. He had to admit that he was feeling unnerved by these two children, but even more by the fading and extinguishing of his flashlight, which left him only the moonlight from the window. Still, he was the adult here.

He didn't know what delusions Sybil had been fostering, but obviously she'd taken a childhood legend and fabricated a world of fantasy all her own — and was now living out that fantasy so completely that there was no way to reason with her. As for Gabi, when you put the two of them together, they could almost convince you there were dark forces swirling around them.

"Girls," he said. "We're not in any danger here, but we do have to get back home. As long as we're in a group, we'll be fine. Now, if you think you can walk, Sybil, I can carry Gabi, and we can make our way back down the trail. I'm sure we won't be meeting any Loogy-Roos or Lemerriants along the way. But we don't have a light, so we'll have to walk carefully."

"I don't need a light," Sybil said, looking misshapen, shrouded in her coat. "But I need my walking stick."

"Where is it?"

"It's outside. I threw it at the Loogy-Roo."

"Yes, all right. Let's go. I'm sure we'll find it." Jeremy picked up Gabi and ushered both girls out the door, then eased through himself. "Where were you when you threw the stick?"

"On the porch."

Jeremy put Gabi down walked a little way. "Is this it?"

Sybil reached out a pale bony hand and grasped the cane. "Yes." Out of nowhere, a dark shape appeared and landed on her shoulder. "Blackjack!"

"All right," Jeremy said. "If we're all set, then let's get going." He turned and then they all froze as a figure materialized in front of them seemingly out of thin air — the figure of a boy with a knife. Sybil gasped, Jeremy just stood there, not sure he could believe his eyes. Later he would tell Willie how, for a moment, he actually thought he was seeing the ghost of the boy in Ulla's photograph — and how easy it is for the most rational man to become Scrooged. The figure in the moonlight, arm upraised and holding a knife, looked menacing enough until Gabi called out, "Matt? Is that you?"

"Yeah." The voice cracked. "Wh ... what are *you* guys doing out here?"

CHAPTER 41

In the deep of the night, the house was quiet as Willie and Jeremy sat in the kitchen having a "decompressing" cup of chamomile tea to help them get to sleep. Both should have been in bed, but the excitement of the day had left Willie's adrenaline working overtime, and Jeremy in enough pain to make him irritable. Celeste and Gabi were tucked into bed; Matt and Sybil (and Blackjack) were back home with Kirsti.

"I may just sleep late tomorrow," Willie said. "I'll have to admit I'm getting too old for this kind of shenanigans."

"Amen to that. It's a good thing Matt came along with a flashlight. That trail is rough going at night. You have to watch every step you take. I think I jarred my sciatic nerve; I'm getting a twinge in my left leg."

"Yes, and you were carrying Gabi. You must be in really good shape for your age."

"I couldn't let her walk. She didn't have shoes. It's lucky we had help getting Celeste back. At least the ankle wasn't broken."

"Nasty sprain, though. Peg taped it up and gave her some pain killers. I hope she's able to sleep comfortably. Tomorrow I'll clear out the junk in there to give her more space."

To keep Celeste from having to climb stairs, Willie had hastily made up her father's old sofa bed in the storeroom, and moved out a few things to allow for a clear path. Luckily, an aluminum walker that Willie's father had used was still in the room, and Celeste found she could hobble around with it. She assured Willie that if she had to get up to use the downstairs bathroom, she would manage; although she was more concerned about Gabi being alone, and wondered if she should be sharing her bed downstairs. Willie assured her that all exits were securely locked, and that both she and Jeremy would leave their doors open, so if Gabi made any sound they would hear her. Celeste would sleep better by herself with no chance of a restless Gabi jarring her ankle during the night.

Jeremy shifted in his chair and rubbed his arm. "Be so good to get this bloody thing off. I'll probably be one of those old men who can predict the weather by the pain in his joints."

"Do you want me to get you a couple of aspirin?"

"I have some Tylenol upstairs. I'll take some if I think I need it."

"Better do it now so it'll have a chance to kick in before you go to bed."

"Don't fuss, Willie. I'll be fine." Jeremy realized that he'd sounded snappish and changed the subject. "I can't image what the Hewetts must be thinking. Here they just moved to what should be the quietest post ever assigned to an RCMP, and they've already had to deal with a cougar kill, a hunting accident, and a missing child. They can't seem to have a meal, or a night's sleep, without being rousted out to haul someone out of the woods."

"I don't think they've even had a chance to unpack yet. Peg was really wonderful with Celeste and Gabi tonight. She took care of Gabi's bruises and scratches and did a great impression of Florence Nightingale. But she *did* ask me if it was always like this on Broom Island."

"I guess you told her it's usually pretty quiet."

"I told her it usually is, except for the bacchanal around the bonfire on *Juhannus*. I told her we had to give up the human sacrifice since we haven't been able to find a virgin in years. It took her a moment to realize I was kidding."

"I guess officially it'll be logged as a kid sleepwalking and getting lost, but I'd like to know what actually happened tonight. Sybil, for instance. I found her cowering in the cabin."

"Did she say anything to you that might explain why she was there?"

"She said a lot of things but nothing that made sense. She said she threw her walking stick at the Loogy-Roo, then hid inside."

"The Loogy-Roo?"

"Oh, she must have imagined it, or maybe heard something in the night that spooked her. She can't *see*. I don't mind admitting that the place was spooky enough to unnerve anybody. Sybil had been babbling about the ghosts of the Lemerriants, so when Matt showed up, for a second there I thought I was seeing the ghost of Elphique."

Willie smiled faintly. "Obviously the Lemerriants are still a presence on this island. If there are any ghosts, this would be a logical time for them to wander."

"Yes, it *is* the anniversary of the fire, isn't it? Seventy years ago today?"

"Actually, seventy years ago *tonight*. The fire took place on the 19th of May."

Jeremy chuckled. "In that case it might have been too early for the ghosts — although both Gabi and Sybil seemed to be hallucinating."

"It's a wonder Sybil even found her way there, although she does get around with the aid of her cane. Did she say why she went to the Lemerriant house in the first place?"

"I get the impression she thinks she's being told what to do by somebody. She had that Indian mask with her, and she said it showed her things and that somebody named — I want to say taxidermy, but that's not it."

"Yaxagama?"

"Yes! That was it. Yaxagama. Who *is* that?"

"Yaxagama is a mythological Native American ancestor, a sort of Eve. The Creator found her beautiful and their children became the ancestors of the Nakamgalisala people. They were one of the Hope Island tribes, called collectively by anthropologists the Kwakiutl, but really the Kwakwaka'wakw. The Nakamgalisala have disappeared, but I'm sure many native women throughout history have borne the name Yaxagama." Willie smiled, a bit smugly. Jeremy gave her an ironic nod of admiration.

"She did say that this . . . Yaxagama . . . tells her things, and apparently that's somehow connected with the mask. That must be why she took it from the shop. She was holding on to it for dear life."

"I don't remember seeing it last night. Did she bring it back? Danielle will have a fit if she's lost it!"

"I didn't notice. I presume she had it with her, but I don't actually remember seeing it on the way back. You know, I can almost understand why Gabi could somehow be tied to the Lemerriants. She does carry the DNA. But what could Sybil's connection be? She's the daughter of Rome and Kirsti Weeks. They're not related to the Lemerriants, are they?"

Willie sipped her tea. "No. But we don't really know Sybil's ancestry either. She was adopted. Both she and Matt were. Kirsti couldn't have children."

"Really!"

"Sybil was adopted as a baby. Her mother was a native woman. She died years ago of alcoholism, and had lived a knock-about life, working in logging camps and fish plants. Nobody knows for sure who Sybil's father was, nor is anything known about her mother's ancestry."

"But the Lemerriants would have died or left the island long before Sybil was born, so it's unlikely there'd be a blood connection."

"It would require another family branch of the Lemerriants. It would mean that Brazeau, or even Elphique, would have had to impregnate an outsider, and sire a child by her."

"And you think that Sybil could be the descendant of such a child?"

"It's possible, but there's no paper trail. Nobody paid much attention to the family trees of native people, except possibly the natives themselves. Sybil had been abandoned by her mother. Back then, things weren't so bureaucratically complicated, and the Weeks just simply took her in. Later they adopted her legally, and adopted Matt as well.

"Sybil was not an easy child to raise. She had all kinds of problems, psychological as well as physical. And then she lost her sight in a tragic accident. She's been on a number of medications, but she's always lived in a world of her own."

"She's very — uh — Biblical, isn't she? But at the same time she's all caught up in ghosts and native spirit guides. She has some fixation on the Loogy-Roo thing, and thinks Gabi is the Loogy-Roo, and that Gabi is evil. Or that somehow Gabi's coming to the island brought the evil back, and that the killings won't stop until the Loogy-Roo is destroyed. I get the impression that, to Sybil, there is a mythical population on the island composed of dead people, and they're all somehow connected to the Loogy-Roo, *attached* to it, held here by it, until it's killed. The ghosts are a malevolent force and the Loogy-Roo uses their power to do evil. When the Loogy-Roo dies, the connection is severed. If it's a psychosis, it's very elaborate, even though it makes no sense . . . unless, of course, it's your churchyard bunch. What were they called?"

"The *Kirkkováki.*" Willie frowned. "We'll have to keep Gabi away from Sybil."

"Do you think she might actually try to harm her?"

"Sybil is unstable. I don't know what she might be capable of."

"And there's even a possibility that Gabi and Sybil could be cousins?"

Willie made a palms-up gesture as if to say, anything's possible. "It's been a strange night. I've got to get to bed. What time is it?"

"Nearly three in the morning." Jeremy yawned. "I'm going to bed too. I just hope Gabi sleeps through the rest of the night this time."

"She was barely awake when we brought her home. After Peg had cleaned off her feet and treated her scratches, I stuffed her into fresh

pajamas and put her to bed. By time I'd tucked her in, she was *out*."
Willie had washed and dried the tea cups and was putting them away.

"Well, the house is secure. Sleep well, Willie. Maybe things will look saner in the morning."

CHAPTER 42

MONDAY MORNING dawned under cloud cover. Willie had slept badly, and then found herself awakened by the sound of squabbling ravens in the trees outside her window. She looked at the clock and saw it was seven-thirty. Sure that the rest of the household would sleep late, she turned over and burrowed under her duvet — but found her runaway brain wide awake. Realizing she wouldn't be able to get back to sleep, she got up and put on her "uniform" of jeans and sweatshirt with the Satama logo. The shirts, originally intended for the tourist trade, came in varying weights, from light summer tees to those thick enough to offer protection from a gale at sea. The shirt logo was changed from time to time, and there was always controversy as to whether the new logo was more or less attractive than the old one. Willie's mid-weight, navy blue shirt was well-worn, and bore a line drawing in white of graceful fishing boats.

Willie remembered that this was the day of the ceremony in the cemetery to honor those who had died in the fire seventy years ago. Would it also be the day of Dory Michaels' funeral? She would have to find out what plans had been made. Amanda Vuorisaari would know, since her husband, Oskar, was the village mortician.

She went downstairs and into the kitchen to find Jeremy already making coffee. He greeted her with a "Good morning, I thought you were going to sleep in."

"Birds were making a racket. I guess Celeste and Gabi are still in bed."

"Gabi was snoozing when I walked by her door. I haven't seen Celeste."

Willie busied herself with slicing a braid of *pulla*. By time Celeste thumped in with her walker, there was freshly-squeezed orange juice, a pot of steaming oatmeal, and a stack of toasted *pulla* with a jar of Willie's seedless blackberry jelly. "Good morning. Did you manage to get any sleep?"

Jeremy had risen to help her get seated, this time more of necessity than good manners, and Celeste eased herself into a chair. "I did," she said. "Whatever Peg gave me must have helped." Willie poured her a cup of coffee. "There's toast, and would you like oatmeal?"

Celeste shook her head. "Coffee's all I usually have." Suddenly she looked anxious. "Where's — where's Gabi?"

"Gabi is fine. I think she's still sleeping. We'll feed her when she wakes up. How does your ankle feel?"

"Hurts. But I think I'll be able to walk on it."

"You'd better stay off it for at least a couple of days. If you like, we'll heat the sauna tonight. A good steam might make it feel better, and it'll be easier for you than trying to stand up in a shower."

Celeste dropped her gaze. "Willie — Jeremy — you've both been very kind. I haven't thanked you properly for going out last night to find my daughter, and for bringing her back safely. But please try to understand that I *have* to get Gabi off this island. There's something . . . *wrong* here. We never should have come. I want to get on the next ferry and go home."

Willie sighed. "I do understand, Celeste, but you can't drive with that ankle, can you? At least not yet. Gabi will be safe, I promise."

"That's what we all thought yesterday! And look what happened."

"We didn't foresee her sleepwalking and leaving the house. Doors will be securely bolted. She won't be able to do that again."

"She could have been killed out there. And that awful woman — girl — Sybil. She's out of her mind, isn't she? She and her hellish bird! What was all that nonsense on the way home about the Loogy-Roo and ghosts. She almost sounded as if she were talking in her sleep. Why was she out there? What does she have to do with Gabi? Did she lead Gabi to the cabin? And how could she have done that? It's . . . it's . . ."

"I think Sybil must have failed to take her medication. She tends to become disconnected when that happens, and I think she just wandered off down that trail behind her house. She suffered a seizure yesterday, and that would have left her feeling disoriented."

"She had another one at the cabin," Jeremy said. "I wondered how I was going to get her home, but she managed to recover enough to be able to walk. It's possible that she's just confused."

"It's even possible," Willie added, "That Gabi may have seen her and just followed her. We don't really know what stimuli a sleepwalker may react to."

"But why would Gabi have been out there at all?"

"We really don't know, but if Gabi was walking in her sleep, she may have been dreaming of going to Matt's house, and, of course, both she and Matt have been on that trail, so it wasn't unfamiliar to her. She may have been re-living that in her dream. When she wakes up, we can ask if she remembers anything about last night."

"It's all just too . . . too. . . ." Celeste was at a loss for words.

"And here's Gabi now," Willie said cheerfully, as the little girl came quietly into the room. "Sit here, dear, and have your orange juice. I'll get you some oatmeal." Gabi slid wordlessly into the chair and Willie put breakfast before her. "Did you sleep okay?"

Gabi blinked, yawned, looked around. She was still in pajamas, blue ones this time, and slippers. "Where's Matt? I've got to tell him something."

"Matt's at home. Do you remember coming home last night?"

Gabi looked at Jeremy. "You carried me."

Jeremy smiled. "Yes, I did. Since you'd lost your slippers, just like Cinderella."

Celeste had been studying her daughter intently, but her voice was almost a whisper. "Why did you go out last night, Gabi?"

Gabi frowned. "I don't remember."

"Do you remember anything about what you saw or where you went?"

"No. I remember it was dark and Jeremy was there and ... and Matt's sister ... and Matt ... and you and Willie. And then a bunch of other people came." Gabi, now brightly awake and hungry, was spooning up oatmeal. "I remember my feet were cold." She bit into a *pulla* toast. "And I remember the man with the knife thing."

"Man with a knife thing?" Willie asked.

"Oh, that's a nightmare Gabi's been having," Celeste added, under her breath, "You remember, the s-c-y-t-h-e."

"Scythe. Yeah, that's what Matt called it. He said old man Lemerriant chopped up his wife with it. Have they found him yet?"

"Who? Lemerriant?"

"No. Dory's dad. He's dead, you know."

"*What?*"

"The Loogy-Roo got him. And the birds are pecking out his eyes."

CHAPTER 43

THE EIGHT o'clock ferry to Port Casper transported Rome Weeks, via ambulance, to the Port Casper General Hospital. Kirsti went with him; Sybil and Matt stayed at home, with the promise that once Rome had settled in, they could visit him later. Yes, their father would be just fine. The bullet had gone all the way through the shoulder, but the wound was serious enough that Dr. Swallow thought it best to send Rome to a better-equipped facility, just in case. Sybil had been reassured, again, that her father was very much alive, and that she wasn't to worry. Having had seizures the day before, it would be best for her to rest, take her medication, and try to sleep. Kirsti told Matt to keep an eye on his sister, that she might be groggy and have trouble remembering things, and if there were any problems, he was to go over and get Willie; and that she, herself, would be back on the next ferry, if at all possible.

***

In Pearl's Café, a group of men watched the ferry depart as they sat eating breakfast. "Damn shame about Rome," Oliver Sylvester said.

"Yeah. But I hear he's going to be okay." Butch Westerlake was polishing off a plateful of ham, eggs, and hash browned potatoes.

"I wonder how long he'll have to stay in the hospital." Veikko Kuusiniemi held up his cup to Pearl who came over with a pot to refill their coffees.

"Maybe just a couple of days, unless there are complications. We can all go see him, give him a bit of a hard time about punkin' out on the hunt."

"Has anybody seen Eddie this morning?"

"He was supposed to come in on the early ferry. I told him we'd be here, so unless he missed it, he should be here any minute. He's probably parking his truck."

"I suppose we'll have to go over and get Schittle — I mean Michaels." Oliver said.

"If there's one guy I'd rather not hunt with, it's Michaels," Veikko made a grimace of distaste. "I think we can safely leave him out of it. If I'd just shot somebody, I don't think I'd feel like hunting the next day."

"Yeah, gives the term loose cannon a whole new meaning. Oh, hi, Eddie. 'Bout time you got here." Butch scooted over to make room.

Eddie Smithson slid into the booth and waved at Pearl who hurried over to bring him a cup of coffee. She smiled at Eddie flirtatiously. "What'll it be this morning, big guy? Haven't seen you for a while."

"Oh, missed my favorite girlfriend." Eddie grinned. "Sugar, you make the best pancakes on the West Coast. I'll have a stack o'buttered."

"Coming right up." Pearl smiled, winked, and headed for the grill.

"We were just saying that we'd rather not have Michaels with us," Butch said. "Be a lot better if it was just us four."

"Maybe he won't even want to go after what happened yesterday." Oliver looked hopeful.

"Maybe. But we'll have to go past his road. He might see us." Veikko said.

"No, we won't. We could start at the other end of the Lemerriant trail, work our way down, past the old house, on up to quarry and the lake, and if we haven't found the cat, then we could keep on going and check out Michaels Acres. We didn't get into the high hills yesterday, and there a good chance the animal's up there. Maybe found a cave in the rocks. Anyway, the weather's better today."

Pearl put a plate of hotcakes in front of Eddie. "There you go, handsome. And here's some real maple syrup, just for you from my private stash." Eddie favored her with a blinding smile that displayed even white dentures under his neatly trimmed salt and pepper moustache. "Thank you, darlin'; you are, indeed, a Pearl among women."

Oliver eyed the flapjacks hungrily. "Damn, those look good! But I'm not allowed to eat them anymore. Dr. Swallow tells me my numbers are too high."

"Yeah, Barb won't let me have them either. She's always watching my cholesterol and BP."

Eddie grinned and poured on syrup. "Fine woman, your wife. You're a lucky man. But sometimes being single has its perks."

"Isn't this the day there's supposed to be some kind of ceremony in the cemetery?" Oliver asked. "I know I saw something in the paper about it, and now I'm wonderin' if they're still gonna have it, what with the funeral for the little girl."

"According to my wife, the funeral won't be for at least a couple more days. The Michaels haven't made arrangements yet. Sanni was talking to Amanda Vuorisaari who told her there would be a gathering in the cemetery at eleven o'clock this morning. Charlie Peterman is supposed to say a few words, and Amanda will read a selection from the *Kalevala* in Finnish, and then Hilda Widjeskoog will read the translation in English. Sanni said it would be a short ceremony."

Veikko rolled his eyes. "Doesn't sound short to me."

"What has the *Kalevala* got to do with the fire?" Eddie asked.

"On this island, it's traditional," Oliver said. "We call ourselves the

Kaleva People, so everything has to do with the *Kalevala*. They'll find some passage appropriate to the occasion — probably a long one. And the ladies will be reading it in two languages just to double the fun."

Veikko drained the last of his coffee. "I think it's more important that we go get that cougar, right?"

Eddie grinned wickedly. "The ladies or the cougar?"

"I'll take the cougar." Oliver said.

Veikko nodded. "What's more important, a ceremony for the long dead or making sure nobody else get killed?" He signaled to Pearl for the bill. "Put your wallets away, gentlemen. Breakfast is on me."

* * *

As the men were filing out of Pearl's and heading for their respective vehicles, Danielle Herron drove up in her yellow Volkswagen Rabbit, and parked next to her shop. Weena Michaels was with her, and listlessly lent a hand as Danielle opened the metal security gate, unlocked the door, turned on the lights, moved a couple of rental bicycles back out onto the landing, plugged in the coffee maker, and flipped up the "Open" sign.

Weena was feeling depressed, almost to the point of inaction. She'd have been content to remain at Danielle's, but Danielle wouldn't hear of leaving her alone. Weena realized that, unless Chad had already done so, she'd have to make arrangements for Dory's funeral. *Dory's funeral.* The words were like a spike in her heart. Of course it would be more appropriate for her and Chad to do that together, and perhaps she'd been too hasty in walking out last night. It might have been better to wait until . . . it . . . was all over. Still, things had gone the way they'd gone, and there was no going back. She'd been adamant enough the night before, but now the aftereffects were crushing in on her. She'd left the truck at Danielle's, knowing Chad would be looking for it, and for *her*, and she just couldn't bring herself to face him right now. She'd have to make plans, find a new road, and it would be easier if she didn't have Chad trying to bully her.

Deep in thought, Weena was roused by Danielle's handing her a cup of coffee. "You don't have to try to do everything right away, you know."

"But I *do*. I have to arrange for the funeral, and I can't stay with you forever."

"First of all, you're welcome to stay with me as long as you like. As for Dory's funeral, why not let me call Oskar Vuorisaari. He'll know exactly how to proceed and will take care of all necessary arrangements. We can make an appointment to choose a casket — you may have to go to Port Casper for that, and, if you like, I can also call Chad. He should be part of it. Perhaps the two of you could set aside your differences long enough to get through the service. Do you think Chad will be able to do that?"

"I don't know. Maybe. If he's taken his medication, and he probably hasn't. You never know with Chad."

"In that case, perhaps I'll have *Oskar* call and talk with him. Chad doesn't like me, and a call from me would just antagonize him. Oskar has a lot of experience with the bereaved, and he might hit just the right note with Chad, pointing out how he'll be the focus of all eyes in the community, and how his courage and dignity will be an inspiration to us all."

"Uh, yeah! That might even work." Weena was trying to picture Chad as the embodiment of courage and dignity.

"Good, then that's what we'll do. Meanwhile, I do have a favor to ask of you, but if you don't feel up to it, it's okay."

"Of course! Whatever you need. You know that."

"I have a couple of important things to do this morning, and I wondered if you could watch the store for an hour or two."

"Certainly."

"There's a memorial at the cemetery, at eleven, for the early settlers who died in the fire. I should put in an appearance, even if I don't stay for the whole thing. And then I have to stop off at the Weeks house to pick up a valuable native mask that Sybil took home with her when she was minding the shop."

"Why did she do that?"

"I have no idea. She could have taken any of the other masks, but no, she picked the one that's worth a lot of money. I was going to go get it yesterday but Sybil was sleeping off a seizure — and then there was the hunting accident with Rome, so I thought it better to wait. But I'd best go collect it before anything happens to it. Are you sure you'll be okay here alone? I could call someone to keep you company."

Weena sighed. "Don't be silly, Danielle. I may be stressed out but not so much that I can't handle this. It's a good place for me to hide out from Chad. I don't think he'd come looking for me here."

Danielle looked at her watch. First she wanted to get the mask, then she'd stop in to see Oskar and ask him to call Chad — but of course the Vuorisaaris would be at the cemetery; she could have a word with Oskar there. Danielle was rather hoping she wouldn't run into Chad Michaels anywhere. She knew he'd be trying to find Weena, and she didn't relish a confrontation with the man.

Luck was with her. Downtown Satama was all but deserted. There would be few, if any, customers at Danielle's this morning. Everyone would be at the memorial. There were only a couple of cars in the lineup, and there wasn't the usual crowd standing on the ferry platform. While the Co-op was open, despite the holiday, there wasn't a group of people chatting in front of it either. Normally, at a time like this, the chat group would have been a large one, as it always was when there was any island hubbub. It was a shifting forum whose membership, like the Radio City Rockettes, kept changing. Those who had gleaned the latest, would drift away as others would join to hear or declare the most recent bulletin.

Danielle pulled out and headed up Kaunio Road. She'd drop by the Weeks house, then go to the cemetery on her way back.

There was no vehicle in the Weeks driveway, but Danielle got out anyway and rang the bell. She gathered her face into a presentation smile which fell flat when Matt opened the door. "Hello, Matt. Is your mother at home?"

"No, she's in Port Casper with my dad. They took him to the hospital this morning."

"Oh, I'm sorry . . . is your father — uh — all right?"

"My mom says he's going to be okay."

"I see. Well, is your sister at home?"

"Yeah."

"Could I see her?"

"I think she's in bed."

"Is she not well, Matt?"

"Mom says she's supposed to rest today. She had a couple of fits."

"Oh dear. I'm sorry to hear that. Matt . . . uh . . . would it be possible for me to just look in on her and see how she's doing? If she's asleep, I won't wake her."

"Yeah, I guess so. Her room's upstairs. Door on the right. Don't let Blackjack out."

Danielle scuttled up the stairway. She hoped Sybil would be asleep so that she could just take the mask and leave. As she knocked lightly on the door, it swung open and Danielle slipped inside. Sybil was dressed, but lying on the bed with her eyes closed, her head propped up by pillows. Danielle looked around for the mask but it wasn't anywhere in sight. *Damn.* She walked over to the bed. "Sybil? Are you asleep?" Sybil opened her eyes. "Oh, good, you're not asleep. How are you feeling?"

Sybil made a move to sit up. "Oh, don't get up, dear. I just wanted to see how you were. Matt told me you were lying down, so I gather you're not feeling well." Sybil said nothing.

"Uh, Sybil, while I'm here, I thought I'd take back that mask you borrowed from my shop. It's rather valuable, and I need to have it back. Where is it?"

"Yaxagama."

"What?"

"Yaxagama ancient mother, help me find the ..." her voice trailed off.

"Sybil, I need you to listen to me. Please try to focus." Danielle knew that wasn't the right term to use with a blind girl, but she was becoming exasperated and a little panicky. "Where is the mask, Sybil? Is it somewhere in this room?"

"Yaxagama mighty mother, standing guard against the evil, waiting for the. . . ." Once again, Sybil's thin voice faded away.

Danielle reached out to take Sybil by the hand, and then uttered a shriek as, with a *whoosh* of wings, Blackjack landed on the bed. She hadn't noticed the raven that had been sitting on a beam above her head. Now the bird eyed her balefully as if threatening to strike. Danielle saw that she wouldn't be getting anything out of Sybil in her present state, and hastily left, closing the door so as not to let Blackjack out.

Matt was downstairs, waiting. Danielle made one more try. "Matt, did you see a carved wooden mask that Sybil brought home?"

"Yeah."

"Well, do you know where it is?"

"No."

"Do you have any idea what Sybil did with it?"

"No."

"Could she have hidden it?"

"I dunno."

"Could she have taken it somewhere?"

"I dunno."

"Do you think it's somewhere here in the house?"

"I dunno."

Danielle shut her eyes and tilted her head back as if seeking strength from above, then gave Matt a look that said: this is why I never wanted children. "What time is your mother coming home — and don't say 'I dunno'!"

"I — I think she said the next ferry."

"Thank you, Matt," Danielle hissed and headed for her car.

CHAPTER 44

THE GROUP in the Satama cemetery wasn't as large as had been expected. There had been some uncertainty as to whether the commemoration ceremony would be held at all, and those who attended had learned of it by word of mouth. Others had opted to bypass it for various reasons, the main one being that the significance of it paled, compared with the tragedy of Dory Michaels. Willie had chosen to stay home with Gabi and the immobilized Celeste; Jeremy had willingly skipped the proceedings in his role as host.

Peg Hewett, over her husband's protests, had decided not to go, saying she'd been awake most of the night, and that if he felt it mandatory, as the village RCMP, to be there, *he* could represent the family. Sanni Westerlake, the postmaster, and Barb Kuusiniemi did attend, even though their husbands were absent. Pearl Rista chose to stay and keep her café open, but Larry and June Nyquist of the New Broom were present. So were most of the seniors on the island, including Ulla Kampsula, who had gotten a ride with Grace Maddox.

Originally, the plan had been to have the crowd stand at the memorial statue, but since a number of seniors would be present, it was decided that folding chairs be brought in from the school auditorium. They proved to be unstable on the uneven ground, and not all that secure even on the blacktopped walkways, so most of the crowd preferred to remain standing, while a few octogenarians, like Ulla, seated themselves very carefully.

Everyone kept a wary eye on the sky which was becoming more cloudy. By time Danielle slipped into the crowd, Charlie Peterman was well underway with his opening address, harking back to the history of the island, the hardships of their forbears, reading the names of those who had perished in the fire, and holding them up as a symbol of all the brave men and women who had died in the early years of settlement, many at sea, many from lack of medical care, many in accidents, or just simply worn out by the arduous task of wresting a life from the wilderness.

Danielle glanced around for Oskar Vuorisaari and saw him standing with his wife on the edge of the crowd. Amanda caught her eye and gave her a cool nod. *You're late.* She was holding a large book in her hands, and Danielle realized that there would be yet another reading from the *Kalevala*. Hilda Widjescoog was standing next to her, also holding a book, and Danielle groaned inwardly. Were they going to do a reading and a translation? She couldn't comprehend the *Kalevala* in either language, and had never understood the Finns' preoccupation with it. Danielle was beginning to hope it would rain, and, indeed, she thought she felt a drop.

Amanda and Hilda were, by now, stationed next to the memorial stone. Hilda, her wild, luxuriant mass of hair tightening its curl in the damp air, announced that they would be reading *Runo* 48, "The Capture of the Fire," and that Amanda would read the text in the original Finnish, and that she, Hilda, would read the English version.

Amanda cleared her throat and began:

Vaka vanha Väinämöinen,
Tietäjä iän-ikuinen

Tuosta tuumille tulevi,
Ajeleiksen arveloille

Danielle glanced around at the group. Helen Laine from the Inn was standing next to Rosemary Gray and Pauliina Ukkonen. They were looking politely attentive although Danielle knew they didn't understand a word of it. Pauliina was a Finn, but, as with many, the language had pretty much died out for her when her parents did, and the old language of the Kalevala required a glossary.

Amanda hesitated. She seemed to have lost her place. Uttering a couple of "ahems," and adjusting her bifocals, she returned to the reading.

Jopa tuikahti tulone
Pääsi käestä Päivän poian
Poltti parran Väinämöisen
Sepolta sitäi pahemmin
Tuli poltti poskipäitä

Danielle sneaked a peek at her watch. Apparently it wasn't going to be a simultaneous translation, like at the UN — and that meant that, whenever Amanda was finished, they were only halfway through. She was wondering how the seniors were managing to stay awake — but look! One of them was obviously touched by the reading. Ulla Kampsula was dabbing at her eyes with a handkerchief. Poor old dears. To Danielle, the old Finnish women all looked pretty much alike, and she could never get their names straight. But Satama wasn't a bad place to be a senior. There was a sense of family, and the villagers looked after their own. Even those in the seniors' home were freer and more able to interact with the community, unlike in cities, where old people tend to be warehoused and isolated.

Most of the old people in Satama continued to live in their own homes until they died, their living assisted by family or friends. Many passed away peacefully in their own beds, and Danielle, in her shop, had heard many deathbed stories that gave her pause. More than once, it seemed that, with their last breath, the dying appeared to be greeting a spouse or parent long dead. So, at the point of death, *did* a loved one appear to guide the dying? Did the dead actually return — or were they hanging around waiting? Did the dead really survive at all or was it just hallucination? More likely it was just some short circuit in the brain that kicks in just before anyone kicks off, and is responsible for all those famous last words. Danielle remembered one funny story about old Aino Ruotsela, who at age 97 was lying on her deathbed, attended by village women who, thinking she was in a coma, were remarking on the smoothness of Aino's skin at such an advanced age. One was saying that she should have asked Aino for her beauty secret while she was still conscious. At that, the old woman opened her eyes, uttered one word before she died: "Noxzema."

Danielle's mind had wandered through Amanda's reading and a good bit of Hilda's as well. Hilda was reading with dramatic flair, her hair almost crackling and writhing like flames:

Uncontrolled the wildfire bounded
Through the billows of Lake Alue;
Flashing through a bush of juniper,
Burned a heath of juniper;
Running through a firwood forest,
Burned up all the stately spruces;

Danielle almost wanted to tap her foot to the rhythm; it did have a rollicking cadence. She noticed that some of the cemetery ravens were infiltrating the crowd. Danielle found it amusing but also a bit macabre. The whole scene was bizarre. It was just another of those things Danielle was forever encountering on Broom Island, where in a deceptively ordinary culture, she kept coming across caves and hollows that she would never be able to explore or understand. It went beyond generations, since each generation seemed to be less ethnic, but she had come to sense that Finns are a breed apart.

"Rain down ice and rain down hailstones,
Rain the best of ointments for me

On my fire wounds, on my blisters"
This is how smith Ilmarinen
Quenched the fire, soothed the burning.
He recovered from his fire-wounds
And is the man he was before
In spite of all the burns he suffered.

And then it was over. But now there seemed to be some disturbance. Sanni Westerlake looked up, surprised, then started making her way toward her husband, who had arrived and was edging through to Constable Hewett. Danielle could see there was some serious matter at hand. The constable and Butch left immediately, and Danielle hurried over to Sanni. "What's going on?"

"They found Chad Michaels in the woods. He's dead."

CHAPTER 45

Kirsti Weeks arrived on the one o'clock ferry. Since she'd gone across in the ambulance and returned as a foot passenger, she needed to get back to the clinic where she'd left the truck. It wasn't a long walk, but she was almost immediately offered a ride by Sali Johnson, a neighbor of Oliver Sylvester. Sali, like Oliver, was one of the Old Finns. His name was actually Kalle, but in logging camps they'd always called him Charlie, and "Sali" was as close as he, with his accent, could come, so Sali he became. "I go right by your place, so hop in."

"Thanks, Sali, but I'm not going home. I have to get my truck at the clinic."

"Fine. I'll swing by there. I just came in to wet my whistle at The Sea Hole. That ceremony this morning was pretty dry. If you just came in on the ferry, I guess you haven't heard the news yet!"

"News about what?"

"You know that guy, Schittle, who calls himself Michaels?"

"Of course. He's the one who shot my husband. What's he done now?"

"They found him dead this morning."

"*What?* What happened to *him?*"

"Party of men out looking for the cougar came across his body just off the Lemerriant trail, on that section that goes up to the lake."

This was stunning news indeed! "Did the cougar kill him too?"

"I dunno. Mighta. Body was pretty well messed up, but they don't know whether he was attacked or if he died of exposure and then some animals found him. The guy was barefoot and I guess he was wearing pajamas or something. I didn't get all the details."

Kirsti was trying to get her mind around the news. "What would he have been doing out in the woods? When did all this happen?"

"Don't know how long he'd been out there, but it musta been some time last night. Mighta been drunk or just out of his head, wanderin' around, maybe got lost. Greenhorns don't know how to act in the woods."

"Oh, my god, what a week! It's like a bad dream. One thing after another. Just drop me off here, Sali, you don't have to pull into the lot. Thanks for the lift."

"Anytime, Kirsti. Say hi to Rome when you see him. How's he doing?"

"He'll be all right. Just takes time. Damn fool must've used an elephant gun." Kirsti headed for her truck, thinking she should probably not have called Chad Schittle a damn fool since she didn't like to speak ill of the dead. Chad's dying was, nevertheless, the least of her worries. Good riddance.

Back home Kirsti found things much as she'd left them. Sybil was still sleeping and Matt was fidgety, confined to the house. "Anybody call while I was gone?"

"No. Just the lady from the shop came by, is all."

"Danielle Herron?"

"Yeah. She wanted that mask Sybil brought home."

"Oh, good. Then I don't have to worry about returning it."

"I didn't give it to her."

"Why on earth not?"

"It's not here. She looked in Sybil's room but it wasn't there."

"It was there yesterday! Are you sure?"

"I think She asked Sybil about it but I guess Sybil was half asleep and couldn't remember. Anyway, she said she'd be back later when you got home."

Kirsti sighed. "Oh, all right. Have you had lunch?"

"I made myself a peanut butter sandwich."

"Would you like something more?"

"I'm not hungry. Can I go outside?"

"With that cougar around I don't want you anywhere near the woods."

"Can I just go to Willie's to watch TV with Gabi? They have satellite."

Kirsti made a face as if to say she didn't like the idea, but it might work with a few qualifications. "I suppose so. But you go straight to Willie's, understand? And the two of you stay in the house. No wandering around. That cougar is dangerous. I heard it might have killed someone else last night."

Matt's eyes widened and his mouth made an "O" as he asked, "Who?"

"Dory's father. Chad Michaels."

"Wow!" This was something he couldn't wait to tell Gabi. "Did it rip him to pieces?"

Kirsti found her son's reaction a little annoying. "I don't know how it happened, but they found Mr. Michaels this morning somewhere off the Lemerriant trail. Right now that's all I know, but it's enough. So you children stay inside."

Matt nodded, then bolted out the door.

"Wait a minute. I'll walk with you." Once in sight of Willie's house, Kirsti waited until her son had disappeared inside, then returned home.

Matt had been hoping he'd be the first with the news about Dory's dad. It turned out, he wasn't.

After Gabi's dire pronouncement that morning, which nobody had believed, Willie had, nevertheless, made a discreet call to Amanda Vuorisaari, ostensibly to offer apologies for not being able to make it to the cemetery, citing her house guest's injury. Amanda had coldly replied that she understood, but had also pointed out that it was a shame that the president of the Historical Society was unable to be there on such an important occasion; but of course, it wouldn't seem so important to Willie, would it, since *she* hadn't actually lived her whole life on the island, had she? Not like some who had toiled to preserve the island heritage year after year. Willie was well aware that Amanda resented her having been elected president, and that Amanda felt it had hinged on the perceived glamor and stature of Willie's life *off* the island. "No one is a prophet in her home town," Amanda had said to her husband.

Willie apologized, regretted heartily that she would miss Amanda's reading of the *Kalevala* in its native tongue, and was relieved that Amanda was saying nothing at all about Chadwick Michaels. Gabi had probably been dreaming again. So, around noon, when the phone rang, she was caught off guard to hear, this time from Sanni Westerlake, that Michaels had indeed been found dead in the woods by her husband and the hunting party.

There was no way to keep the news from Celeste, so Willie simply announced it to everyone. Gabi just shrugged. Celeste received it with a haunted look. Jeremy said little, as if the less said the better. Willie set about preparing lunch which everyone ate in near silence. Matt's arrival seemed a matter of course, and the two children slipped away almost unnoticed.

When Matt and Gabi had been left alone by the TV set, both of them were bursting with the news. "Did you hear about Dory's dad?" Matt asked.

"Yeah. I told them he was dead, but they didn't believe me until somebody phoned."

"How did you know?"

"The birds tell me things. I guess there really is a Loogy-Roo after all."

"They said it was the cougar."

Gabi's tone was weary, as if to say, cougar, schmougar: "Doesn't matter what they call it, does it? The birds tell me there'll be fresh blood, and somebody gets killed."

"That's weird."

"Yeah, guess so."

Matt seemed to be mulling something over in his mind. "Okay, then, when the birds tell you stuff, do they talk out loud? I mean the day we went in the woods there were birds all over the place. Were they talking to you then?"

"Yeah."

"How come *I* couldn't hear them?"

"I dunno."

"They seemed to be following you around. We saw that big bird on the hill. Did *he* talk to you?"

"He was the one who said there'd be fresh blood."

"Then, after that, when we took our bikes on the trail, there were birds following us. Like the birds that showed up when you were talking to Dory's dad at the gate. Did the bird at the gate say anything?"

"I don't remember. I don't think so."

"They seem to show up whenever you're around. Can all of them talk to you?"

"I don't know. I just hear them and I know what they're saying."

"You mean they're just talking bird language to each other and you can understand them?"

"Something like that."

"Cool! What else do they talk about?"

The question seemed to surprise Gabi. "What do you mean?"

Matt was looking keenly at Gabi. "The day we went to the lake there were birds there. And when we went to the old house, birds were there. Then when we went to Dory's house and her dad caught us at the gate. Birds there. We went up the hill and saw the big black bird, and when we went back to the lake and the quarry, lots of birds there. If you can understand bird talk, then you must have heard them say all kinds of stuff. What do birds talk about?"

Gabi gave a little shrug. "Oh, I dunno. Mostly they told me about the kids that got killed by a cougar and what it was like."

"What do you mean? What *was* it like?"

"Oh, they said it was windy and the blood was fresh and they pecked out their eyes."

"Cool!"

"And they said there'd be more blood and then Dory got killed."

Matt frowned. "Okay, did the birds say anything about my dad getting shot?"

"The birds didn't tell me that. The singing girl told me, remember?"

"Tell me more about the singing girl."

"I told you. I woke up and I could hear her voice singing the rainy day song."

"The one Dory Michaels used to sing."

"I couldn't really understand all the words but then I heard 'a man with a gun will be shot on a rainy day.' And it happened, didn't it?"

"What I want to know is how come you hear this stuff? You hear birds talking, dead kid singing."

"I don't know if it was a dead kid. All I heard was a voice."

"So what are you, psychic or something?"

"Umm . . . maybe. Whatever that is."

"My sister's psychic. I overheard my mom say so. Somebody called Sybil crazy. Mom got all upset and said that Sybil was psychic. I guess that means not crazy but something else just as weird. She's always hearing stuff too. Did the birds tell you about Dory's dad?"

"Uh-huh."

"When?"

"This morning. There were lots of them in the yard. I could hear them through the window."

"And what were they saying?"

"They said they'd find the barefoot man who called the cougar."

"Called the cougar? What does *that* mean?"

"I don't know, but that's what they said."

"How did you know it was Dory's dad?"

Gabi looked puzzled. "I don't know. I think I just knew."

"So did the cougar kill him?"

"I don't know that either."

"Did the birds say anything else?"

"Stuff about the moon and the mud and the cougar, so I guess maybe it did kill him."

"Cheez! This is starting to creep me out."

"You think there really *is* a Loogy-Roo?"

Matt swallowed. "My sister thinks so."

"Did she say anything about last night?"

"No. She's been sleeping like she usually does after she's had a fit. She used to get them a lot when she was younger." Matt again fixed Gabi with narrowed eyes. "What were you doing at the old house last night? Did you go there with my sister?"

"I don't remember anything about it till Jeremy found me. I guess I was sleepwalking. I do that sometimes."

"Whoa! You mean you just get up and walk around while you're still asleep?"

"Yeah."

"How do you do that? Can you see where you're going or do you bump into stuff?"

Gabi shook her head. "I don't know. I never remember."

Matt stood up, shut his eyes, held his hands out in front of him and started walking. "Man, that's — " he bumped into a chair. "Okay, are your eyes open or shut?"

"I told you, I don't know. Nobody's ever told me."

"People see you do it? Could *I* watch you sometime?"

Gabi was becoming exasperated. "My mom sees me sometimes, and no you *can't*. I never remember anything about it and I never know when it's going to happen."

"Can you talk in your sleep too?"

"I don't know. So just forget about it, okay?"

"So you walked to the old house in your sleep last night. I wonder how Sybil got there. And why."

"Why don't you ask her."

"Oh, I will. Not that she'd tell me. But I wonder if she took the mask with her."

"Mask?"

"She had this Indian mask yesterday. The lady from the shop came by to take it back but we couldn't find it."

"What's that got to do with anything?"

"I'm not sure. But something. Sybil was hanging on to that mask and wouldn't tell me why, except that it had something to do with the Loogy-Roo. Maybe it's part of her psychic stuff. I'll bet she took it to the old house. I'll bet she left it there. I'll bet if we went there we'd find it. Maybe we could even figure out what it's for."

"If it was that important, why would she leave it?"

"I don't know. But it's not here unless she hid it someplace."

"Well, we can't go looking for it now. They'd never let us out of the house." Gabi glanced through the kitchen doorway and saw her mother looking back at her. "They're watching us like hawks."

"Yeah. I don't want a cougar jumping on me anyway."

Gabi smiled a little remotely. "No cougar is ever going to jump on *me*."

CHAPTER 46

Danielle Herron was once again driving her Volkswagen along Kaunio Road, heading for the Weeks house. She had just gone through a harrowing hour with Rowena Michaels.

After the ceremony, when Sanni Westerlake had told her the news about Chad, Danielle realized that she would have to be the one to tell Rowena that her husband was dead. She'd gone back to the shop, shut the door, flipped up the "Closed" sign, and poured the puzzled Rowena a glass of sherry from a bottle she kept in her desk drawer. Then, as gently as possible, she had told her the news about her husband.

Rowena had taken it harder than she'd expected. As if watching a water main blow, Danielle stood by as Rowena screamed, dropped the sherry, then burst into loud and uncontrolled weeping. Danielle recognized it as a delayed reaction and let her cry it out. Then, when Weena had grown calmer, Danielle bundled her into the car, locked up the shop, and drove her back to her house on Kaunio Road. There, in a comfy chair, soothed by another glass of sherry, Rowena had leaned back, closed her eyes, and finally fallen asleep from exhaustion.

Now what? The shop was closed. *Damn!* She should go back and open it, but could she leave Rowena alone? No, not really. Still, Rowena seemed comfortable, and was even snoring softly. Danielle lifted the foot rest of the recliner to put Weena's feet up, and covered her with a knitted afghan. She glanced at her watch. Maybe she could find someone to keep the shop open. Not Sybil, certainly. Maybe somebody else would be available. At any rate, she still had to go find that transformation mask. *Double damn!* Kirsti would know where it was. She may even have had the presence of mind to put it away in a safe place. But could Danielle just leave Weena alone, asleep? Well, maybe she could leave a note. Finding paper and pencil, Danielle wrote: "Weena, if you wake up before I get back, call me at the shop at 973-6396." She removed the empty glass and left the note in its place.

The truck was in the driveway so obviously Kirsti had returned. Danielle rang the bell; Kirsti opened the door.

"Hi, Kirsti. I guess Matt told you I'd be stopping by. How is Rome doing? We've all been so worried about him."

"Come on in, Danielle. Rome will be all right, thanks. I'll tell him you were asking. It's a bad wound but he'll recover."

"Terrible accident. How on earth did it happen?"

"Sounded like stupidity to me. Greenhorns with guns. They'll shoot at anything that moves. Then they get themselves killed as well. I suppose you've heard."

"About Chad Michaels? Yes. I was at the cemetery this morning when they news came that they'd found him. I had to break it to Rowena. She was very upset."

"She shouldn't be out there by herself."

"She's not at home. She's at my house. I left her napping. She was emotionally drained, poor thing."

Kirsti sighed. "Yeah, I can imagine. I thought I was going to lose a husband myself. I was just about to make coffee. Can I offer you a cup?"

"Thanks, Kirsti, but I really can't stay. I had to close the shop and I'll need to find someone to mind it and then get back to Weena, although I might as well have shut down for the holiday. Doesn't look like I'll have any customers. Anyway, I thought I'd stop by and pick up that Indian mask Sybil borrowed. It's rather valuable and I'd hate to have anything happen to it."

Kirsti looked uncomfortable. "I'm sorry but the mask doesn't seem to be here. I don't know what Sybil could have been thinking when she brought it home. Matt told me you'd stopped by earlier so I looked all over for it, but it's not in the house unless Sybil has it hidden. I did ask her about it, but she's so fuzzy-minded after her seizures that she doesn't seem to remember anything. I'm sure when her memory clears up she'll be able to tell us."

Danielle tried to hide her annoyance and glanced at her watch. "Well, then I guess there's nothing we can do right now. I just want to impress upon you that that particular mask is worth *$15,000*. It's the most valuable one in my collection. It would have been fine if she'd taken one of the reproductions, but this one is an original."

Kirsti looked shocked. "Good heavens! I'm sure Sybil will have put it in a safe place." Kirsti wasn't sure at all, but hoped fervently that that were true. "I'll certainly try to find it, and I'll call you the minute I do."

Drat the woman, they each thought as they parted, Danielle for her car, Kirsti for Sybil's room. What in the world had possessed Sybil to steal a valuable artifact? Was the girl totally out of her mind? Didn't she know what she was doing? And, good grief, if the damn thing turned out to be broken or lost, she and Rome would have to make it good somehow. Fifteen thousand dollars! She'd had no idea! Kirsti remembered casually tossing the thing aside. Maybe Danielle was exaggerating. But that wouldn't matter, would it? She could say it was worth twenty thousand, or thirty thousand, and how could they prove otherwise? With a husband in the hospital, and a daughter recovering from seizures, Kirsti didn't need this additional aggravation.

She knocked softly on Sybil's door, and, not getting a response, she opened it. "Sybil? Are you awake?" Sybil, lying propped up on pillows, opened her eyes.

"Would you like something to eat? You missed breakfast and it's past lunch time." Sybil blinked, then shifted position. Blackjack hopped over and landed beside her on the bed. "How do you feel? Do you think you can get up if I help you?" She put an arm around her daughter to steady her.

"I need to pee." Kirsti helped her down the hall to the upstairs bathroom. Sybil relieved herself, then allowed her mother to wipe her face and hands with a damp washcloth. "You're looking better. But you need to get some food down you. You can have it up in your room if you like."

"I'll come down." Sybil's voice was faint and her movements listless.

"Good. Can I help you?"

"I can make it. I was a bit dizzy but I'm all right now."

Looking concerned, Kirsti walked down the staircase ahead of Sybil, ready to catch her if she swayed. Sybil managed, holding onto the railing. Kirsti heated Sybil a bowl of leftover beef and vegetable stew, and when Sybil had eaten, Kirsti seated herself at the table, across from her daughter.

"Sybil, what do you remember about yesterday — about last night?"

"Last night?"

"Yes. You went to the old house on the Lemerriant trail. You remember that, don't you?"

"Old house?"

"Yes." Kirsti said evenly. "The old Lemerriant farm. You went there. Why?"

Sybil's expression was wary. "I guess I don't remember."

"Do you remember an Indian mask that you brought home from Danielle Herron's shop?"

"Uh. No, I don't think so."

"Danielle wants it back. It's very valuable. It's worth a lot of money."

Sybil said nothing but indicated with a shake of her head that it meant nothing to her.

"You had it in your room yesterday. Where could it be now?"

"I . . . I don't know." Something in her manner made this sound unconvincing.

"If it's not found, Danielle could have you arrested for stealing. If it's not found, your father and I would have to make good the cost, which Danielle says is *fifteen thousand dollars.*"

Sybil bit her lip but said nothing.

"So, my girl, you just try to remember where that mask is. I'm sure it'll come to you. And the sooner the better."

Sybil looked uncomfortable. "I think I'll go back to bed. My head hurts." She got up and made her way back up the staircase while her mother watched her through narrowed eyes.

. . .

Danielle Herron checked her watch again. Torn between friendship and commerce, she was trying to decide whether to go back to her shop or home to Rowena. Well, just this once, she guessed the shop could wait. It wasn't high tourist season, and given the holiday, and given that the town was in shock over the deaths of Dory and her father, it seemed unlikely that there would be customers this afternoon. Her biggest concern now was the mask. Perhaps, after checking on Rowena, she could come back again to see if Sybil had remembered what she'd done with it. She headed homeward along Kaunio Road, but when she pulled into her driveway she saw that the Michaels' truck wasn't there. Rowena had gone.

Danielle went inside to find a message scrawled on the note she'd left for Weena: "I've got to go back home. Don't worry. I'm fine. I'll call you."

Danielle went out again, got in her car, thought momentarily of following Weena, but then decided she'd go back to the shop. If Rowena felt strong enough to leave on her own, then so be it. She'd wait for her call or ring her later. Meanwhile, Danielle was feeling a bit light-headed and remembered that she hadn't had lunch. She could nip over to the New Broom — no, come to think of it, the Nyquists wouldn't be opening their restaurant now until dinner time; she could get a sandwich to go at Pearl's. But first she'd open the shop and make that call to Oskar Vuorisaari, the mortician, so that she'd have some information for Rowena next time they spoke. All this was *so* distressing! Broom Island was supposed to be the most peaceful of places. Nothing ever happened here except for a bit of teen vandalism or a drunken brawl at The Sea Hole. Suddenly there was a rogue cougar and people dying and her valuable mask missing. None of this was good for business!

CHAPTER 47

Elphique Lemerriant knew the cougar was watching him, but felt no fear of the beast, even though his only protection was the knife on his belt. He couldn't see the cougar, but he could feel its presence; and he could almost hear it breathing in raspy little puffs while it remained hidden, observing Elphique's every move. Elphique doused his campfire, rolled up his blanket, and packed up his gear. He wanted to see if the cougar would follow him, so he started walking slowly across the sandy quarry, up the embankment, on upwards toward the ridge that lay like the backbone of the cat-shaped island of Broom. A bird — a raven — flew across his path, uttering a raucous cry, as if in warning.

Elphique kept moving. He could feel the cougar following. Was it stalking him? Yes. Was it hungry or just curious? Elphique knew that a cougar can be curious enough to follow you, just to see what you're doing, simply in order to pass the time of day. Elphique had already encountered this cougar. It was the one he'd fed at his campfire, the one he'd "called" by imitating its cry. Elphique was not afraid of animals, although he showed them respect and treated them with the same wariness that they treated him. He was more frightened of people. Except for the shadow people on the hilltop, people were incomprehensible to Elphique; animals he understood. There were times when Elphique felt he was more animal than man.

Elphique had found that he could, at first only occasionally, then with more and more facility, understand their language — not just the twitters and growls, but animals spoke with their bodies: twitch of tail, pricking of ears, the way they moved, and the flash of their eyes. At first their noise in his head had been just background sound, but gradually it had begun to make sense to him. Now he could listen to the ravens and know what they were saying. Not that they seemed to have anything important to chatter about; mostly it was about food, or the weather, or what was going on in the forest. Same with the starlings. Starlings were constantly in voice, just as they seemed to always be on the move, like anxious passengers, squabbling with each other, while trying to keep track of tickets and luggage and changes in scheduling, although Elphique would have known nothing of such things. He just considered them to be unnecessarily noisy. Their level of chatter had little interest for him; although birds were a good early warning system, letting him know whenever a stranger or the village boys were around. Otherwise he wasn't all that interested in hearing about a hatch of winged ants, or whether a dead animal had washed up on the beach, or the birds' concerted effort to drive away an owl or hawk.

Cougars were different, and Elphique really wanted to know more about *them*. One was following him now, and he knew why: the cougar also wanted to know more about *him*.

Elphique chose a place next to a large rock, put down his gear, then sat quietly waiting. He could hear the faintest rustle as the big cat crept closer. Elphique sat and waited, so still that he was barely breathing. Then, slowly, ever so slowly, the cougar emerged from behind a thicket of salal. He stopped and stared at Elphique. Elphique made eye contact, and for a moment animal and boy were locked into each other's gaze.

Then, as if it had been struck, the cougar leapt back and vanished into the brush.

Elphique smiled. For a moment, he'd been a cougar! He had thrown his mind into the mind of the animal. He had felt what it was like to look out through a cougar's eyes, had experienced the lithe body, the comforting fur, the pulsing strength, the keen senses, and sheer power of the beast.

It wasn't the first time Elphique and been able to project his consciousness into another creature, but never a cougar. He'd done it with ravens, an eagle once (and that had been breathtaking!), and even into a banana slug as it seemed to sleep on a stump. (That had been so strange and alien that Elphique had instantly pulled back.) He'd done it with the island deer, and in each case he was always surprised by the clarity and richness of the experience. It was like a huge splash of *nowness*, as if the *now* of an animal was different — much bigger than the *now* of a man. Elphique could never maintain it for more than a second or two, but it was vivid and shocking, like being dipped into an icy stream, all his senses jolted wide awake and amplified.

Elphique also knew that this time it had been different. Not only had *he* experienced being a cougar, but he knew that the cougar had also experienced being Elphique! While his mind had entered the mind of the cat, he had felt the cougar probing his own. *That* had never happened to Elphique before, and it left him feeling as startled as the cougar must have been. It had only lasted a second, but Elphique sensed that some permanent change had taken place, some level of understanding had been established. From then on the two would be linked. He would never have anything to fear from this cougar — nor any cougar. He could sleep anywhere, undisturbed, and he'd be protected. A little of the cougar would always be with him, just as he would always be part of the cougar. If either killed the other, they'd be killing themselves.

Elphique did not articulate any of this. His mind worked more in pictures than in words, and perhaps that made the connection with animals easier. Nor did Elphique ponder any of it for long. For all he knew this was normal. He accepted such things, even the shadow people, the way he accepted the wind and the rain. His solitary path gave him no standard for comparison with others of his species. Since his lifestyle was more animal than man, he existed brilliantly in the present moment, with little dwelling on memories of the past, when his father would work him and whip him like an ox, nor visions of the future — because what future did Elphique have that would be different from his present?

World events didn't intrude. The trappings of civilization were peripheral, and something to be avoided. Elphique couldn't read; what he'd learned in his brief early schooling was long forgotten. He knew of such things as automobiles and airplanes and ships, for he'd seen cars on the island, planes flying overhead, and ships passing by in the strait. He accepted them with little curiosity, as something that belonged to the outside world, although he would always stop and watch the boats until they disappeared from view.

People? He avoided people. For years he'd hidden from them. Now he displayed ferocity and that seemed more effective. His rage and his strength had freed him from his father's domination on the day when he found he was strong enough to leave his father lying in the dust, screaming that his son had gone mad.

Even his mother and his sister had become irrelevant to him. He did visit his home now and then, but usually only at night when everyone was sleeping. He would wander through the farmstead, the outbuildings, and sometimes sleep curled up in the hay in the barn when the weather was bad, then leave early, before anyone saw him. Sometimes he would find food left for him on a stump. He always knew who had left it, recognizing his mother's *pot au feu* or her French bread and cheese. The neighbor's girl would leave a loaf of rye, a braid of *pulla*, and sometimes even a bowl of fragrant *kalamojakka*, a chowder made with fresh salmon, halibut, or cod. She liked to spy on him, but they never spoke. For a time she always seemed to be hanging around, hiding in bushes or behind trees, and he wanted to warn her to stay away, but never did. Then, after a while, he didn't see her anymore, but accepted her absence the way he accepted everything else. Elphique hadn't even known her name.

CHAPTER 48

Celeste Ooms-Possum was feeling restless and frustrated, sitting alone at the kitchen table, while Willie was upstairs tending to housework and Jeremy was out in the yard. Her ankle was still too painful to walk on, but as long as she sat still it was no longer actively aching. Peg Hewett had wrapped it in an elastic bandage and given her Ibuprofen, so despite the occasional twinge during the night, Celeste had managed to sleep. She'd apologized to Willie for not having made her bed, and had been told not to be silly, and to go find the most comfortable chair. That turned out to be one of the wooden ones in the kitchen, as it was easier for her to get on her feet — foot — with aid of her walker than from a soft, overstuffed sofa. Willie had given her a cup of tea and permission to use her office and her computer whenever she wanted.

Now, all Celeste really wanted to do was to get herself and Gabi off the island; and she desperately wanted a cigarette. Willie had been right, of course. She wouldn't be able to drive. Well, perhaps she could, but it wouldn't be safe for her to be operating a car just yet. Maybe by tomorrow morning she and Gabi could get on the ferry and leave all this behind.

Meanwhile she was keeping a watchful eye on Gabi, who wasn't doing anything more than sitting on the floor in front of the TV set with Matt Weeks. They seemed to be innocently watching a movie on tape; it all seemed safe enough, at least for now.

But what horrors lurked outdoors, luring her daughter into the jaws of danger? Celeste was not one to believe in the supernatural, but what *was* this beast that had killed two people in the short time she'd been on the island? The chant — the children's chant — about the Loogy-Roo kept playing over and over in her mind as a persistent earworm.

Beware the laughing blackbirds
And the Loogy-Roo
If they don't stop laughing
Then they've come for you.

Loogy-Roo . . . *loup garou* . . . werewolf . . . superstition . . . laughing blackbirds . . . Lemerriants . . . *Le Merle Riant.* It all added up in a strangely gothic way. But it had been such a long time ago! What possible connection could there be anymore? Had the Lemerriants, one or more of them, had some kind of genetic trait that they'd passed on? A mental aberration intensified through incest? They'd all been considered mad! Perhaps all they had was ESP.

Celeste grudgingly accepted psychic ability as a gift that some people may have, but if it were genuine, then it had to be a natural condition that simply was not yet correctly understood. In the time of the Lemerriants, it would have been considered witchcraft or possession or madness. Could such a thing be passed on genetically? And why not? The genes contain coded information that can actually be traced to groups of ancestors thousands of years past, and probably to a prehistoric common ancestor, should there actually have been such a worthy. Genetically archived information was a lot more enduring than computerized data which could be destroyed, corrupted, or simply find itself obsolete, in that the new technology could no longer access the old floppies.

The cougar, of course, was a coincidence. She'd gotten the impression that whenever a cougar surfaced on the island, the old Loogy-Roo stories resurfaced as well. No doubt some of it was just a bit of island lore, something to chill and thrill a tourist, a fey connection to the fanciful, like tales of "the little people" in an Irish village, or the ghost in the castle.

At any rate, Celeste felt she should be doing something other than just sitting around waiting for her ankle to heal. Since Willie had so generously given her leave to use her computer, Celeste, with the aid of the walker, limped into Willie's office, settled herself in front of the Mac and turned it on. She clicked on the icons of Ulla Kampsula's photos. There, full screen, stood Brazeau and Dauphine, frozen in time, yet seemingly in motion in the wind that whipped their clothing and bent the grasses.

They were not unattractive people. Brazeau was stocky, built like a bull, but there was a hint of brutish good looks that must have attracted Dauphine in her youth. Dauphine, standing unconsciously posed like a dancer, had the delicacy of an aristocrat, despite her drab clothing and humble setting. Tall and willowy, she must have been quite beautiful as a young girl. Celeste tried to picture the two as being young, in love, courting. Or maybe that's not the way it had been. All marriages are not for love. Brazeau, according to the dates on the tombstones, had been thirteen years older. Had Dauphine, for whatever reason, been forced into a marriage of convenience — a marriage against her will? Had Brazeau always been crazed and domineering? Or had something happened to make him that way?

Celeste stared at the photo, trying intuitively to wring every nuance of information from it. What lay beyond the edges? What had happened immediately before the snapshot was taken — and immediately afterward? They were all dead now, and had died on the same day, exactly seventy years ago today, the day of the fire that had killed Elphique as well.

She opened the photo of Elphique. Somehow, he was the key to it all, wasn't he? He *was* the Loogy-Roo, at least in the eyes of the villagers at the time. He did look menacing, scowling in the sun with a knife on his belt, poised as if he might draw it and stab you with it. Why was he doing that? Had he heard Ulla creeping up on him? Did he hear the click of a shutter? Perhaps he knew she was there, and wanted to scare her a little — show ferocity, the way an animal will snarl in warning. Ulla's mother used to send food to him, so maybe the two, Elphique and Ulla, *had* known each other. What was their relationship? Wary? Friends at a distance? Certainly not playmates, but Ulla didn't seem to be afraid of him, at least not the way other children had been.

The writer in Celeste was telling her that all this could become an interesting novel. She'd always wanted to write one, and this had all the elements of a good story. It wouldn't be the first time she'd tried to write a book; she had at least three unfinished efforts in a desk drawer. Somehow, though, she'd never been able to follow through to produce a full-length manuscript. Celeste had always worked with assigned word counts — a three-thousand word article on the Bahamas or a page on the Galapagos Islands. Whenever she'd tried a novel it always seemed to bog down, then languish on a back burner until it no longer interested her. This might be different. It would be a story of her own ancestors — fictionalized, of course. She toyed with a title: *The Lemerriants of Broom Island* by Celeste Ooms-Possum — or perhaps *The Mad Lemerriants* by Celeste Ooms-Possum. No! It would be *The Mad Lemerriants* by Celeste *Lemerriant*. Call that the working title. She would have much research to do on their ancestry, and she'd scrape up every bit of information here — in fact, she might just spend the summer on Broom Island to immerse herself in her history. Well, maybe not, but it bore thinking about.

As usual, when the muse grabbed her by the scruff of the neck, Celeste transcended all else. Gabi would be fine. They'd get off the island whenever they got off the island. Meanwhile, she did want to talk with Ulla again. *Damned ankle*, but that, too, would be okay in a day or two. In fact, it was probably the best thing to have happened or otherwise she'd be gone by now. She would start with an outline. Glancing into the living room she saw Gabi and Matt apparently in conversation, paying little attention to the screen. Good to see Gabi had a friend. Kids watch too much TV anyway. She opened a new document in Microsoft Word, and smiling, typed in: Chapter One.

* * *

Jeremy was feeling rather restless himself as he walked around the yard and noted that the weather seemed to be clearing. It hadn't actually rained, although a few drops had fallen; it would be a pleasant afternoon for a hike. The post office would be closed on Victoria Day, but he could stop at the Co-op and pick up a paper. He stuck his head in the kitchen door and called, "I'm going into town. Anybody need anything?"

"Can we come with you?" Gabi and Matt were racing toward him. "We've been in the house *all day*."

"Well, I don't know. You'd have to ask your mothers."

"My mom won't care," Matt said. "As long as I'm with you."

Gabi was already in Willie's office. "Mom, can I go into town with Jeremy and Matt?"

Celeste looked up. She's been so engrossed that it took her moment to zero in. "Gabi, I told you to stay in the house today."

"We'll be with Jeremy. Can I please, *please!*"

Celeste looked up to see Jeremy smiling helplessly at her from the doorway. "Jeremy, are you sure? You *don't* have to take them with you."

"I think we could all do with a bit of fresh air and exercise. They'll be fine. I won't let them out of my sight. And we won't be long. Will you let Willie know that we've gone into Satama, and if Mrs. Weeks calls before we get back, please tell her Matt is with me."

"Uh, okay." Celeste's attention was already focused back on the computer. She probably should have switched to her own laptop, but Willie's machine had an Internet connection and she wanted to do some surfing, saving information and making notes as she went. No matter, she could use Willie's CD burner to transfer everything to a disk for easy transport. She did, definitely, want to talk with Ulla Kampsula again. She thought of recording a conversation with her, but instinct told her the situation would be delicate, and she didn't want to come off as conducting an inquisition.

"I see you're hard at it." Willie had come downstairs. She'd taken a shower and changed into fresh jeans and a sweater.

"Yes, I just had the idea that my family, the Lemerriants, might make an interesting novel." She looked up at Celeste to see what impact this might have. It was a little like saying, "I'm pregnant," and she found herself waiting for the joyful congratulations.

Herself a writer, Willie knew just what to say at such a time. This was not the time to mention the commitment, the hours — years — of labor followed by the frustration of dealing with Publication Hell. "That is *so* exciting. It would make a wonderful story and you'd be the perfect person to write it."

Willie had considered doing something similar herself, but her own book seemed to be taking forever to finish. The island was a fount of interesting tales, and she might, one day, if she lived long enough, do an anthology of Broom Island legend and lore.

"I was looking at the pictures Ulla took, and wondered if maybe she might have more information on Elphique and his family. Do you think she'd talk to me again?"

"The only way to find out is to ask her. I'll call her, and if she's willing, I'll drive you."

"I hate to be such a nuisance. Do you think it would be better if I talked with her alone? Sometimes people are more relaxed one-on-one. And do you think it would be better if I didn't try to record the conversation?"

"I can drop you off and pick you up again in an hour or two, since I have a few things to do in the village. As for recording, I think I'd just chat, at least for now. Once Ulla knows you better and trusts you, it probably won't matter. I don't even know if she has anything more to contribute, but people tend to clam up when you put a microphone in front of them."

"Right. I kind of thought so. Oh, by the way, Jeremy went into town and took Gabi and Matt with him. He said they'd be back soon."

"Good. I do need a few things from the Co-op. I'll give Ulla a call and also ask her if she needs anything from the store."

"Oh, but we'll have to wait for Jeremy and the kids to get back, won't we? I can't just leave here and expect Jeremy to babysit my daughter."

Willie glanced at her watch. "If Ulla is at home, and if we go now, I'm bound to run into Jeremy and the children in the village. We can find something to do for an hour or so, then I'll pick you up and we can all ride home together."

Celeste smiled. "Thanks, Willie. You are, indeed, the gatekeeper!"

CHAPTER 49

Danielle Herron crossed the road and climbed the short flight of wooden steps to Pearl's Café. She didn't like Pearl's, but today she had no choice. She always felt — or was made to feel — like an intruder, as the place was often filled with men. The sight of a woman always seemed to silence them, as if they now had to edit their language, even though they didn't bother to put out the cigarettes that filled the place with a haze of smoke. It was never what Danielle might have considered a classy crowd: itinerant loggers, local fishermen, retired farmers, work and construction crews. If a pretty young woman entered, the men generally did *not* whistle, hoot, or overtly leer. Islanders knew each other, and there was an unwritten code of conduct that mandated a show of respect among people who did, after all, have to live near each other in a limited space. (An outsider would quickly be clued in.) Still, Pearl's was the nearest thing on Broom Island to a men's club. The "Closed" sign that was always in the window tended to repel tourists and assure its integrity.

Pearl Rista enjoyed her element. She liked being the queen bee in her café, and didn't particularly encourage the presence of other women, although she treated them with cool courtesy. She liked to flirt with the customers, and, to her, a café full of her "boys" made her feel like the hostess of a salon. Men, in turn, enjoyed the atmosphere of freewheeling masculine camaraderie that Pearl's afforded.

A bit gingerly, Danielle opened the door to find Pearl's nearly empty. Only one booth was occupied, and that by Jeremy Banks, Gabi Choate, and Matt Weeks! Gabi and Matt were spooning down helpings of ice cream while Jeremy seemed to be enjoying a cup of coffee.

Jeremy smiled, made a move to rise. "Miss Herron."

"Oh, stay seated, please! And I think it's time you started calling me Danielle. Everyone does." She smiled sweetly. She didn't know Professor Banks all that well, but she found him attractive with his Old World charm . . . and handsome, too, although he was probably much too old for her. He must be wealthy, or if not rich, at least financially comfortable. She wondered idly what his relationship might be to Willie Haapala.

"Of course, and I'm Jeremy. Won't you join us?" He slid over to make room. "I just walked into town to pick up a few things and get a little exercise. Gabi and Matt were kind enough to keep me company."

Danielle slid into the booth and eyed the children speculatively. "Yes, it's not safe these days for children to be out on their own. Such terrible things have been happening." She dropped her voice and leaned closer to Jeremy. "Did you hear about Chad Michaels? Were you at the ceremony this morning?"

Jeremy nodded solemnly. "We heard, but no, we were sorry we couldn't make it to the commemoration. Gabi's mother had a bit of an accident and sprained her ankle, so we all stayed home."

"Oh my goodness, what a shame! How did it happen?"

"She tripped and fell," Gabi said, her big blue eyes on Danielle.

"Did she? How did she do that?"

"On the trail in the woods," Matt said.

"She was out hiking?"

"We all were," Matt said.

Something in Matt's manner piqued Danielle's curiosity. "All? Who was all?"

"Me, my sister, Gabi, Willie, Jeremy and Gabi's mom."

"Your *sister* went hiking on a trail?" Danielle was trying to make sense of this.

Jeremy intervened smoothly. "Gabi had gone for a walk, and since we didn't consider it safe for her to be out there, we all went to find her." He was sorry the subject had come up at all, and for some reason felt uncomfortable giving Danielle Herron any details.

"And Sybil went looking for her as well?"

"No," Matt said. "She was at the old house."

Danielle's lips were moving as if repeating what she'd just heard. "You don't mean the old Lemerriant house, do you?"

"Yeah." Matt scraped up the last of his ice cream.

"What would your sister be doing at the old Lemerriant house? How could she even find her way to it?"

"I dunno. I guess it doesn't make much difference to Sybil if it's dark out."

"It was dark?"

Jeremy tried to manage a reassuring smile. "We all had a bit of an adventure. It was late in the evening. We discovered that Gabi was missing. Her mother thought she might have been sleepwalking, and since she and Matt had been on the trail earlier, we thought she might have gone that way again. Happily we found her. No harm done. Right, Gabi?" Gabi blinked wordlessly.

"Oh *my*, that must have been a scare, what with the cougar around. But I still don't understand how Sybil came to be there."

"Nor do we," Jeremy said. "We found her in the old house. She seemed to have taken shelter there, and we escorted her back."

Danielle was putting two and two together. Sybil had been out in the night, at the old Lemerriant place (preposterous as it sounded) and today she'd been recovering from a seizure, and so confused that she could recall nothing. Or at least she *pretended* to recall nothing. Sybil had stolen a valuable piece of native art. Surely she knew she'd be caught! Had Sybil taken the mask to the Lemerriant house? Had she hidden it there? Could the silly girl have possibly gone to such lengths to hide the mask so she wouldn't have to return it? It didn't matter why Sybil was so fixated on it, it only mattered that Danielle get it back. "Do any of you remember seeing Sybil carrying anything last night?"

"No," Jeremy said, so quickly that he wondered why he was lying. "Sybil was using her walking stick. I was carrying Gabi, and I was quite amazed at how easily Sybil was able to maneuver." His eyes met Gabi's solemn gaze. Gabi had seen the mask that Sybil had been gripping — hugging it to herself — when they were in the cabin. She must have seen it, or maybe not! Gabi had been in a very strange mental state herself. So, Gabi, if you do remember, and if you now choose to say so, then we can both recall that Sybil did, indeed, have it in her clutches while she was in the cabin, though she may or may not have had it on the way back. Gabi said nothing.

Danielle's eyes slid over to Matt. "Do you remember seeing her with the mask last night?"

"Nope. She had it at home, but last I saw of it was when she took it to her room and kicked me out."

Danielle was staring straight ahead. That mask was at the Lemerriant house. She just felt it. She was so focused on this thought that she started when Pearl appeared at her elbow. "What'll it be?"

Danielle smiled abstractedly, "Oh, nothing, thanks. I won't have time after all. I have to go."

CHAPTER 50

Ulla Kampsula had lived alone for over thirty years, but now she ruefully mused that sometimes, lately, the house had begun to seem too crowded. Old friends, family members, faces from the past sprang up in her mind's eye unbidden, like surprise guests. Sometimes they seemed all too real, and incidents long forgotten, events she thought safely buried, appeared out of context like yesterday's weather. At the same time, she was capable of drawing a mental blank when it came to the name of a plant or a person she knew well. Sometimes it was becoming hard for Ulla to pinpoint the present. She would be moving around, her mind focused elsewhere, then catch sight of herself in the hall mirror — and hardly recognize the old woman who looked back at her. Time had become . . . unreliable. "You, old voman, you going to die soon, aren't you? Vell, dat's okay. You about done vit all dis!"

Ulla had no fear of death itself. She just hoped God would take her easily, so she wouldn't have to lie in a hospital bed or rot in a nursing home. Nor did she want to leave her cozy little house to move in with her sons and their rambunctious families. It was enough to see the grandchildren on their visits, and a big relief when they all went home.

Although most regarded Ulla as a religious woman, she had long since left the concept of Heaven and Hell behind; both seemed illogical to her. One short lifetime here, and you'd go on to an eternity of burning in Hell, or worshiping in Heaven; neither sounded like any fun. The Christian faith into which she'd been born seemed inefficient. One historical son of a god who lived a couple of thousand years had to save your ass from hellfire. That simply *couldn't* be right. Yet, Ulla saw God in everything: sunsets, flowers, animals, young faces, old faces, spring grass, and in herself. If I'm a child of God, why do I need to be saved by a *son* of God? It seemed suspiciously chauvinistic.

Ulla didn't discuss her beliefs. She felt no need to impose them or to defend them. In the early years of her widowhood, when all eyes had been on her, judging her every move, and advice on how to conduct herself had been forthcoming from every quarter; she had maintained her independence, sometimes using salty language of the logging camps to make people back off. Still, she had her own standards of propriety, and nobody had ever witnessed anything even faintly scandalous in her behavior. Now, in her old age, she was a respected figure, one of the last of her era, and what passed on Broom Island for a grande dame.

Ulla did have a few secrets; one was her drinking. She faced it without equivocation, but kept it strictly to herself — well, almost. It had started about a year ago when she'd had an episode of angina. It proved to be nothing serious, but the doctor, almost in jest, had told her and her son, Lauri, who had been with her that afternoon, that a glass of red wine a day might be good for Mum to keep her arteries clear. Lauri had then brought her a bottle of chianti which, to her uneducated palate, tasted like battery acid. Then, unexpectedly, an old friend visiting the island had presented her with a bottle of Burgon Rouge. Ulla suspected that Lauri had put him up to it, but the choice was a happy one. The wine was sweet and rich and Ulla found that she really enjoyed a glass of it in the evenings before bedtime. It helped her sleep and became a pleasant way to end the day.

Now, of course, she had a problem. She could hardly be seen going into the Co-op to buy booze! The community would immediately be buzzing with the news that Ulla Kampsula, of all people, a member of the Circle of Light, was a closet drunk! Her son lived on the mainland, and didn't visit all that often — besides, his taste in wines was lousy!

Enter Willie Haapala. One day, when Willie had dropped by to see how Ulla was faring, and when Ulla had told her that she often had trouble getting to sleep at night, Willie had actually made the same suggestion about red wine! This gave Ulla the opening to mention the Burgon Rouge, but that she couldn't bring herself to go buy any at the liquor store. Since that day, Willie had discreetly made sure that Ulla always had a bottle of her favorite wine in the house. One small glass a day was all Ulla drank, but, with a theatrical sigh, she had to acknowledge that now she was addicted to alcohol. An evening without her glass of sweet wine would have loomed bleak indeed!

Ulla laid out cups and napkins and put a pot of coffee on the stove. Her mind was on the Lemerriants. Their great-granddaughter was coming to call, and Ulla wondered what she wanted now. What more could she tell her? What else did she hope to find out — and why? They'd be alone. Willie had offered to do Ulla's shopping, and Ulla had made her a short list, knowing that she didn't need to write down the Burgon Rouge.

When Willie and Celeste got out of the car, Ulla saw that Celeste was limping. She opened the rarely-used front door with the shorter flight of steps and held it open while Willie assisted Celeste inside. Greetings, explanations, an offer of coffee that was turned down by Willie, who said she'd be back in an hour or so — and Ulla and Celeste were alone, sitting at the table, with a view of hummingbirds at the feeder and the delicious smell of fresh coffee. There were plates of cucumber and salmon sandwiches, cookies, Ulla's homemade jelly roll, pots of jam and slices of *pulla*, all laid out on an intricately worked lace tablecloth that was covered by a sheet of transparent plastic.

"Now," Ulla said, "Vat can I tell you?"

Celeste, who had rehearsed what she would say, suddenly found herself tongue-tied, and unprepared for her own reaction. This old woman actually had lived in the time of her ancestors; this motherly, earth-goddess woman now represented a window into her past. She was almost afraid to look through it.

Ulla dabbed at her watering eye with a tissue pulled from a box she always kept within reach. "Child, vhy don't you just talk to me."

"I want to know about my family. I need to know everything about them. I know they were considered . . . strange . . . perhaps even mentally disturbed, but I want to understand them, or at least try to."

"You vant to vrite about them, don't you?"

Celeste was surprised. "Yes. Yes, I think I do."

"Because until you do, you never get rid of dem, yes? I vish I could help you more, but I don't know much. I vas just a kid."

"How well did you know Elphique?"

"I used to vatch him."

"Did he know you were there?"

"Yah, he knew. He knew much more dan people tought. He tried to scare me."

"Why do you think he did that?"

"I tink he vas trying to protect me."

"From what?"

"His father."

"Brazeau Lemerriant?"

"A cruel, violent man."

"You did say that no woman was safe around him."

"Yah, I saw dat myself von day."

Celeste said nothing, just waited, while the wall clock ticked.

"It vas late summer. Blackberries vas ripe. One of de island girls, a native, vas out picking. Brazeau had been vatching her. I saw him attack and rape. It could have been me. I never vent back after dat."

"Did you tell anyone? Did the girl bring charges?"

Ulla laughed dryly. "No. I told nobody. Not even my family. You're de first. In dose days, young girls didn't talk about sex. Ve veren't supposed to *know* about sex. I couldn't say notting. It vould have been as shameful to me as if it had been *me* got raped. Had to stay pure and innocent, you see.

"De Indian girl, I know who she vas. Less dan a year later she had a boy, Nick. Could have been Brazeau's. De mother vas alcoholic. Kid grew up to be hellion. He got killed in a knife fight."

"Then, from what you tell me, it's likely that there are other descendants of Brazeau Lemerriant on the island."

"Oh, yah! May be lots of dem. I dunno how many vomen got raped by Brazeau or how many kids he got. But even if de Indian girl — her name vas Marie — even if she vas de only one — her boy — he got around, let me tell you. Good-looking kid, but vild! Girls vas crazy about him. He didn't have to rape. Vell, I dunno, maybe he *did* rape, but he didn't have to! He might have picked on a girl vit jealous boyfriend because dey found his body in de quarry."

"And of course his gene pool continues."

"Lots of crazy young people on de island. Age straightens dem up sometimes. Kids get bored here and act out. But some are *different*."

"How?"

Ulla took a moment as if trying to decide whether to stay on the topic or to change it. "Sybil Veeks, for von. You know her."

"Oh, yes!"

"She's different. And so vas her mother."

"Kirsti Weeks?"

"No. Her real mother."

"You knew her real mother?"

"Jennie. Part Indian voman. She vas addicted to alcohol too, but she used to see tings."

"You mean like delirium tremens?"

"Ghosts. She could see ghosts. And she could tell who vas going to die. Nobody paid any attention because everybody tought she vas out of her head vit drink. She vas the one dat said the Lemerriant farm vas haunted. She said it vas meeting ground for island dead people, and after she saw dem, she never vent near de place. Ve worked in the same camp one summer so I got to know her. Tvice she told me who vas gonna get killed in logging accident and tvice she vas right."

"What happened to her?"

"She died. Kirsti and Rome took her little girl to raise."

"Do you think *she* might have been a descendant of Brazeau Lemerriant?"

"Hard to say for sure. Lots of kids born who don't know who vas de father. It vas a rough time. Loggers, camps, drinking, prostitutes. Nobody kept records. Nobody cared. Finns vere classed as Christians or Communists, ven de truth vas dat most of dem vas neither. Everybody vas surviving best they could." Ulla was ticking off her fingers: "Sybil, Jennie, Nick, Marie. If she's related at all, she could be a great-grand-daughter to Brazeau."

"If Sybil was adopted, what about Matt? I couldn't help noticing how much he looks like the photo of Elphique Lemerriant. I'm sure people must have noticed the resemblance."

"Not many left who even remember vat Elphique looked like, but Matt's mother died ven he was born. She vasn't married. Nobody knew who vas de father. So yah, is possible. In place like dis, you get inbreeding, and, like in small country like Finland, if you go back far enough, you find everybody is related."

"The island must have been a different place back then."

"Ve had notting. No phones. No electric. Everyting vas hard labor. Logging done vit horses. No automation. Vinters brutal. Much colder dan now. People died young. Look in de graveyard and you see how many drowned in storms and got killed in accidents. Vomen died having

babies. Children died from diseases nobody gets no more. Life vas hard."
Ulla sat silent for a moment, remembering. Celeste tried to picture that
existence.

"Ulla, do you think it's possible to inherit — what would I call it?
ESP? Second sight? From some remote ancestor?"

"Vhy not? You can inherit blue eyes or shape of nose, so vhy not?
But vhy you ask?"

"Because I think my daughter, Gabi, may have inherited something."

"How old is she?"

"Ten."

"Vat makes you tink she got de gift?"

"She knows things before they happen, and she says she hears things."
Ulla nodded slowly. "And you? Do *you* have de gift?"

"I don't think so. I used to have nightmares as a child, and Gabi
has them. I used to sleepwalk, and Gabi does too. I've sometimes had
a premonition of danger, but I think most people do."

"All people do. Some just don't listen to demselfs. Or dey scared
dey going crazy."

"I'm wondering about Brazeau Lemerriant. Was he really crazy or
did he have some form of ESP that drove him out of his mind? Did *he*
see things? Hear things? Did he drink because of it?"

"I dunno, but I don't tink he needed a reason to drink." Ulla chuckled.
"People vit de gift don't have to be saints. Dey can be real bastards! Dey
call it gift but it can just as easy be curse. You usually tink of de old vise
voman who is village prophet — not de roaring drunk!"

"I don't know how to handle it. I don't know what to do about my
daughter. She's gotten into fights at school, behaved like someone out
of control. Doctors only prescribe drugs. I thought if I could learn
more about her history, I might be able to help her. Now I find that
her ancestors were wild and violent people."

Ulla got up and poured coffee. "Have a sandvich, and dat's fresh
pulla I just baked yesterday."

Celeste smiled faintly. Apparently coffee and *pulla* were the Finnish answer to stress. She dutifully nibbled a cucumber sandwich. "What if Gabi grows up to be mentally disturbed like her great-great-grandfather?"

"She von't."

"How can we be sure?"

"You are vriter. Ven tings get heavy, you vrite about dem and you get rid of dem. I take pictures. Ven tings pile up on me I put dem in photographs, then I put dem avay. I don't have to carry dem no more. Someday I may show you. Brazeau drank and made life hell for everybody. Gabi vill go her own vay, but she vill use her gift better — or she'll lose it."

"Willie said she might just outgrow it."

"Villie is vise woman vit gifts of her own."

"I just want Gabi to have a normal life."

"Yes. Of course. If *anybody* really has one. People who do tings — paint pictures, play music, dance, vrite books, carve vood or stone — all have de gift dat has to be used. Everyting that happens to dem gets put in de art, dis I know. If you don't use de gift? Can drive you crazy. Maybe dat's vat happened to Brazeau, but Gabi vill find her art, I tink."

"So you don't think I should worry about her?"

"Oh, child, you're her mother. You vill vorry. I just tink it's going to be okay. I can see her as happy normal kid."

"You can?"

"Yah. Look out de vindow. Dere she is wit Villie and her friend Matt — oh, and dat professor friend of Villie's is vit them. I tink maybe ve need another pot of coffee."

CHAPTER 51

"This always happens when you have coffee with Ulla," Willie was saying as they drove homeward down Kaunio Road. "You don't have to worry about fixing dinner. You won't be hungry, and in any case, she always sends you home with enough food to see you through the night."

They were all carrying something: Celeste, on her lap, had a tray of sandwiches covered with plastic film; Gabi was holding a tinfoil-wrapped jelly roll; Jeremy had a fresh braid of *pulla* packaged for transport; and Matt carried a bag of cookies and a jar of icicle pickles that Ulla had told him to take home to his mother.

"I suppose the village is still in shock," Willie remarked.

"We didn't talk to anybody except Miss Herron. She came into Pearl's while the kids were having ice cream," Jeremy said.

"I didn't run into anyone either at the Co-op except Goldie Slumber. She saw me buying a bottle of wine and gave me The Look."

"There's something wrong with buying wine?" Celeste asked.

"Not for you. Maybe not so much for me either, since I'm sure I already have a *reputation* — what with a single man living in my house!

Alcohol, in any form, in a Finnish community, is a touchy subject."

"Why? Don't Finns like to drink?" Jeremy asked.

"That's the trouble. They like it too much! Finnish men tend to come in two categories: they either don't drink at all (the minority) or they don't stop till they fall flat on their faces."

"What about the women?"

"There's the cliché of the drunken husband and the pious wife. Everyone sympathizes with her efforts to try to get her spouse to sober up, but nobody expects that he will. She comes to hate alcohol in any form, and never touches a drop herself."

"You mean Finns never drink socially?"

"Oh, they do! Go to a *Mittumaari* — midsummer festival — or a *Vappu*, Mayday, and you'll find a wild party. And, nowadays, with the modern generation, wine may be served at meals with no stigma. It's the older generation — mine — and Goldie Slumber's — that's scandalized at the thought of a woman taking a drink. They all know that one drink will spiral you into addiction and depravity."

"Is Slumber a Finnish name?" Celeste asked.

"Originally. Goldie's husband was named Nukkuvainen, which means sleeper. He anglicized it, but didn't like Sleeper so he became Slumber. That sort of thing happened a lot in the old days."

"From what Ulla was saying, it must have been a puritanical society back then."

"More like hypocritical. It was all about appearances, and the most scandalizing of creatures was the Drunken Woman. A woman was supposed to be pure, godly and selfless. The only alcohol that should ever touch her lips was Communion wine.

"It's not that way today, even in staunchly Lutheran Finland, but traces remain. Once, when I was there, I was visiting one of my married cousins, and she and her husband took me out to a lounge in Kajaani for a drink, but swore me to secrecy because she didn't want word of it to get back to her father. Her father, in fact, was a total lush, but for a woman to drink was worse, even, than for her to enjoy — uh . . ." Willie stopped, remembering the children in the back seat. They had reached the Weeks house; she pulled over. "Here we are, Matt. Your mother will be expecting you. I called to tell her we'd be bringing you home." She watched as Matt sprinted up the driveway with his cookies and pickles, and waited till the door slammed behind him before she put her car in gear and moved on.

"So were you able to get more information from Ulla?" Willie and Celeste were back inside, in Willie's office. "Any more photographs?"

"Yes and no. No, I didn't see any of her photos, and yes, I did get more information on Brazeau — and I wish I hadn't."

"Oh?"

"The man was a rapist."

"Didn't we already know that? Didn't he father Fidelia's child?"

"He may have sired many more descendants."

Willie looked out the window at the lengthening shadows on the grass. "She told you about Nick?"

"You knew? Ulla said she'd witnessed the rape but never told anyone."

"It wasn't Ulla who told me. It was Marie. Nick was a beautiful boy with black, curly hair. He looked like a gypsy with huge brown eyes, but he was a wild child, full of the devil. He was only eight or nine when I left the island, and I heard he'd come to a tragic end."

"So did his mother."

"So did a lot of people from that era. Did Ulla tell you more about him?"

"Only that he had a chance to sow his wild oats liberally on the island, and that there may be many more descendants of Brazeau carrying the crazy Lemerriant genes. Apparently promiscuity was only frowned on if you were a woman."

"When it comes to the double standard, Finns were on the cutting edge. A woman who wasn't a virgin was a whore. If she had a child out of wedlock, it was branded a bastard. If a man married and found his bride wasn't a virgin, nobody really blamed him if he killed her."

"Ulla said she never told anyone about the rape because it would have stigmatized *her*."

"And it would have. She'd have been tainted. She would never have been just Ulla, the pure young maiden. She'd have been Ulla, the girl who knew too much and therefore was no longer innocent."

"But it must have been an agrarian society. Surely, everyone had seen farm animals copulating. How could sex have been such a secret?"

"It wasn't the seeing — or even the doing — it was the pretending that you hadn't. That's why Ulla said nothing."

"But that's so — "

"Isn't it, though? And I take the stand that if your ancestor was crazy, then so was most of the island."

"Sybil Weeks may be a descendant of Brazeau." Celeste was studying the photo of the Lemerriants onscreen, trying to detect a family resemblance, but concluding that Matt Weeks looked more like Elphique, than Sybil resembled Brazeau.

"Yes, I've often wondered about Sybil."

"She could be cousin to Gabi."

"Every family has a few nutty relatives. It doesn't necessarily mean a thing."

"Ulla seemed to think that the artistic temperament is often accompanied by eccentricity, and that perhaps Gabi will find an art form into which she can pour her psychic energies."

"Ulla said *that*?"

"Not in those words, but that's what she thinks. She said it's a gift that has to be used."

"Ulla is a wise woman, and a gifted one herself. If you want to go on using my computer, go right ahead. I noticed that your foot seems better. Does it still hurt?"

"Uh, no, not as much!" Celeste had been starting to put weight on the ankle without wincing. "I think it's going to be okay. I might even be able to drive by tomorrow."

"Do you think a hot sauna would help? It takes a couple of hours to heat, but we could fire it up?"

"Thanks, Willie, but I think I'll just take a shower tonight. I'm sure I can manage it now."

The phone rang; Willie picked it up, "It's Kirsti," she whispered. "Yes, Kirsti . . . What? Are you sure? . . . No, I haven't seen her. I thought she was at home, spending the day in bed. She couldn't have gone far, could she? . . . No, I haven't heard anything about the cougar. I don't know if the men went out again today. They probably did. Just try to stay calm, Kirsti, I'll be right over." Willie hung up. "Sybil's missing again."

Celeste looked up, alarmed. "Where's Gabi?"

"Gabi is fine. Gabi is with Jeremy. She's helping him refill the hummingbird feeders. But I've got to go see what's happening at the Weeks'. Kirsti sounded really stressed. She's worried about Rome, of course, and now she can't find Sybil and she's upset."

"I would be too, with that killer cat roaming around. I hope Sybil hasn't gone back to that old house again. I can't imagine why she went there in the first place. She's *blind*. What was she thinking?"

"I don't know. I'll call back here if we need Jeremy to help us look for her."

"Maybe I could — "

"No, you couldn't. Not with that foot. You stay here with Gabi and man the phone. We may need someone to make calls. I'll be back as soon as I can."

CHAPTER 52

BACK IN her shop, Danielle Herron was quietly fuming. She needed to get her transformation mask back; and now it looked like that silly twit of a girl had hidden it away, in — of all places — the old Lemerriant house. How was she going to retrieve it? That is, if she could even *find* it. It was a valuable piece, but Danielle couldn't picture Sybil performing a heist in order to sell it for profit. The girl was obviously deranged, and had carried it off the way a crow will steal your watch or your glasses and take them to its nest.

Danielle couldn't get the police involved; on this island it would be professional suicide. No, she wouldn't press charges, but she'd do everything in her power to get her property back. And now she faced the horrible realization that, to do that, she'd have to go to the Lemerriant house.

Danielle was a not a hiker. Trekking through woods was *not* her cup of tea, but she could hardly trust anyone else, could she? She checked the clock. She *could* close up a little early. Hardly anyone had been in the shop all day. Everyone was preoccupied by the deaths and the cougar

— and, oh dear god, there was a killer cat in the equation! Did Danielle really want to be walking in the woods where Chad Michaels had just died or been killed? No! Wouldn't it be better to wait until somebody shot the animal? But suppose they never found it at all!

She wondered how close she could get to the old house in her car. On Quarry Road, the one she's taken to Weena's, the trail entrance was near the water tower. She went over to a rack, rummaged through some island brochures, and found a map of the hiking trails. There it was: the Lemerriant Trail — but it was a long walk from the water tower to the Lemerriant farm which seemed to be situated at about the halfway point. She studied the map, tracing it with her finger, and saw that, at a spot farther up, past the turnoff to Weena's, between the quarry and the lake, the distance to the old house was shorter, only half as far to go. A sketchy mark on the map might even indicate that there was a path. Did she dare? She might be able to park on Quarry Road and cut through to the trail on foot, but it was still a hike. *Damn Sybil Weeks!* Still, if a blind girl could do it, how hard could it be? She wished she had someone who could come with her, a big strapping man, for instance.

Her mind quickly ran over the short list of possibilities. Rome Weeks was out of commission. Matt was too young — and for all she knew he may have been in on the whole thing. There was the new constable, Grant Hewett, but she didn't want to involve the law, and he might not consider her errand important enough to take him away from his duties. Jerry Nyquist would be working at the New Broom. There were a couple of old geezers, her neighbors on Kaunio Road — Sali Johnson and Oliver Sylvester — but they were so rickety they'd probably only slow her down — or pick that time to have a heart attack or stroke so she'd have to drag them back. Veik Kuusiniemi was still a fine figure of a man, but he'd have to come all the way from the lighthouse. Butch Westerlake might do it. Or, her mind slid silkily over the name she'd saved for last, the way she saved the double chocolate raspberry truffle with its single thin slash of red icing in a box of Godivas . . . maybe .

.. perhaps . . . since he's *such* a gentleman . . . Jeremy Banks. Yes, she wouldn't mind at all hiking the trail if Jeremy were with her. It could even be — well — kind of romantic.

To reach him, she might have to go through Willie. She wished she had his cell phone number. She didn't know, of course, if he even had a cell phone. She rang Willie but didn't recognize the voice that answered, cleared her throat and used her most professional tone: "This is Danielle Herron, and I was wondering if I might speak with Professor Banks."

"I'm sorry, but he just stepped out. This is Celeste Ooms-Possum. May I take a message?"

"Oh, then you must be the visiting writer. I did meet your dear little girl when she and Matt Weeks came into my shop."

"Yes, of course, Danielle's. I've been meaning to come in and look for some literature on the island — brochures, maps, anything local."

"You're welcome anytime. I'm sure we can find what you're looking for. Do you expect Professor Banks back anytime soon?"

"I really don't know. We have a bit of a situation. Apparently Sybil Weeks has run off somewhere, and everyone is out looking for her. You haven't seen her, have you? She hasn't made her way to your shop, has she? I know she works there sometimes."

Danielle gasped. "No," she said faintly. "No I haven't seen her since this morning. I thought she wasn't feeling well. I stopped by."

"Well, I'm sure they'll find her. Meanwhile, if you do see her, please call me back. Her mother is worried."

"Of course."

"Oh, was there a message for Professor Banks?"

"Uh, no. I . . . I'll call back later."

Sybil Weeks had run off somewhere. There was only one place Sybil Weeks would run to: the Lemerriant farm. She's gone there to get the mask. Danielle hastily locked the shop, got into her car and headed on out.

CHAPTER 53

CELESTE HUNG up the phone, wondering if she'd said too much to Danielle Herron. She didn't know the woman, but she'd been told that Sybil occasionally worked in her shop. Gabi had met Danielle, but she'd referred to her as the lady with the bleached hair in the shop with the broken bikes, and that didn't quite line up with Danielle's description of Gabi as a "dear little girl." Well, anyway, surely it hadn't done any harm to alert Ms. Herron to Sybil's disappearance.

And that, of course, was the matter at hand. Where could Sybil have gone now? Willie had called to say they were all going to look for her. It had sounded as if she, Kirsti and Matt were all going to head down the trail to the Lemerriant farm again. What was it about that place that made it such a magnet for the deranged? Or the psychically gifted, she quickly amended, remembering that the last time it had been Gabi they'd been looking for.

Jeremy had left immediately to join the posse, saying that, given what had happened to Chad Michaels, it would be safer if he went as well, if only to swell the ranks. A part of Celeste would have wanted to go along too. Now that the idea of a novel about the Lemerriant family had taken hold, she would have liked to be part of the intrigue, but of course that was impossible; she could barely hobble. At least Gabi was safe this time, although a bit at loose ends. She had asked Jeremy if she could go with them, but a resounding double "no" from both him and Celeste had silenced her.

Now the dear little girl was in Willie's office, sitting on a wooden chair while her mother was at the computer. Fretful and restless, she wished Matt were with her. *Matt* got to go along and look for Sybil. Boys always got to do cool stuff. It was going to be a boring night. She didn't want to watch TV or play games. Celeste gave her a hard look. "What's the matter, Gabi?"

Gabi realized that she'd been repeatedly kicking the leg of her chair, making a thumping noise that must have been annoying to her mother. She stopped.

"Why don't you go see if there's anything on TV?"

Gabi shook her head.

"Are you hungry? Would you like something to eat?" Nobody had thought about dinner after the coffee with Ulla. "There are sandwiches — or maybe you'd like cake and ice cream."

Gabi shook her head again.

"Well then," there was a sigh in Celeste's voice, "What would you like to do? You know you can't leave the house. And yes, I realize that we're not at home where all your stuff is. We're visiting here, but we'll be going back soon, so if you could just *try*. Pretend you're an anthropologist visiting a tribe of natives and you have to follow their customs or you die."

Gabi's lips twitched as she tried to suppress a giggle.

"But whatever you do, *don't smile!*"

Gabi grinned outright and rolled her eyes. "It's just so boring. Everybody's gone."

"*I'm* here."

"Yeah, but you're busy and . . . hey, can I go out on the porch and watch hummingbirds?"

"Uh, I don't know, Gabi. I can't see you out there from here."

"Please! Jeremy and I filled the feeder and he said there'd be dozens of hummingbirds at it tonight. He said they go into a feeding frenzy just before dark and I'll probably never see so many in one place anywhere else."

"I'd really rather you stayed in the house," Celeste said slowly. "Can't you watch them through a window?"

"Not as well. I could sit in the porch swing. I promise not to leave the porch. I will not put *one foot* off the porch. I will *absolutely* stay on the porch. I promise, I promise, I promise!"

There had been a time when a promise from Gabi was acceptable — but now? "If I say it's okay, you will come in before it gets dark or the second I call you, whichever happens first."

"I'll even make some noise so you'll know I'm okay."

"Won't that scare away the hummingbirds?"

"Jeremy says they're not scared of anything. He says they've landed on the feeder while he's been filling it. He calls them attack birds because they'll fly right at you sometimes, although they never hit you."

"In that case, I may come out later myself and watch them with you. I just need to finish this first."

Moments later she heard the reassuring squeak of the rusty porch swing while she contemplated the screen in front of her. Celeste needed to do more research on her family name, but didn't feel she could tie up the line by connecting to the Internet. Broom Island had only recently gotten a connection, and it was the basic dial-up which meant that when the computer was online, she couldn't be reached by telephone. And since she was manning the phone tonight, she had to keep it open. So, instead, Celeste was organizing information that she'd downloaded earlier — rather interesting stuff about a plague that had almost wiped out a whole village in France. If she could find a firm family thread, it might be a dramatic opening for her novel to start with that time period — then weave in the werewolf legend that had sprung up among the superstitious villagers as a counterpoint to the Broom Island legend later. Yes, that might work.

CHAPTER 54

As DANIELLE drove through the village and on toward the island bush, she realized that she didn't have a clear plan. Her only thought had been: get to the Lemerriant farmstead before Sybil could remove the mask. Now, thinking things through, she had no idea of whether that was even going to be possible. When had Sybil gone missing? She could have been there and gone by time Danielle could get to the farm. And exactly how was she going to do *that*? She wasn't all that sure just where the entrance was — somewhere near the water tower, but there was that shortcut on Quarry Road, past Weena's.

As shown on the map, the Lemerriant trail snaked across the island to another head on Tranquil Bay Road, but the island was also patterned with old footpaths, like the one behind the Weeks house, paths that children had been using for years, as well as loggers' roads and animal trails — and Danielle was not a woodswoman. Did she really think she could navigate a walking trail in a rainforest? In her shop shoes? She hadn't thought to bring a pair of boots or even sneakers. Good lord, she was wearing *heels* for chrissake! Okay, they were only two-inchers but not something for a trail hike. Besides, would any artifact be worth dealing with a man-eating cougar? She thought not. But then, they may have found the cougar by now. Surely they wouldn't stop till they'd killed the beast! Perhaps she might even run into the hunting party and have the protection of a bunch of guys with guns. Yes, that would be good. She hadn't even brought a flashlight. *Nice going, Danielle.* Not that she'd be needing one for some time yet, but she might need one to search inside the cabin. There wouldn't be electricity. Should she turn back? No, she had a better idea; she headed straight for Michaels Acres.

When nobody answered the door, Danielle went around to the greenhouse and found Weena tending tomato plants, pruning out unwanted sucker shoots. "Good heavens, Danielle, you didn't have to come all this way. I was going to call you as soon as I finished up in here. I appreciate everything you've done, but you don't have to worry about me. I really am okay."

"I just need to borrow a pair of boots." Danielle burst into nervous laughter and Weena, surprised, laughed too.

"Sure, do you need anything else?"

"Maybe a flashlight — and maybe a jacket."

"Okay, let's go in the house and you can tell me exactly what you're up to."

Over coffee poured from Weena's retro Farberware electric-perk pot, Danielle explained about going to find the mask that Sybil had stolen.

"You're not seriously planning to go out there by yourself *now*, are you? Have you ever been on that trail?"

"No, have you?"

"Not all the way. You must have passed right by the main entrance, but there's another path off Quarry Road that leads into it. Dory and I walked part of the way when we were looking for Bruno after he disappeared. We had Turk with us. But you can't possible go there alone now. Good lord, Danielle, my husband was just killed on that part of the trail. There's a *killer cougar wandering around loose!*"

"I was sort of hoping I might run into the hunters. Maybe they've already shot the cougar."

"If they're out there, I haven't seen them. But even so, it's much too dangerous. You could get lost. I think that's what happened to Chad. He must have taken a wrong turn. Otherwise why would he have gone off the road and onto that trail at night?"

"You're probably right, but it's still light enough to see, and if I make it to the old house, I'll probably meet a mob of people. Kirsti Weeks and her boy and Willie Haapala and her professor friend are all out there looking for Sybil. I have a feeling I won't be alone for long. I just want to get that mask back before somebody loses it or damages it. It's authentic and very valuable. If the trail looks too bad, I can always turn back."

"In that case I'm coming with you."

"Oh, Weena . . . you don't . . . I mean what with Chad. . . ."

"Yes. They wouldn't let me see Chad . . . yet . . . but I think I'd like to go see where . . . what might have happened last night."

Danielle didn't try to dissuade her; truth was she was relieved not to be going alone, and admitted to herself that she had been hoping that Weena might offer to come along. "We can drive up the road in my car and park next to the entrance. We might even run into Sybil."

"I don't know how a blind girl can be running all through these woods."

"I don't know either, although Sybil's grown up on this island and she's always roamed around. She and her bird. I didn't realize that she'd be able to find her way on a hiking trail, though. They say the blind develop other senses to make up for their lack of vision."

"It's awfully easy to go the wrong way. I got lost once on our own acreage when I followed a path and didn't notice another joining it. When I turned around to go back, there was this fork and I didn't know which way I'd come. I don't think a blind person would have a chance. But, if you're determined, then we'd better get going while we still have plenty of daylight."

Danielle drove up along the road Chad had taken, a little past the lake and the quarry. "Here. Stop here." Weena said.

Danielle pulled over. "Is that the trail? I don't think I would have noticed it. It's not marked at all."

"The main entrances are marked — the one near the water tower and the one that comes out on Tranquil Bay Road, but the area is covered with footpaths and old logging roads, so this is just another path that connects with the official Lemerriant trail down the hill."

There was little indication of a trail, just a hole in the vegetation and bit of graveled entryway that probably had led Chad Michaels astray in the dark. The path headed downwards and into the umbrage of evergreens, where the underfoot changed to spongy peat strewn with vegetation, hazardous with tree roots.

"I wouldn't have been able to do this in my pumps," Danielle said. She was already a little out of breath. Weena was carefully inspecting the trail as she walked. They were coming to a wet spot where mud sucked at their boots, and then they found that someone had put down a series of tree rounds that allowed them to bypass the mud but were, in themselves, treacherously slippery. Danielle stopped to catch her breath, pretending that she was pausing to listen. Weena turned to look at her. "Did you see something?"

"I was just hoping to hear someone else on the trail," she said a bit nervously. "This place is giving me the willies." Just then a raven flew through the trees, shattering the quiet with its raspy call. Danielle put a hand over her heart.

"Birds will be heading for the lake," Weena said. "You'll see it on your right when we go by. Swimming hole for the island kids."

"Isn't that the same lake we passed up on the road?"

"Yes. This trail skirts the other side of it."

Danielle disinterestedly noted that yes, they were going by a ridiculously small body of water to be called a lake. "How much farther do you think it is?"

"I don't know. I don't remember if Dory and I came this far when we were looking for Bruno. It must still be some distance though."

"I wish I'd brought the map of the trail," Danielle said. "Anyway, it looks clear enough. We can't really get lost, I suppose."

Weena had crouched down to pick up something that had been wedged between a couple of the lily pads. She straightened, slowly, staring at the thing in her hand. Danielle caught up with her and saw what it was: a muddy and misshapen man's house slipper. "Oh god, Weena!"

"Chad's." Holding on to the slipper, she made a move to continue walking.

"Maybe we should go back," Danielle said. "Let's just go back now."

Weena appeared not to hear her and kept striding forward. She stopped again as she found the mate to the slipper and picked it up. Then, as if drawn, she continued on down the trail with Danielle hurrying to keep up while trying to persuade her to stop. Then, suddenly, Weena did. She stopped dead and stood looking at something on the ground at the edge of the trail. Danielle saw what it was — a rifle.

"Oh my god! Is that his gun?" Danielle reached out to pick it up.

"Leave it," Weena said.

"But — "

"Leave it."

"But why would it be still here? Why didn't the men bring it back?"

"They didn't come this far. They must have come through the Tranquil Bay Road entrance. When they found Chad they took him back the way they came."

"But why was he here at all? He wasn't dressed for the trail. Why did he have a *gun*? Did he hear a noise and follow it?" Danielle gasped. "Do you think it was the cougar?"

"Yes. That must have been it. I left him in the shower. Perhaps he came out and heard the cougar and followed it. That must have been what happened." Weena didn't say what she was really thinking, that when Chad came out of the shower and found her gone, perhaps in his addled state of mind (and he must *not* have taken his medications after all), he might have been looking for her. The gun might have been meant for *her*, not the cougar. She'd taken the truck. He might have been just crazy enough to try to make it on foot along the shorter route to Danielle's. Only he'd made a wrong turn and ended up on the trail instead.

"But why didn't he keep his gun with him?"

"I don't know. He probably lost it along with his slippers. He must have been disoriented and stumbling around in the dark."

"Do you . . . do you think the cougar killed him?" Danielle whispered.

"We don't know yet. Dr. Swallow says there will be an autopsy. It could have been that he just fell and hit his head and died of hypothermia." Weena turned and once again headed up along the trail.

"Weena, can't we just go back?"

"Just a little farther." She was scanning for signs — any signs — of what might have happened, but beyond the gun there was little to see. They came to a spot that might have been where Chad was found. There were lots of boot prints in the mud, but that was all. She tried to picture what had happened; she hadn't seen the body, and didn't know if she could even bear to see it at all after the horror of what happened to Dory. She tried to clear her mind. "We must be fairly close to the old house by now, if you still want to go looking for your mask. If we keep going, we should connect with the main trail that takes us there."

"No! Let's just go back, please. It's not important anymore. I just want us to get out of here."

Weena sighed. "All right, let's go." They started back the way they'd come.

As they passed it, Danielle asked "Do you want to take Chad's gun back with us now?"

"No. I don't ever want to see it again. I hate guns."

The way back always seems shorter than the way *to* anywhere, although this time they had to climb a hill to the road, and Danielle found herself puffing harder. Grateful to reach the car and get inside, she looked sideways at Weena who sat silent and remote. "We'll go to your place and make a nice cup of tea," she said, turning they key in the ignition.

Nothing happened. She tried again. Same result. No response at all. Was the battery dead? She kept trying, starting to feel a little panicky, but the Volkswagen might as well have been carved out of yellow cedar.

"Looks like we'll have to walk," Weena said. "It's okay, it's not that far."

Danielle fumbled around in her bag and took out her cell phone. "Maybe I can catch Hank at the garage before he goes home. Maybe he could bring the tow truck."

"I don't know if that's going to work way out here." Weena got out of the car. "We can walk back to the house and call him on the landline."

Sure enough, the cell phone wasn't working either; Danielle didn't know whether it was the battery or the area that was dead. They started back on foot, Weena studying the terrain, aware that she was retracing Chad's walk of the night before. He would have been heading toward town. He'd have guessed she'd be at Danielle's, and had taken the shorter route — dear heaven, had the man been mad? — started after her in his joggers and bedroom slippers and his *rifle*. She never should have left him alone. The guilt was hers. If she'd stayed, he'd be alive. And if she hadn't had the music playing in the greenhouse that day, perhaps she would have heard something — the dog barking or whatever — and maybe Dory would be alive. She'd killed her own family as surely as if she'd fired Chad's rifle at them. If she'd only managed to talk Chad out of buying that gun, he wouldn't have wounded Rome Weeks. Weena's guilt trip was interrupted by a gasp from Danielle who had stopped dead.

"What's the matter?"

"I thought I saw something."

They had just passed the quarry and were standing on the roadbed next to the lake. A deeply rutted sandy section of road led down a hill toward the water that was glassy and black as a pool of obsidian.

"Where?"

"Over there, ahead of us, on the road."

"What did you see?"

"I don't know. But I saw something move."

"A bird, maybe? The lake area is a rookery." Weena stood looking and listening. It seemed strangely silent. Usually, in the evening, if Weena stood out in the yard, she could hear the chattering of the birds in the distance.

"No, it was on the road. I think it was an animal."

"Somebody's dog, probably. Lots of them on the island."

Danielle clutched Weena's arm. "Look, there, did you see it?"

"No."

"See those bushes moving? There's something in there. I think it's watching us."

Weena peered into the distance. There *was* something on the road, cutting off their way home, but she couldn't make out what it was. Danielle was gripping her arm. "It's the cougar. We should run, go back, and get in the car."

"I don't know what it is," Weena said softly, "But I know you can't outrun a cougar." Don't cougars attack from behind? Weena had seen a documentary on tiger attacks in India where workers in the jungle actually wore masks of faces on the *backs* of their heads. "Maybe it hasn't seen us. Maybe if we just stand still it'll go on about its business."

"I think it's coming toward us."

Weena still couldn't make out what it was, but slowly, ever so slowly, grasping Danielle by the arm, she edged to the side of the road, allowing them both to melt into the growth of hemlock. There she momentarily lost her footing and they both found themselves sliding in the loose sand. Weena regained her balance and stood still, listening, but heard nothing. She looked in the direction of the lake and saw the dinghy at the edge of the pond. If she and Danielle could get to the boat, they could row out onto the lake. Did cougars swim? Yes, she told herself distractedly, they must, or how else did they get to the island at all? Still, she didn't think one would actually be so bold as to swim out after them.

It probably wasn't even a cougar they'd seen — or *hadn't* seen. It could have been one of the island deer or even a black bear. Why not just get back on the road and make a lot of noise? Wild animals, she'd been told, were usually more frightened of you than you of them. If she and Danielle charged down the road, whooping and hollering, whatever was out there would run for the hills, wouldn't it? Whatever was out there could also be a rogue animal that may have killed two members of her family.

"We should have brought the gun," Danielle whispered.

"Do you know how to shoot it?"

"No."

"Neither do I. I think we should get in the boat and row out to the raft."

Danielle looked stricken. "Row?" she quavered. "I've never rowed a boat."

"How hard can it be?" Weena took Danielle by the arm and began moving toward the water's edge. Then they both froze in terror as, from the thicket of salal, emerged an animal. There was no doubt any longer as to what it was, nor any question as to whether it had seen them. It was as if the beast had deliberately circled around to meet them head-on. It stood between them and the boat, facing them, tail twitching — a full-grown, sleek, tawny female cougar, beautiful and menacing, the embodiment of death by fang and claw.

CHAPTER 55

"Well, obviously she's not here!" Willie, Jeremy, Kirsti, and Matt had covered every inch of the trail and there had been no sign of Sybil. They had walked about, calling Sybil's name, looked into the old barn, and thoroughly searched the Lemerriant cabin and surrounding area.

"Where could she possibly have gone?" Willie was at a loss.

Kirsti looked at Matt. "You're her brother, where do *you* think she could be?"

Matt shrugged. "I dunno, maybe she's hiding."

"Hiding from *us*?" Jeremy asked.

"Maybe." Matt was fidgety with all eyes on him.

"Matt, do you know something you're not telling us?"

"No, Mom, honest. I don't know where Sybil is. I guess she just went someplace else this time. I don't know why."

Kirsti looked narrowly at her son. "You know these trails better than we do. If she's been here, where else could she have gone?"

"If she stayed on the main trail, she'd go all the way to Tranquil Bay Road. If she went the other way, she'd end up at the water tower — or she could take a path to the lake and on up to where we rode our bikes to Dory's house. And there are lots of old paths that lead to different places." Matt pointed to a narrow footpath that led off the trail. "That one comes out across the road from the cemetery."

"In other words there are several directions she might have taken." Willie said. "She could be anywhere, and we've got to find her before it gets dark."

"She could have wandered off the trail completely and gotten lost," Jeremy said. "I don't know how she ever managed to find the old house in the first place."

"Or the cougar could have got her."

Once again all eyes turned to Matt. "Don't say that! Your sister has not been attacked by a cougar or anything else. She may be lost. She might even be hiding, though I can't think why, but we're not going back home without her."

"The reality is," Willie said with a sigh, "that she could be anywhere in these woods. With her limited sight, it's more than likely that she's gotten hopelessly lost out here, and if she's on the move, she could be far off by now. We're going to need help."

"Maybe we should split up." Kirsti said. "I could comb through the woods and double back onto the trail. Maybe, you, Willie, could go back and call Constable Hewett. Matt knows the trails, so he and Jeremy could check out the lake area."

"I don't think that's a good idea." Jeremy said. "Matt and I will continue the search, and we'll check out the lake and the other end of the trail. But it would be safer for both you and Willie to go home together and get a search party going. You might even find Sybil on the way back."

"Is there any way to get word to you if we do?" Willie asked. "Do you have a cell phone with you?"

"Cell phones aren't much use out here," Kirsti said. "Nearest phone would be at Schit ... uh ... at Michaels Acres. You could try calling there."

"We'll check Michaels Acres too. Matt can guide me." (Matt nodded.)

"There might even be hunters in the woods looking for the cougar. If we meet them we can ask them to help us look for Sybil."

"Be careful," both Willie and Jeremy said in unison as they set off in opposite directions.

* * *

The hunting party, gathered at Pearl's, now consisted of four — Eddie Smithson, Butch Westerlake, Veikko Kuusiniemi, and Oliver Sylvester. They'd had to do a lot of hiking, and Oliver was feeling the strain. After they'd found Chad's body, they'd hiked back to notify Constable Hewett, then hiked back again to show him where it was — and then helped transport the body out of the woods. "I hate to admit it, but I'm getting a little too old for this."

"Yeah, we all are," Veik said. "I wouldn't mind going home and putting my feet up. You know, I never knew what's so great about putting your feet up, but Barb is always saying that. Maybe it's a woman thing. Anyhoo, right now it's beginning to sound good to me."

"Go ahead," Butch said. "Eddie and I can check out the ridge. You two take a break. If we don't find anything we can all go out again tomorrow. Or we'll recruit more manpower."

"We could just call it a day, couldn't we? That cat will still be there tomorrow." They had just polished off a lunch of sandwiches and coffee, and Oliver was thinking how nice it would be to go home and take a little nap.

"But *I* won't," Eddie said. "I gotta be getting back to Alert Bay on the ferry tonight. So if it's all the same to you guys, I'd just as soon spend the afternoon tracking. Be good if we could find that animal before it attacks anyone else."

"In that case, I'm in," Butch said.

"Me too," Veik agreed.

"Well, I suppose — " Oliver began.

"Suppose nothin' old man. You go home. We may need you bright-eyed and bushy-tailed tomorrow," Veik told him.

Oliver smiled his crooked smile. "Yeah, okay then. It's different for you, you're still in your prime what with ridin' a motorbike and all. . . ."

Heading back to the hills, the three of them had opted to bypass the hiking trail and had all squeezed into Eddie's truck. Guided by Butch, they followed a network of logging roads as far as they could go, then left the vehicle and hiked to the highest point of the island.

"If I was a cougar, this is where I'd be." Veik said. "Great view and nobody to bother you."

It was true. The view of blue water, distant mountains and canopy of greenery was beautiful; and it also brought home the fact that, although the island was small, trying to find an animal that didn't want to be found could be difficult. The high terrain was dry and rocky, studded with boulders and small caves where an animal could easily hide, live, and breed, for that matter.

"Not the best place to find tracks, so we'll look for scat or any sign of a kill," Eddie said. "We can walk the ridge, then circle back again." This time Eddie had brought a rifle as well; this cat meant business. "We can space ourselves within calling distance. Anybody finds anything, give a holler."

The search proved fruitless. All they found was one dead crow and some animal scat that, by its color, was too old to be important. "Damn! Where the hell could that critter be holed up?" Butch Westerlake shielded his eyes from the late afternoon sun that hit the hilltops long after the valley lay in shadow.

"It's almost like a ghost," Veik Kuusiniemi muttered. "Strikes, then disappears into thin air."

"Do you think it was the cougar that killed Michaels?" Butch asked. "Doc Swallow said maybe not."

"You saw the body," Eddie said. "Pretty badly chewed up. Cougar could have killed him or just found him afterwards. By the time it and the birds got through with him, it was hard to tell."

Butch shrugged. "I guess anything coulda happened. I thought he was going to have a stroke when we were out in the woods. Maybe he just dropped dead and the animals got him afterwards. If ever I saw a man on the edge, it was him."

"It was weird. Why would a man be walking along a hiking trail in the dark in his bare feet?" Eddie mused.

"Could something have been chasing him?"

"Or was he chasing something?"

"I think he was just buggier than a prison mattress," Veik said. "Hey, what's that?"

"What? Where?"

"Down there, on the road." They all looked over the edge of the bluff.

"Looks like a parked car." Eddie said.

Veik looked more closely. "I know that car. It looks like the yellow Volkswagen that belongs to the Herron woman who owns the gift shop by the ferry dock. It's usually parked in front."

"What would she be doin' out here?"

"I dunno, unless some kids nicked it and took it for a joyride. Wouldn't be the first time," Butch said.

"Funny place to leave it, though." Eddie leaned over to get a better look.

"The lake's nearby and so's the quarry. Could be a bunch of teenagers hellin' around. Maybe we should go down and have a look-see." Veik hesitated. "We should probably go back to the truck and ride down. I don't feel like climbing down this hill and then back up again."

"Amen. It's gettin' late and we should be going back anyway. Too bad we didn't find anything."

"Yeah, we can come out again tomorrow. Oh, that's right, Eddie you're not gonna be here, are you?"

Eddie shifted his gaze. "I got this thing tomorrow," he mumbled, and started walking back down the slope in the direction of the Ford.

Veik sensed something, and picked up on it. "So, what's so important in Alert Bay? You gotta woman in trouble?"

"Hah! I wish!"

Butch grinned. "Nah, it's not that. Eddie's gonna be made chief of the tribe. Chief Two Feathers. Heap big ritual, right Eddie?"

"Nothing that glamorous, I'm afraid, boys."

"Okay, so are you going to tell us what the big thing in Alert Bay is?"

"It's not in Alert Bay. I have to go to Port Casper in the morning."

"God, this is like pullin' teeth. So what's in Port Casper?"

"The doctor."

Veik's eyes widened in surprise. "Hey, you're not sick, are you, Eddie?"

Eddie gave them an exasperated look. "If you must know, I have to get my ass to the doctor to see about getting some rectal polyps taken care of."

Butch winced. "Oh Jesus!"

"It's no big deal. Once they schedule the operation, I should be out of there in a couple of days."

"Polyps, huh?" Veik sounded a bit nervous. "How'd you know you had any?"

"Well," Eddie said airily, "When I noticed my shit was nearly white and I kept having to *go* all the time, I called the doctor. You guys may have noticed me hittin' the bushes fairly often on this trip."

Veik and Butch made faces that clearly said they were sorry they'd asked. Butch Westerlake was painfully visualizing the surgery while Veik began to adopt the symptoms as his own, wondering if *he* could have polyps, trying to remember if *his* bowel habits had changed recently, and vowing to check the color of his feces ASAP.

Leaving their rifles in the back, they climbed into the truck. With shrubbery whipping at the sides of the pickup, they navigated the old and unused logging road, then made their way, via a number of turns guaranteed to get a greenhorn lost, down to Quarry Road.

They identified the car as the four-door hatchback Danielle Herron owned, but there was no sign of anyone, although the keys were in it. "Gotta be kids," Butch said as Eddie drove on down past the quarry and to the lake. They stopped the truck and got out, taking their rifles with them. This was, after all, cougar country, and, as Veik Kuusiniemi said, "If we have our guns with us, we're less apt to get an argument from a bunch of punk kids."

They walked to the sandy hillside road and started down it, stopping short as they got within sight of the shore. "Oh, my god!"

***

Willie Haapala and Kirsti Weeks were making their way back through the deep woods, each glad not to be alone. Willie was noticing that, as the sun sank and the shadows deepened, the trees themselves seemed to grow taller and more menacing. Or was it just that she, herself, felt smaller and more vulnerable?

Willie had grown up on the island and was no stranger to the rain-forest, but she'd also been away a long time, and wasn't at all sure she could even find her way around anymore. Years of logging and logging roads, as well as a couple of generations treading forest paths, had rendered the woods unfamiliar. The village was another world. One could live there all one's life without exploring the interior. Fortunately the trail they were on was wide and clear of underbrush. Here and there a fallen giant had toppled to block the way, but had been sliced through with a chainsaw with the obstructing part removed, so hikers could walk through the gap as though between two giant wheels of cheese. All they had to do was walk carefully so as not to trip over roots and stones in their path.

Kirsti was an island woman who had also roamed Broom in her childhood, but now rarely went into the forest. When was the last time? Must have been three or four years ago when she and Sanni Westerlake had gone looking for chanterelle mushrooms. Many islanders still picked salal to sell to the florist industry, but Kirsti hadn't done that in many years either. She had plenty to do outdoors just taking care of her vegetable patch and flower beds.

"Have you ever been on this trail before?" Willie asked.

"Can't say that I have. I don't get out in the woods much anymore. Have you?"

Willie laughed. "No, not all of it. Like a lot of people on this island, I've been meaning to hike it, but just never got around to it. A group of us went out to take a look at the Lemerriant farm, but we took the short way by the quarry. Now this is the second time I've been on this trail in two days!"

"It seems an easy trail, although I wasn't paying that much attention on the way in. I was following Matt."

"So was I. He was the one who led us to the old house last night and back again. Well, not quite all the way to the house in my case. When Celeste sprained her ankle, she and I had to wait for help. On the way back it was dark, but there was a bunch of us, so I just followed the crowd." Willie was looking around and suddenly nothing looked familiar, although the trail lay wide and open before them. *Too* wide and open! It had seemed narrower going in. "We should be looking for the path that takes us to your house, shouldn't we? This doesn't look like we're on it, does it?"

Kirsti stopped and looked around. "The light's fading. I'm not sure where we are. We may have missed our turn."

"What happens if we just keep going the way we're going?"

"We'll end up at the entrance by the water tower."

"Maybe we should turn back and see if we can recognize anything."

"It's getting later and we could end up lost. And I'm not sure we've even passed our cutoff. If we come to it and recognize it, we're home. If not, it may be better to keep going. At least we'll come to a road."

"Is there anything out there? Does anybody live up that way where we might get to a phone? Or will we have to hike all the way back to the village?"

"We'll come out near Burt Strunk's place. He has a sawmill on Quarry Road. We could use his phone and maybe get him to help look for Sybil."

"Burt Strunk. I must have gone to school with his dad, Mike. We used to tease him by yelling, 'Mike's drunk again!'"

"Mike was Burt's grandfather. His son was Andy. Andy married one of the Salmi girls and had three boys, Karl, August, and Burt. Karl and August left the island. Burt runs the sawmill. Andy died a few years back of a heart attack. Mike's long gone."

Typical island history — knee-jerk genealogical recitation whenever a name was mentioned. Willie knew about the sawmill but hadn't had occasion to go there, nor, until now, made the connection. Mike had been the *grandfather*. Willie felt old. "Guess we'd best keep on moving while we can still see without our flashlights."

"Are you going to be all right, Willie?"

"I'll be fine." *Now she thinks I'll be dropping dead of old age any minute to join old Mike Strunk. I hope she's wrong.*

* * *

Jeremy and Matt continued on the part of the trail that would lead them first to the lake, then onto Quarry Road, and from there to Michaels Acres. Jeremy, who had made his way along the trail all the way to the Lemerriant farm in the dead of night, was glad to have Matt along. That night Jeremy had been following footprints with the aid of panic and a flashlight, and was now realizing how easily he could have gone astray. There seemed to be any number of ways to take a wrong turn, especially where the edge of the forest appeared thin. The woods were apparently well traveled, but by whom? Berry-pickers? Kids? Deer? An animal path could look like a human footpath. Of course Jeremy hadn't come this far or in this direction.

"It's a good thing you're a woodsman, Matt. I literally would be lost without you."

Matt grinned. "I go to the lake all the time. Lots of paths used to lead to it like the one behind our house. Then they put the new trail in so now everybody shortcuts into it. You have to kinda watch out or you'll miss your place though."

"Are the kids here allowed to just run around in the woods without adult supervision?"

"Not all of 'em. New kids — city kids — aren't allowed to do lots of stuff. Me and my friends come here all the time."

"Isn't it dangerous? Aren't your parents worried?"

"Guess they did it too when they were kids so they don't care."

"But you could get hurt out here and nobody would know. And what about wild animals?"

"There's usually a bunch of us at the lake. Right now we're not allowed 'cause of the cougar, but I'm not scared to go alone. I take my hunting knife," Matt said with bravado calculated to impress.

The thought of a kid with a hunting knife wasn't particularly reassuring. "Do you have it with you?"

"No. I couldn't find it. I keep it in my room but when I looked for it, it was gone."

"Gone?" Something about that rang a warning bell in Jeremy's brain. "That was the knife you had with you last night?" Jeremy remembered how the appearance of Matt with the knife had looked so much like Elphique Lemerriant in the photo that Jeremy, for a second, had thought he was actually seeing a ghost. "What do you think happened to it?" Question casually framed, carefully asked.

"I dunno. It's always in my room. It's s'posed to be in a pouch hanging on a hook on the wall so's I can put it on my belt. But it wasn't there."

"When did you notice that it was missing?"

"When we came out to look for my sister. I was going to bring it but I couldn't find it."

"Maybe you put it someplace else."

"No. I put it there last night and it was there this morning."

"Matt, I think we should go back."

"Huh?"

"Yes. I don't think your sister came this way. I think we need to get back."

"You know where she is?"

"Maybe. More important, I have to make sure about where she *isn't*."

CHAPTER 56

GABRIELLE CHOATE sat watching hummingbirds. She'd rather have been out on the trail with Matt, but, as it was, hummingbirds were, again, the best show going.

Now, in the gathering dusk, sitting on the porch swing with one leg folded under her, she pushed with her extended foot to start the creaky swing moving, and watched as three or four tiny birds arrived, a bit tentatively, at the feeder. There wasn't enough light to illuminate their ruby throats, but their numbers kept growing. Now Gabi could count twenty — thirty? They kept arriving, hovering, zipping away and returning to circle the feeder like a swarm of insects. Gabi watched as some coasted into position, fanning their little tails to brake or to balance. Now and then a male bird would zoom in, sending all the females to flight, then another male would give chase and both would fly off while the females instantly returned to feed. It was a Cirque du Soleil of hummingbirds, astonishing to Gabi who couldn't have guessed that there would be so many. They made no sound except for the *vvvvt!* of their flight and the hum of their hover.

Gabi thought of calling her mother to come watch, but she knew how Celeste would react when interrupted while working. Getting her attention could sometimes be like trying to wake someone from a sound sleep. Besides, Gabi didn't know how long it would all last, and didn't want to miss any of it. It was as if the birds were frantically tanking up before nightfall and might suddenly be gone.

She let the swing come to rest and focused on the show, not noticing that another bird had appeared like an apparition on the porch rail: a large black bird. It had materialized silently — or had Gabi simply failed to hear the sound of its wings? Now, from the corner of her eye, she caught the motion as the bird shifted position on the railing.

Startled, Gabi turned to look. The bird was regarding her solemnly. Gabi looked back at it, puzzled but no longer frightened. Then, in the gathering gloom, she saw another black shape behind the bird — a figure in a long black coat, holding something in its hand in front of its face. Gabi saw that it was a wooden mask. It looked vaguely familiar; had she seen it somewhere? Gabi recognized the figure as Sybil, Matt's sister. She had a momentary impulse to run and yell "Mom!" but something, she wasn't quite sure what, stopped her, and all she did was gaze back at the mask that seemed to be looking back at her. She had a fleeting impression of a theater stage, as the outer panels of the mask hung open, and the painted eyes of a raven seemed to rivet her to the spot.

Gabi became aware of a murmuring sound and realized that the girl behind the mask was talking, chanting, almost singing, although Gabi couldn't make out what she was saying. It sounded like something partly in a different language, but it had a strangely soothing sound, almost like a lullaby. Gabi stared, fascinated, into the dark eye holes in the raven's face.

Slowly, deliberately, still holding the mask with its face pointed at Gabi, Sybil Weeks stepped onto the porch and stood in front of the little girl. *Yaxagama, Yaxagama, guide my hand, O Ancient Mother. Give me strength to slay the demon, strike to death the Loogy-Roo.* Gabi saw that while one hand held the mask, in the other she caught the gleam of metal — a knife.

Gabi felt an iciness run through her body like an electric shock. And then — where did it come from? — a voice in her head: "Fresh blood," it said, "Fresh blood!" Suddenly she was no longer a prisoner. She swiveled her head and looked at Blackjack, the raven, who was staring back at her. Then Gabi felt something powerful pass between them.

As Sybil raised the knife and advanced toward her, Gabi could feel her mind fly forth into the mind of the bird, and for a split second they were one. There seemed to be a flash of *something*, then Blackjack leapt into the air as if propelled and landed on *Sybil*, claws digging into her neck, wings flapping, beak open and jabbing. Gabi ducked under the porch rail and jumped the short distance to the ground. Sybil gasped and tried to fight off the bird, flailing about with her knife, and finally managed to thrust it into the raven who fell dead at her feet. She had dropped the mask when Blackjack attacked her, but quickly retrieved it; then, holding the knife stained with the blood of the bird, she tried to follow Gabi who had ducked into the dark of the shrubbery.

At this point, neither of them could see the other. Gabi moved quietly, barely breathing. Sybil was panting from exertion, trying to see with the aid of the mask but it seemed awkward, and she dropped it. "Yaxagama, help me," she whispered, feeling her way, trying to find her walking stick which she'd earlier let fall on the grass.

It was not yet wholly dark. The sky above them was still light and stars had not begun to show. It was still possible to make out the red of the rhododendrons, although shadows that formed in the shrubbery swallowed up everything at their feet to form wells of blackness. Sybil had the advantage, even without the aid of her mask. She knew what she had to do, and drew upon every bit of her cunning.

Gabi, sensing that Sybil would hear her slightest sound, was barely breathing, crouching in the shadow of a lilac bush. She listened but heard nothing. Had Sybil gone? No, a flicker of shadow from the light of a window told her she was still there, searching for her, but that she was moving in the wrong direction. If Gabi could just make her way around the corner to the flagstone walk that led to the kitchen door, she'd be safe. But she didn't dare make a move. Sybil was still too close. Carefully, she moved her foot to take a step and felt herself almost fall. She'd stepped on something — Sybil's walking stick. Gabi bent down and grasped it in her hand. She had a weapon!

Sybil had heard the noise in the bushes. She turned, listened, and knew where Gabi was. She raised her knife and slowly, soundlessly, moved toward the stand of lilac. Gabi didn't see her until the shadow rose up in front of her, arm upraised: *Yaxagama, Yaxagama, make my blade strike swift and true!* Sybil's arm came down in a sweeping motion, aimed at Gabi who reflexively stepped aside to avoid the thrust, and then felt herself being pushed out of the way as the knife came down and made contact — with a plaster cast. Jeremy!

With darting speed Jeremy grabbed the knife, then dropped it as he tried to subdue Sybil who was fighting like a madwoman and screaming incoherencies. The noise brought Celeste who threw open the kitchen door to see her daughter sprawled in the shrubbery — and what looked like a wild apache dance going on between Jeremy Banks and Sybil who, black coat flapping like the wings of a bird, arms raised, kept flailing at Jeremy and screeching. Celeste moved toward Gabi, helped her to her feet, and held on to her, as Jeremy finally managed to pin Sybil's arms behind her back while she was still kicking out with her feet, threatening to topple both of them.

Celeste shot Jeremy a what-the-hell's-going-on? look while he, over Sybil's shoulder, returned it with one of, what do I do now? There seemed to be no answer to that, so Jeremy just relaxed his hold, preparing to defend himself if Sybil should attack again. The sudden release caused Sybil to lose her balance. She raised her arms, swayed, and for one moment her eyes seemed to lock onto Gabi's, then she pitched forward onto the grass.

"She's having another seizure," Jeremy said.

"Oh my god! What should we do? Can we get her inside?"

"I think it's best to wait till it passes. Do we have a blanket we can throw over her?"

"There's one in my room," Gabi said and vanished into the house.

"I'd better call her mother," Celeste said. She went indoors into Willie's office to phone Kirsti. Matt answered. "Is your mother at home, Matt?"

"No."

"Sybil is here. If your mom phones, have her call me right away, okay?"

Almost instantly after she hung up, the phone rang. It was Willie.

"Oh, thank god it's you. Is Sybil's mother with you?"

"Yes, has Sybil come back home?"

"She's here, Willie, but I'm afraid she's having one of her seizures. What should we do?"

"Where is she?"

"She's out in the yard on the lawn. We put a blanket over her to keep her warm, but should we try to get her into the house?"

There was mumbled conversation at the other end, then Kirsti's voice: "Just wait a few minutes. It's best to do nothing till it passes. We'll be right home. Burt Strunk is giving us a ride. Thank God she's safe."

Safe, yes, Celeste thought as she watched Sybil in throes of a seizure. But is anyone safe from *her*? She seemed totally out of control. *I wonder if that's part of a seizure disorder. I've heard that people can become violent just before they have one.*

The three of them, Gabi, Jeremy, and Celeste stood quietly waiting for Sybil's *grand mal* to pass. Only one of them knew what had actually taken place. Jeremy had arrived just in time to intervene; Celeste hadn't come upon the scene until after the drama with the knife.

"Exactly what happened here tonight?" Celeste asked.

Jeremy was about to speak when, to his surprise, Gabi leapt in. "I was on the porch watching the hummingbirds and I heard a noise. Then I saw Sybil and she was holding a wooden mask and she was reciting a poem or something. Then Jeremy came and Sybil started acting funny. She was kind of starting to dance around and she bumped into me and pushed me over, and Jeremy tried to catch her, and then you saw what happened. She went all ballistic and then she fell down." Gabi's eyes were wide and blue and convincing.

Celeste shot Jeremy a look as if to say, is that what happened? And once again Jeremy had been effectively silenced by a ten-year-old. Oh, he could have told a different story of hurrying back with Matt to find nobody at the Weeks house, and of having a gnawing fear that Sybil had taken Matt's knife and that Gabi's life might be in danger. He could have told her how he'd rushed over to find Sybil stalking Gabi in the darkness, and how, through the grace of God, he'd managed to push her out of the way and deflect the blow that had landed harmlessly (he glanced down — well, almost harmlessly) on the cast on his arm. But why had Gabi chosen not to mention any of that?

Gabi had also chosen not to mention the dead raven that was still lying on the porch and which, at the earliest opportunity, she planned to kick into the bed of lady's mantle beneath it.

Sybil's spasms had stopped and the girl now seemed to be sleeping. They heard a car, a shouted "Thanks, Burt," and Willie and Kirsti arrived on the run. Kirsti rushed over to her daughter. "Sybil, it's Mama. Can you hear me? Can you wake up now, Sybil?"

Sybil opened her eyes. She seemed unfocused, as usual, but with no sign of the murderous rage she had shown earlier. She stirred, and Willie, Kirsti, and Celeste helped her up, wrapped her in the blanket, and supporting her while they guided her in through the kitchen door.

"Where's the knife, Jeremy?" Gabi asked.

"I don't know, Gabi. I think it fell in the grass somewhere."

"We have to find it. I'll look on the porch to make sure it's not there."

"It can't be up there, Gabrielle. Now what's all this about?"

"You're right, Jeremy. It's not here." (And neither was the raven, although there was a bloody spot, but she couldn't do anything about that now.) "Oh, there it is!" Gabi ran over and picked up Matt's knife and gave the blade a quick swipe against the grass. "I'll give it back to Matt when I see him."

"Perhaps you'd better give it to me."

"Okay," Gabi made a motion to hand it over, then stopped. "Or maybe I should just give it to Mrs. Weeks. She can take it back. Matt's probably wondering where it is. I can tell her he left it here."

"Gabi, Sybil was trying to kill you. Don't you think we should tell her mother — and also tell the police? She's dangerous. She could hurt someone else. She would have hurt you if I hadn't been there."

Gabi smiled. "Maybe. Maybe not. I had a stick. I'd have whacked her with it." She retrieved Sybil's stick and leaned it against the wall by the kitchen door.

She was sounding like Matt Weeks with his knife. *The child is in denial. She's been through a traumatizing experience. Of course she'll try to make it seem as if it never happened. But I can't be party to that.* "It's okay, Gabi. It's all over. Sybil will get the help she needs. We don't want her to be a danger to anyone else."

"She's not going to be dangerous for long." Gabi was again searching around in the grass.

"How can you know that, Gabi?"

"I just know." Gabi ran back toward the porch steps, looked around, then picked up something: the mask. When dropped, the outer panels had snapped back into place and the face was again that of the shaman — deathly white with the thick red lips and black staring eyes.

"That, I believe, belongs to Danielle Herron, and she'll be grateful to have it back."

"We'll give it back, but please, Jeremy, don't say anything to my mom about the knife. She'll only get all upset and worried. And Sybil won't be able to hurt anybody anymore."

"How can you know that?"

"I just *do*. She may try but she can't do anything to me."

"Why are you trying to protect Sybil?"

Gabi shrugged, the way a kid shrugs when asked a question she doesn't want to answer. "I dunno. But you're not going to *tell*, are you?"

"I make no promises, Gabi, but I know that tonight everyone is tired and upset and perhaps it would be better for us all to get a good night's sleep — including Sybil. We can sort this out tomorrow."

They went inside to find Sybil sitting on the couch, staring dully into the middle distance, while Willie, Kirsti, and Celeste were talking excitedly.

"So we just missed our turn. Things look so different in the woods when it starts getting dark," Kirsti was saying. "Not that I've been out there since they put the Lemerriant trail in. That's what threw me off. It used to be a straight path to the lake."

"And it was starting to get dark so we just walked on to the water tower and Burt Strunk's sawmill. Lucky that Burt was home." Willie said. "Burt was going to call some of his friends to join the search."

Gabi was still holding the mask and Sybil's eyes flickered toward it. Kirsti went over and took it from Gabi. "Thank God this turned up! It belongs to Danielle Herron and it's — well, she *says* it's worth fifteen thousand dollars. I don't know. Maybe it is." The mask was a bit worse for wear, but intact. It seemed to be missing some of its "hair" and the cedar bark ties had vanished, but Kirsti hoped Danielle wouldn't notice, or at least she'd be so glad to see it that she wouldn't make a fuss. "I'll make sure Miss Herron gets this back first thing in the morning."

"Well, after all that," Willie said, "I think we should all go to bed early and get some sleep." She looked at Kirsti. "Maybe it would be better if Sybil stayed here tonight. She must be weak and exhausted, and we have room. Would you like to stay here tonight, Sybil?"

Jeremy looked alarmed, but then relieved when Sybil said "I want to go home. I need my stick."

"Stick?"

"Her walking stick," Kirsti said. "She uses it to find her way. Where did you leave it, Sybil?"

"It's outside the door," Gabi said, once again looking directly at Sybil who seemed to return her gaze with a look of wary puzzlement.

"Then we'll say goodnight," Kirsti said, "Can you walk, Sybil? Do you need help?"

By way of reply, Sybil stood up and walked over to her mother.

"I just want to get her home, get her cleaned up, and into bed."

Gabi opened the kitchen door and silently handed Sybil her cane. She couldn't tell whether Sybil could see her — or how much of her she might be able to see — but Gabi gave her a long look.

"Wait!" Willie hurried after them. "Take a flashlight."

The group clustered, framed in the light of the doorway, to watch Sybil and her mother enter the patch of woods that separated the two houses. They could see the intermittent gleam of the flashlight as the two woman made their way home; then, when they couldn't see the light anymore, they all went inside.

"It's not all that late yet. Would anyone like a cup of tea or a snack? We never did have dinner. Is anybody hungry? We have a refrigerator full of Ulla's sandwiches and goodies." Willie looked from one to the other, and nobody seemed to be refusing. "That settles it. I'll put the kettle on. Gabi, would you like a glass of milk or a cup of cocoa?"

"Cocoa, please," Gabi said, and climbed into a chair.

"Can I help you, Willie?" Celeste asked.

"Sit. You're still walking wounded. There's nothing to do anyway." She brought a platter of sandwiches from the refrigerator, rounded up cake and cookies, and then, with the grace of a magician, set the table with cups and plates and napkins. Gabi's cocoa materialized from the microwave and the handsome china teapot took center table.

"Jeremy, what on earth happened to your cast?" Willie asked.

Jeremy had been reaching for a napkin, and now in the moment of silence that followed, he was aware that Gabi was watching him carefully. "Oh, that. Yes, I must have whacked it on something." The cast was broken nearly through. "It's supposed to come off anyway." Jeremy took hold of the ragged edge, gave it a wrench and cracked it off completely. He noticed, for the first time, that it seemed to have a small stain. Blood? But no, it couldn't be. He checked his wrist and there wasn't a scratch on it. "See? He flexed his hand. Good as new." He glanced at Gabi who was contentedly sipping her hot chocolate. "Feels great to get that thing off!"

"There was a call for you," Celeste said to Jeremy. "Danielle Herron phoned."

"Really? Did she say what she wanted?"

"No. She sounded a little mysterious — and disappointed that you weren't here."

"I can't imagine what she'd want with me. I just saw her in town earlier today. She didn't say anything much then, although she *was* asking about that Indian mask."

"She's been very upset about that," Willie said. "Kirsti told me she'd been over there twice looking for it. But I don't know why she'd be calling you. I guess you'll have to ask her."

"She did say she'd call you back," Celeste said.

"If it's about the mask, Kirsti will return it to her now that it's turned up," Willie said. "What on earth could Sybil have been doing with it?"

"It helps her see."

Everyone looked at Gabi. "What do you mean it helps her see?" Celeste asked.

"When she looks through the mask she can see."

"Did she say that?"

"No. But I could tell."

"Gabi, how could that be possible? It's just a piece of wood — a carving. How could it help anyone see anything?"

"I don't know how, Mom, but when she looks through the eyeholes, she can see."

"You can't know that, Gabi, because it's not possible. And, young lady, if you've finished your cocoa, it's time you were in bed. It's time I was in bed too. If it's okay, I think I'll go upstairs tonight. My foot's feeling a lot better, and I think I'd like to be close to my daughter. But first, the dishes?"

"No need, I have the help of a two-handed man tonight. Off you both go, then, and sleep well."

"More tea. Jeremy? There's still a drop in the pot." There were still sandwiches left and Willie was moving them to a smaller plate and covering them with plastic wrap.

"No thanks, Willie." Jeremy carried dishes to the sink.

"What did you do to break that cast? Did you fall?"

"No, it came in contact with a sharp object."

"Oh?"

"You were right about Sybil. You did say that when she's off her medication, things can become unpleasant!"

Willie covered up the sandwiches and put them back in the refrigerator. "Okay, so tell me about it."

"She went after Gabi with a knife."

"*What?*"

"If I hadn't gotten back in time, God knows what might have happened!"

"Good Lord!" Willie stood with her mouth open.

"Sybil is obviously mentally disturbed. She needs professional help, and probably more than just medication."

"But . . . but why didn't anyone say anything? I thought she'd just had a seizure. *Kirsti* thinks she just had a seizure — and, good heavens, she and Matt are under the same roof with a homicidal maniac! How could you have not said something?"

Jeremy sighed. "I'm wondering about that myself, except of course Sybil has never been a danger to anyone but Gabi. She's fixated on her, thinks of her as evil incarnate that has to be destroyed. She thinks she's saving the world from her."

"And that's insane!"

"Yes, of course it is. But what's even stranger is that it was *Gabi* who begged me not to say anything to her mother."

"Why would she do that?"

"I don't know, but she's convinced that Sybil won't be a danger to her anymore."

"Jeremy, Gabi is ten. She's a kid. Okay, she may be a psychically gifted kid, but she's not the Delphic oracle."

"Of course not. Everyone will be told the truth, but I just made a decision not to upset Celeste or Kirsti tonight. Kirsti's been through a lot already, and Sybil will probably just sleep after her seizure. I told Gabi we'd sort it all out tomorrow."

"Well, I hope you're right. Truth is, I'd really hate to call Kirsti and get her all upset tonight — although a part of me says I should. I don't understand why you chose to keep it a secret."

"I haven't kept it a secret. I just told you, didn't I? And if you think you should call Kirsti or the cops or the men in white coats, I'll stand by your decision. I just thought that we might all see this more clearly in the light of day tomorrow."

Willie sighed. "Yes, it's been a quite a night. I'd expected something to mark the anniversary of the great fire, but I didn't think it would be this . . . intense."

"Well, at least we're all done with that now. I didn't see any Lemerriants walking around last night, although Matt did give me a turn."

"Technically, *this* is the anniversary of the fire. May 19th. And I guess Sybil's contribution tonight was creepy enough."

"I suppose we can all relax now, at least about the Lemerriant ghosts."

"I'm off to bed. Didn't sleep much last night, so I'm going up early."

"Right, Willie. The house is secure."

* * *

Celeste looked at the sleeping form of her daughter. Who was this child, and how did she always seem to be in the middle of trouble? Was she destined to become — Celeste hesitated, even mentally, to use the word — some kind of freak of nature? Or was it, as Willie had suggested, something that would blow over? Or was Gabi really the last of the Mad Lemerriants? Celeste had more reason to research their madness than just getting book material. Gabi's future might depend on what she could find. If, indeed, there was some psychic ability that ran through the family, it wouldn't necessarily be demonic, would it? Although it could certainly have been seen that way by superstitious peasants. If the madness had an organic cause, like ergot poisoning, then the Lemerriants may not have been any madder than anyone else. Brazeau may have just been a son of a bitch who abused his wife and children to the point of irreparable damage, but it didn't have to affect his descendants, did it? It would all look different once they were back home, off the island, and Celeste vowed they would leave the next day.

* * *

Kirsti, too, had tucked her daughter into bed. Sybil had been subdued and sleepy on the way home, picking her way slowly through the woods, but needing no help except that of her walking stick. Kirsti, had lit the way with Willie's flashlight, while she carried the native mask. (What an immense relief to have that ugly thing turn up!)

The mask was now in Sybil's sleeping grip, like a monstrous teddy bear. Kirsti would have rather put it into a cabinet downstairs, but Sybil had picked it up and hung onto it so tightly that Kirsti decided to humor her. She was tempted to pry it loose and put it elsewhere — something about it gave her the creeps — but she didn't want to risk waking Sybil. The hellish thing would go back to Danielle Herron tomorrow in any case; she'd see to that!

As she had done countless times, Kirsti stood looking at her daughter while she slept. Sybil's waking persona was so eccentric that it took sleep to neutralized it. Now she looked young and innocent and even pretty. If she'd only dress like a normal young lady and do something with her straggly hair! Of course, poor thing, she couldn't see well enough to know how she looked. It really was too bad! Kirsti wondered for the umpteenth time what might become of her. She and Rome wouldn't live forever; only by the grace of God was Rome still alive at all. Sybil would never have a normal life. Marry and have children? Kirsti couldn't even picture it. Nor would it be fair to Matt to end up having to care for her one day. Sybil wasn't stupid (Kirsti knew that better than anyone), but she had too many problems to be able to hold a normal job and support herself. She could end up in an institution, living in a world of her own; she pretty much did that now, she and her pet bird. Kirsti looked around. Where *was* Blackjack, anyhow? Oh well, he'd be back. Now and then the bird would fly off, but he always came back to Sybil. Kirsti turned out the light and closed the door.

* * *

Matt Weeks was having a restless night. Matt wasn't normally given to nightmares and usually fell asleep like a tired puppy — instantly — to awaken with no memory of, or curiosity about, the world of dreams. Tonight was different. Someone was calling to him and he was walking through tall, dark, woods, knowing that he was also being followed by someone. He couldn't see what it was but it kept coming, and, in turn, he kept on going although his legs were getting so heavy he could hardly lift them. But he knew he had to keep moving toward whoever was calling his name. One painful, struggling step after another, he toiled on, feeling that at any moment he would fall exhausted, and whatever was behind him would overtake him. He woke once, gasping, trussed up by a sheet, struggled and kicked himself free, then flipped over on his side and pulled the blanket over his head — only to fall again into the same fitful dream.

* * *

Sybil, on the other hand, had only been pretending to sleep. What had gone wrong? She had brought the mask home, hidden it under her pillows. She had taken Matt's knife from its sheath, and she and Blackjack had carefully slipped out without being seen. She'd made her way to the Haapala house to wait, inside the greenhouse, for an opportunity. Through the eyes of the raven, she'd been able to see the woman through the window, and that the Loogy-Roo was with her. Sybil had to find a way to get her alone. But how? Gripping the handle of Matt's knife, she'd planned to wait — wait all night if she had to. Wait till it got dark and everyone had gone to bed. Then she would creep into the house, find the devil child and strike her down. But then — *thank you, Yaxagama* — the girl had came out to sit in the swing. Sybil had slipped out and crept silently closer, awkwardly using her stick to guide her steps while she hugged the mask and held the knife with her other hand. The girl, intent on watching hummingbirds, had heard nothing. It was the perfect time! She'd let her stick fall, didn't need it now, and raised the mask to her face and advanced.

But what had gone wrong? Blackjack! But of course, the Loogy-Roo was powerful! Sybil hadn't counted on her being able to command the bird to attack her. Poor Blackjack. She would mourn him later, find him and give him a funeral. Now, while she still had the mask, there might be one last chance to rid the world of the Loogy-Roo. Yes, the Loogy-Roo was powerful, but so was Yaxagama. But Sybil knew she needed someone else to help her. She got out of bed and dressed to go out. Holding the mask, she made her way downstairs and out the door without being seen. She found her walking stick and vanished into the darkness.

CHAPTER 57

Gabi opened her eyes. Had someone called her name — or had the girl been singing again? She thought she'd heard something. She sat up, and in the dim light she could make out the shape of her mother sleeping in the next bed. Wide awake now, Gabi got up and went to the window, leaned her elbows on the sill, and looked out.

Night was a strange and mysterious time. You never knew what might be out there! Monsters? Wild things? Right now everything looked peaceful with the moon casting shadows on the clipped lawn — but what was that? Someone was out in the yard! Was something moving? Or was it just a bush or a shadow? No, it was something else. Some*one* else. Matt! Matt Weeks! What was Matt doing standing on the grass looking up at her window in the middle of the night? She almost called to him, but realized it would wake her mother.

Quickly and quietly Gabi got dressed — pulled on jeans, sweatshirt, and sneakers — then tiptoed out the door, closing it silently, and made her way downstairs, through to the kitchen door. She reached up and slid back the bolt, slipped outdoors through the mudroom, and looked around. "Matt?" she hissed. "Matt, where are you?" She'd clearly seen him; he had to be there! Yes, there he was in the shimmer of moonlight. He'd moved back toward the woods, and now he seemed to be leaving. She raced after him, "Matt, wait!"

Matt stopped, looked back at Gabi as if to see if she was following, then turned and continued on his way. Gabi was becoming upset. "Matt Weeks, stop playing dumb games and wait for me!" She broke into a run, but Matt kept on going through the woods toward his own house. Gabi hesitated. Should she just go back? Once again, Matt stopped and turned toward her. Something about him seemed weird — it looked like he was wearing pajama pants and had no shoes on. "Matt, you dork, why don't you wait!"

They were coming to the Weeks house, but Matt kept on going, moving past it, down toward the entrance to the trail. "Matt, we're not supposed to be out here. Do you hear me?" Gabi couldn't tell if he *could* hear her. Was he walking in his sleep? Gabi knew that sometimes *she* walked in her sleep and never remembered anything afterwards. Should she go back? But she couldn't just leave him out there. If he was sleepwalking, she'd have to catch up with him and try to wake him up and bring him back home. But no matter how fast Gabi ran, Matt was always a good distance ahead of her. If she stopped, so did he, to look back at her, and as soon as she tried to get closer, he moved on. They were in the dark of the trail now, and her only guide was Matt's pale, retreating figure. Gabi was near tears of frustration, but so focused on Matt that she didn't think to be frightened, only furious. "Matt, you big fuck, *stop!*"

He obviously wanted her to follow him, but why? "Matt, come back. Let's go home. We're not supposed to be here. There's a cougar loose. *Matt!*" Matt appeared not to hear her although she was yelling. Should she go home and wake everybody? Or should she go knocking on Mrs. Weeks's door? Grownups would know what to do, but if she left Matt out there all by himself, he might go anywhere and they'd never find him. And the cougar could get him. "*Oh, man!* Matt, get your big dumb ass back here!"

It seemed to Gabi that they'd been walking for hours. She'd walked the trail several times by now, and she and Matt had wandered through the woods a couple of times, before they'd even known there *was* a cougar. And that last time had been *really strange.* Matt was the one who was supposed to know the area, but that day, he'd followed *her.* Of course that had been in the daytime. Gabi couldn't remember walking the trail in her sleep, and barely recalled being carried back by Jeremy. Walking in her sleep like that big dumb kid, Matt, who seemed to know she was there because he kept looking back at her! If he was just doing this to play with her head, she'd kill him. Well, asleep or not, she couldn't leave him — and she didn't really want to go all the way back in the dark by herself either. They were heading for the old Lemerriant farm.

And there it was. Dark buildings in a moonlit clearing. What was Matt doing now? *Oh shit!* He was going into the cabin. Well, at least she'd catch up with him there.

Thinking dark thoughts about what she'd like to do to Matt Weeks, Gabi got a scratch from a blackberry bramble, and she gave the door an angry shove that jarred it open yet wider. "Matt, you idiot, I don't know what you're playing at, but — " Gabi stopped. The figure in front of her wasn't Matt. In the light of a flickering candle on the table, the figure was partly in silhouette, but Gabi recognized it immediately: Sybil Weeks.

Sybil stood facing her. She was holding the wooden mask and Gabi noticed a strong smell in the cabin.

"What are *you* doing here and where's Matt?"

"Matt isn't here."

"What do you mean he isn't here? I followed him all they way from Willie's house and I saw him come in here." She looked around.

"You can see he's not here."

"What do you want, Sybil?"

"I know you. I know what you are."

"I'm Gabrielle Choate."

"You're the devil's spawn and you must be destroyed!"

"You can't do anything to me, so why do you keep trying?"

"Because you're the Loogy-Roo. The sins of the fathers!" Sybil was almost whispering. "The sins of the fathers."

"I'm just a kid." Gabi's blue, innocent eyes held just the faintest flicker of cunning.

"Why did you have to come back?"

"I've never been here before."

"This is your lair, isn't it? You've been made flesh again and you're out for blood, aren't you?"

"I told you. I've *never* been here before."

"Then why do the birds know you? Why did Blackjack recognize you? Why does Yaxagama know you? How is it that the birds can talk to you?"

"I don't know."

"But they *do* talk to you, don't they? And they follow you around, don't they?"

"Yes."

"And you know when someone is going to die, don't you?"

"Sometimes. But *I've* never killed anybody. I'm just a kid."

"You're in the body of a child, but you make it all happen, don't you?"

"How?"

"You made Blackjack attack me. You made the cougar kill Dory. You made that man shoot my father."

"No, I didn't. I don't know about Blackjack; it happened so fast. But I never made anybody kill anybody."

Sybil said nothing at first, then gripped the mask. "Maybe you don't even know. But Yaxagama knows who you are. We know your power, but we'll fight you."

"Sybil, look at me. *I'm just a kid.* I'm not even going to *be* here. My mom and I will be leaving tomorrow. And that's just an old wooden

Indian mask. This is just an old dusty farmhouse, and nobody lives here anymore. It's empty. Let's just go home."

"The Devil is a liar! You *are* the Loogy-Roo!"

"Because I sometimes know stuff before it happens? Because I can hear birds talking? What about you? *You* know things too, don't you? And you may be blind but you can see when you look through that mask, can't you? And you can make people do things, can't you? You made Matt come here tonight, didn't you?"

"I called him."

"Then where is he? I saw him come in here."

"It wasn't Matt."

"It *was* Matt. I *saw* him. He looked like he was walking in his sleep."

"I called him and his spirit form came and brought you here. If you could *see* his spirit form that *proves* you're the Loogy-Roo! While you're alive, the Loogy-Roo will go on killing."

"Even if there was a Loogy-Roo, why would it want to kill anybody?"

"Because the Loogy-Roo is of the devil. You're ancient evil, and you command the beasts to do your bidding."

"But I don't even *live* here. I'm not going to be around to command anything."

"It doesn't matter. Do you think distance makes any difference? You're alive. You're the Loogy-Roo. Your power will keep growing every time someone dies."

"That's just dumb. The Loogy-Roo thing happened a long time ago. I wasn't even born then, and neither were you. Anyway, who made *you* the boss?"

"Yaxagama."

"That *mask?*"

"Yaxagama shows me things *through* the mask, but Yaxagama isn't the *mask*. Yaxagama is the Ancient Mother, and she lives in *me* like the Loogy-Roo lives in *you*. I always knew you'd come back, and I'm ready. We're ancient enemies, you and I . . . and one of us will have to die . .

. I didn't know what form you'd take . . . but I knew I had to make . . . with word of God and magic spell . . . a way to send you back to Hell."

"Yeah, okay. But we're sort of alike, you know. You see things and hear things. So if stuff like that makes *me* the Loogy-Roo, then so are *you*."

For a moment Sybil looked uncertain. "Don't try to confuse me with your lies."

"All I said was maybe *you're* the Loogy-Roo. Or maybe we both are. Maybe we don't really know what the Loogy-Roo *is*. So far, you're the only one I've met, but there might be other people like us. I don't want to hurt anybody, but sometimes I get in trouble. I don't think you want to hurt anybody either. I don't think we're *bad*. Maybe we're just *different*."

Sybil's features twisted, almost as if she were about to burst into tears, then she smiled again. "Oh, I know you're powerful, and you'll try to trick me."

"Let's just go *home,* Sybil."

"I can't. This place is foul. I must destroy it. Many spirit forms are bound here. I've seen them all my life."

"Sybil, you're *blind*. How can you see anything?"

"Spirit forms aren't seen with eyes . . . but they follow those they recognize. They come in the night and find you. They whisper . . . and they wail . . . and they sing. . . ."

"Why?"

"Because they're tortured souls, bound to walk the earth for the sins of their fathers."

"That doesn't sound fair."

"They *carry* the sins of their fathers, and when the Loogy-Roo is alive in flesh, they have the power to do evil. The Loogy-Roo is the host, and when the Loogy-Roo dies, the connection is broken . . . until it is born back into flesh again. They use the power of the Loogy-Roo to kill, and each death gives them more power, so the evil grows and grows. They recognize you and they know you can hear them. *I* know you can hear them!"

"All I heard was the birds talking . . . and a girl singing."

Sybil laughed triumphantly. "See? I knew it. They've attached them-selves to you. You'll never be free."

"She was singing about a man getting shot on a rainy day. But it wasn't *my* fault your dad got hurt."

"You're the host. You may not even know it, but you're the host. My mission is to destroy you!"

Sybil had picked up the candle and was circling toward the door. Gabi saw that she'd put the old mattress next to it, and Gabi realized what the smell was — gasoline. Sybil had splashed it all over the cabin.

Gabi stood her ground. She realized now that Sybil intended not only to kill her, but herself as well. "Sybil, don't do this. Let's just get out of here."

"It's too late! *Yaxagama, Ancient Mother, help me to fulfill my mission!*" Sybil applied the candle flame to the mattress setting it ablaze. Gabi made a move for the door, but Sybil lunged at her, knocked her over backwards and fell on top of her, her weight pinning her down while the fire spread and the room filled with choking smoke. Then, suddenly, someone else was in the room. Gabi could feel Sybil's weight rolling off her, or being lifted off and she, herself, was crawling toward the door, catching her breath in the last smoke-free space next to the floor boards. Was someone dragging her, or was she moving on her own? Who was it? Gabi's eyes were stinging and she couldn't see, but her lungs were now filling with air and she knew she'd managed to get through the doorway. She got up and ran down off the porch with the cabin now completely engulfed in flames. She turned. "Sybil," she whispered, knowing that for Sybil it was now too late. Just as she'd known that it would be. . . .

But who had helped her? Matt! It had been Matt. She saw him now, standing in the clearing, looking at her. She walked toward him, and this time he stood waiting. "Matt, I. . . ." and then as the boy looked at her, she realized that he looked different. He looked a lot like Matt, beefy of build, but bigger and older than Matt, and he wasn't dressed like Matt. He was wearing trousers and shirt and he had a knife on his belt. "Matt?"

There was no answer. The boy looked at her, and then, with the faintest of smiles, he just vanished. One moment he was there, the next, he . . . wasn't. Gabi was alone in the clearing with the burning building which now was sending sparks high into the sky, dispersing them over the woods, threatening to ignite the forest.

Suddenly Gabi was once again just a kid alone in a scary place, and she began to cry. She stood sobbing and watching the flames that warmed the cold night, but presented a danger if the fire spread. She wished she were safe at home, and realized that nobody even knew where she was. She stopped crying and stood still. The fire was beautiful, as fires are, and Gabi found herself transfixed by the fanciful shapes of the flames. Then, to her surprise, she saw she was no longer alone. A figure stood next to her, watching the fire. She was about to call out when she saw another, then another, and soon Gabi was part of a gathering throng. Nobody spoke. The figures looked like ordinary people—men, women, children—but there was something *thin* about them, as if they weren't really solid. They weren't paying attention to her, nor were they moving about; they stood apart from Gabi and from each other, all just silently watching the flames. There was something almost comforting in their presence, and for some time Gabi stood among them, wondering who they were, and where they'd come from, and whether they were real or not. Were these the ghosts that Sybil had talked about? Ghosts that had been somehow tied to this place? Whoever they were, there were many, and for a moment she thought she saw one that looked familiar — a fat, bald man standing next to a girl — but they vanished from her sight as the crowd thickened.

And then, instantly, they were gone. But something else was happening. She could see lights, not on the trail, but coming from a different direction. It was vehicles. People! Men! Men in cars and men in a fire truck!

CHAPTER 58

It had been Burt Strunk at the sawmill who spotted the glow in the sky. Telephone lines lit up as volunteer firemen were summoned, and within minutes the bright red tanker truck was making its way into the hills and onto the long-unused road that led to the Lemerriant property. Fire, on the heavily treed island of Broom, was something everyone dreaded; when anyone spotted smoke, it triggered instant response. Now the operation was energetic, though not quite as efficient. The regular firemen were also fishermen, and they were at sea. The second string of less- experienced firefighters had trouble with the hoses. Instead of driving the tanker to the fire, they parked it by the well (the only additional water source) and dragged out the hoses, only to lose precious time when they found they had the wrong ends. The cabin, by then, despite its solid construction, was burnt flat, as well as the barn that had already been near collapse. The good news was that they were able to wet down the area to contain the fire before it spread to the woods.

Nevertheless, to Gabi the firemen were angels from heaven. She was cozily wrapped in a blanket and driven home by Larry Nyquist of the

New Broom. In the network of emergency notification, Willie's phone was one of the first to ring in the night, and she duly called others on her list of people to alert. Not all Broom islanders lived in Satama or Tranquil Bay. There were several settlers whose homes were in wooded areas where the threat from a fire was greatest; they had to be alerted.

Jeremy awakened, and so did Celeste, and everyone panicked to find that Gabi was, yet again missing — but then, to immense relief, she arrived home safely, moments later, to be hugged, cleaned up, fussed over, and given a warming cup of cocoa. Willie had quietly put the kettle on and produced a pot of herb tea, and now the hubbub had died down, as each in his own way reacted to the night's events. Celeste, who had been near tears, was now angry. "I thought you said the doors were bolted and that she couldn't get out."

"I'm sorry," Jeremy said. "I'm sure we *did* bolt the door. Gabi must have opened it. It didn't think she could do that while sleepwalking. That slide bolt is up above her head and I didn't think she'd even noticed it was there. I'll put a hook and eye on that door tomorrow well out of her reach."

Celeste sighed. "Don't bother. We'll be leaving. I'm sorry too. You've both been kind, but it's all been, well, it's all been just *too much*. It's not your fault, I know, and I shouldn't be blaming you." (If only she could light up a cigarette to calm her nerves!)

"Well, I'm sorry too," Willie said. "I should have been more alert. We're not used to having a child in this house, and it didn't occur to either of us that this could happen. But at least nobody got hurt."

They sat, for a moment, in silence.

"Sybil is dead," Gabi said.

"What?" Willie looked stricken.

"She got burned up in the fire."

Celeste looked hard at her daughter and spoke quickly, "Gabrielle Penelope Choate, I think you'd better tell us everything. First of all, why were you there? How did you get there?"

Gabi took a moment. She had followed Matt Weeks — only it might not have been Matt Weeks — although she was *absolutely sure* it *had* been Matt, but then there had been the other boy who looked like Matt. Or was he just one of those things nobody else could see or hear? A spirit form, like Sybil had said. How was she going to explain any of it? "I . . . I don't exactly remember how I got there."

"Were you sleepwalking again?"

"Uh, yes, I guess I must have been."

"Then what about Sybil?"

"She was there, in the cabin."

"And that part you remember?"

"Yes, I guess I must've woken up."

"What was Sybil doing there?"

"I . . . I don't know. She was there the last time too. I don't know why."

"Did she say anything to you?"

"No. Yes. I think she told me she knew who I was."

"She said she recognized you?"

"Yeah, well, it's wasn't so easy for her . . . she can't see . . . and it was dark except for the candle."

"Sybil had a candle?"

"Yes. That's what started the fire. I guess it was an accident."

"Exactly how did it happen, Gabi?"

"I think Sybil must have knocked over a can of gasoline and it got on the old mattress and Sybil dropped the candle . . . and then there was fire everywhere and I tripped and fell . . . and there was smoke and flames . . . and I crawled to the door and got out. But Sybil didn't. I think she had another one of her fits and that's why she dropped the candle."

"Oh, sweetheart, you could've been killed!" Celeste moved to gather Gabi up in her arms and hugged her so tightly that Gabi squirmed to get loose.

"Did the firemen find Sybil? Did they know she was in the cabin?" Willie asked.

Gabi looked surprised. "I don't know! Nobody asked me anything. They just wrapped me up and the man from the restaurant said he knew who I was and that he'd take me home. I guess I should have told them about Sybil!"

"It's all right, honey. You need to go to bed now. I'll take you upstairs. We'll talk in the morning."

Jeremy had been listening thoughtfully, and wasn't exactly convinced by Gabi's story. Sleepwalking? The girl had taken time to change clothes. The night that she'd really been sleepwalking, she'd walked the trail barefoot. Tonight she'd come home wearing blue jeans, shirt, and sneakers. And the door *had* been bolted, that Jeremy knew. Would a sleepwalker know how to unbolt it? But all that just raised more questions. Why had Gabi gone to the Lemerriant farm in the night — with a cougar prowling? What — or who — could have led her there? Wouldn't she have gotten lost? But Willie was saying something . . . he snapped to attention.

"I was just wondering whether Kirsti knows anything about this yet."

"If what Gabi says is true, wouldn't the firefighters have found Sybil's body? Wouldn't they have notified Kirsti?"

"That's just it. *Did* they find a body? Would they have known to look for one? Or did they leave the burn to cool down, planning to come back later to determine the cause of the fire? These fellows weren't the regular fire crew."

"It must have seemed odd to them to find Gabi there alone. Wouldn't that have made them curious?"

"They may have thought that Gabi started the fire and was lucky to get out before it got out of control. And, remember that this is Broom Island. Everyone here knows about Gabi's sleepwalking by now. It would be all neat and tidy. The child was sleepwalking and went to the Lemerriant farm, *as she's done before*. She woke up, took shelter in the cabin, lit a candle and accidentally burned the place down."

"In that case, Kirsti may still not know."

"No," Willie said heavily. "So I should go over there."

"Willie — uh — can we be absolutely sure that Gabi's story is true? Is there a chance that she was — uh — imagining things? It would be terrible to alarm Mrs. Weeks when her daughter may be perfectly all right."

"Good point. The kid could be lying," Willie said, rather uncharitably, for her.

"She was lying about sleepwalking. She wasn't dressed for sleepwalking."

"You're right. She went to bed in pajamas. Okay, I still have to go over there. They never lock their door, so I could possibly just sneak in and take a look. If I'm caught, the worst I can be called is an old fool. But if Sybil's not there, then I'll have to try to find a way to prepare Kirsti."

"Fine, Willie. Go. Do what you have to. I'll wash the cups. I'm wide awake now so there's no point in my going to bed. If you need me, call me. What time is it anyway?"

"Three o'clock. I'll either be back right away or I'll stay as long as I need to. God, I hope I find Sybil tucked into bed . . . but I'm afraid I won't. I don't think Gabi was lying about that."

* * *

Not bothering with a flashlight, Willie took the path through the woods. Although the sun wouldn't be up for another couple of hours, the darkest part of the night was over and she knew the way. There were no lights on in the Weeks house and Willie was beginning to feel a bit foolish. *I feel like a cat burglar — or Goldilocks! Maybe I should just go back.* But then Willie pictured Kirsti's panic if she found Sybil missing. She'd be calling everyone to ask if anyone had seen her. If not for Gabi, it might take a long time before anyone even found the body buried under the charred timbers, but the villagers would be searching everywhere for Sybil. And eventually Gabi's story would come to light.

And Kirsti would know that she, Willie, had known all along. Willie was about to bypass the front door and enter, as she usually did, through the kitchen, when she noticed something up on the porch. Puzzled, she made her way up the steps to find a huddled form sleeping, out in the open, on the porch floor.

"Matt?" Willie touched the boy's shoulder. He'd be cold as ice out here! "Matt, wake up!" The boy stirred. He was barefoot and wore only thin pajama pants with a sweatshirt. "Matt, you have to go inside. What on earth are you doing out here?"

Matt opened his eyes, saw Willie, then started to shiver violently. Willie quickly took off her jacket and threw it over his shoulders, then tried to get him to his feet. She was a bit frail to be lifting a kid of Matt's size, but he managed to get his balance, and Willie led him into Kirsti's kitchen, put him in a chair and put the kettle on. She found an afghan on the living room couch and wrapped him snugly in it, then began rubbing his feet and hands. "Oh, you poor thing. How on earth did you end up out there?"

"What's going on?" Kirsti had come down the staircase and stood watching, astonished.

"I don't know," Willie said. "But I found this one out on the porch freezing to death. He was sleeping on the bare wood. I'm heating water for hot lemonade."

"Matt?" Kirsti looked as though she couldn't believe her eyes. "What on earth were you doing out there? Are you all right?"

"I'm okay, Mom," Matt mumbled, blinking to clear his vision.

"Does Matt ever walk in his sleep?" Willie asked.

"No, he never has."

"Well, that's what it looks like to me. He must have gotten as far as the porch, then curled up and gone to sleep, not realizing he wasn't in his bed."

"I don't understand," Kirsti said. "Matt's never done anything like this before. Sybil's had problems but . . ."

Willie spoke carefully. "Is Sybil here?"

"She's upstairs, asleep," Kirsti said slowly. Then she turned and rushed up the steps; Willie followed. Kirsti threw open Sybil's door and gasped when she saw the room was empty, the bed unmade. "Where is she, Willie?"

"I'm afraid there may have been an accident."

"Sybil's been hurt?"

Willie was near tears. "I don't know what happened exactly, or where she is now, but Gabi told us that Sybil was at the Lemerriant farm again tonight. Gabi was there too. There was a fire. Gabi said Sybil had a seizure and accidentally dropped a candle. Someone had spilled gasoline and the cabin went up in flames. Gabi managed to crawl out the door."

"And Sybil?" The question was a whisper.

"Gabi was nearly overcome by smoke, and she didn't actually see what happened to Sybil."

Kirsti sank slowly to sit onto Sybil's bed. How could any of this be true? How could Sybil possibly have gone anywhere? She'd been sleeping after a seizure. She always slept for hours after a seizure. Kirsti had tucked her in. She'd been holding onto that wooden mask. Kirsti looked around for it, but of course it was gone too. "Who brought Gabi home?"

"Larry Nyquist. Apparently someone spotted the fire and the volunteers went out in the tanker truck while others went by car. They found the cabin in flames and Gabi there alone. There was no mention of Sybil. Gabi was too traumatized to say anything, and Larry recognized her and brought her back. Gabi told us later that Sybil had been there."

"If she died in the fire, they'd have found her. Where is she now? Where's Sybil? I want to see my daughter."

Willie put an arm around her friend's shoulder. "Right now, Kirsti, we don't know. I haven't heard. All I really know is what Gabi told us."

"Then there's still a chance she may have escaped, isn't there? If Gabi got out, maybe Sybil did too!"

"We can pray. All we really know for sure is that she's missing."

"But the firefighters would have found her, wouldn't they? If she was alive?"

Willie didn't know what to say. Kirsti needed that shred of hope, and, of course, *anything* was possible. "I'll call Burt Strunk. He may be home by now, and I'll tell him that Sybil is missing. He'll get the rest of the firemen out looking for her. If somehow she got out and wandered off into the woods, they'll find her. They wouldn't have known to look for her last night."

"I need to go with them."

"Kirsti — " Willie began gently.

"No. You go home, and take Matt with you. I'll drive over to Burt's. I want to see for myself what's happened to my daughter."

Neither of them had noticed that Matt had appeared in the doorway and had been listening to the conversation. Downstairs the tea kettle was whistling endlessly. Willie looked up, "I'm so sorry, Matt."

Matt said nothing, just turned and walked back downstairs. He must have turned off the kettle; the whistling abruptly stopped.

CHAPTER 59

WILLIE HAD made a call to Burt Strunk, to hear Bella, his wife, tell her that Burt was still at the fire. There was no way to reach him, but she'd give him a message as soon as he got home. Willie told her that they needed to look for Sybil, and that she might have perished in the blaze — and that Kirsti wanted to join the search. Plans were hastily made that Kirsti should drive to the Strunks, and that Benny, their teenaged son, would drive her over the back roads to the Lemerriant farm. Matt had wanted to go too, but Kirsti said no.

Back at Willie's there was hot coffee. Jeremy hadn't gone to bed either, and had set out breakfast dishes. Matt was given a cup of cocoa and *pulla*, then Willie suggested he might want to doze on the couch or just stretch out and watch TV until he felt like napping. He was still wearing his sleep sweatshirt, but had hastily slipped into jeans and a pair of sneakers before Kirsti ushered him out the door.

"My god, what a night!" Willie poured herself black coffee.

"How is Kirsti? I take it Sybil. . . ?"

"She wasn't there. Kirsti insisted on going with the firemen to join the search. She's desperately hoping Sybil somehow escaped."

"She could have, couldn't she? Gabi did. And Gabi might not even have known if Sybil survived."

"Someone would have found her. But if, by some miracle, she did escape, then we can all be thankful."

"If not, I was just picturing the shock to Kirsti — such a terrible thing for her to have to see." Jeremy poured himself yet another cup of coffee to dispel that inner chill that comes with not having slept.

"It seems to be one tragedy on top of another. Everyone's being affected. I'm sure it had something to do with Matt's experience last night. I found him out on the Weeks porch, curled up asleep in the cold, poor kid. Kirsti said he's not a sleepwalker, but he must have done so last night. Luckily he only got as far as the porch."

"Matt was sleepwalking?" It was Gabi.

"Good morning, Gabi. I thought you'd still be sleeping," Willie said.

"I woke up. Was Matt sleepwalking?"

"We think he was. I found him on the porch when I went over to see Mrs. Weeks."

"I wonder what made him do that."

Willie gave Gabi a glass of orange juice and a bowl of cereal. "I don't know, but you can ask him yourself when you've had a bit of breakfast. I think he's napping on the couch in front of the TV."

"How come he's here?"

"Mrs. Weeks has gone with the firefighters to look for Sybil."

"Sybil got burned up in the fire."

"Are you absolutely sure, Gabi?" Jeremy asked. "Could she possibly have gotten out after you did?"

"She didn't. I got out because the boy helped me."

"Boy? What boy?"

"He looked like Matt but it wasn't Matt."

Willie and Jeremy exchanged looks. "Do you know who he was?" Willie asked.

Gabi spooned up the last of her corn flakes. "Well, I thought it was Matt, because I followed Matt. I woke up, looked out the window, and Matt was standing in the yard, so I got dressed and went out. At first I didn't see him, but then I saw him standing by the woods so I chased after him. I called but he wouldn't stop so I just kept following him all the way to the old house."

"Are you sure you didn't dream it? I don't think Matt was on that trail last night."

"I'm sure it was him."

"So you weren't really sleepwalking, were you?" Willie said.

Gabi thought a moment, bit her lower lip. "You know, sometimes it's hard for me to *tell*. Things get weird. And people don't believe me. I'm telling you guys what I remember, but I'd really like it if you didn't tell my mom because she'll only freak out." She gave a sigh. "I can't stop you from telling her, but I hope you won't."

"Then why are you telling *us*?" Willie asked gently.

"I don't know. Maybe I trust you guys not to spaz out. Maybe I'm hoping you guys know about stuff like this. Anyway, it's kind of good to tell somebody. You probably won't believe me either, but it doesn't matter. After today we won't be here."

"Is there anything more you'd like to tell us about the fire?" Willie asked.

"Well, it wasn't an accident. Sybil burned the place down on purpose."

"Do you know why?"

"Sybil thought I was the Loogy-Roo. She tried to kill me. I knew she was going to try, because she already tried to kill me with Matt's knife. She was using the mask to be able to see, and she might've done it except for Blackjack."

"Her bird?"

"Blackjack helped me. He flew at Sybil and she killed him. Then she came after me, but Jeremy stopped her."

"Why didn't you — " Willie began, but Jeremy laid a restraining hand on hers. "Go on," he said softly.

"When Sybil had that fit on the lawn, I knew she'd have to try it again, but I knew she couldn't do anything to me. I thought maybe I could help her."

"How did you know that she couldn't hurt you?" Jeremy asked.

Gabi smiled, then laughed. "Because I *am* the Loogy-Roo."

Jeremy looked at her reproachfully while Willie said, "Oh, Gabi, you know there's no such thing as the Loogy-Roo."

"I'm ten. I know there's no such thing as Santa Claus or the Easter Bunny either. But I think . . . I think the Loogy-Roo isn't what everybody thinks it is. It looks different up close, like those stone birds on the beach. From far away they look like birds. Up close they're just rocks. I saw stuff last night."

"What did you see?"

"People."

"You mean the firefighters?"

"No. It was before they got there. I saw people."

"You mean the flames were taking shapes that looked like people?"

"No. They were just people. But they were kind of misty."

"What were they doing?" Willie asked.

"I was standing watching the fire, and they just showed up. They didn't do anything. They just stood there."

"Did you see where they came from?"

"No, but there were lots of them. They started coming, and then they were all over the place, and then they all disappeared. Sybil said something about ghosts that were stuck there because of the Loogy-Roo, and they couldn't get free until the Loogy-Roo was dead. She wanted to kill me because she thought I was the Loogy-Roo and I'd killed Dory Michaels. She said the Loogy-Roo was the devil."

"There *is* no Loogy-Roo, Gabi," Willie said firmly.

"I don't think there's a devil either."

"The Loogy-Roo is just a story that sprang up when your

great-great-uncle, Elphique Lemerriant, was alive. He was different. People were frightened of him, so they called him that."

"I think it's more than that," Gabi said. "Sybil said we were old enemies. I don't know what she meant, but maybe we were. It was like we always knew each other."

"Is that why you didn't want to tell us when she attacked you?"

"Yeah. When you get in a fight with another kid, you don't tell the grownups. I knew how it was going to come out. I'm sorry she's dead, but I *did* try to talk her out of it. We were both different. And I think that's what being the Loogy-Roo is. You're different so people are scared of you. I don't think the Loogy-Roo killed anybody, at least on purpose."

"Those people at the fire, what did they look like?" Willie asked.

Gabi thought a moment. "Trees. They just stood still, like trees, kind of apart from each other. They didn't talk or move around. They just watched the fire. Some were old. Some were kids. All kinds of people."

"How were they dressed?"

"I saw some guys wearing hats and coats, like they were going some-place. Some had on work clothes. I saw women with long skirts like maybe they were going to a costume party. Others looked just like any-body else. Just a big crowd of people, but I knew they weren't *really* real."

"And you're sure you actually saw all that. Flames and shadows can play tricks on your eyes." Jeremy had been listening thoughtfully.

Gabi shrugged. "I dunno. I think I did. Can I be excused? I want to go see Matt."

"Yes, dear, of course." Willie looked at Jeremy. "Well, what do you make of that?"

"I don't know, but my gut feeling still is that there's nothing wrong with that young lady, in spite of how unbelievable all that sounds."

"You mean we shouldn't speak of this to her mother?"

"The day will come when Gabi will tell her herself. But I think she needs time to figure out who she is."

"The Loogy-Roo?"

"For want of a better term," Jeremy said dryly. "She's learning to cope with abilities most of us don't have. She protects herself instinctively. Or maybe she's learned to do so. I understand she's been evaluated and medicated."

"Yes, that's what Celeste told me. Celeste doesn't like any of it, but she's also worried about Gabi and doesn't know what to do. Every time there's an incident, she feels she has to do something."

"If psychic ability is normal for Gabi, there's nothing she *can* do, or even should do, except to help her find ways of living with it."

"But she's only a little girl. She's too young to be coping with it alone."

"She's not alone. Her mother loves her. But they both need time."

"So you think we shouldn't say anything to Celeste?"

"About what?" Celeste had come into kitchen. "What is it that you shouldn't be telling me, Willie?"

"Oh, Celeste, good morning. We were just talking about the tragedy last night. It's so upsetting, and they haven't found Sybil yet — and what a shame it is that all this is happening while you're here." Willie's attempt to cover up was mercifully saved by the bell when the phone rang. She ducked into her office to take the call. Jeremy poured coffee.

"Have you found out any more about what happened last night?" Celeste asked.

"Nothing for sure. We're all hoping that somehow Sybil might have escaped after all. The firefighters are going to search for her and Kirsti is going with them."

"Oh god, and she'll find her daughter's body in the ashes. I don't understand any of this. How did either of them manage to get to that . . . place . . . in the middle of the night? And what in heaven's name were they doing there?"

"Maybe Gabi will remember more about it later."

Willie came back into the room. "At least they got the cougar!"

"Well, it's about time! How did it happen?" Jeremy was glad of the distraction.

"That was Amanda Vuorisaari on the phone. She heard it from Sanni Westerlake at the post office who got it from Barb Kuusiniemi. It was her husband, Veik, who shot the cougar."

"Well, that *is* good news. We can all stop worrying about another attack." Jeremy said.

Willie smiled a bit wickedly. "Oh, there's more to that story!" She waited, for effect, and made a show of pouring herself fresh coffee, then settled into a chair.

She was the focus of two pairs of eyes. "Well?"

"Well! It seems that Butch Westerlake, Veikko Kuusiniemi, and Eddie Smithson had been on the ridge, looking for the cougar, when they noticed that there was a car parked at the bottom of the bluff. They went to investigate and recognized the car as Danielle Herron's. They thought some kids might have stolen it and taken it for a joyride, so they walked over to the lake, and guess what they found!"

"Oh, come on, Willie," Jeremy urged impatiently.

"They saw two women on the raft in the middle of Big Lake — Danielle Herron and Weena Michaels! And on the shore, in plain sight, was the cougar."

"Oh my *god!*"

"Veik took one shot, and it was all over."

"How did the women get to the raft? Was there a boat?"

"There's a dinghy, but that's not what they used. I don't know if you've ever been down there, but there's a big tree with a ladder thing — lengths of two-by-four nailed to the trunk — that the kids climb, and a rope they slide along to drop off onto a raft or into the water."

"What were the women doing out there in the first place?" Jeremy asked.

"Something about going to the Lemerriant farm to look for the Indian mask, but they didn't get that far. For some reason they'd decided to turn back.

"Anyway, when Danielle's car wouldn't start, the women decided to hike back to Weena's but they met the cougar on the road. They ducked into the bushes and headed for the lake. They were going to get in the dinghy and row out — but the cougar had circled around and gotten between them and the boat. I guess it was Weena's idea to shinny up the ladder, but the cougar was coming after them into the tree. So somehow they managed — " Willie couldn't suppress a laugh.

"Go on!" Jeremy urged.

"They — ha-ha! — they managed to both grab the pipe and hang on and slide out over the water. But Danielle lost her grip, fell off into the lake, and had to swim for the raft. Weena dropped off onto the raft surface and managed to drag Danielle out of the water. Of course they were both freezing and yelling for help. And right then, Veik, Eddie, and Butch showed up."

"The cavalry to the rescue!"

"Eddie put the dinghy in the water and rowed out to collect the women. They all ended up going to Weena's where Danielle got dry clothes. She hitched a ride into town with Eddie and Butch. Veik hiked back home to the lighthouse on foot. And then Eddie took Danielle home . . . and *hasn't been seen since*. Amanda said that he was supposed to be on the ferry last night but his truck wasn't in the lineup!"

"Who's Eddie?" Celeste asked Willie.

"Eddie Smithson? He's a Métis gentleman who lives in Alert Bay. His native name is Two Feathers, and he's done a lot of tracking and hunting — mostly with a camera. Bit of a devil with women, I hear."

Jeremy was laughing. "Maybe the sight of Danielle Herron in a wet T-shirt drove him mad with desire."

"My guess is that Danielle locked him in." Willie pantomimed dropping a key down her bosom.

"Oh, we shouldn't be laughing," Jeremy said. The women were in real danger and they must've been terrified."

"No. Of course we shouldn't. But I think we all badly needed a laugh! It was probably too late for Eddie to make the ferry so Danielle offered him a berth for the night. But now, of course, everyone will be saying they're an item."

"Speaking of ferries," Celeste said, "Gabi and I will be leaving on the next one. I'm never, ever, going to forget how kind you've been to us."

Willie looked at her a bit wistfully. "It's been lovely having both of you here. I'm only sorry it's all been so unsettling. You'll keep in touch, won't you?"

"Oh yes, if I may! I'll probably make a nuisance of myself consulting you about all sorts of things when I get going on my book. Right now I'm eager to get Gabi away from here, but a part of me is going to miss this place."

"Come back whenever you can."

Celeste smiled, nodded, then got up. "I have to go pack."

CHAPTER 60

THE TV was turned on to a morning talk show, although the sound was so low as to be nearly inaudible. Matt had kicked off his sneakers and was lying under a crocheted afghan on the couch, his eyes closed, but when Gabi switched off the set, he opened them to stare at her in some confusion.

"Hi, Matt. What are you doing here?"

Matt blinked a few times. "Uh, my mom sent me. She's not home."

Gabi sat next to him and looked long at the kid who didn't really seem to be all that focused. "Wake up, Matt. I need to talk to you."

"What do you mean? I *am* awake."

"You need to be really awake. You need to remember stuff."

Matt sat up, his knees to his chest, and pulled the afghan around him. "Okay, then, I'm awake. What do you want?"

"What were you doing last night?"

"Sleeping, I guess. What do you mean?"

"What were you doing out in the yard?"

"What?"

"Come on, Matt, you gotta remember this. What were you doing outside my window?"

Matt shook his head. "I . . . I dunno. Was I really there? I thought I dreamed it."

"Try to remember, Matt. What did you dream?"

"I dreamed . . . uh . . . something about walking. It was nighttime. It was dark. I was walking along the trail. Somebody was calling me."

"Do you remember seeing *me*?"

"Uh, yeah? Maybe. Somebody was following me. Was that you?"

"Where were we going, Matt?"

"To the old house, I guess, but I don't remember if we got there."

"Why were we going there?"

"I dunno."

"Try to remember, Matt. Why were we going? What were we going to do?"

"Uh . . . Sybil. *Sybil* wanted me to go there."

"Sybil told you to go there?"

"Yeah. Sybil. She was calling me . . . but I don't remember why. I guess I just got up and went, in the dream that is. I was following her voice."

"Do you remember anything about the fire?"

"No."

"Do you remember anything about Sybil, or helping me get out of the fire?"

"No."

"Do you remember coming back home?"

"No. All I remember is dreaming I was on the trail, and I guess you were too, and then I woke up on the porch when Willie found me."

"So you really were on that trail last night."

Matt thought for a moment, then said slowly, "I don't think so. I was in my pajamas. I'd have been all muddy or something." Matt pulled aside the afghan to show his bare feet. "I didn't have my shoes on, and my feet weren't wet or dirty or scratched or anything. You were on the trail in your bare feet that first time. Were your feet clean?"

Gabi kicked off a sneaker and raised her foot to display a few scrapes and a black and blue marks. She remembered that Peg Hewett had applied Polysporin to her scratches. Matt's feet had been bare last night. How could they be so clean and white?

"My mom thinks I was sleepwalking, got as far as the porch, then just fell asleep again. I know it was really *cold*. I guess I had the dream, and got out of bed and went on the porch, and then just laid down and kept on dreaming."

Gabi waited, not knowing what to make of any of it, not knowing what to ask next. "Did you have your knife with you?"

"I don't even know where it is."

Gabi looked puzzled, then sighed. "I guess you heard about Sybil."

"That's where my mom went. To look for Sybil."

"Sorry. Sybil's dead. She was in the fire."

"How do you know for sure?"

"We were in the cabin. Sybil lit it on fire. I got out. Somebody helped me. I thought it was you. Sybil didn't get out."

"But she might've. *You* got out, didn't you? Maybe my sister did too."

"There was gas poured all over the place. When Sybil took the candle and lit the mattress, everything just . . ." Gabi made a gesture that said more than words.

"Are you saying she did it on purpose?"

"Yes."

"But why?"

"She wanted to kill me. She thought I was the Loogy-Roo."

Matt narrowed his eyes. "And are you?"

Gabi smiled faintly. "Yeah, I guess I am. I think Sybil was too. And there may be others. Lots of others. We see stuff. We hear stuff. Stuff other people can't hear or see. And sometimes we know stuff before it happens."

Matt was hugging the afghan like a security blanket. "Like you knew my dad was going to get shot?"

"Yeah. Like I knew about Sybil."

"How do you know these things? I mean, what happens?"

"Sometimes I hear things — like the birds talking."

"Yeah, so you said. Can you talk to *them*?"

"Sometimes I just hear them talking to each other. Sometimes they say things to me. And, yeah, I can talk to them in a way. Sybil had your knife. She tried stabbing me with it, but I must've made Blackjack attack her. And you know something? Sybil could see through that wooden mask. She could see anything she wanted to see, even stuff that was far away. And she could look through the eyeholes, and when Blackjack flew, she could see everything *he* saw."

"How do you know that?"

"I told you. I know stuff." Gabi realized that she could tell Matt anything. In a few hours she'd be gone, and if Matt told anyone, nobody was going to believe him anymore than they ever believed her. It was sort of fun, and the expression on Matt's face was . . . well, she wished he could have seen it himself. "There really are ghosts around that cabin. At least there were. They may be gone now since the place burned down."

"You *saw* them?"

"I saw them. I think one of them pulled me out of the fire. He looked like you, but he had a knife. I think it was that kid in the old photo my mom has. You know who he was. He used to live in the woods."

"Elphique Lemerriant," Matt whispered through stiff lips.

"Remember the day we went through the woods and up on the bluff and down into the quarry? That's where he used to hang out, talking to birds and animals. I think he was with us that day."

"What do you mean with us? Could you see him?"

"No, but I could feel him. I could feel like I *was* him. Like when we climbed the hill and the big bird flew over us. I'd be me, and then I'd be him, and then me again. It was sorta like dreaming. Everybody was scared of him, but he wasn't a bad guy. He was sort of like me. He heard things and saw things."

"They say he was crazy and he killed some kids."

"He didn't kill anybody. I think his father killed his mother, but he didn't chop her up like they say. He used one of those hay fork things. Stabbed her with it."

"But didn't Elphique shoot his father?"

"No. Right now I don't know who did, but I know it wasn't him."

"And you really saw their ghosts? That's *so cool!* What did they look like? What were they doing?"

"The kid who helped me looked like any kid, expect he just blinked out. The rest showed up when I was watching the cabin burn down. All of a sudden they were just there, like they all came to watch the fire. There were lots of them. When the guys in the fire truck came, they all disappeared."

"What did *they* look like? The ghosts?"

"I don't know. Just people, I guess."

"Were they old people? Kids? Could you see through them?"

"They just looked like a bunch of people — like a crowd that shows up to watch fireworks. But they looked kind of shady, like they were made of fog."

"Oh, man, now I wish I'd been there!"

"No, Matt, you don't. Anyway, there's nothing you could have done."

"You mean about Sybil."

Gabi nodded. "I don't know how you led me down that trail last night if you weren't there. Maybe I was just seeing stuff again. But it's weird that you'd been having a dream about it."

"Okay, then, you say you saw lots of ghosts. How come so many? If it was the Lemerriants, I count only three. Old man Lemerriant, his wife and Elphique all died back then. Who were the others?"

"I don't know, but Sybil said something about the sins of the fathers. Maybe there were other relatives. I got the feeling that any relative who died could end up as a ghost. That they were all part of the Loogy-Roo thing. Maybe they didn't even have to be relatives. Maybe they were just dead people."

"Yeah, but how about the ones that are still alive — like you? When you die are you going to end up as a ghost at the Lemerriant place?"

Gabi hadn't thought of that. "I don't know. When things get really weird, I never can tell what's real and what isn't. I just know I saw them, but I don't know who they were, except . . . except . . . I *think* I saw Dory Michaels' dad, and maybe Dory. . . ."

"Wow!" Then Matt slitted his eyes. "What did Dory look like?"

"Kind of fat. Long, light brown hair, sort of curly, with barrettes." Gabi indicated the placement of the hair clips over both temples.

Matt hugged his afghan. "*That's . . . so . . . creepy.* You didn't see my sister, did you?"

"No, there were just so many, and they all disappeared when the fire truck came. I don't know who they all were or why they were there. Maybe they weren't even ghosts. Maybe I dreamed it up. I don't know what I saw."

"Guess you don't know everything after all."

"No, of course I don't. But I do know something about you."

"What's that?"

"When you grow up you'll move away from here. I see you on a great big ship."

"You mean like the one we saw?"

"No, it's much bigger. I think you're working on it. It goes all the way across the ocean. Well, I have to go now and help my mom get packed up."

"Yeah. Well, I guess I'll be seein' ya."

"Yeah. Oh, and Matt?"

"Yeah?"

"I'm really sorry about Sybil, but your dad's gonna to be fine. He'll be home by the weekend. You know, when I first saw you I thought you were a dork, but you're not."

* * *

The one o'clock ferry was late — again. The number of people at the dock had swollen, as it always did whenever anything even mildly unusual was happening in Satama. There was speculation as to whether the *Island Empress* had suffered mechanical failure, until Hilda Widjescoog, at Bloomers, got a call from Port Casper that her shipment of nursery plants was on the truck; but that they'd be late, because a flatbed trailer was stuck on the ferry, and they had to wait for the tide before they could unwedge it. And since they didn't know how long it would take, would she please not close up shop till they got there. Hilda passed the news on to a couple of customers and the word quickly spread.

The ferry lineup was a long one. Some had come down early to pre-park for the following sailing and now were hoping to make it onto the next boat out. The line of cars stood empty as most occupants were doing last-minute shopping, having lunch or coffee, or just wandering around the village. Everyone, of course, was talking about the fire at the Lemerriants, the tragic death of Sybil Weeks whose body had been found — mercifully by Burt Strunk and his son — not Kirsti. Kirsti had single-mindedly refused to accept that Sybil hadn't escaped, and had gone off into the woods to search for her — or perhaps she'd decided that she'd rather not be on the scene if the body lay in the char.

Island seniors were clustered outside the door to the Co-op. "Death always comes in threes," Goldie Slumber was saying to Amanda Vuorisaari who sagely nodded her wispy head.

"Yes, it's the curse of the Lemerriants. I, for one, am glad the place burned down. Always been something wild loose on this island, dating back to those people."

"God moves in mysterious ways," Grace Maddox announced.

"And the devil takes the hindmost, so we better get going!" Oskar,

Amanda's husband, had come through the Co-op door. "I want to stop at the hardware store on the way."

"You'll have your work cut out for you this week," Goldie said. "Three funerals! Never thought I'd be going to the funerals of a child, a young woman, and a man in his prime before my own."

"Just goes to show you never know who's going to be next," Grace said, "so we should all be putting our houses in order."

"Right you are, Grace, and, for me, that means fixin' the leaky pipe in the kitchen. Come on, Amanda, let's go beat the devil."

"Wicked, wicked man," Goldie laughed. "I don't know if I want you laying me out when I *do* go."

"I'll be gentle," Oskar cackled.

"Oh! Get your husband out of here, Amanda." Amanda smiled mirthlessly and gave Oskar a long-suffering look."

"Seems awfully cheerful for a funeral director," Grace remarked as they watched the Vuorisaaris leave.

"Why not? Business is booming."

* * *

Business was booming at Danielle's too, although Danielle Herron, herself, seemed uncharacteristically abstracted as she rang up candy bars, postcards, books, souvenir items, and cups of coffee to those waiting to depart. She was keeping one eye on the ferry lineup, specifically on Eddie Smithson's truck now parked solidly in the line. No chance of *his* missing the next sailing. But where was Eddie? He had dropped her off at the shop, parked his truck and then disappeared. *Was he having lunch at Pearl's?* He'd already had a big breakfast of scrambled eggs at Danielle's. Why would he need to go to Pearl's? "That'll be $28.75 with the PST and GST. " *Surely he wouldn't just take off without even saying goodbye!* "Yes, those are genuine Cowichan sweaters, knitted by native women in Alert Bay." *Alert Bay. The next time I'm there, I'm going to find out where he lives.* "The scented candles are imported, but the soaps are made right here on Broom Island." *Maybe he's married. Could he be married? What do I really know about him? Nothing!* "The eagle carving was done by one of our local artists. It's made of red cedar." *Or, maybe he's just one of those selfish bastards that uses up women like Kleenex. Love'em and leave'em. Well . . . leave'em anyway.* "Postcards are on the back wall. Lovely pictures of Broom Island taken by a local photographer." *Broom Island. Oh god, everyone will be talking now. Everyone will know that Eddie Smithson spent the night at my place.* "Hazelnut or decaf?" *And he better not be blabbing about it! But I'll bet he is. And the next time I see him, I swear, I will kill him!*

* * *

Celeste's Volvo was parked in the lineup a half-dozen cars in back of Eddie Smithson's truck. She'd hoped to make it to the earlier sailing, but it had taken a while to get their stuff together, and then Willie had told her that the mid-morning ferry was for hazardous materials only and would be carrying no passengers. She and Gabi were among the very few who were sitting in their vehicles waiting. Celeste was eager to leave, just to get *on* with it. She'd said her goodbyes to Willie and Jeremy, and now, to her annoyance, it looked like they'd have to wait — again. She checked her watch. The ferry should have been here a half-hour ago. Her ankle was still sore enough that she didn't feel like walking around on it, but she would have liked to know what the delay was.

"Mom, is it okay if I go out on the dock?"

"Oh, I suppose so, but stay where I can see you. Maybe you can ask somebody what the holdup is."

"Can I get a chocolate bar at Danielle's?"

Celeste took money out of her bag. "You might as well. I'd planned to have lunch in Port Casper, but it may be a while before we get there."

"You want one too?"

"No." What Celeste wanted was a cigarette. She hadn't thought about smoking as much, lately, and had congratulated herself on how easily she'd been able to quit. Now, with her car pointed toward her old life, old habits were surfacing to bedevil. She kept an eye on Gabi who, looking both ways first, carefully crossed the street and disappeared into Danielle's. There was a faint tap-tap at her passenger side window, and Celeste turned to see Ulla Kampsula's smiling face, the handle of her cane, and a hand making circular open-the-window gestures.

With a happy grin, Celeste reached over and pushed the door open. "Come on in and sit, Ulla. It looks like we're going to be here for a while."

Ulla eased in and handed her an oblong parcel wrapped in tinfoil. It could be nothing other than a braid of Ulla's *pulla*. "Oh, thank you! How lovely of you! But how did you know we'd be leaving today?"

"Oh-hoh! *Everybody* knows you're leaving. And it von't be too much longer. Tide's coming in. Vhere's your little girl?"

"She went over to get a snack. I'm so glad I had a chance to see you and tell you how much I appreciate all your help. The photographs are priceless, and I'm going to send you enlarged copies when I get back to my computer."

Ulla smiled wistfully. "Dat's nice. Pretty soon nobody left to remember. Young people don't remember."

"There seem to be lots of young people here, in any case."

"Dey von't stay. Most of dem vill take off. Not much here."

"But there must be descendants of the original settlers still living here."

"Oh yes, and sometimes dey move avay and come back."

"Ulla, do you think Sybil really *was* a descendant of the Lemerriants?"

"I tink so. You can *tell*."

"How?"

"They're all *hullu*."

"*Hullu?*"

"Yah, *hullu*. Crazy. Vild. Lots of dem now in de cemetery. Crashed cars and killed demselfs. Sybil used to say sins of fathers. Vell, I don't know about sins but someting *is*."

"How well did you know Sybil?"

"Nobody knew Sybil, but she used to come see me. She had dat bird, you know. And sometimes she used to come over and just sit."

"Did she talk to you? Did you talk to her?"

"Not much. I just let her sit. And I used to sit vit her. Sometimes I make a cup of tea. She didn't drink coffee. Sometimes she bring her Bible." Ulla pantomimed reading Braille. "Ve just sit. Nobody says notting. Then she'd just get up and go. Sometimes she came to listen to Ernie."

"Ernie? Was that your husband?"

"No. Ernie vas native man from Alert Bay. Camp cook in logging camps. Used to come over and chop my vood and I show him how to make *pulla*. Oh, Ernie, now *dere* vas a character! Never met nobody like Ernie! He used to make me laugh! Ve get dry summer, and I tell Ernie he should bring rain, and Ernie say, 'Do you have any idea how much a rain dance *costs*?' Ernie vasn't here very long, but he'd been to lots of places, traveled evervhere, vorked in Cajun country, on Petite Anse Bayou. And he had stories about magic spells and spooky stuff. Sybil loved to listen to him."

"How old was she back then?"

"Tvelve . . . tirteen maybe. It vas after her accident, and Ernie vas nice to her. He gave her de raven. He say he von Blackjack in a card game, but I don't know. Ven he left he gave the bird to Sybil, couldn't take it vhere he vas going."

"How did Sybil learn to read Braille? Did she go to a special school?"

"Not much school after her accident, but dere vas a course one summer for seniors and Sybil vent. It vas sponsored by de Lutheran church. Ve had a few old people vit bad ice, and some just vent because it vas someting to do. I almost did myself, but I figured you can't teach old dog new tricks. And it vas true. Not many of dem got to be any good at it, but Sybil — Sybil vas bright girl. She learn fast and that's how she got her Bible. It vas prize."

"Such a tragedy about Sybil. She was so young."

"Sybil vas never young, believe me. She vas old soul trapped in young body. Confused. She knew tings but didn't understand." Ulla gave Celeste a pointed look. "Old soul needs teaching, not drugs. Drugs only make trouble." Was Ulla still talking about Sybil, or was she making a point about Gabi?

"Gabi could have died in that fire as well. Terrible, terrible accident."

"You tink it vas accident? I don't."

"Why would you say that?"

"Sybil only here for short time. She knew. I knew. Maybe dat's vhy she liked to come over. Listen to my clock tick."

"But if it wasn't an accident, was she trying to kill Gabi as well!"

"Maybe. But didn't happened. Your daughter has protection, and she knows dis."

"I don't understand. Why would Sybil Weeks hate my daughter enough to try to kill her? What did Gabi ever do to her?"

"Tings like dis are like ice on a lake. You can skate on de ice, but the vater under it is a different vorld. You don't see it. You don't know how deep it is. You don't know vat lives down dere. Ve don't know vat connections ve all have or how far back dey go. Ve see only de top layer."

"Are you talking about reincarnation?"

"I say ve may have all met before . . . and vill probably meet again." Ulla chuckled, "And, like I said, Sybil vas *hullu*, and every *hullu* is *hullu* in his own vay. Easy to become crazy ven you're different. She lived in her own vorld. It crushed her. Don't vorry. It *von't* happen to Gabi."

"I hope not. But it's hard for me to deal with it. It's one thing to hear about such things, but when your own kid tells you she heard a dead girl singing about somebody getting shot, and then it *happens*, what do you do?"

"Gabi heard dead girl singing?"

"Well, of course she *couldn't* have, could she?"

"But she said it vas dead girl?"

"No, not really. Gabi only said she heard a girl singing, but she found out later that it was a song that Dory Michaels used to sing, and it was Dory's dad who shot Rome Weeks. And then, later, she told us Dory's dad had been killed — and we found out that he *had* been. I can't just dismiss it."

"*Kirkkoväki.*"

"Excuse me?"

"Is very old legend. Dead passing messages. I remember ven I was kid, ve had neighbor, Kusti Väisänen. He vas valking past de cemetery and he heard a voice call out, 'Kusti here next veek on Tuesday.' And he *vas*. Horse kicked him in de head."

"Oh, Ulla, it sounds like one of those spooky stories you'd tell at a campfire."

"It does, doesn't it? I vonder why ve still tell dem, ven ve all so much smarter now."

"*You* don't believe them, do you?"

"Doesn't matter vat I believe. Your life vill bring you vat *you* believe. Best to keep de mind open. Closed mind is alvays under attack."

* * *

Gabi's young nose savored the smells in Danielle's shop as she walked about, waiting to buy a candy bar: scented candles, coffee, the smell of new books, leather, wool, perfumes, and oils; she was like a puppy, sniffing and identifying, while Danielle, at the counter, kept a sideways eye on her to make sure she wasn't touching anything. When the last customer had exited, she smiled, a bit woodenly: "So, Gabrielle, you and your mother are off and away, then?"

"Yes, ma'am." Gabi had long since learned the diplomatic value of a the well-placed "sir" and "ma'am."

Danielle seemed to relax a bit. "Is there something you'd like?"

Gabi chose a Cadbury bar from a box and handed over money.

"Well, I hope you have a nice trip back." Danielle hesitated, then plunged ahead. "I heard about the fire. I'm so sorry, but I'm glad you're all right. It must have been very frightening." Gabi said nothing, just looked at Danielle solemnly.

"Uh, and we're all just so *shocked* to hear about Sybil. She used to work for me, you know, and it's all just so hard to believe."

Gabi continued to stare and Danielle was finding her silence disconcerting.

"The whole village is terribly upset. We'll all miss her."

"It's gone," Gabi said.

"What?"

"The mask. It's gone. It got burned in the fire."

"Uh . . . what . . . I mean . . . of course that's not important now . . ." Danielle was stammering. "Yes, of course, Sybil had borrowed one of my masks, and I'm sure she . . . she meant to bring it back . . . but that doesn't matter now. . . ."

"She had it with her in the cabin and it got burned. Sorry. Gotta go."

* * *

There was still no sign of the *Island Empress*, and Gabi was about to go back to the car when she saw that her mother was chatting with someone in the front seat. So, instead, she walked to the dock to watch the water, sat down on a bench to unwrap her chocolate bar.

"Halfers!"

Gabi turned to see Matt Weeks laughing at her. "What did you say?"

"Halfers. Now you have to give me half."

"No, I don't!"

"Yeah, you do. You didn't say 'holders'!"

"Holders!"

"Too late. You hafta say 'holders' *before* I say 'halfers.'"

"You're making all this up."

"Nuh-uh. It's the *law*."

"Well, *I* never heard of it so it doesn't count."

Matt sat next to her. "So I guess you guys are goin' huh?"

"If the ferry ever gets here." Gabi broke off a section of her bar and handed it to Matt who popped it in his mouth.

"It's coming. See it out there?"

Gabi could now see the boat making its way across the strait. She munched her chocolate and continued to share it with Matt.

"You think you'll ever come back?"

"I dunno. I kind of hope so."

"Got somethin' for you," Matt reached into his pocket and pulled out a tiny cloth bag with a drawstring.

"What's that?"

"Goofer dust."

Gabi opened the top and peeked inside. "What's it for?"

"Take it with you."

"But what *is* it?"

"Something my sister used to make. She had different kinds. I asked her what it was and she told me it was goofer dust. Some guy from Alert Bay told her how to make it."

"What's in it?"

"I dunno. She didn't say."

"But what's it *for*?"

"Sybil said it was magic. She had bags of it in her room, so I took one. Cool thing to have. Like taking some of island with you. I kinda think you'll know what to do with it."

The ferry was pulling in. Gabi pocketed the bag of dust. "Okay, Matt, gimme a high five."

"A what?"

"Lift your hand like this." Matt raised his and she slapped it. "See ya, Matt." She raced off to the car.

* * *

The shop had emptied, the ferry was unloading, and Danielle poured herself a cup of decaf and stepped outside. And there, pulling into her parking space was her yellow Volkswagen with Eddie Smithson at the wheel. He got out, ran up the steps and handed her the keys. "I went over to Hank's and he and I went to Big Lake and towed your car back. It was the solenoid. Good as new now, and everything's taken care of."

"Oh, Eddie, thank you! I tried calling him myself but he wasn't there, and then it got so busy in here. What do I owe you?"

"Just one of your beautiful smiles, sugar! Uh-oh, gotta go!" The ferry was ready to load and Eddie was out the door, down the steps and sprinting for his truck. Danielle stood, one hand raised in farewell, and, as Eddie's Ford drove by, she saw him rakishly blow her a kiss.

CHAPTER 61

"WELL, THEY'RE gone." Willie and Jeremy had just finished dinner. As old people tend to do, left to themselves, they ate early and their meals were light. Although there were still sandwiches and cakes left over from Ulla's largesse, Willie had decided they needed a sensible dinner. She'd made raw vegetable juice according to her favorite recipe: carrots, celery, apple, ginger, and garlic, a combination that, to some sounds revolting, but is, in actuality, surprisingly delicious. Willie had been "juicing" for many years, but had long since stopped suggesting it to friends — friends who, she quietly noted, were having knee and hip replacements, bypass surgeries, and taking medication for high blood pressure and high cholesterol. She suffered from neither. Tonight they'd broiled and split a Delmonico steak, served with a small baked potato, steamed asparagus, and a green salad with oil and vinegar dressing. No dessert, but a tiny glass of port.

"Seems a lot quieter now," Jeremy said. "Not that they were noisy."

"It's good to have company now and then, but it's always nice when things get back to normal."

"Whatever passes for normal on this island. What did *you* make of all this . . . this activity we've been having?"

Willie paused for a moment to consider the question. "On the surface, we had a rogue cougar that may have killed two people. A disturbed young woman became obsessed and went over the edge of sanity. The island will now deal with the tragedies, then move on as it always has."

"But you think there's more to it than that."

"I think that any event we experience is only the tip of the iceberg, and that there are deeper levels involved."

"Gabi?"

"Gabi seemed to be the catalyst. Her history whirls around her like spindrift, stirring up the past and mixing it with the present. There is a metaphysical theory that time is an illusion and that all events happen simultaneously. I'm inclined to believe it. And I'm also inclined to believe that we're all so interconnected that nothing is really hidden or so remote that it can't be accessed."

"So maybe Gabi *did* hear the birds talking about things that happened long ago."

"Maybe she did. At least that's her translation of the way she got the information. And I think her being here may have awakened awareness in many of us. Like having someone remind you of something that you once knew but had forgotten. She may have expanded our consciousness and left some of us more open to paranormal experiences."

"I'll have to mull that over for a while. Why don't we take our port in the living room and check out the news. We've been so preoccupied that we might have missed some calamity."

"Good idea. I'd like to put my back down into my recliner for a while." Willie walked over to the TV set and reached for the remote — then stopped. "Hey, what's this doing here?" She held up an object that had been pushed out of sight behind a stack of VHS tapes. "It's a hunting knife. Whose is it?"

"I think that belongs to Matt Weeks. I thought Gabi had given it back to him. Maybe she forgot."

"Is this the one Sybil used? The one that broke your cast?"

"That's the one. We should return it to Matt." Jeremy looked at it closely. "Thing like this could do a lot of damage. You think it's okay for a kid to be carrying it around?"

Willie settled into her chair and sipped her port. "Island kids are used to hunting knives. Normally, here, they're tools, not weapons."

"It's just as well that Matt didn't have it last night if he was wandering around the trail in his sleep."

"He never made it to the trail. He never left the porch."

"But Gabi was so *sure*."

"Gabi . . . Gabi probably saw his thought form."

"A what?"

"Open your mind wide and picture this: Any time you think strongly or emotionally about a place, you send a bit of your consciousness there in the form of a phantom. We all do it, though we're not aware of it, and not everyone can see thought forms."

Jeremy watched Willie with a half smile on his face. He should be used to this sort of thing by now, but it kept surprising him. "A thought form."

"Yes. So-called primitive people, who don't have cell phones and TV sets and e-mail, have astonishing ways of communicating. In Lapland, a thought form is called the *etiäinen*, the forerunner. A Lapp goes off to visit a friend, and the thought form precedes him. The friend sees the thought form arriving well in advance, and has the coffee on by time his friend actually gets there. I think Matt started out to follow the trail in his sleep, but physically he only got as far as the porch. His thought form kept on going. Gabi saw it and followed it."

Jeremy drained his port. "Have you, yourself, ever experienced any-thing like that?"

"I can't say I've ever seen a thought form, and it's the sort of thing that can get old people put in a home. I've had a few incidents, but the so-called paranormal is hard to pin down. I'll bet a lot of seniors have many experiences that they never talk about. In a way, it's a good thing that old age flies under everyone else's radar."

"When I was younger, everything was simpler. I was a black-and-white kind of guy, and part of me still is. But there's a lot in life that makes me stop and wonder who *is* that little man behind the curtain?"

"Producing all the special effects? Yes. It can be staggering to contemplate the infrastructure of our own existence. Just the workings of our bodies! We take it for granted that we can breathe and walk and talk and see, and that our hearts pump and our blood flows. But what do we really know about how we function?"

"Religion would call us God's creations."

"Yes, but it's a bit of a blank wall, isn't it? I've always wanted to take a closer look at His blueprints. Our world is magical and beautiful. There's an order to the universe that escapes us, amazing in its complexity and size, inhabited not only by fleshly humans but all sorts of entities beyond our range or ken."

"You sound like my Irish aunt who believed in the little people."

Willie grinned. "I'm not at all sure that I don't!"

"Gabi would agree with you. I wonder what it was that she really saw at the old farm. Sybil had some cockamamie theory that all the Lemerriants were ghosts somehow tied to the Loogy-Roo. And that as long as the Loogy-Roo was alive, they were held captive. She'd got it into her head that Gabi was the Loogy-Roo incarnate, and if she died they'd all be free and their evil would go away."

"I think Sybil was trying to assimilate a lot of *unofficial* information, and I think she was seeing it in the black-and-white context of good versus evil. The Lemerriants became the embodiment of evil, with poor Elphique as the focus. In a larger sense, they represented the arbitrary and cruel oppression of the authoritarian culture in Europe — the very thing Finns had come to North America to escape.

"Sybil had grown up identifying with native culture, with all its mystic lore, as well as the Finnish tradition of the *Kalevala*. Add to that Christianity! Christianity imposed itself on the early belief systems of both.

"It was the perfect medium for a myth to emerge. I believe that the Loogy-Roo is a genuine, homegrown, honest-to-goodness Broom Island myth."

"Yes, of course."

"No, I mean that it really *is* a myth, not just a folktale. A myth always has a greater and more durable reality than any historical event. All religions are based on myths and that's what gives them their power."

"The Loogy-Roo story is based on historical fact, surely."

"Yes, but look at it more closely. There are all kinds of conflicting stories about the Lemerriants and their history. Events have become clouded while the drama has been embellished. So much psychic energy has been invested that it's taken on a life of its own. It's become a metaphor for the history of the island, particularly the Finns."

"But the Lemerriants were French, weren't the?"

"Exactly. They were The Others. They represented evil and disruption. They became, in a sense, the devil, and even today, rebelliousness and recklessness in the young is seen as stemming from their genetic influence. Sybil was acting out the drama of exorcism."

"And died in the process."

"Martyred to her cause."

"What about the killings? And the ghosts?"

Willie hesitated, then went on: "The ghosts are an ancient myth of the Finns, dating back much farther than the Lemerriants. I was listening to Gabi describe what she saw, and *I have no doubt at all that she saw it*. She actually *saw* the *Kirkkoväki*. I'm sure that Sybil had seen them too, judging by her talk about spirits bound to the Loogy-Roo. That would have been her interpretation. The *Kirkkoväki* goes back to ancient times, long before Christianity gained power, although the term became used only after they started burying the dead in churchyards."

"I remember your mentioning the bonehouse . . . the *luu* something."

"*Luutalo.* We were a lot more hands-on with the dead back then. There were many customs of burial, some dictated by climate. The dead were, in some areas, placed into the branches of trees — not unlike the raised platforms used by First Nations tribes. Broom Island, of course, is steeped in the lore of both Finns and native tribes, and there's a natural affinity between the two. Islands were often dedicated as cemeteries, and bodies stored in a trees would be transported there when the ice formed. Like Charon ferrying the dead to Hades.

"The *Kirkkoväki* consisted of the souls of the dead who had not yet moved on. In a sense, they *were* bound, and they were also feared. They were believed to have power that could do you harm, but their power and protection was also sought. A shaman, or anyone else practicing magic, would try to solicit the power of the *Kirkkoväki* to add to his own. The idea was to enlist their aid against all the horrors that might beset you. How do you protect yourself from a wildfire or a storm or an illness — or a cougar attack?

"It was a time of spells and rituals. You could bake a cheesecake from the milk of a newly calved cow and feed it to your stock to insure their safety from predators. You could circle your land three times, carrying an ax and an urn to form a barrier that would keep your property protected."

"But surely none of that mumbo jumbo actually worked!"

"Yes, but there was still a sense of empowerment to it, and if you believe something strongly enough, it *can* work. But whether it worked or not, you were at least *doing something.* Christianity came along and labeled it witchcraft, for which you could be punished, even killed. All you could do then is try to appease a capricious God and meekly accept adversity as His punishment for your sins — and then invent a devil to take up the slack. It was easy to call a cougar attack the work of the devil and personify him as the Loogy-Roo."

"But surely now, in a scientific, technological age. . . !"

"Christianity, at least, gave us a get-out-of-jail-free card called

Salvation. Science claims we're here through some cosmic accident, and that life has no meaning. Psychiatry teaches that our subconscious is a seething cauldron of uncontrolled impulses that we have to keep a lid on. Medicine insists that we're constantly in danger of being ambushed by illnesses — and the six o'clock news shows us that we're at the mercy of anyone's random violence. It's a Catch-22 that has us convinced we live in mortal danger."

"But don't we? Look around you at the state of the world."

"Exactly. If we *believe* the world is a dangerous place, that's all we'll see. We'll totally miss the underlying loving cooperation upon which our reality rides."

"Isn't that all rather . . . Pollyanna?"

"I think that may be the message of the *Kirkkoväki*. We all lived and died, but we're still here. We survive, so will you. There is nothing to fear. Earthly life is the hallucination; ours is the *real* reality."

"Well, I guess the Kirk — uh — whatever — would then be like the gods on Olympus or the Tooth Fairy. But surely nobody today really believes that you can actually see them."

"Those who've had contact with them, *know* they exist. Belief doesn't enter into it. Those who haven't, will either disbelieve or wonder. It's like any paranormal experience. You tend to reject it until it happens to you."

"But Willie, *you* can't possibly believe that the dead continue to live in the local cemetery!"

"No. Why would they? I think the dead have far more freedom than that, and that they face brilliant challenges. I don't think they do much eternal resting or worshiping. I don't think they *dwell*, but I *do* think they might *return* and gather to view any event that might interest them, particularly on this psychically charged little island."

Jeremy shook his head. "I guess I'll have to just chalk that up as a cultural thing. Do you think it's all over now?"

"I doubt it. It takes a lot to kill a myth. It may surface again in another four generations, with different actors in the passion play."

"Complete with a cougar killing people?"

"So far, there's always been a cougar. Maybe Elphique had a pet cougar, who knows? If there's a connection to the past among the birds, then why not beasts as well? It doesn't have to be evil; it just has to be *there*. Remember the flatworms and the calves. Cougars don't live here. They always come from somewhere else, but when they arrive, they may be tapping into the island's collective consciousness — the very consciousness that may have drawn them here in the first place. The cougar accepts the role and dies when the drama is over."

"It's still macabre. It may be a drama, but real blood has been spilt."

"Yes. On our planet we seem to like to spill blood. Maybe we need the *Kirkkoväki* to remind us that it *is* drama. They're the actors who have left the stage and become part of the audience. I also think that anyone who has a connection with them is being singled out."

"Like Gabi?"

"Gabi, for one, Sybil, for another. Elphique, probably. There may be many more. Each will react to the experience in his own way, and interpret it according to his own frame of reference.

"As for the myth of the Loogy-Roo, it's an island treasure — our very own! It'll go on as long as there's an emotional need to keep it alive. This island is a bubbling stew of creativity, so I think the myth will only keep growing. As a by-product, Celeste may end up with a good novel, and Gabi will help her write it. A myth spawns events the way a glacier "calves" icebergs. The ramifications can be immense."

Jeremy yawned. "I'm sure they're huge, and it's not that I don't believe you, but I think I'd have to still see for myself."

Willie grinned, a bit wickedly, harking back to a naughty old British witticism: ". . . As the actress said to the bishop."

Jeremy got up. "It's probably old age, but I'm *tired*. Maybe because I was up most of the night. I think I'll skip the news and go up for a soak in the tub, then just go to bed and read for a while." He set about making the rounds and locking the doors.

"We should have heated the sauna. With all our hiking and running around, our muscles could've used hot steam. I think I'll make an early night of it as well — but I'll go check my e-mail first." Willie took the empty port glasses into the kitchen. "Sleep well, Jeremy."

"You too, Willie. The house is secure."

EPILOGUE

GABRIELLE PENELOPE Choate stood on the deck of the *Island Empress* and watched the village of Satama recede in the distance. As the boat had pulled away from the ferry dock, she'd spotted Matt Weeks standing on the platform, waving at her. Now the village was becoming smaller and smaller, and Gabi could see stretches of shoreline on both sides. She could make out Willie's house with its three stories and big windows on Kaunio Road; backtracking with her eyes, she spotted the cemetery, partly visible through trees along the water side where there was no hedge to hide it. She could still see the large building that was the Broom Island Inn where they'd briefly stayed, and scanning past it, she could pick out the water tower on the hill on Quarry Road. It all looked warm and peaceful with the sun lighting up the blossoming broom. Had it all really happened? Or had she dreamt it?

Gabi put her hand in the pocket of her jacket and pulled out the small bag of — what had Matt called it? Goofer dust! Funny name. She loosened the drawstring and looked inside. It looked like dirt — or sand — or ashes, maybe. She moistened a finger and dipped it in and looked at it closely. On impulse, she put a few grains on her tongue. It was gritty and salty. She spat it out. Sybil had made this! Sybil — her "ancient enemy" had made this dust. Had Sybil also somehow *made* Matt give it to her? Was this a parting gift or was it something she should be throwing away? Was Sybil still trying to destroy her, or was she seeing things differently now? Sybil had told her that she was the Loogy-Roo, and would always be bound to the island. What if she threw the bag into the sea? . . . But of course she wasn't *tied* to this place, and would probably never come back again. Or would she?

Would she *want* to come back again? It had all been . . . sort of magic . . . weird and mysterious and scary and beautiful and wild — and also strangely familiar! Somehow Gabi felt that she *owned* Broom Island, maybe the way Alice owned Wonderland. She'd explored the woods and taken a sauna and patted a dead seal and seen shadow people and talked to birds. *Beware the laughing blackbirds and the Loogy-Roo. . . .*

Was she the Loogy-Roo? If Sybil had been right, then she *would* come back, wouldn't she? But Sybil had also said that distance meant nothing, so maybe she'd be the Loogy-Roo whether she came back or not. It was like being "It" in a game of tag. Gabi looked at the bag of dust. Of course! Sybil had just tagged her, and now she was It! Like being handed the baton in a relay race.

But Gabi's race would be different from Sybil's. She didn't know how, but she sensed that there was a lot more to it. *Okay, let's just pretend that I am The Loogy-Roo. Sybil said the Loogy Roo is powerful, but what does that really mean? Okay, then, could the Loogy-Roo even kill somebody — accidentally? Could I make a cougar kill somebody? No, I don't think it works like that, and why would I want to do that anyway? She thought about Elphique. Could he have made a cougar kill a kid? Maybe, if he was in danger, a cougar might help him the way Blackjack helped me. It was probably something like the birds talking to me. There's a place where it doesn't matter if I'm me or if I'm a bird. That day, when Matt and I were in the woods, I could find my way around like I lived there. I felt different, like I was somebody else, but I was still me too. Is that what being the Loogy-Roo means? You can be more than one person at the same time? If I'm the Loogy-Roo, what else can I do? Is it like being a superhero? They usually have a secret identity. Sybil talked about the Ancient Mother.* Gabi didn't have an Ancient Mother. At least none that she knew of. She wondered about the shadow people. She hadn't been afraid of them. They hadn't said anything to her, but they'd seemed . . . *interested* . . . as if they were standing by her. She held the bag of dust tightly in her hand until it began feel warm and made her palm tingle. Would she now hear birds talking no matter where she went? Could the shadow people find her anywhere?

Gabi gripped the bag and hesitated. She sensed that in that moment she could go either way — accept or reject whatever lay before of her. *Should I toss this over the side and pretend none of this ever happened? Or should I keep it and see what happens next?*

Looking around, she saw her mother who was busy taking last photographs of the now-distant island in the sun. Smiling, Celeste turned her camera on Gabi to get shot of her standing at the rail. Gabi smiled back, struck a pose . . . and carefully pocketed the bag of dust.